RUIN & Renewal

Volume Three of CRESCENT CITY

JACK CALDWELL

RUIN AND RENEWAL: VOLUME THREE OF CRESCENT CITY

White Soup Press, c/o Jack Caldwell, 3140 Sunset Beach Drive, Venice, FL, 34293.

info@cajuncheesehead.com

https://cajuncheesehead.com
http://whitesouppress.com/
http://austenvariations.com/

ISBN: 978-0-9891080-5-8

Front Cover: "St. Louis Cathedral" © dndavis

Back Cover: "Police Line Do Not Cross" © Thomaspajot
New Orleans, LA, September 4, 2005—A view of the roof of the Superdome which was damaged as a result of Hurricane Katrina.
Jocelyn Augustino/FEMA

Layout & design by Ellen Pickels

Dedication

For Barbara

For those who are gone and for those who remain.
May America never forget.

Author's Note

Ruin and Renewal is Volume Three of the *Crescent City* series. The story resumes immediately after the end of Volume Two, *Elysian Dreams*. The author strongly suggests that story be read before this one.

Crescent City

Prologue

Why does violent weather like a hurricane occur? It is because of the sea.

Two-thirds of the Earth's surface is covered by water. Day in and day out, the seas and oceans absorb the heat of the sun, storing enormous amounts of energy like gigantic batteries. But all the energy cannot stay there.

The laws of thermodynamics state that, when two systems are put in contact with each other, there will be a net exchange of energy between them unless or until they are in thermal equilibrium; that is, they contain the same amount of thermal energy for a given volume.

One form of energy exchange between the oceans and the atmosphere is water vapor. Parcels of air, traveling close to the surface of the oceans, take up moisture. Warm, ascending air expands and cools, releasing moisture and rain during condensation.

Thank goodness for it. For without rain, we would surely die.

However, the oceans can store so much energy that the rather benign process of water-to-condensation-to-rain is not sufficient to process all of it. Remember, the energy must be released. When conditions are right—when there is a lack of shearing winds that would normally retard the growth of storms—the process continues to expand, growing larger and larger, like a nuclear reaction out of control. A miniature weather system develops with higher and higher winds spinning around an area of low pressure. Scientists call this tropical cyclonic activity, and its product is a tropical storm.

The vast depths of the seas are the birthplace of these systems. The life-giving waters give off stored energy, forming enormous engines of death. Tropical storms follow steering currents in the sky, generally east-to-west with Atlantic and Pacific storms, and south-to-north in the Indian Ocean. As they move, they feed off the waters beneath them. If those waters are particularly warm, the storms grow so large they are known by new names: hurricanes, cyclones, and typhoons. The winds increase, and the area of lowest pressure becomes an eye, open to space. Once on shore, these storms lose their support system, weaken quickly, and drop their millions of tons of rain onto the land.

Without oceans, humans would perish, for the seas are the source of weather and rain. However, there cannot be oceans without hurricanes.

Thus, the trade-off between life and death.

Volume Three

Ruin and Renewal

Dramatis Personae

Leon Anderson VP at Delta Global Shipping, lives in Algiers.

David Baugham Special Agent with the FBI, New Orleans office.

Annie Betancourt Exotic dancer known as "Spice," resides in Las Vegas, NV.

Catherine Bingley Wealthy widow, lives in Baton Rouge.

Charles "Chuck" Bingley Senior lender for Gallic National Bank of New Orleans, lives in Covington.

Jane Boudreaux Bingley Wife of Chuck Bingley, daughter of T.B. Boudreaux, part-time nurse in Mandeville.

Elizabeth Boudreaux Communication Manager at Economic Development/New Orleans, fiancée of William Darcy, lives in Metairie.

Thomas "T.B." Boudreaux Owner of a small oilfield service firm, lives in Chackbay.

Frances "Franny" Boudreaux Wife of T.B. Boudreaux.

Mary Boudreaux Third daughter of T.B. Boudreaux, English teacher at E.D. White Catholic High School in Thibodaux.

Catherine "Kit" Boudreaux Fourth daughter of T.B. Boudreaux, attends community college in Houma.

Lydia Boudreaux Youngest daughter of T.B. Boudreaux, exotic dancer known as "Sugar," resides in Las Vegas.

Dr. Chris Breaux Psychiatrist, LSU Medical Center, New Orleans, lives in Uptown.

Carrie Bingley Buford Wife of John Buford, daughter of Catherine Bingley, works for the Louisiana Department of Administration, lives in Baton Rouge.

Capt. John Buford Captain in the Louisiana Army National Guard, lawyer in Baton Rouge,.

John "Trey" Buford, III Son of John and Carrie Buford.

Marianne "Mari" Dashwood Insurance company clerk, part-time jazz singer, lives in the Faubourg Marigny.

Scott Davis Student at UNO.

William Darcy President/CEO and majority stockholder of Delta Global Shipping Inc. (DGS) of New Orleans, lives at Dansereau Plantation in St. Charles Parish and at a condo in the Warehouse District.

Gina Darcy Sister of William Darcy, student at Auburn University, Auburn, AL.

Edward Denham General Manager of Jean Laffite Resort & Casino, Gulfport, MS.

Anna Elliot Assistant to the mayor of New Orleans.

F. Edward Fitzwilliam Chairman of Delta Global Shipping, uncle to both Richard Fitzwilliam and William Darcy, lives in Fort Lauderdale, FL.

Richard Fitzwilliam Captain in the New Orleans Police Department assigned to the Third District, cousin of William Darcy, lives in Mid-City.

Olivia Fitzwilliam Wife of Richard Fitzwilliam.

Jan Hill Administrative assistant at Economic Development/ New Orleans.

Kaywanda Johnson Secretary at Economic Development/New Orleans, lives with her mother in Gentilly.

Emma Weinberg Katz Wife of George Katz, daughter of Abe Weinberg, lives in Lakeview.

Dr. George Katz Surgeon and instructor at Tulane University Medical Center and Medical School.

PO3 Donald Lauck Petty officer (third class) and aviation survival technician (AST), US Coast Guard.

Charlotte Lucas Economic developer at Economic Development/New Orleans.

Justin Middleton Producer with Action NOW News, Hartford, CT.

LTJG Jeremy Price Lieutenant (junior grade), US Coast Guard and helicopter pilot, lives in New Orleans East.

Airman Marcus "Randy" Randle Airman (E-3) and rescue swimmer, US Coast Guard.

Betsy Reynolds Long-time housekeeper at Dansereau Plantation.

Lucy Steele Entertainment coordinator at Jean Laffite Resort & Casino, Gulfport, MS.

Adam "Bubba" Teresina Biology teacher and assistant football coach at E.D. White Catholic, fiancé of Mary Boudreaux.

Bryan Thorpe Reporter, Action NOW News.

Cathy Tilney Realtor, lives in Baytown, Texas.

Henry Tilney Husband of Cathy Tilney.

John Waguespack Assistant manager for entertainment, Jean Laffite Resort & Casino, Gulfport, MS.

Sam Watson Cameraman, Action NOW News.

Abe Weinberg Retired architect, lives with his daughter and son-in-law in Lakeview.

LCDR Fred Wentworth Lt. Commander, US Coast Guard, helicopter pilot and squadron leader, lives in Belle Chasse.

Gregory "G-Daddy" Wickham Unemployed small-time drug dealer in New Orleans.

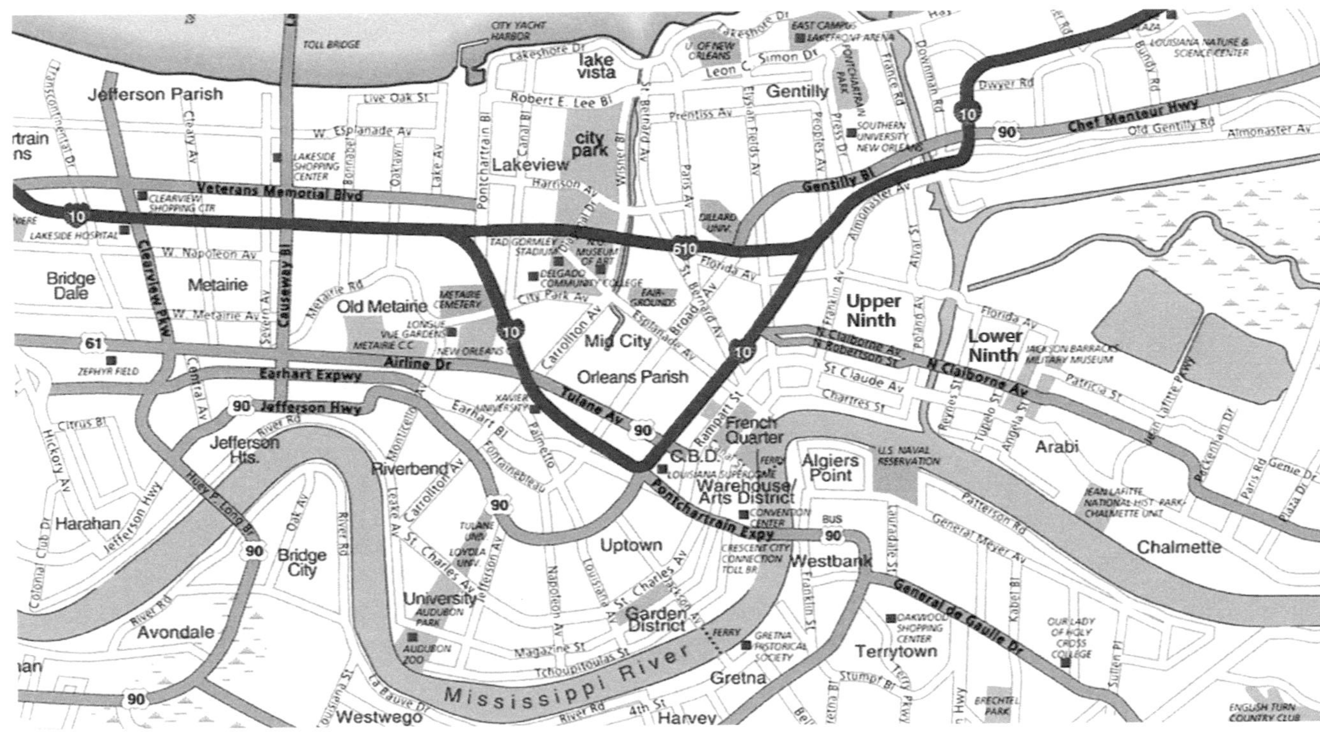

Jefferson Parish
Metairie
Bridge Dale
Old Metairie
Lakeview
city park
lake vista
Gentilly
Mid City
Orleans Parish
Upper Ninth
Lower Ninth
French Quarter
C.B.D.
Warehouse/ Arts District
Algiers Point
Arabi
Chalmette
Uptown
Garden District
University
Riverbend
Jefferson Hts.
Harahan
Bridge City
Avondale
Westwego
Gretna
Harvey
Westbank
Terrytown
Mississippi River
Veterans Memorial Blvd
Causeway Bl
Clearview Pkw
Airline Dr
Earhart Expwy
Jefferson Hwy
Tulane Av
Pontchartrain Expy
Chef Menteur Hwy
Gentilly Bl
N Claiborne Av
General de Gaulle Dr
Lakeshore Dr
Robert E. Lee Bl
Pontchartrain Bl
Canal Bl
St Charles Av
Magazine St
Tchoupitoulas St
Carrollton Av
Esplanade Av
Broad Av
St Claude Av
Chartres St
Rampart St
Elysian Fields Av
Franklin Av
Almonaster Av
Florida Av
Jean Lafitte Pkwy
Paris Rd
Huey P. Long Br
Lakeside Shopping Center
Clearview Shopping Ctr
Lakeside Hospital
Zephyr Field
Metairie Cemetery
Delgado Community College
Xavier University
Dillard Univ.
Southern University New Orleans
U of New Orleans
Pontchartrain Park
Louisiana Superdome
Convention Center
U.S. Naval Reservation
Jean Lafitte National Hist. Park-Chalmette Unit
Audubon Park
Audubon Zoo
Tulane Univ.
Loyola Univ.
Gretna Historical Society
Oakwood Shopping Center
Our Lady of Holy Cross College
Louisiana Nature & Science Center
English Turn Country Club
Jackson Barracks Military Museum
Ferry
Toll Bridge
City Yacht Harbor

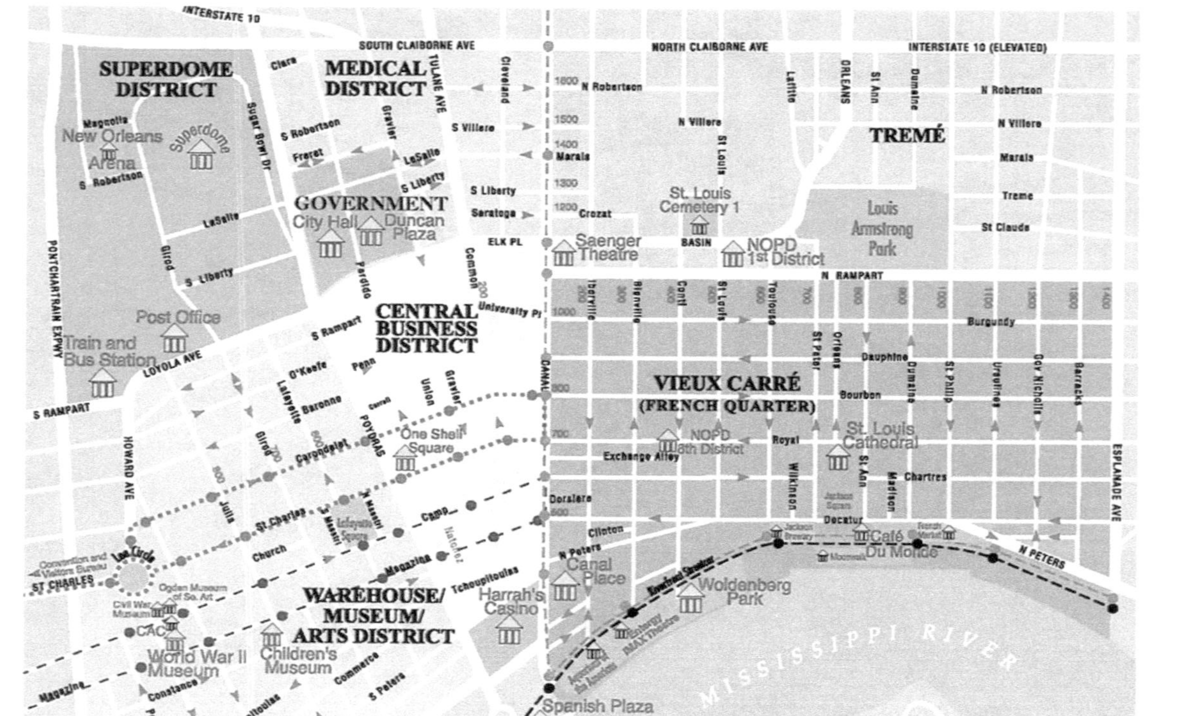

INTERSTATE 10
SOUTH CLAIBORNE AVE
NORTH CLAIBORNE AVE
INTERSTATE 10 (ELEVATED)
SUPERDOME DISTRICT
MEDICAL DISTRICT
TREMÉ
New Orleans Arena
Superdome
GOVERNMENT
City Hall
Duncan Plaza
St. Louis Cemetery 1
Louis Armstrong Park
Saenger Theatre
NOPD 1st District
CENTRAL BUSINESS DISTRICT
Post Office
Train and Bus Station
VIEUX CARRÉ (FRENCH QUARTER)
NOPD 8th District
St. Louis Cathedral
One Shell Square
Café Du Monde
Canal Place
Woldenberg Park
Harrah's Casino
WAREHOUSE/ MUSEUM/ ARTS DISTRICT
Ogden Museum of So. Art
Civil War Museum
CAC
World War II Museum
Children's Museum
Convention and Visitors Bureau
Lee Circle
Spanish Plaza
MISSISSIPPI RIVER
PONTCHARTRAIN EXPWY
LOYOLA AVE
S RAMPART
HOWARD AVE
ST CHARLES
TULANE AVE
CANAL
N RAMPART
ELK PL
BASIN
ESPLANADE AVE
N PETERS
Clara
Sugar Bowl Dr
Magnolia
S Robertson
LaSalle
Girod
S Liberty
Freret
Gravier
S Villere
Cleveland
Saratoga
Perdido
Common
University Pl
S Rampart
O'Keefe
Penn
Lafayette
Baronne
Union
POYDRAS
Carondelet
Julia
St Charles
Church
Camp
Magazine
Natchez
Tchoupitoulas
Constance
Commerce
S Peters
N Robertson
N Villere
Marais
Crozat
St Louis
Lafitte
ORLEANS
St Ann
Dumaine
Treme
St Claude
Iberville
Bienville
Conti
Toulouse
St Peter
Orleans
St Philip
Ursulines
Gov Nicholls
Barracks
Burgundy
Dauphine
Bourbon
Royal
Chartres
Decatur
Exchange Alley
Wilkinson
Madison
Dorsiere
Clinton
N Peters
Jackson Square
Moonwalk

Part One: RUIN

He knew too what it was to live through a hurricane with the other people of the island and the bond that the hurricane made between all people who had been through it. He also knew that hurricanes could be so bad that nothing could live through them.

— Ernest Hemingway, *Islands in the Stream*

Chapter 1

Friday, August 26, 2005
K minus sixty-five hours:
Lafayette, Louisiana

"Honey, listen to me. This is damned serious. Our private weather service just sent us an advance of the 5:00 p.m. National Hurricane Center advisory, and it's bad. The expected track of Katrina just shifted three hundred miles to the west. It's headed for New Orleans."

Elizabeth Boudreaux, in Lafayette for the next day's wedding of her friends Dr. Chris Breaux and Marianne Dashwood, could hardly believe William Darcy's words over the cell phone.

"What? I thought the storm was heading for Florida!" She turned on the hotel room television set, her cell glued to her ear.

"So did the weather service until just a couple of minutes ago." Her fiancé's voice was terse. "It's a Cat 2 now—winds at about one hundred—and they expect it to strengthen."

"Oh, no!" The five o'clock news led with Hurricane Katrina. The new track had moved to the mouth of the Mississippi River since the last advisory, placing New Orleans squarely in its crosshairs. "They're just announcing the warning now."

"Lizzy, DGS is declaring a full emergency. We've got to get the ships we have in New Orleans out of here, and we have to reroute all of our other traffic."

The implications hit Elizabeth. "You're not coming to Lafayette."

"I can't, babe. I've got to see to my people here."

Elizabeth got control of herself. "I understand. You do what you have to."

"I've got to go. I'll call later. We've got to make some decisions."

"Okay. There are decisions to be made here, too. When will you call?"

"Late—maybe ten o'clock. I love you."

Elizabeth placed her free hand over her heart. "I love you, too."

Metairie, Louisiana

Chuck Bingley navigated the Friday rush hour traffic while calling his wife.

"Jane, have you heard the news? They say Katrina's headed here."

"I just turned on the TV. When are you getting home?" Jane's voice was nervous.

"I'm just on the interstate now. Traffic's not too bad. I should be home at my regular time."

"What are we going to do?"

"We'll talk it over when I get home. Let me go, now. Love ya."

Baton Rouge, Louisiana

Carrie Buford watched the hurricane coverage as she sat on her living room couch, holding hands with her husband, John. Their son, Trey, was playing on John's lap.

"Good lord, they've already developed the graphics," Buford observed as the words "HURRICANE KATRINA" flew across the screen with a whoosh of sound.

"The local stations live for this," agreed Carrie. "I swear the weather boys get a hard-on every time there's a storm in the Gulf." She glanced at her husband, a captain in the Louisiana National Guard. "Are they going to call you up?"

"Oh, yeah. Just a matter of time."

Right on cue, the phone rang. The two shared a look before Buford deposited Trey into Carrie's arms and answered the call.

He spoke in a low tone, listening more than responding, and rang off after a minute.

"Well?" Carrie blurted.

"A heads-up. The brass thinks the governor will activate us by noon tomorrow. Excuse me, honey, but I better warn my officers and NCOs."

Carrie bit her lip as she watched her husband walk into the kitchen to retrieve the small directory where he kept his National Guard contacts. She had a very bad feeling about this.

Lakeview, New Orleans, Louisiana

THE KATZES' SHABBAT WAS INTERRUPTED BY THE NEWS ALERT about the hurricane. Dr. George and Emma Katz watched the broadcast with concern while Abe Weinberg, Emma's father, sat quietly. Finally, George passed a hand over his face and turned to his wife. She spoke first.

"Why don't we have the Shabbat now? They'll be talking about the storm all night."

George nodded his agreement and rose to follow Emma into the dining room.

"When are we leaving?" asked Abe.

The two stopped dead in their tracks and turned in unison to the older man.

"We're evacuating, aren't we?" Abe was standing next to an armchair.

"We haven't discussed it yet," Emma said, glancing at her husband, "but it would probably be for the best."

"I agree." Abe walked past them into the dining room, an astonished pair in his wake. Only last year, Abe had stubbornly refused to evacuate when Hurricane Ivan threatened New Orleans. Now, the old man had done a complete turnaround.

Everyone sat at the dinner table. "I appreciate the change of heart, but what brought this on, Abe?"

Fear was evident on his father-in-law's face. "I've been thinking a lot about what Hurricane Ivan did to Pensacola last year—how it tore up those bridges. Do you know how much one of those bridge spans weigh? Tons! And water floated them off the supports. Water!"

"Floated? Concrete *floats*?" George was flabbergasted.

"Under the right conditions, anything can float." The retired architect pulled his ever-present pen out of his shirt pocket and sketched on a paper napkin a cross section of a bridge span, speaking as he drew. "The Escambia Bay Bridge was a low-level trestle just like the Causeway and the I-10 Bridge to Slidell. The spans aren't secured to the pilings by bolts because salt water and spray would corrode them in no time. The engineers thought the bridges would last a lot longer without the invitation to corrosion from metal. The sheer weight of the spans keeps them in place. All of them meet federal highway standards." Abe looked his family in the face. "Trouble is, the design has a fault."

He gestured at his crude drawing. "See how the span section forms an inverted U? The Escambia Bay Bridge was fifteen feet above high tide, but the storm surge turned out to be about twenty. The rising water trapped air under the sections, just enough to lift them a couple of inches. That was sufficient for the surge and the winds to move the sections out of alignment before the air escaped. They lost what little buoyancy they had and sank into the bay."

Abe leaned back with a stricken look. "Almost every bridge and elevated highway from Florida to Texas is designed this way: solid horizontal concrete sections without holes for air to escape and built as low as possible to save money. The Causeway and the I-10 Bridge are just like the Pensacola bridge. It's a disaster waiting to happen. If Ivan had hit here, half the entrances to the city would have been cut off."

"But we've had storms in the past," Emma pointed out. "Why hasn't it happened before?"

"Storm surge wasn't high enough. You get an eighteen-foot surge or more, those bridges are toast." Abe took a breath. "The levees here are as good as anywhere in the world, so we can take a hit by a Cat 3, but if those two bridges are cut, it's going to be a *lot* more than three days to get everything okay again. How can help get here? Assuming the I-55 survives, trucks will be backed up for miles trying to get in from the west. The levees in Plaquemines and St. Bernard aren't adequate. They're going to get hurt if that storm comes anywhere near here. And the coast—" He shook his head. "If we're out of power for only three days, we'll be lucky. It could be a week or more. And no power means no water from the city. Why put up with that? Best to empty the refrigerator and hang out in a motel in Texas until the dust settles." Abe looked at George. "Besides, it will make Emma happier if we just get the hell out of here."

Emma leaned over and kissed her father's cheek. "Yes, it will. Thank you, Papa." She gave George a watery smile. "I'll call Mari in Lafayette and tell her we can't make the wedding. Then we'll have dinner." She walked into the kitchen.

George could see that Abe, for all his declarations, was frightened by the thought of evacuation. But the older man had let solid science and common sense overcome his dread of traffic, and the doctor could appreciate that. He patted Abe on the shoulder, trying to let him know he understood what his decision had cost him. With that, he went to help Emma in the kitchen.

Gentilly, New Orleans

Harmony may have reigned at the Katz household in Lakeview, but things were different with the Johnsons in Gentilly. Kaywanda Johnson's boyfriend, Scott Davis, was trying to convince them to evacuate, and Mrs. Johnson was having none of it.

"Miz Johnson, you really should be planning to get out of here."

The large, overweight woman shook her head. "No, no. This is my house. I'm not goin' anywhere."

"But, there's a hurricane coming."

"Now look here. I've been through more storms than I can remember. I got through Betsy, didn't I? I ain't leavin' so some hooligans can break into my house—no sir!"

"Kay, can't you get her to see sense?"

Kaywanda was torn. "Scott, her mind's made up. We'll be okay."

"*You're* not planning to stay, are you?"

"I can't leave my momma!"

"Crap, you're both crazy!"

"Watch your mouth!" Mrs. Johnson cried. "You don't talk that way in my house!"

Scott threw up his hands. "That's it! I'm done. I'm outta here. I'm not hanging around in a bowl waiting for a hurricane to come and drown me! Kay, you can come with me or you can stay. What's it gonna be?"

Mrs. Johnson crossed her arms over her enormous chest. "I'm stayin' right here, and so's my baby girl. You just take off, white boy. We don't need you, anyhow."

Scott looked at Kaywanda, but she wouldn't meet his eyes. "Fine, okay. I'm gone." He spun on his heel and walked out the front door. A moment later, Kaywanda followed, catching up with him on the sidewalk beside his beat-up car.

"I'm sorry, Scott, but I can't leave Momma. Can't you see that?"

Scott was so furious he was breathing hard. "All I see is two insane women. I ain't waiting here for a storm to come and kill me. If you were smart, you'd come with me."

"Leave Momma? Are you crazy?"

"If she wants to die so bad, let her."

"No! I ain't leaving her, an' that's final!"

Scott stared at her for a moment and then, with a curse, climbed into his car.

"Please say you understand!"

He shook his head. "I wish you good luck, Kaywanda. You're gonna need it." With that, he slammed the car into gear and peeled out.

A tearful Kaywanda returned to her mother, who was still mumbling. "Smart-ass Yankee tellin' *me* what to do! Babygirl, you're better off without him. You need a man, not a coward."

Kaywanda didn't respond. She only sat on the couch, trying to stem her tears.

Lafayette

CHRIS BREAUX HUNG UP THE PHONE JUST AS THE DASHWOODS and Elizabeth arrived.

"That was Will," he told Marianne as he hugged her. "He's not gonna make it."

Marianne kissed his cheek. "Lizzy's already told me. Neither are George and Emma."

Chris greeted the others as they joined the Breaux clan in the den. Eventually, everyone was seated in a rough circle.

"Okay, we've been thrown a curve ball," Mr. Breaux said. "What do we do?"

Chris turned to his intended. "Babe, what are you thinking?"

"We're still going to get married tomorrow, aren't we?" Marianne cried without pause.

"If you want to. I'm just worried about the wedding. With this storm out there, I don't know how many of our friends are going to be able to attend."

"I don't care about that! I'm marrying *you*!"

Chris jerked his head towards the kitchen. "Excuse us a minute, folks." The two left the den and closed the kitchen door behind them. "Honey, are you sure? This is your wedding. I just want it to be the way you want it."

Marianne hugged him. "All that's important to me is that you and I want to get married. The rest is just a party. As long as my mother and sister are here, I'm happy."

Chris kissed the top of her head. "All right. Let's go tell the others." They returned to the den and saw his mother on the phone.

"That was the Bufords," she reported as she hung up. "They think John's going to be called up, so they're canceling."

"I talked to Jane earlier. She and Chuck aren't coming, either," Elizabeth added.

"Doesn't matter," said Marianne. "This gig goes off as scheduled tomorrow."

"The boss has spoken. But, I'm going to need a new best man." Chris turned to his brother. "Would you do the honors?"

"Sure," Mike Breaux agreed. "Who takes my place and escorts Lizzy?"

It was agreed to use Chris's uncle, who was acting as an usher.

Mr. Breaux checked his watch. "Let's get down to the church for the rehearsal. Father Gerald's waiting for us. How many cars are we taking?"

Gulfport, Mississippi

An all-managers' meeting had just ended at the Jean Laffite Resort & Casino in Gulfport in which they planned for the orderly evacuation of the guests and the shutdown of the facility. Corporate headquarters in Las Vegas participated via teleconference.

"Any guest who wants to leave tonight, we don't charge 'em. Got that?" Edward Denham reminded his people. "We want them to remember we took good care of them, so they'll want to come back. Tomorrow, we start clearing out the hotel rooms. Standard emergency procedures for reservations and refunds. The gaming floor remains open until noon Sunday. Advise all your non-essential employees to evacuate. I want this place locked up tight by three o'clock Sunday afternoon. We'll have another meeting at nine tomorrow morning." He turned to the microphone on the conference table. "Anything you want to add, Vegas?"

"No, you've got everything covered, Ed."

"Thanks. That's all, people. You're dismissed." Denham disconnected the call to Nevada as the managers filed out of the room. Only John Waguespack hung back.

Denham glanced up. "What's up, John?"

"I thought I'd volunteer to stay here and monitor the building. You know, keep an eye on things."

Denham shook his head. "Not needed. Security will have that handled. They'll man the place until early Monday morning and then pull back inland until the storm's over. Thanks for the offer, but you just get out of here."

"Are you pulling out?"

"Yeah, the wife's packing right now. We've got rooms in Atlanta."

"Atlanta's pretty far away. Wouldn't it be a good idea to have a manager close by?"

"John, I said security's got it covered. Look, there's a line between being gung-ho and being stupid. You just do your job and take care of yourself. We clear?"

"Yes, sir."

Waguespack returned to his office. Lucy and the rest of the staff were already talking to the acts booked that weekend, canceling their gigs. He went into his office, closed the door, and pulled out the corporate directory to find the number of the VP of Mississippi Operations at the corporate office. He dialed the Nevada number and introduced himself.

"Yes, sir, we met at the last company conference. I'm glad you remember me. … Yes, we've got a storm bearing down on us. That's the reason I'm calling. I think we need a senior manager on site along with security. … Umm, most of our security people are good, but you never know. … Right. You know how it is. … Well, I'm a Mississippi native, and I've been through these things before. I'd be glad to stay behind. … Denham? He's pulling out—his wife is scared. I'm single, so that's not an issue. … Yeah, the casino will be closed, but my place is a quarter-mile away. … Sure, it's safe. It survived Camille. … Camille was a Category 5 storm that hit near here some years ago. I'll be fine. … Yes, sir, I'll keep you advised as things go along. Thank you for your confidence, sir. Good night."

Waguespack grinned as he hung up. The idea of staying behind to watch over things had come to him during the meeting. It was dangerous to go behind Denham's back, but Waguespack wasn't going to pass up this opportunity to impress the corporate bigwigs. If he pulled it off, he was on the fast track to Las Vegas.

Damn, Katrina just might be the best thing that ever happened to me.

K minus sixty-two hours: Mid-City, New Orleans

Richard Fitzwilliam closed the trunk of his wife's car. "You have everything, honey?"

Olivia Fitzwilliam finished securing their daughter in the car seat. "I'll gas up north of Hattiesburg, and we'll break up the trip at a rest stop somewhere in Alabama for a few hours before continuing to Atlanta." She and Megan were evacuating to her parents' house outside of Atlanta. By leaving on Friday night, they hoped to avoid the massive traffic jams well remembered from Ivan.

Fitzwilliam nodded and leaned in to kiss his daughter. "Be a good girl, now."

"Come with us, Daddy!"

"No, sweetie. Daddy has to protect the city. You have a good time at Grandma and Grandpa's, and I'll see you real soon. I love you." He kissed her again and closed the door. He then took his wife into his arms.

"When do you report?" she asked.

"Right after you leave. I'll be at Third District for the duration."

"I wish—oh, Fitz, I wish you were coming with us. Goddammit, I hate your job."

Fitzwilliam said nothing; he only held her close. A couple of breaths later, they shared a kiss.

"Call me when you stop, okay?"

"I will."

Fitzwilliam thought of something. "You have the charger for the cell?"

"Right in the car. I'll plug it in as soon as we leave." Olivia kissed him again and then got in the driver's seat.

Fitzwilliam stood in the driveway of his home and watched his family drive away, his mind already focused on the job ahead.

K minus sixty hours: Lafayette

Elizabeth was back in her hotel room by the time William called again. She told him Chris and Marianne had decided to go through with the ceremony the next day, and they talked about how quiet the rehearsal dinner had been.

"What time does the wedding end?" William asked.

"It starts at one, so we should be at the reception hall by two-thirty. Why?"

"Okay. I can have the jet land at four. Will that be long enough?"

"Jet? What are you talking about?"

"The DGS jet. We're flying out of here with Lakefront Airport being so low. It'll hole up in Oklahoma City until we can bring it back. I can have it pick you up at Lafayette Airport at four o'clock."

"You're going to Oklahoma City?"

"I'm not—you are. I've got to stay here and manage things."

Elizabeth almost dropped the phone. "I'm not leaving! I'm staying here with you!"

"Honey, please. You'll be safer out of here."

"And what about you?"

"I'm staying in the city until Sunday. I'll hunker down at Dansereau during the storm."

"Let me get this straight. It's too dangerous for me to stay, but it's not too dangerous for you? That makes no sense!" Elizabeth tapped down her anger at William for making plans without her input again.

"Look, I'll feel better if you're somewhere safe."

"I'm not leaving. Either we both leave, or neither of us does."

"Lizzy, please, listen to me—"

"No." She knew that facts, not screaming, were the best way to change William's mind. "You've told me Dansereau Plantation is built like a tank. It has a natural gas generator that can run the whole house. All that satellite equipment is there. If it's safe enough for you, it's safe enough for me."

"Yeah, but what if we got hit by a tornado? The house can't stand up to that! If something happened to you—"

Elizabeth pleaded, "Will, don't you see? What makes you think I would want to be somewhere else if something happened to you at Dansereau? Do you think I would want to live without you?" There was silence on the other end. "Baby, if we had children like Jane and Chuck, it would be different. But it's just you and me. I want to be with you. I *need* to be with you. Don't do this; don't cut me out."

There was a pause. "You're making this real hard, Liz."

"I'm not trying to be a problem, but I'm not abandoning you, and I'm not going to let you leave me behind. Besides, I have my work, remember? EDNO will need me if we get hit. So, there you are. You'll just have to put me up for the duration."

Another pause. "All right, you win."

"Will, this is NOT about winning or losing. It's about us being a couple, being a team." It was important that he understood that.

"I DO think of us as a team." She could hear him sigh. "What are you going to do tomorrow?"

"After the reception, I'll drive to Dansereau. I'll be going against traffic, so it shouldn't be too bad."

"I'll have Mrs. Reynolds open up the house for you. She'll be staying with us."

Elizabeth tried to lighten things up. She hated fighting with William. "Will, it'll be all right, you'll see."

"Yeah, I just love you so much it's scary."

"It's scary for me, too. We'll get through it together."

"I better go. I've got to have the flight plan changed, and then there's this call I've got to put in to London at midnight."

"Okay, honey. I love you. Don't work too late."

"I'll get some shut-eye after the call. Talk to you tomorrow."

Elizabeth's mind was still unsettled after she hung up. She understood William's concern, but he was wrong. She only hoped she handled it properly, that she didn't insult him. The old Elizabeth would have gotten angry and stormed about. The new, more mature Elizabeth used reason instead of emotion, and it seemed to work much better.

As she undressed for bed, she knew she still had work to do. She had convinced William she would not be a burden during this emergency. After she got to Dansereau, she would have to prove it.

Upper Ninth Ward, New Orleans

Greg Wickham watched the hurricane coverage with a smile on his face. The governor had declared a state of emergency and had recommended that people in the New Orleans area evacuate. Wickham had no intention of following the governor's advice, but he hoped others would.

Wickham had found it impossible to rebuild his drug dealing

empire in New Orleans. Other gangs, large and violent, had a stranglehold on the drug trade. But this storm might be just the chance he needed to take a few of them down.

Wickham knew where several of the gangs stored their product. If a major hurricane threatened the city, some of the gang members might flee. The drug caches would be only lightly guarded. If one heavily armed man was daring and fearless, he could reap a fortune.

He glanced at his closet. He still had a half dozen hand grenades from the Columbian boat massacre so many months before. That kind of firepower should give him an edge.

Wickham sat back and tossed a few potato chips into his mouth. If everything went right, G-Daddy would spread a little chaos in the city in a few days.

Chapter 2

Saturday, August 27
K minus fifty-three hours:
Gulf of Mexico

At dawn, the armada set out.

Offshore of Louisiana and Texas, in the western Gulf, lay the bulk of the oil and natural gas reserves of the United States. Thousands of people on hundreds of production platforms worked day and night to provide the petroleum and natural gas the American economic engine required. Combined, the two states produced 2.8 million barrels a day, a third of America's domestic production.

The people who labored to extract this black gold from the shale and sandstone beneath the Gulf were hard and hard working. With twelve-hour shifts, seven to fourteen days at a time on massive platforms as much as one hundred miles from land, the men and women of the oil field were not afraid of hardships. But as massive as rigs were, the roughnecks knew they could be destroyed by hurricanes. Just like the storm now churning off Florida.

At first light, hundreds of helicopters from Venice, Grand Isle, Intracoastal City, and other heliports across the region took flight to evacuate the roughnecks, engineers, and roustabouts. Workboats ran flat out for the rigs close to shore and in the marshes. The pilots and crews all risked their lives laboring to retrieve the most precious component the oil exploration companies had—their highly trained workers.

Meanwhile, on the rigs, all hands secured operations. The procedure was well rehearsed, for it occurred every time a storm was in the Gulf.

Multiple trips by the boats and 'copters were needed to retrieve everyone, but there was no panic. It was a familiar, orderly process. The pilots and crews were professionals, and the workers knew their brothers and sisters would not rest until everyone was safely ashore.

By nightfall, the Gulf of Mexico was devoid of human life.

K minus fifty-one hours:
Miami, Florida

The data stream into the National Hurricane Center (NHC) confirmed the previous day's computer model predictions. The tropical system named Hurricane Katrina, heading for the mouth of the Mississippi, had grown in intensity. Sustained winds were now 115 miles per hour, placing the storm in the third category of the Saffir-Simpson Hurricane Scale.

Katrina was officially a monster.

K minus forty-eight hours:
Washington, DC

The President's emergency declaration the day before authorized the Federal Emergency Management Agency to ramp up in preparation to respond to the hurricane. FEMA was created by the Robert T. Stafford Disaster Relief and Emergency Assistance Act of 1988, and it was the most misunderstood organization in the federal government. A part of the Department of Homeland Security since 2003, it was kept small on purpose by Congress to save money. There existed only two thousand permanent FEMA employees. In case of an emergency, FEMA was to call on other government agencies—Coast Guard, USDA, EDA, HUD, SBA, EPA, and others—to lend it personnel as needed. Private contractors could be hired.

It made sense on paper. An earthquake would need different experts than a forest fire or a terrorist attack. It was expected the "borrowed" employees and contractors would work cooperatively with FEMA officials. However, there was nothing in the law that gave FEMA authority over any employees but their own.

At 1000 CDT, an hour after Plaquemines and St. Charles parishes ordered a mandatory evacuation, the director of FEMA appeared on television from Washington to encourage people in the affected area to leave. He then left for his command post in Baton Rouge. He would arrive near mid-day on Sunday.

Covington, Louisiana

Chuck hung up the phone and turned to Jane. "All right, everything's set. You and the kids will stay at Mom's house. Carrie will join you there Sunday night. Mom's getting the rooms ready for you."

"Does your mother know we're bringing Rufus with us?"

Chuck shrugged. "She should. I told her I was staying but everyone else was headed for Baton Rouge." He reached over and rubbed the Great Dane's ears. "Who can resist my big boy, huh?" Rufus simply gazed at his master with adoration.

Jane grimaced. "Your mother might."

"How could she? She's got that walking dust mop of a Persian. Rufus is as much a part of our family as Chin Chan is of hers. Besides, he's completely housebroken. He hardly sheds at all. Tell you what—offer to have her place professionally cleaned afterwards. That'll take care of it."

Jane wasn't so sure. "I wish you were going with us."

Chuck shook his head. "I've got to stay here and watch the house. If any of those trees fall, somebody's got to patch things up before the water damage gets too bad." He hugged her. "I'll be fine."

"Until the power goes out."

"So what? It'll be like camping out. C'mon, let's get the car packed. If you can get on the road tonight, you can beat all the traffic."

K minus forty-six hours:
Baton Rouge

CAPTAIN JOHN BUFORD, DRESSED IN GREEN BDUs[1], WALKED OUT of the office of the National Guard Armory in Baton Rouge, his orders in hand.

"Where are we going, sir?" asked the lieutenant of Second Platoon.

"Superdome. We're to assist in security." He put on his beret.

"With no weapons?"

"Won't need 'em. The NOPD will back us up."

"That ain't bad," remarked the First Platoon lieutenant. "At least we get air conditioning."

"You're not going to be sitting on your ass enjoying it," Buford shot back. "We'll be patrolling the facility constantly as long as there are people in there. The state doesn't want the place torn up this time."

"Roger that."

Buford eyed the troops milling about. "All right, let's get our people loaded up and get this show on the road." He walked over to his command Humvee, Sergeant Mack already behind the wheel.

"Here we go again, sir."

"Yep, it sure seems that way, Mack," Buford said as he sat down.

Told of their assignment, Mack asked, "And where's the staging area for the rest?"

"Governor's sending them directly to Jackson Barracks."

Mack frowned. "In the strike zone?"

Buford shrugged. "Not my call. Let's just focus on our assignment."

"Like in Kabul?"

"Correct, Sergeant."

"Can do, sir."

AS FOUR THOUSAND MEMBERS OF THE LOUISIANA NATIONAL GUARD moved towards New Orleans, a sizable number of other military units were leaving the city. The US Coast Guard could not leave

---

1 Battle Dress Uniform

their invaluable helicopters in the path of the oncoming storm. Saturday found Lt. Commander Fred Wentworth leading a flight of USCG helos towards their staging area in Alexandria, safely deep in the central part of the state. Similar flights were leaving the Mississippi Coast. They would return to conduct search and rescue as soon as weather permitted.

Meanwhile, their comrades assigned to boats and shore duty were busy securing the ports and harbors. They were scheduled to pull out the next day.

The civilians of the central Gulf Coast had their duties, too. The special sound of an approaching hurricane arose—that of power saws and hammers, of cars dashing to supermarkets and hardware stores, of cash registers ringing, and credit card readers dispensing receipts.

It was the sounds of boarding up and preparation. Plywood was cut and nailed over the windows of houses and businesses. Loose items like planting boxes, water hoses, and children's toys were stored away lest they become missiles in one hundred plus mile-per-hour winds. Shoppers bought out the stocks of water, milk, batteries, bread, and canned meat. Anyone who had lived in this part of the country for more than five years knew the drill.

For those evacuating and those staying behind, it was not quite business as usual. The forecasters were scared of this storm, and that fear was successfully transmitted to most of the population.

Most, but not all.

K minus forty-four hours: Lafayette

The newly wedded Mr. and Mrs. Christopher Breaux walked out of the church sanctuary into a sunny afternoon just as the clock struck two. The small party waved as Chris and Marianne climbed into the waiting limo before following in their own cars to the reception hall down the road. Within a few minutes, Elizabeth was posing for the requisite wedding photographs, hoping her smile hid her disappointment. She missed William terribly.

What followed was the most downbeat South Louisiana Catholic wedding reception Elizabeth had ever attended. Almost half the guests were no-shows. Nothing could get the few attendees out of a forced-cheer stupor. Not the bouquet toss, which hit Elizabeth squarely in the chest while all the other young women ducked as per Marianne's request. Not the required Money Dance. Not even the heartfelt toast to the couple from Mr. Breaux. The looming threat of a hurricane hung over the crowd like a persistent fog.

When the time came for Marianne to change, Elizabeth accompanied Margaret and Mrs. Dashwood into a back room to help the bride.

"What are you going to do now that your honeymoon's canceled?" asked Margaret as she unzipped her sister.

"*Postponed*, Margaret. We still have our reservations at the hotel in Lafayette for tonight," Marianne said with perfect composure as she shrugged off her gown. "With the storm in the Gulf, we'll just put off our cruise until another time." She smiled as she reached for her going-away dress. "That's why we got the travel insurance."

"I got in touch with the cruise line, and we can reschedule," added Mrs. Dashwood. "I pulled a couple of strings and called in some favors, so the company won't charge us a rebooking fee."

Marianne slipped the dress over her head. "Even if we wanted to go, our flight was canceled."

"Are you staying here?" asked Elizabeth as she zipped up Marianne's dress.

"Yes. We'll wait out the storm with the Breauxes." She turned to her mother. "Mom, I wish you would change your mind and stay. They have plenty of room."

"I've got to get back to Jackson and prepare the house. We'll be okay—we're pretty far inland." The Dashwoods had checked out of the hotel and were planning to leave Lafayette right after the reception.

"And you're driving back to Dansereau?" Marianne asked Elizabeth.

"Yes. Will says it's built very strong, and the generators will run the whole place, even the air conditioning."

The ladies engaged in some lighter chitchat while Marianne refreshed her makeup and changed her jewelry. Mrs. Dashwood carefully put away her daughter's wedding dress.

"All right," Marianne said as she finished, "group hug!" The four women embraced. "This is a happy day. Let's not worry about hurricanes or any of that stuff. Let's everybody drive safely, okay?"

Elizabeth asked, "Ready?"

Marianne grinned. "The question is—is Chris ready?"

"Mari!" her mother scolded.

Marianne just waggled her eyebrows and left the room. Elizabeth helped the Dashwoods move Marianne's belongings to one of the Breauxes' cars to return to the house.

Tulane Medical Center,
Downtown, New Orleans

"HELLO," GEORGE KATZ SAID INTO HIS CELL PHONE AS HE SAT IN his small office at Tulane Medical Center.

"Hi, honey. I just wanted you to know I've returned from getting the last of the stuff Papa and I will need before we head out."

"Good. When are you leaving, Emma?"

"We'll pack tonight and then get some sleep. We'll leave early tomorrow morning."

"Is the car all gassed up?"

He heard a chuckle. "Yes, dear, and I checked the tires. I had the oil changed a couple of weeks ago. We'll be fine. Don't worry about us." Emma's light tone turned serious. "How's everything at your end?"

George leaned back in his chair. "Busy. We sent off all but the most critical patients. That leaves us with about one hundred twenty. We've got plenty of diesel for the generators, so we'll be okay if the power goes. Plenty of food and water—kitty litter, too."

"Kitty litter?"

"Fifteen hundred pounds of the stuff in case the toilets stop working."

"Uggh!"

"They opened up the Park Plaza Hotel a couple of blocks away for staff families, and a bunch of them took advantage of it."

There was a pause on the other end. "Do you want us to change our plans and come downtown?"

George sat up. "No, don't do that. I've already got your reservations in Houston. They're probably the last ones available. And besides, I'll feel better with you and Abe over there than right next door."

"All right. I've got to fix Papa dinner now. Can I call you later tonight?"

"Please. I love you, honey."

"I love you. Bye."

George ended the call as a sound caught his attention. Two hospital guards walked by armed with shotguns, the click of their hard-soled shoes against the tile floor echoed through the hall. George was unnerved by the sight. He never knew the guards owned firearms other than handguns.

He fingered the green wristband the hospital had handed out to staff and dependents. *Green for Tulane.* It was a security measure, he knew, but he couldn't help but recall a wisecrack he had overheard as he was putting it on.

"It's so they can identify our bodies after the storm."

New Orleanians were renowned for their black humor, but this jest hit a bit too close to home as far as George was concerned. One never knew what one of those storms could do.

Louisiana Superdome

BUFORD AND HIS MEN CARRIED THEIR GEAR INTO THE SUPERDOME. In an open space, Buford had Mack round up the company.

"All right," he called out, "you're going to be part of a five hundred fifty-man security team. You'll be told where to stash your gear. After that, I want squads formed. Study your maps and charts. Start familiarizing yourself with this place. Get to know it like the back of your hand.

"At 0800 sharp tomorrow, we start letting people in. Everybody gets searched, and I mean *everybody*. The only weapons in the Dome will belong to NOPD. We have no idea how many folks are going to come, but we'll have plenty of MREs and water. Enough for three days. Trucks will arrive soon. When they do, I want them unloaded and everything stowed away in a secure area.

"Any questions? No? Good. Platoon leaders, take over."

K minus forty-two hours: New Orleans

Louisiana had learned its lesson from Hurricane Ivan the year before. At 4:00 p.m., the barriers were removed from the interstates, and the tolls were suspended on the Causeway over the lake and the Crescent City Connection over the river. Contraflow was put into effect, and all lanes of I-10 in Jefferson became westbound.

An hour later, Anna Elliot watched her boss, the mayor of New Orleans, hold a joint news conference with the governor of Louisiana. Four hours before, Alabama's governor had ordered an evacuation of all low-lying areas near the coast. Now Louisiana should be doing the same.

Only it didn't.

The governor made a passionate plea for the citizens to listen to their local officials and follow the evacuation plan. The mayor declared a state of emergency and recommended the people of the city leave. Busses were available to carry folks to evacuation centers out of the strike zone, but it fell far short of a mandatory evacuation.

Anna sighed. There had been heated discussions in City Hall about this very issue. She and others had pressed the point that the mayor had the authority under state law to order an evacuation. But the lawyers disagreed, and the mayor sided with them.

She prayed the people would take this opportunity to flee. As for herself, she could go nowhere. She would be with the emergency response team in City Hall. After the news conference, she'd go to her apartment, pack what she would need for the next few days, and get some rest.

It was certain she would get little in the days to come.

K minus forty-one hours: Lafayette

Marianne and Chris let themselves into their hotel room, carrying only an overnight bag. Chris tossed it onto the dresser before turning to his new wife.

"Well, here we are, babe. I'm sorry it wasn't quite what we had planned."

Marianne wrapped her arms around herself. All day she had maintained a cheerful demeanor, not wanting anyone to know how disappointed she was. Now, safely in her hotel room, her façade fell away.

"I know I shouldn't let it bother me, but…oh, damn it!" Chris took her into his arms. "Why does everything happen to us?" she said into his shoulder. "Our wedding, our reception, our honeymoon—all ruined!"

Chris knew better than to try to say anything. He simply held her in silence. To be honest, his feelings weren't very far from hers.

Marianne sniffed. "Even the guys in the band couldn't make it. Why did this have to happen now? Why couldn't God wait a week before screwing us all over?"

Chris caressed her hair. Spent, Marianne chuckled into his chest.

"You're just waiting me out, aren't you? Puttin' up with my moaning and groaning until I'm amenable to you jumping my bones."

"Well, you *are* my wife now. It's kinda in the contract. The bit about 'love, honor and *obey*.'"

She looked up at him. "That wasn't in the ceremony."

"Really? Must have been an oversight. I think it's on the marriage certificate."

She shook her head. "You guys are all the same. There's only one thing you want."

"Mmm-hmm."

She looked up at him, her hands cupping his cheeks. "Well, since we're here and we've got nothing better to do…" She started undoing the buttons on his shirt. "C'mon, Cajun-boy. Let's see what you've got."

"Anytime, Mrs. Breaux."

Elizabeth left the reception hall minutes after Marianne's family. It took time to get to the interstate. Lafayette's traffic north towards the I-10 had grown steadily more congested since it was an evacuation route. The traffic lights were turned off, and police at the intersections attempted to enforce order on fleeing residents from points south.

Elizabeth made decent time once she went eastward on the I-10 towards Baton Rouge. The only traffic she encountered were first responders, the odd trucker making one last haul, and locals seeking the last bit of plywood for the windows or bottled water for the house. The stream of westbound vehicles was something dreadful to behold. An endless line of thousands of cars and trucks of all kinds crawled bumper to bumper. The monotony was broken by the occasional sheriff's deputy or state trooper passing on the left shoulder.

She wondered whether any of her friends were caught up in that mess, but Elizabeth resisted the urge to pull out her BlackBerry and find out. The cellular system had to be overloaded.

Within ninety minutes, she was at the outskirts of Baton Rouge, and she had a decision to make. Normally, Elizabeth would continue eastward through the city on I-10 until she reached either the Sunshine Bridge near Donaldsonville or the Veterans Memorial Bridge in Gramercy. But Baton Rouge traffic was a pain on ordinary days, and this day was far from ordinary. It had to be horrible. Contraflow stopped at Laplace, and there was no telling what the conditions were on those bridges over the Mississippi.

So Elizabeth exited I-10 and headed south on LA 1. The traffic was heavy and all the intersections were manned, but slow and steady was the best alternative. Once she reached Donaldsonville, she jumped on the River Road, LA 18. Now, unless the highway was blocked, nothing would stop her from reaching Dansereau Plantation.

At Vacherie, she got a scare. Traffic control was so horrendous that Elizabeth feared the road was blocked, and she thought of turning on LA 20 towards her parent's home in Chackbay. But she took a chance and was rewarded. Traffic thinned out after the

Gramercy Bridge, and minutes later, she was before the closed gates of Dansereau.

Flustered, Elizabeth remembered she did not have a remote to operate them. She began to reach for her cell to call William when she noticed the keypad/intercom stand next to the driveway. She lowered her window and pressed the call button.

A few moments passed. *"Hello?"*

"Mrs. Reynolds, it's Lizzy Boudreaux."

"Oh! Hold on a second."

The gates swung open, and Elizabeth drove to the house. It was twilight, but the mansion was well lit and inviting. She saw Mrs. Reynolds just outside the kitchen door as she pulled up.

"How was the drive from Lafayette, Miss Lizzy?" the housekeeper asked after she greeted her.

"It wasn't too bad until I got on Highway 1. But you should have seen all the people headed in the other direction!"

"I know. It's been all over the TV. Can I help with your things?"

Between the two of them, Elizabeth's belongings were in the house in quick order. Refusing anything to eat, she joined Mrs. Reynolds in the den to watch the hurricane coverage.

Fifteen minutes later, the phone rang. The women shared a look.

"That will be Will," Elizabeth predicted.

"I'll bet you're right." Mrs. Reynolds smiled as she answered the phone. "Darcy residence. Oh, Mr. Will!" She winked at Elizabeth. "Yes, sir, she's right here. Shall I put her on? Hold on, please…" She tried to hide a smirk as she handed the receiver to Elizabeth.

As expected, William asked her about the drive and the wedding and reception. Elizabeth happily chatted about her day, pleased to hear William's voice, even if it was on the other end of a phone line.

"Man, that's tough about the honeymoon."

"I know. Mari's taking it real well, though."

"Glad to hear it. She's a strong lady. Reminds me of somebody else I know."

"Oh?" Elizabeth grinned. "And who might that be?"

"It's somebody you know. She's smart, she's beautiful, and she can talk me into damn near anything."

"William—"

"It's just a joke, honey."

"Right." Elizabeth rolled her eyes. "When are you coming home?"

"Tomorrow. I'll work until noon and then prepare the condo. I thought I'd run by your place and empty the refrigerator. By the time I leave, the traffic should clear. Look for me at about six."

Elizabeth shook her head. Sir William was at it again. "You don't have to do that."

"It's no trouble. Besides, if you lose power, you'll never get the stink out of the icebox."

"All right. Thank you, sweetie. Get some rest tonight."

"Is Mrs. Reynolds still there?"

"Yes."

"Then I won't embarrass my lovely fiancée by saying what I would like to be doing to her instead of resting."

Elizabeth blushed. "Good night, William."

She heard his laugh. "Good night, Lizzy. Love you."

"I love you, too."

An hour later, Mrs. Reynolds returned to her own house, leaving Elizabeth alone in the huge estate. In the months she and William had been dating, Dansereau Plantation had become a second home, but this was the first night she had ever spent alone in the place.

The first but certainly not the last, she thought. *Mrs. Darcy won't be able to attend every out of town trip. I might as well get used to it.*

K minus thirty-eight hours: Baton Rouge

Catherine Bingley, alerted by Jane's phone call, waited in the driveway as the minivan pulled in. She greeted her daughter-in-law with a hug.

"Jane, what took you so long? I've been worried sick over you!"

"I'm sorry, but traffic was awful, especially in Baton Rouge. Oh no, Hailey!" The pregnant woman dashed back to the open van door to grab Rufus's collar. "You almost let Rufus out. You have to be careful, dear, or he might run in the street."

Hailey hung her head. "I'm sorry, Mommy."

Jane hugged her daughter. "That's all right. Take Rufus by his leash and say hello to Grandmother while I get Brett out of his car seat."

Jane retrieved her young son while Hailey carefully led the Great Dane over to Mrs. Bingley. Rufus dutifully followed his young mistress. Jane couldn't miss the look of unpleasant surprise on Catherine's face. The older woman kissed her grandson and gave Jane a look.

"You brought the dog?" It was clear she was not happy.

"Yes, Chuck didn't tell you, did he?"

"No, he didn't."

"I'm sorry, but we couldn't leave him in Covington. Chuck will have enough to do without watching Rufus, especially if a tree falls on our fence. He'll be no bother, I promise."

Rufus sat wagging his long tail and panting happily at Mrs. Bingley, looking goofy with his huge tongue hanging out of one side of his mouth.

Unimpressed, Catherine asked, "Where is it going to sleep?"

Jane gestured to the van. "We brought his crate." She giggled. "It takes up most of the back of the van!"

"I'm sure it does," she said dryly.

"He's completely housebroken and hardly sheds."

Catherine blinked. "You mean to bring that—" She glanced at her granddaughter, who had her arms around the Great Dane's neck. Rufus didn't mind the attention one bit. Catherine started again. "I'm not used to having a dog like that in my house, Jane."

"Grandmother," injected Hailey, "can I bring Rufus in to meet Chin Chan? They're going to be such good friends!"

Catherine knelt down. "Chin Chan is very sensitive, dear. This dog may frighten him."

"Oh no, Grandmother. Rufus likes cats, and dogs, and everybody. We sol—so—" She screwed up her face to remember the word. "*Socialized* him. He's met lots of cats. He's nice!"

Catherine sighed. "Very well. Let's all go in together." She stood up. "We'll get your belongings later, Jane, as well as that crate. Where did you plan to put it, by the way?"

"It should fit in the washroom."

Catherine gritted her teeth. "We'll see."

K minus thirty-six hours: Gulf of Mexico

The monster was moving steadily north-northwest at about twelve miles per hour. It hadn't increased much in power, but it was steadily drawing energy from the incredibly warm waters. The sun was beginning to go down, but it would do nothing to retard its growth. It wasn't just pulling energy from the Gulf; its winds were pushing water along with it.

By 2200 CDT, the NHC had upgraded the Hurricane Watch area to Hurricane Warning, indicating the storm was moving, inevitably, towards landfall.

Onward the monster advanced, pulling more and more water in its wake.

Chapter 3

Sunday, August 28
K minus thirty-three hours: Gulf of Mexico

The monster had fed well. The winds whipping around the eye were now moving at over 140 mph. It was now a powerful Category 4 storm, moving towards the Gulf Coast at twelve miles an hour, and there was nothing but more warm water before it.

Third District Headquarters

THE LEADERSHIP OF THE NOPD THIRD DISTRICT READ THE DAILY duty roster in dismay. The announcement was clear. A state of emergency existed. All hands called in for special duty. All leaves and vacations canceled. Yet, fully one-third of the district's personnel had failed to show up for roll call. Most of the missing were either civilian employees or desk jockeys. That was not surprising. However, patrol officers were absent too, including veterans. No one wanted to say there were deserters in the ranks, but these people were definitely AWOL.

The precinct captain gave the list of no-shows to a lieutenant. "Get some people on the horn, and get these stragglers in here."

"Screw 'em," cried Richard Fitzwilliam to his boss. "I'll get my people on the street and get ready for this thing. We'll do the job. Take care of those assholes later."

"Get going, Fitz. Leave this personnel shit to me."

Fitzwilliam nodded and left for the duty room to issue the orders for the next shift.

K minus twenty-seven hours:
Gulf of Mexico

Atmospheric pressure technically is the pressure at any point in the Earth's atmosphere. In common usage, atmospheric pressure, or barometric pressure, is the air pressure at ground level. Meteorologists worldwide have long measured air pressure in millibars (mb). In the United States, mercury barometers, which measure air pressure in inches of mercury, are still commonly used by TV forecasters for the same reason Americans have retained the Fahrenheit scale for temperature—it's familiar. One atmosphere of pressure is equivalent to 29.9 inches, or 1,031 mb. This is considered normal.

If there is one truism about the weather, it is that it is never *normal.*

Atmospheric pressure is in constant flux, intricately tied to weather systems. Generally, high pressure means fair weather, while low pressure is associated with storms. The range of pressure is relatively narrow. The highest barometric pressure ever recorded at sea level was 1,086 mb, while the lowest pressure outside of a tornado was 870 mb during a typhoon in the Pacific. This makes the range of possible pressure approximately 216 millibars, or 6.37 inches of mercury.

Roughly, a tropical storm can exist at a pressure of about 1,000 mb, and a Category 1 hurricane starts somewhere south of 990 mb. The stronger the storm, the lower the pressure.

An hour after Hancock County, Mississippi, ordered a mandatory evacuation, the reports out of the NHC confirmed the wisdom of the edict. Incredibly, incoming data showed the internal pressure of the monster had dropped from 930 to 909 millibars, and the maximum sustained winds at the eyewall were 167 mph.

The monster was now a Category 5 horror, and it had not deviated from its track towards the Louisiana/Mississippi line. The eye was two hundred fifty miles SSE of the mouth of the Mississippi River, still traveling at twelve miles per hour.

New Orleans

AT 0800, THE TROOPERS OF THE LOUISIANA ARMY NATIONAL Guard took up their positions. Buford walked around, reviewing his final instructions to his people. The Guard expected no problems, even though the vast majority were unarmed. Only NOPD and MPs carried side arms. The others were protected only by the sense of authority that camouflage BDUs commanded.

"Okay, open it up," Buford ordered.

The doors opened, and the first of the enormous horde of people outside began to trickle into the stadium.

Lakeview

EMMA CLOSED THE DOOR TO HER CAR AND GLANCED AT HER FAther. "Ready, Papa?"

He took a breath. "Ready as I'll ever be, princess."

She started the engine. "It's going to be a long drive. You do know that, right?"

"I know. We'll be lucky to make it to Houston before nightfall."

Emma gave Abe a tight smile and reached over to peck his cheek. "Let's prepare for the worst and hope for the best." She fastened her seat belt.

Abe grunted. "C'mon, we're burning daylight!"

Emma laughed as she backed out of the driveway.

A FEW MINUTES AFTER TALKING TO THE PRESIDENT, THE MAYOR ordered the first mandatory evacuation in the history of the City of New Orleans. Thankfully, it was redundant, for the greatest mass departure ever in the United States was already underway.

Over two and a half million souls lived in the strike zone—the Greater New Orleans and southeastern Louisiana area, the six southern counties of Mississippi, and the two counties that made up Mobile, Alabama. The lessons learned from Camille, Andrew, Georges, and Ivan were well heeded: Get out now.

By the thousands, cars and trucks streamed in three directions. Louisianans to the north and west, the others to the north and east. Most took the interstate highways and fought enormous traffic jams. Others, more familiar with their surroundings, stuck to the local roads, in an attempt to make better time. For some, the drive was short—only a few score miles inland to high ground. For others, their destinations were hundreds of miles away in other states. But the withdrawal was managed without major incident. This was not the first evacuation for most Gulf Coast residents.

Cooperation between the states was the key. Mississippi and Louisiana coordinated on Contraflow rules for I-59 from Slidell to Poplarville and I-55 from Laplace to Brookhaven. When Baton Rouge initiated Contraflow the day before, it was a decision made in concert with Jackson. Alabama worked their part of the plan, encouraging their people to head east. Within hours, the coastal cities of the region became ghost towns.

Later, it was estimated ninety percent of the people in the coastal areas fled in the thirty-six hours before the monster's landfall, including about one million in the New Orleans area alone, a feat the experts had deemed impossible.

But not everybody left.

Those who remained had also learned lessons from the previous storms—very different lessons. Too many times had they heard the local forecasters go ballistic over "the big one" headed right for their door, only to see it fizzle or turn away. They were tired of uprooting their families, driving for hours, and spending hundreds of dollars for motel rooms, food, and gas, only to return to an undamaged town and a looter-ransacked house.

They knew better than their neighbors. Hadn't they survived Betsy, Camille, or Andrew? Certainly, they had been told a Category 5 hurricane would destroy them. But would it? Hurricane Camille did wipe Bay St. Louis off the map, but it was so small that New Orleans barely felt it. Hurricane Andrew devastated Homestead, Florida, but nearby Miami remained virtually unscathed. The odds of Katrina having a direct hit on New Orleans were astronomical. Yes, the levees could be overtopped, but the pumps were designed to handle that. It was better to take a chance, stay, and protect their property, they decided.

Others had a different excuse. They were homebodies, used to their ordinary, unchanging lives. Anything was better than spending days cooped up in an uncomfortable shelter, elbow-to-elbow with a bunch of smelly and untrustworthy strangers. Mostly elderly, they preferred to sit quietly in a favorite chair in their kingdom of denial, while Armageddon approached at a dozen miles each hour.

Some had no way of getting out. The city provided buses to the Superdome, but not transport out of the city. To many, the prospect of being cooped up in the Dome was worse than the storm. They remembered was it was like during Ivan. If they didn't have family, or friends, or neighbors who could give them a lift out of town, they stayed put.

Some had to stay because of their jobs in law enforcement, public service, health care, or hospitality. Yes, *hospitality*. Someone had to run the hotels for the guests who couldn't get out and serve the new guests coming in—for a small army was arriving.

The national and international press descended in force upon New Orleans, drawn to what promised to be a major story of the year. These hardy reporters and correspondents, cameramen and sound engineers, intended to brave Nature's fury and capture the destruction for posterity. But not in discomfort. They filled prime rooms in fancy French Quarter hotels. They would stand witness to a devastating hurricane while sleeping on 600-thread-count, Egyptian cotton sheets.

French Quarter

JUSTIN MIDDLETON RELUCTANTLY FOUND HIMSELF BACK IN A CITY he had forsaken many years before. Bryan Thorpe, an up-and-coming reporter for a local network affiliate in Connecticut, had demanded to cover the hurricane, and the news director, seeing a chance to steal ratings from the other stations in the market, agreed. Justin was Thorpe's producer, and where the talent went, so did he.

"You got all the stuff, Justin?" Thorpe asked as he carried his hanging bag over his arm as he walked into the Napoleon Quarters Hotel.

Justin glanced at the jerk as he and the cameraman, Sam Watson, struggled with the rest of the gear in the trunk of the taxi. "Oh, yeah, Bryan," he answered with thinly disguised sarcasm, "we got it covered. Don't we, Sam?"

Thorpe waved as he went through the doors.

Watson chuckled. "Asshole probably thinks this will be his ticket to New York City and the network. He's got the hair for it."

Justin snickered as he paid the driver. He took in the sight along the street. The damn Quarter was just as humid and smelly as he remembered from his Loyola days. All the biggies were there: the networks, the cable news outlets, and of course, the Weather Channel. Everybody wanted a piece of the action just in case they got lucky and the city took it in the shorts. The dish trucks jockeyed for a clear line towards the satellites orbiting high above. Justin had already arranged for time on the network's dish so Thorpe could beam his reports back home.

"Hey, Justin," said Watson, "you've been through these things before, huh?"

Justin shrugged at his nervous co-worker. "Nothing to worry about. I went to college down here, you know. Never had a bad storm hit us. Some say there's this heat sink around the city, protecting it. Like Miami during Hurricane Andrew. We'll be down here for a few days, enjoy some beers in the Quarter, and eat good food. Be like a vacation. Come on, let's get this shit in the rooms."

With no bellhop around, the two men lugged their gear into the hotel.

Upper Ninth Ward

Greg Wickham stood on the small balcony of his house, smoking a cigarette and watching the neighbors leave. He had to be patient and wait until the storm was almost there. Then he would make his move.

"Hey, Steve!" A skinny black man from across the street tossed a black plastic garbage bag of belongings into the bed of a rusted pickup truck. "Ain't you gittin' out?"

Wickham took a puff before he answered. "Maybe later. Traffic's too bad right now." According to his neighbors, he was "Steve Martin." Everybody thought having the same name as the famous comedian was hilarious. As for Wickham, he knew the best way to hide was in plain sight.

"Shit, it'll be worse when the storm gits here. I'm gittin' my black ass to Baton Rouge." He climbed into the cab.

"Hope you took a leak, dude. You're gonna be sittin' in that truck for the rest of the day."

The man flashed him a toothy grin and drove the pickup down the street. Wickham flicked his cigarette butt off the balcony and returned to the house, escaping from the heat of the day. He decided to get a little rest. He was going to be busy later.

Preparations continued throughout the area at a fevered pace, nowhere more intense than at the utilities that provided energy for the region. They knew their power poles would fall before the might of the storm, so they called in linemen from utilities all over America. Usually competitors, they became lifesavers during emergencies. It wasn't free, of course. The locals would eventually pay for the assistance at overtime rates. But next time it would be Louisiana and Mississippi shipping their workers to help out Oklahoma, Florida, or California.

At the nuclear power plant in St. Charles Parish, the workers began the process of powering down the facility. Generating over one thousand megawatts of power, it was the major producer of electricity for New Orleans. The emergency plan called for the plant to be shut down if a major hurricane approached the area, and Katrina fit the bill.

So, it wasn't a matter of *if* New Orleans and the region would lose power but *when*.

Covington

Chuck Bingley smiled as he fired up his new gasoline-powered portable generator. The saleswoman had told him the 800 watt unit would run for eight hours on a six-gallon tankful of gas and could easily power his refrigerator, freezer, a television, and a couple of other items. She also said it was easy to start, and Chuck was relieved to see she was right. He reached down and turned off the engine to preserve fuel.

Chuck had three six-gallon tanks of gas, along with another three two-gallon cans. With the fuel in the generator, he had power enough for forty hours—almost two days. He knew he couldn't have the thing on the whole time the power was out. Using the machine sparingly, he would be able to keep the food cold in the icebox for three days or so until the power was restored. He could always get more gas if it took longer.

He moved out of his packed garage and took one more walk around the yard. He had spent the last two days dragging loose patio furniture and other items into the half of the garage reserved for Jane's minivan. What was too heavy to move, he turned over or propped next to a tree. The trash cans were jammed underneath the bushes. A bonfire was smoldering, turning the last of the large branches on the ground into harmless ash.

Chuck wiped his sweaty, soot-stained face with the bottom of his t-shirt. It wasn't too hot for a Louisiana summer's morning, but he had been working hard. Now that his job of preparing his beloved home was done, he thought about taking a shower while he had the time.

Ought to wash my clothes. Run the dishwasher, too. Could be a few days before I can do that after the storm passes.

Chuck took one last look about his yard. Jane jokingly accused him of loving his home more than his family. She was wrong, of course. The house came in second. A very strong second, he had to admit. In his mind, they were inseparable. He loved the house because it was the home of his family. They were part and parcel of each other.

With a last check of the front gate—he secured it not to keep people out but to prevent it from banging open in the wind—he went inside, pulling off his sneakers first. It was Jane's demand that dirty shoes be removed by the back door, and even though she wasn't there, he did it automatically. On the dining room table were a box of matches, a battery-powered radio, several flashlights, and every battery he owned. Candles were placed strategically about the house. Extension cords snaked from the appliances to the doorway into the garage.

He stripped off his shirt as he turned on the shower, thinking he had nothing else to do. He was ready. Might as well watch a football game after he called Jane.

In case of emergency, each community on the Gulf Coast had its own command center. Usually located in the county or parish seat, it was built like a WWII bunker and had the finest electronic communications gear money could buy. The top political and law enforcement officials took their places to await the storm. Police, EMTs, and other First Responders were strategically located throughout the various parishes and counties.

Secure links were established with state officials. Communication with neighboring governments, however, was spotty and haphazard. The cooperation between the North Shore and the bayou region was excellent, but the South Shore was the hole in the doughnut. Orleans and Jefferson parishes had little contact with anyone else, other than the capital and each other.

St. Tammany's command center was in the old courthouse in downtown Covington. St. Bernard's was right in the middle of its massive government complex in Chalmette. In Mississippi, similar facilities were manned and provisioned.

Jefferson Parish's command center was located in Gretna on the West Bank. Every vital group of public employees was represented, except one. For reasons no one could later explain, the parish president followed a "doomsday plan" and ordered the evacuation of the workers who manned the parish's drainage system. Torrential rains were expected, and there was *no one* who could turn on the pumps.

Jefferson Parish was not the only government entity to do something irrational.

Downtown

Anna Elliot crossed Poydras Street from New Orleans City Hall to the Hyatt Regency Hotel. The city's command center was officially in City Hall, and it was staffed with the police chief and the city's director of emergency preparedness. The plan called for the mayor to be there too, but he wasn't.

The mayor's proudest achievement in his first term was to bring city government into the twenty-first century in terms of technology. It took three years, but now New Orleans was one of the most cyber-ready cities in the nation. It had gone as paperless as possible. The web site, with its ability for citizens to do much of their business with government in a virtual environment, had won national awards. All top staffers were equipped with BlackBerries and were encouraged to use e-mail as the preferred means of communication.

There was still more to be done. The NOPD had a shocking lack of satellite phones. They were waiting on appropriations from the federal government, and the city didn't have the cash to front the cost and wait for reimbursement.

Despite the shortfall, the electronic revolution at City Hall remained impressive—so impressive that the mayor saw little reason to hang around the command center.

The procedure during an emergency was for city government to use a suite of rooms provided by Hyatt management. The massive X-shaped hotel was right next door, and its beds were far more comfortable than cots. All rooms were fully wired for Internet. Using this excuse, the mayor and his staff relocated to the hotel, staying in contact with the command center via voice and Internet connections.

Anna entered the towering, glass-covered atrium, the main feature of the building. Adjacent to the Superdome and attached to it by a skyway, the atrium had been the scene of countless events, from wedding receptions to Superbowl parties. Within minutes, Anna was on the floor reserved for the government of the City of New Orleans. Staffers were working the phones and pounding on laptops.

"Anna," called out one of her co-workers, "are the RTA buses making their runs to pick up people for the Dome?"

Anna checked the notes on her pad. "A lot of the drivers failed to show, but we've been assured buses are running." Exactly how many people were being picked up no one knew.

"How come they're missing drivers? It's an emergency!"

"I've been told that, without a contract, many of the operators refuse to work overtime." The RTA drivers had been without a labor agreement for some time.

Anna took a moment to look out the window. It faced the Dome, and she could observe hundreds of people waiting in line to enter the single set of doors open into the stadium. More and more people streamed in from the streets. NOPD stood guard to prevent the crowd from entering the Hyatt.

"I wish those people had gotten out," she murmured to herself.

The RTA buses were taking people to the Dome; they weren't taking them out of the city to shelters in Baton Rouge. No solution had been found for the impasse with the Orleans Parish School Board, so the school buses were idle, their drivers evacuated.

Anna had to be satisfied that the first-ever mandatory evacuation of the city was going as well as it was. The jammed highways were not as congested as last year during Hurricane Ivan. At least there was that.

Still, there were thousands who couldn't or wouldn't leave the city. Everything depended on the levees.

K minus twenty-two hours: Gentilly

KAYWANDA JOHNSON DROVE THE FEW BLOCKS FROM THE LOCAL convenience store back to her mother's house, a small bag of last-minute items in the seat beside her. The last thing she expected was to see a certain beat-up sedan parked in front.

She just knew Scott was back to bully her into abandoning her momma, and she needed all her willpower to resist him. After parking her car in the short, one-lane driveway on the side of the house, she took a couple of deep breaths. With a grim look, she marched into the house, bag in hand.

"Baby," called her mother. "Look who's here."

"I know, Momma, I saw—" she said before she lost the ability to speak.

Scott Davis was sitting next to Mrs. Johnson on the sofa, a duffle and a sleeping bag on the floor next to them.

"He came back," Mrs. Johnson said proudly as she patted his hand. "He's gonna stay with us."

Kaywanda could only gape.

Sheepishly, Scott got to his feet. "Umm, Miz Johnson, excuse me. Can I talk to you a minute, Kay?"

Kaywanda nodded. He took the shopping bag from her hand, and the two retreated into the small kitchen. As he placed the bag on the counter, she recovered her ability to speak.

"What're you doing here? I thought you'd be long gone!"

Scott kept his back to her. "So did I. I was gonna leave, I really was. But every time I got in the car to drive outta here, something held me back."

Kaywanda bit her lip. "What was it?"

He took a deep breath and turned around. "You. I couldn't just leave you—I couldn't." Shoving his hands in his pockets, he stared at Mrs. Johnson's clean kitchen floor. "Look, I've never been brave. I've run from most things in my life. But I couldn't run away from you. That storm scares the shit outta me; I ain't gonna lie. But if I left you and your mother here all alone, well…I couldn't live with myself. So, either we all leave or we all stay."

"You don't need to do this, Scott."

"Don't I?" He crossed the room to take Kaywanda into his arms. Feeling no resistance, he kissed her soundly. "Still think I shouldn't have come back?"

"Yes, I do." She kissed him back. "But I'm glad you did."

Baton Rouge

Carrie pulled next to Jane's minivan in the driveway of her mother's house. Max stared whining from the rear seat, ready to jump out.

"Hush, Max," she told the Boxer as though he understood English. "I've got to get Trey out of his car seat first."

With Trey on her hip and Max on a leash, Carrie entered what used to be her home to be greeted by the low bark of a Great Dane. It was not appreciated by the Boxer. The riot of barking dogs heralded the appearance of Catherine Bingley.

"Carrie, you're here," she said unnecessarily. Her smile for her grandson faded. "Oh, Carrie, couldn't you have left the dog at home?"

"No, Mom." There was only one way to handle Catherine Bingley. One stated one's case and stood one's ground. "I told you I was bringing Max, and I meant it. Is that Rufus making that ruckus? Where is he?"

"That monster is in his box where he belongs! And so will that thing!" Catherine cried, pointing at Max.

Carrie smiled. "Sorry, Mom. No room for the crate in my car. Guess he'll just have to sleep with me."

"*Carrie...*" Catherine growled.

Just then, an overweight Persian waddled into the hallway, hissing at the latest intruder. Max immediately assumed a play stance, low in front and hindquarters raised, cropped tail wagging and barking in return.

Catherine, with a yell, scooped up Chin Chan. "For heaven's sake, restrain that animal!" She hugged the wiggling cat to her chest.

"Mom, they're just greeting each other. Haven't you seen animals play before?"

Jane and her children arrived on the scene, setting Rufus off again. It would take some time before the animals were settled. Using the excuse of quieting Max, Carrie fled into her old bedroom with the dog and Jane, leaving Catherine with her grandchildren.

"So, how has it been?" Carrie asked her sister-in-law as all three sat on her bed.

"It's been a bit...difficult."

Carrie's eyebrows rose. Jane was the nicest person she had ever met. For her to mention a complaint, things must be bad indeed. "What happened?"

Jane explained things had gone downhill since early that morning. Rufus, after eating breakfast, had taken residence on Catherine's sofa, basically claiming the whole thing. At Catherine's request, Jane had shooed the dog off the couch. He then decided to lie on the floor and chew on one of Chin Chan's toys, which set Catherine off again. Exchanging the toy for one of Rufus's, the crisis was over until Chin Chan decided he wanted the dog's toy. Rufus defended his property with a growl, which was the last straw for Mrs. Bingley.

"Rufus has been banished to his crate for the duration," Jane reported.

"That big old sweetie? I'm so sorry."

"I know this is Catherine's house and we're the guests, but I feel bad for poor Rufus. He didn't do anything to deserve this. The animals were just settling their boundaries. Catherine just doesn't understand."

"Jane, you are too good. You know my mother. She's had her mind made up, and there's nothing you can do to change it. She's being unreasonable." Carrie patted Jane's hand. "Hopefully, we can make the best of it for a day or two. I'll do what I can."

Jane absently rubbed the Boxer on the head. "Thank you."

Carrie frowned. "Is there something else bothering you?"

"I wish Chuck had come with us." She looked at Carrie. "I hope you're not worried about John."

"Of course not," she lied. "John can take care of himself." There was not a moment she did not fear for her husband's safety.

"Well, let's put Max in the washroom with Rufus for now and pay our respects to the old battle-axe."

"Carrie!" Jane laughed.

K minus twenty-one hours:
Gulf of Mexico

THE MONSTER HAD GROWN IN INTENSITY. THE HIGHEST SUSTAINED winds were 173 miles per hour—almost three miles each minute. Worse, the internal pressure had fallen to 902 mb. Like God's own vacuum cleaner, the low air pressure literally sucked up billions of gallons of seawater, forming an enormous bulge in the Gulf. Rogue waves of seventy-five feet and more raced about the surface of the sea, smashing into abandoned oil platforms and ripping them loose from their anchors.

Relentlessly the monster headed north-northwest, without a goal and without a reason. Cooler waters would eventually weaken and kill the monster.

However, there were no cooler waters ahead. Only land.

Chapter 4

K minus nineteen hours:
outside of Lake Charles, Louisiana

Emma and Abe had been fighting the traffic along I-10 since they left at eight that morning on their three hundred fifty-mile trek to Houston. Traffic had been bumper-to-bumper the entire time. Contraflow helped until it ended at Laplace. They managed between twenty to thirty miles an hour until Baton Rouge. It took hours to get across the Mississippi River bridge. Traffic rolled well to Lafayette, where things came to a standstill again.

Now, at three in the afternoon—seven hours on the road—they were between Lafayette and Lake Charles, a trip that should have been made in three. Traffic was tightening up once more, and they had over one hundred fifty miles to go.

Abe glanced at the road sign. "Iowa?" he snorted.

"I think it's pronounced 'eye-oh-way,' not 'eye-oh-wah,' Papa."

"'Eye-oh-way?' What's the matter—the *shmendricks* can't pronounce the name of their own town?"

"Take it easy."

"I *have* been taking it easy! Can't they move any faster? *Oy gevalt*!" Abe cried, the brake lights on the SUV directly in front of them shining again.

"Papa, please! This is hard enough without your bitching!"

Abe turned to her. "I'm sorry, princess, but you know how much I hate traffic."

Emma had to admit he had been on his best behavior, at least at the beginning of the trip. By the time they got to Lafayette, however, his patience had reached an end. She couldn't blame him; hers was at a fraying point, too. The low afternoon sun shining directly in their eyes only added to the aggravation.

"Papa, do you need to go to the bathroom?"

"No, I'm fine."

"Really, I can stop at Iowa."

"I've been taking it easy with the water. I'm good for a while. Unless—"

"We'll keep going." Emma really didn't want to stop. For one reason, she was in the left lane. She would have to fight to get into the right lane to exit. The second reason was she wasn't looking forward to trying to get back onto the interstate afterwards.

"I'm sorry I'm so useless."

"You are not useless, Papa."

"I can't help you out with the driving, can I? What do you call that?"

"I call it 'my turn.' You did all the driving when Irene and I were little. Now I get to return the favor."

"And I call it being old and useless!"

Emma bit her lip while Abe continued to grumble. She was tired, something she wouldn't admit to her father. For a moment outside of Lafayette, she had thought about cutting the drive short and asking Chris Breaux's parents for refuge. She dismissed the thought almost immediately; showing up unannounced at someone's doorstep was plain rude. Now, she wondered whether it had been a mistake.

"Emma, do we have any antacids?"

She glanced at Abe out of the corner of her eye, noticing a light sheen of perspiration on his forehead. "I think I've got something in my purse. Are you warm? Is your stomach upset?"

"Heartburn," he grumbled as he dug in her handbag.

"You see?" Emma scolded. "You see what getting upset does for you? It's given you indigestion."

He grunted as he popped a couple of tablets into his mouth.

"If you're not careful, you could give yourself a case of acid-reflux," she continued. "You have to learn to relax. Let it all go. Center yourself—"

"Aarrggh!" Abe cried.

Emma jumped in her seat. "Papa? Papa, what is it?"

Abe thrashed in his seat, arms clutching at his chest. His face white and lips blue, he gasped for air.

"God…God help me!" he gasped.

"PAPA!"

Emma immediately assumed a heart attack. She had to get Abe to a hospital—now. She whipped her head around, looking for a break in the traffic. She leaned on the horn, opened her window, and screamed, "Let me in! Let me in!"

Of course, the other drivers couldn't hear her. It was useless.

"Papa, Papa, how are you?"

An ashen Abe had slumped back against his seat, as still as death.

"NO!"

Emma jerked the wheel to the left and floored the accelerator. She drove down the inward half-shoulder of the interstate, one hand blowing the horn. For the next two minutes, she drove as fast as she dared, potholes jarring the car, dust flying. She had almost reached a small bridge, and the shoulder was not wide enough for her to pass on the left. Would someone let her in?

Just then, she heard a siren's wail. The rear view mirror was filled by a Louisiana state trooper directly behind her, light bar flashing.

For an instant, she considered ignoring the trooper, before remembering they had radios. *He can call for help!* Emma pulled fully off the shoulder into the median before coming to a stop, yards away from a canal. Throwing the car into park, she turned to her father, trying to see if he was still breathing.

"DRIVER IN THE CAR! SIT UP STRAIGHT! TURN OFF YOUR ENGINE, AND PLACE YOUR HANDS ON THE WHEEL!" The trooper's loudspeaker reverberated through the car.

Emma lowered her window instead. "Help! My father's had a heart attack! Call for an ambulance! Quick!"

In her side view mirror, she could see the trooper in his

flat-brimmed hat slowly approach her car, one hand on his unclamped service pistol. "Keep your hands where I can see them!"

Emma calmed her rising panic and forced herself to obey the commands. A moment later the trooper was beside her window.

"Shut off the engine, please! Slowly!" he commanded her.

Emma shakily did as she was told. "My father! I think he's had a heart attack! Please help us!"

"All right, ma'am, take it easy. Now, I want you to get out of the car."

"But my father!"

"Out of the car, please!" he demanded.

Emma unbuckled her seat belt and opened the door. Quelling her growing anger, she slowly climbed out, her hands in plain view, tears running down her face.

The trooper gestured. "Ma'am, please sit down right here in front of the car." At her wild look, he added, "It's for your safety. The sooner you comply with my requests, the sooner I can check on your father."

Emma sat down in the dry, dusty grass, manicured hands clenched hard to her knees, stomach roiling in fury and fear. Once the trooper was satisfied, he carefully peered in, one eye on her. Emma could hear him trying to talk to Abe. A moment later, the trooper was squatting beside her, his gun now secured.

"Ma'am, may I have your name, please?" His voice was now gentle, instead of the bark of command.

"Emma Katz. That's my father, Abe Weinberg. We're from New Orleans, evacuating from the hurricane. My license is in my purse," she added.

"We'll talk about that later." He pulled out a notebook. "Does your father have any history of heart disease?"

"He had a triple by-pass six years ago. How is he?"

"He's breathing, but he's unconscious. I'm going to call this in." He stood up.

"Can I go to him?"

The trooper hesitated. "All right. But don't move him."

"Can I start the car to run the air conditioning?"

"Not yet. Wait until I get back." He jogged back to his cruiser, lights still flashing, as Emma opened the passenger-side door, traffic crawling by only feet way. The other drivers were gawking at them, she was sure, and she didn't care.

The sight before her almost completely unraveled her grip on her emotions. Her dear, strong, funny, proud father, once the most important man in her life, was lying helplessly on the fully-reclined passenger seat of her car, skin pale and damp. He was fighting for his life.

She sobbed. "Please hold on, Papa. Help is coming." She kissed and caressed her father's clammy face, murmuring in his ear until the trooper returned.

"Ma'am, there's an EMT on the way now. They'll be here as soon as they can." He put a hand on her shoulder. "Why don't you turn on the ignition so we can get the AC running?"

The EMT finally arrived—within ten minutes, claimed the trooper, but it seemed like forever. Along with them were a half-dozen police cars and a fire truck. By the time Emma had the presence of mind to call her husband, the paramedics had begun to work on Abe. Emma reached George, and offered her cell phone to one of the EMTs.

"My husband's on the line. He's a heart surgeon at Tulane," she explained when the paramedic demurred. No one commented on the irony of his absence.

The female paramedic took the cell, and after a couple of questions, began speaking in earnest as she and her partner worked on Abe. The trooper took Emma over to the side and continued to gather information from her. She knew he was keeping her occupied, and she allowed him to do it. Minutes later, the female paramedic returned to her.

"We have your father stabilized. Vitals are acceptable for now. We're calling in a MEDIVAC. Here's your husband, ma'am."

The trooper left to organize the landing zone while Emma spoke to George. "Honey? How's Papa doing?"

"It's hard to say. The EMTs are doing everything they can. They're flying him out?"

"They're calling in the helicopter now."

"Okay. How are you doing?"

Emma ran her free hand through her tangled hair. "Tired. Scared. Oh, I wish you were here!"

"I wish I was, too, babe. I'm sorry—"

"No! Don't be! I shouldn't have said that. I'm sorry. You have to be at the hospital, I know."

"I feel awful I can't be there to help. Look, hon, you best go now. Call me the minute you get to the hospital."

"I will." She fought the tears that threatened reappear.

"Don't hang up yet. Where are they taking him?"

She asked the paramedic. "Lake Charles Memorial Hospital."

"Okay. I'll put in a call to the emergency room. I love you, Emma."

"I love you, too."

"Abe's in great hands, honey. Don't you worry, okay? Bye."

Emma pocketed her phone, praying her husband was right.

AS SOON AS THE MEDIVAC HELICOPTER BLADES STOPPED MOVING, the paramedics rushed Abe, now secured on a stretcher, into the aircraft.

"I have to go with him," Emma told the trooper.

"I'm afraid that's not allowed, Mrs. Katz. Only the patient and the crew. Don't worry, we'll get you to the hospital."

Emma watched the copter take off and fly towards the western sun. She then looked at the traffic jam inching its way towards Lake Charles. "How are we going to get through that?"

The trooper grunted. "We don't. We head east." At Emma's surprise, he explained. "There's an exit a couple of miles from here. We know a few back ways into Lake Charles. You follow us. We'll get you to Memorial in no time."

Emma got in her car and buckled in for the longest, most miserable shortcut of her life.

K minus eighteen hours: New Orleans

CONTRAFLOW HAD BEEN IN OPERATION FOR TWENTY-FOUR HOURS, and for all the agitation the drivers experienced, eighteen thousand vehicles had moved through the system each hour. Eighty percent of the population of the city had fled, a feat many said couldn't be done.

However, an estimated hundred thousand people remained in the region, most of them in New Orleans.

Lake Charles

BY THE TIME EMMA REACHED LAKE CHARLES MEMORIAL HOSPITAL, she knew George's phone call had gotten through. Never had she been treated so well by hospital staff. After a short wait in the hospital chapel, she was personally escorted to Abe's bed in the ICU.

Emma's heart was in her throat as she approached her father. Tubes and sensors snaked everywhere. She could barely see his face behind the oxygen mask. Lighted panels flickered in the cold, sterile atmosphere, and in the background was a low hum of equipment and the murmur of staff.

"Oh, Papa," her voice cracked behind her crumbling façade. She was given permission to sit next to him and hold his cool hand.

Oh, merciful God, she prayed, *please watch over us, and deliver my father from this illness.* She pulled out the small book of Psalms she had found in the chapel and let the words comfort them both as she waited for the doctor.

Moments later, a doctor summoned her outside and began to give her a prognosis. She held up her hand, asking if she could call her husband first. Soon, the physician was giving a detailed report to George and Emma.

"So, to recap, Mr. Weinberg has suffered an acute myocardial infarction," he concluded. "We won't know the total damage until we've had a chance to completely stabilize him for an MRI. We might have to do a coronary angiography, as well. Then we can look to treatment. The EKG is not great, but it's steady for now. We'll continue with a course of MONA until then. Yes? … Thank you, doctor. We'll keep you briefed. … Right. Here's your wife. Watch yourself over there. Good luck." The doctor handed the cell phone back to Emma.

"George?"

"He knows his stuff, Em. Abe's in good hands. Look, there's

nothing else to do right now. You need to get some rest. Is there a place to crash?"

Emma repeated George's question to the attending physician. "There's a couch in the doctors' lounge. I'll take you there as soon as you're finished."

After Emma told George of the offer, they spent a little time talking about the car and her sister Irene in Maryland. He said he would update his in-laws and asked, "Do you know anybody in Lake Charles?"

"No, I don't. Do you?"

"No. Damn, let me think—"

"George, how's the weather there?"

"No rain yet. The mayor's just ordered a curfew. We've been pretty busy around here. Just to be on the safe side, we're moving the emergency room, the pharmacy, and the food service from the first floor. And we just got some patients from the Superdome. We're hunkered down nice and tight."

"When does it hit? I haven't seen a report in hours."

"Mid-morning tomorrow. They're now calling for between Slidell and Waveland."

Emma bit her lip. "Be careful."

"I will. Get some rest."

"You get some rest, too—you hear me?"

"I will. Call me if there's any change. Love you."

K minus sixteen hours: Gulfport

It was six o'clock, the sun peering through fast moving clouds, when John Waguespack arrived at his condo on foot. He had been at the casino, watching security lock up the building. He wanted to hang around longer, but the head of the team assured him they had everything under control. The guards were planning to withdraw inland by midnight. So, with nothing else to do, Waguespack called Las Vegas to give a status report as he hoofed it the quarter mile back to his place. He left his car parked on one of the higher levels of the casino's parking structure.

Gulfport was nearly deserted; only a few hardy souls were planning to defy the warnings to leave and stay in their homes. Waguespack doubted the wisdom of doing that. Unlike his condo, most of the homes on the Mississippi Gulf Coast were one-story slab houses.

But his place—now, that was different. Built of brick and situated across the road from the beach, the place had survived the greatest of all hurricanes, Camille, so he was told. Of course, the place was on the eastern side of Gulfport, almost in Biloxi, and for all its power, Camille was a small storm. Still, Waguespack's unit was on the third floor, so even if the storm surge was high enough to cross US 90, he would stay high and dry. He had stocked up canned food, water, and scotch, so he figured he was set.

He wasn't prepared for the surprise that awaited him at his doorstep.

"Lucy?"

"Hey there, John!" Lucy Steele, wearing jeans and a sleeveless blouse, waved from her spot sitting cross-legged on his doormat, a small duffle bag next to her. "I heard you were having a hurricane party, so I thought I'd join you!"

"I'm just keeping an eye on the casino." He helped her to her feet, which placed Lucy between him and the door.

Lucy wound her arms around his neck. "Then we'll make it a party. You got some stuff?"

Waguespack thought about his cocaine supplies. "Yeah, a little."

"No problem, I brought some of my own." Her hands drifted down to his crotch. "As long as you bring *this*, we'll have a good time. So, open up the door and let a girl in."

Waguespack shrugged. It would be pretty boring waiting for the storm to come. If there was one thing Lucy was good for, it was for passing time interestingly. He smiled as he unlocked the door and opened it.

"After you."

Lucy picked up her bag and walked into the condo, wiggling her ass at Waguespack. Accepting the challenge, he swatted her on the butt, which earned a giggle. He grinned as he locked the door behind him.

Chapter 5

K minus fifteen hours:
Gulf of Mexico

The law of entropy works for spinning tops and hurricanes. The internal pressure of the monster rose only a hair, to 905 mb, but it was enough to cut the maximum winds by twelve miles per hour. She was still a very dangerous creature at 161 mph, but there was a sliver of hope she would continue to weaken.

What scientists didn't know was that the slight pressure increase wasn't necessarily a good thing.

Metairie

Carrying a Styrofoam ice chest, William let himself into Elizabeth's apartment and moved straight to her refrigerator. He put the eggs, dairy products, produce, and uncooked chicken in the chest, and then turned his attention to the freezer. He debated taking the half-eaten carton of chocolate swirl ice cream with the unopened frozen food, and decided to err on the side of bringing too much rather than not enough. Besides, chocolate swirl was Elizabeth's favorite. He dumped about half of the ice from the icemaker on top of the food and the rest in the sink. All of the leftovers and opened condiment jars went into the trash. He left the diet drinks and water bottles.

Once both the refrigerator and freezer were empty, he unplugged the appliance and propped the doors open. He carried the ice chest to his car, placing it next to the one from his condo. It took two more trips to pack the dry food in the trunk and toss several trash bags into the dumpster, already full from other residents who had done the same.

William quickly returned to the apartment one last time, using his cell phone to call his fiancée. "Hey, babe, I've got the fridge emptied. Do you want anything?"

"Oh no, I've got all my personal stuff here. Don't worry about it. It's only going to be for a couple of days."

He looked around the room. "How 'bout if I grab your jewelry box?"

"If it's no trouble. Just get yourself home."

"On my way," William said as he walked into the bedroom.

"How's the traffic?"

"Pretty clear so far. Everybody who's leaving must have gone already. I ought to make it home in fifteen or twenty minutes after I leave."

"Be careful."

"I will. Love you."

William found Elizabeth's jewelry box was still guarded by her Riptide Beanie Baby. "Well, buddy, I guess you come with me." Box and Beanie under his arm, he left the apartment, locking the door behind him.

As he placed the last items in the trunk of his BMW next to his photo album, he noticed the door of a neighboring apartment cracked open, a dim face watching him from the shadows within.

Oh, great. Miss Crazy Cat Lady is checking me out, wondering if she should call the sheriff's office.

He straightened up and called out. "I'm Lizzy Boudreaux's boyfriend, bringing a couple items to her! If you're not evacuating, can you keep an eye on her place?"

An elderly female voice grumbled. "All right."

William pulled out his business card holder. "Do you want the number where we're staying?"

He could just make out her shaking head. "Don't need it. I figure a thief don't drive a fancy car." She turned away from the door, talking to something inside. "Get away from the door. The dogs'll get you if you run outside."

William hesitated before leaving. "Ma'am, do you have any way of getting out? Can I call someone?"

The woman returned, holding a cat. "I ain't leaving." A second cat looked at him from between her legs. The reek of unemptied litter boxes filled the air.

"Here, take my card if you change your—"

By then she had shut the door. William impulsively stuck the card in the jam.

As he had told Elizabeth, traffic was almost non-existent. He noted a convoy of National Guard trucks heading towards the city on I-10. He crossed the Mississippi River via the I-310 Hale Boggs Bridge, turned on LA 18, and was soon at the front gates of Dansereau Plantation.

Elizabeth and Mrs. Reynolds were waiting for him outside the kitchen door as he pulled into the detached garage, the welcome from his fiancée properly warmer than from his housekeeper. The three of them made quick work of carrying the food and other items from William's car, Elizabeth laughing as she pulled Riptide out of the trunk. Above their heads, wisps of clouds were dashing across the darkening sky from the north-northeast.

Food and luggage put away and a quick dinner of hamburgers consumed, William and Elizabeth cuddled on the couch, watching the storm coverage, while Mrs. Reynolds retired to the guest bedroom she was to occupy for the duration. The two said little, both feeling a need to simply be in each other's company.

William kissed the hair on the top of her head. "I'm glad you talked me into this. I like having you here."

"Does that mean I was right?" Elizabeth's eyes danced with mirth.

"Yes, you were."

She snuggled closer. "Usually, I would be home at my parents, helping put plywood over the windows. It feels a little funny being somewhere else. Oh, I'll get used to it." She wrinkled her nose at him playfully. "After all, *this* will be my home someday."

"I hope we won't have to go through this too often."

Just then, the cable blipped.

"Wind must be moving the satellite dishes at the cable company," William explained.

"What happens if we lose cable TV?"

"I'll switch over to my DIRECTV dish."

"Won't the winds affect it?"

"Yeah, but I can reset it easy."

Elizabeth sat up. "I'm going to call my folks and then go to bed. Tomorrow's going to be a stressful day."

"Good idea." William moved over to the windows that lined the den and triggered a switch, lowering the hurricane shutters. Dansereau Plantation was as ready as it was ever going to be.

K minus fourteen hours: Lake Charles

EMMA HAD BEEN CATNAPPING ON THE DOCTORS' LOUNGE SOFA FOR a couple of hours when she heard the door open. She peaked out of one eye to get the biggest surprise of her life.

"Cathy?"

Cathy Tilney closed the door behind her and moved toward Emma. "My God, Emma. How are you doing?"

Emma sat straight up. "What are you doing here?" She had not seen her former friend since college, and they had parted on bad terms.

"George called us. He told us what was going on. I came to—"

She was cut off by Emma jumping off the sofa to embrace her. "Oh, I am so happy to see you! I didn't know you lived in Lake Charles."

"We don't. Henry and I live in Baytown, Texas."

Emma pulled back. "Baytown? That's next to Houston. And you came all this way? Oh, my God!" She burst into tears.

Cathy led her back to the couch, where they sat until Emma could get control of her feelings. The two talked, first about Abe's condition and then about George calling the Tilneys after he hung up with Emma. Cathy almost immediately decided to drive the three hours to Lake Charles to support Emma while Henry made provisions to stay home from work the next day and watch the kids.

Emma held Cathy's hands. "It's been six years. You look great."

Cathy smiled. "So do you, Emma."

Emma wiped her eyes with the palms of her hands. "Yeah, right—I must look a fright."

"Oh, Em, after what you've been through?" She paused. "I'm sorry how we ended it back at school. Can you forgive me?"

Emma hugged her again. "Oh, that's all done and forgotten. I am *so* happy to see you." Emma needed distraction from what was happening in the ICU. "Tell me what you've been doing with yourself. How many kids do you have?"

The two former and future friends settled back and began six years' worth of catching up.

AMTRAK HAD TRAINS IN NEW ORLEANS. THERE WERE PEOPLE IN the city who may have wanted to leave. Why not offer to use the empty cars to get people out?

It was a brilliant idea because it was simple, like most brilliant ideas. Perhaps too simple, because the city never responded to numerous calls offering the trains for evacuation.

No one at the time, or later, could give a comprehensive answer to why New Orleans ignored the offer. Perhaps officials thought the trains would be overrun with refugees. Or they feared abandoning people in stations like Jackson, Memphis, and Chicago with no shelters waiting for them. Except for Contraflow, there was little coordination between Louisiana local officials and cities out of state. Politicians and bureaucrats were terrified of bad press and lawsuits.

Hubris was firmly established. The US Army Corps of Engineers had constructed the greatest series of levees in the world. While the National Weather Service had issued dire warnings, forecasting catastrophic damage, and while computer models had suggested a potential cataclysm, no one really believed the levees would fail.

For whatever reason, two and a half hours after the mayor declared a dusk-to-dawn curfew, the last Amtrak train left New Orleans, mostly empty.

K minus twelve hours: Superdome

IT WAS A LITTLE AFTER TEN, AND JOHN BUFORD WAS EXHAUSTED. For over twelve hours, the Louisiana National Guard and the NOPD had been working the endless line of refugees streaming into the Dome. Each had to be searched for weapons and contraband. He noticed several young men, usually in long, starched white t-shirts, turn away from the door and walk away once they saw the armed MPs and police standing guard outside.

Gangbangers, he thought. *Good God, we don't need that kind in here.*

Buford dearly wished he had his trusty M-16 rifle securely strapped over his shoulder rather than sitting back at the armory in Baton Rouge. Even his M-9 Beretta pistol would have been better than nothing. Why Baton Rouge sent them to the Dome unarmed was a question he couldn't answer.

Even with over five hundred troops working, it took a long time to search ten thousand people. The last couple of hours were the worst as the first rain bands swept over the city, inciting a bit of panic. But now in the dim streetlights, he could see the end of the line. Another thirty minutes or so and they could secure the doors. And not a moment too soon. The wind and rain was freshening every minute.

Buford took in the confused mass of humanity milling around the hallways as the security people tried to guide them into the seats of the arena. The aged and the infirm had cots waiting for them on the field. The Wildlife and Fisheries people had moved the seriously ill to Tulane Medical Center, four blocks away.

Suddenly, there were loud shouts. Yet another argument had broken out. While most of the people were grateful for the shelter, there were always those who demanded to establish territory in the chaos. It led to the usual pushing and shoving. A mixed squad of troops and NOPD moved in to settle the situation. It was not the first incident, and it certainly wasn't going to be the last.

Buford rubbed his face. It was going to be a long night.

In 1956, the local shipping interests convinced Congress to authorize the construction of a new shipping channel to serve the Port of New Orleans. The project, named the Mississippi River-Gulf Outlet Canal, started at the Intracoastal Canal in the middle of the city and ran seventy-six miles east into Lake Borgne, cutting though the marshes on the northern edge of St. Bernard Parish. Completed by the US Army Corps of Engineers in 1965, the MRGO was six hundred fifty feet wide and thirty-eight feet deep. Shortening transit to the port by thirty-seven miles, it was intended to make New Orleans more competitive in the new container-style shipping industry, providing more jobs for the people.

The road to hell is paved with good intentions. The engineers could not have picked a worse spot to dredge a canal. Unlike the thick, heavy clay found in the Mississippi River basin, the route's marshy soil was sandy, and erosion was constant. The MRGO's channel grew to over fifteen hundred feet. The Port spent $13 million a year for dredging, but the depth was impossible to maintain. By 2005, only a ship a day was using the thing. The MRGO was a financial disaster.

The Port, the Corps, the politicians, and the people argued for years about what to do. The shipping interests wanted to spend millions to save the MRGO by shoring up the banks of the canal with massive earth-and-concrete levees. The Corps wanted to put massive European-style storm gates at the mouth of the channel. The environmentalists and the citizens of St. Bernard Parish fought back, settling for nothing less than the closing and filling in of the MRGO. The stakeholders clashed, so the politicians did nothing.

Everything was in place for a disaster forty years in the making.

Chapter 6

Monday, August 29
K minus ten hours:
Gulf of Mexico

The monster couldn't maintain the incredible power it held. The pressure overnight had risen again, and the winds had fallen. The change was only slight, but it was enough for her to slip from Category 5 to Category 4. Still, at over 160 mph, the thing was strong enough to kill a city. As the winds slowed, the forward momentum sped up. Now, moving at fifteen miles per hour, it was 130 miles from landfall.

Around midnight, the first bands of rain began to fall on the Mississippi Gulf Coast, and the tide began to rise.

St. Charles Parish

SOMETHING WOKE ELIZABETH.

She looked around in the darkness of the bedroom she shared with William. The clock radio was blinking and the ceiling fan was revving up as if someone had just turned it on. Had the power blipped?

Listening, she could hear the wind blow against the house. And there was another noise—a low humming she had not heard before.

"Generator's on."

"Will! Did I wake you up?"

He denied it, and a frightened Elizabeth took it as an invitation to embrace him. She knew, in an abstract way, that the hurricane was approaching, but the sounds of the wind and the generator made it real. The storm wasn't just coming. It was *here. Now.*

William's lips were near her ear. "It's okay, honey. I'm right here."

He slowly stroked her back, trying to comfort her. But she needed more. Answering a primitive call from deep inside, she kissed him hungrily. He seemed surprised at her urgency, and it took a moment before he responded in kind.

Skin touched skin. Hands grasped. Legs intertwined. Kisses grew in intensity until neither knew where they ended and their partner began. Lightheaded from lust and need, Elizabeth found herself lying full over her fiancé. She groaned, grinding her pelvis into his. It was all the invitation he needed.

In the next moment, they had switched positions. He developed a hard and fast rhythm, feeding off her cries. Both knew Death was just outside the strong walls of Dansereau, and they needed to reaffirm to themselves and to each other that they were alive in the most basic way possible.

On and on William drove, plunging deep inside his woman. Elizabeth, almost incoherent, cried his name again and again. Finally, with a mighty groan, he collapsed onto her. She wrapped her arms about him, pulling him as close as possible.

"Are you all right, Lizzy?"

Elizabeth couldn't catch her breath at first. "Don't…don't pull away. I need you."

He kissed her face again, this time with gentleness. "I'm here. Nothing will harm you. I won't let it."

The small smile on her lips was hidden in the darkness. "I know, as long as you're here with me. But I need to touch you. Don't roll away, please."

"I won't." He kissed her eyelids. "Go to sleep, now. I'll keep you safe."

"The wind—"

"Can't touch you. Sleep, love."

And so she did.

K minus nine hours: Lake Charles

Emma and Cathy had talked until almost midnight; then Emma returned to Abe's ICU room while Cathy attempted to get some sleep in an armchair. Emma kept vigil, sitting next to her father, closing her eyes every few minutes.

In her half-sleep state, she dreamed.

She was a little girl again, walking hand-in-hand with Papa beside the lagoon in City Park, watching the swans glide over the water. Nearby, a couple in a pedal boat softly laughed at some shared joke. A father and son floated by in a canoe. Shouts drifted over from a touch football game underway in the next field. The warm sun peeked through the canopy of the oak trees.

Father and daughter walked along happily, swinging their hands, enjoying the weather. Emma, in a pretty pink dress, giggled at Papa's grin. He was so handsome is his seersucker suit. They came to a fork in the sidewalk, and Papa came to a stop.

"Papa, what is it?" Emma asked.

He said nothing; he just stared straight ahead.

Emma turned. Standing on one path was a disheveled, teen-aged George Katz, dusty from the football game, holding the ball in one hand. On the other path was her mother, Ruth Weinberg, dressed as if she were going to synagogue, pearls at her throat, waiting patiently.

"Papa?"

Abe turned to Emma, a small smile at his lips. "Princess, why don't you go play with George for a while?"

"Where are you going?"

He looked at Ruth. "I'm going to go with Mama now. I will see you later." He bent over and kissed the top of her head.

"Papa, can't I go with you?"

His fingers stroked her dark hair. "Now's not the time. You go on." At his urging, she walked towards George. To her surprise, she saw her older sister, Irene, playing behind him. She turned again to Papa, only to see he was far down the other path with her mother. They were holding hands and smiling.

They waved at her, and she raised her hand—

She was startled awake by a sharp, beeping sound, and a moment later, everything went to hell. People in scrubs and lab coats rushed into the room. Hands from nowhere guided her gently but firmly out of the room. Above the chaos of noise, one shouted phrase stood out:

"CODE BLUE! Get a resuscitation team in here—stat!"

Emma watched in horror as people and machines moved and wheeled all around her motionless father. She couldn't make out their faces, but she could tell they were working—fighting—doing everything in their power to stave off the inevitable.

"Clear!"

The mechanical noise of the defibrillator was accompanied by the jerk of Abe's body. The team huddled about him and then prepared to use the machine again.

Inevitable...

Emma knew. Without a doubt. The dedicated team was wasting its time. Katrina had claimed her first victim.

Abe Weinberg was gone.

K minus six hours: St. Bernard Parish

The monster moved steadily towards the mouth of the Mississippi River. Its counter-clockwise rotation pushed a surge of water from the east to the west, right up the MRGO. The water rose rapidly in the channel, all the way up to the Industrial Canal, seventy-six miles away. By 0430 CDT, the storm gates in the storm walls in New Orleans were beginning to leak water into Gentilly and New Orleans East.

This was anticipated, and the pumps could handle the worst of it. But downstream, along the weak levees of the MRGO, the surge was beginning to overwhelm the sandy barriers. Now, only the 40 Arpent Levee stood between St. Bernard Parish and the maelstrom.

Chapter 7

K minus four hours:
Buras, Louisiana

Buras, Louisiana, located at 29°21′6″N by 89°30′50″W, was a sleepy little village along Louisiana Highway 23, hard against the west bank of the Mississippi River in southern Plaquemines Parish. Most of its thirty-three hundred inhabitants earned their living from the riches of the Gulf, be it fishing, shrimping, harvesting oysters, or extracting oil. Its one landmark was its tall, blue-and-white water tower situated in the middle of the town. It was a sight that had welcomed boaters for decades.

One had to love Buras to live there. Over fifty miles southeast of the Crescent City, it was as close to the end of the world as one could find in the United States. The people of Buras were a stubborn and hardy breed. They had lived there for generations, and many would live nowhere else.

The residents weren't fools. Hurricanes were a constant threat to their village. The people took storms seriously. The cost of living downriver was the need to evacuate several times a year during hurricane season.

Therefore, there was no one around to welcome the Category 4 monster when she roared ashore at 0610 CDT, making her second landfall. The storm brought more than just 140 mph winds. Twenty-five feet of water inundated the hamlet. Abandoned shrimp boats were flung at their owners' homes. The highway itself was torn asunder. Nothing could resist the monster's power, not even the beloved water tower.

It would be days before the flood receded, and the only evidence Buras had ever existed was the wreckage of that blue-and-white structure, surrounded by the waters of the Gulf of Mexico.

Superdome

A hand shook John Buford awake.

"Sorry to wake you, sir," said Mack, "but I thought you should know the generators are on."

Buford rubbed his face in an effort to awaken. "The power's out already?"

"Yes, sir."

Buford swung his feet to the floor and sat up in his cot, trying to function on four hours sleep. He racked his mind to remember how much fuel there was for the Superdome generators and couldn't.

"Hand me my kit, will you, Sergeant?"

"You're getting up, sir?"

"Might as well. It's gonna be a long day anyway. No use in putting it off."

The water continued to rise in the MRGO and Industrial Canal. The channel formed a funnel, multiplying the power of the surge. The levees protecting the vital NASA facility at Michaud were as tall and strong as any in the area, but the same could not be said for the protection offered along the canal and the swamps of the Bayou Sauvage National Wildlife Refuge for New Orleans East. It was only a matter of time before those lesser levees were overtopped. This was an event for which, while foreseen, the city was ill prepared. No pumps could handle that much water. The eastern part of the city, home to poor and middle-class blacks, whites, and Vietnamese, was flooding.

What was not foreseen was something that was happening far away at the Orleans/Jefferson line. The 17th Street Canal was built on that line to serve pumping stations for both parishes. The canal was not quite half full, yet something odd was happening.

The walls were leaning in.

K minus three hours:
Lower Ninth Ward

Ernie Washington had lived in the Lower Ninth Ward all of his sixty-five years. He went to school until his momma allowed him to drop out at fourteen. He then went to work cleaning hotel rooms, and he rose through the ranks from bellhop to bell captain. Hospitality was his profession for fifty years, and he was proud of it until his back gave out. There was a woman once, but that didn't work out. Ernie didn't think too much about it because it didn't bother him to be by himself.

Now disabled on Social Security, Medicare, and a small pension, he made his home in a run-down rental shotgun house four blocks from the place where he'd grown up. Ernie didn't have much to his name except his dignity. The gangsters who tried to rule the street gave Mr. Washington a wide berth for two reasons: first, because the old man didn't have anything to steal, and second, the long-time deacon of the neighborhood Baptist church would turn a *brotha* in to the five-o so fast it would make your head spin.

It was safe to say that Ernie Washington was scared of nothing. He had marched with the NAACP in the 1960s and faced the white bigots with their water hoses, dogs, robes, and burning crosses. What were gangly punks in pants half down their hips to him? Live and let live, but "what's mine is mine," he always said. On his little corner of the world, life was hard, but it was peaceful.

Ernie had known about the storm coming. It had been all over the TV that sat on the table and blocked his window, the better for the rabbit ears to pick up the local stations. He had thought about getting out, but the word on the street was the RTA buses were only taking folks to the Superdome. That didn't sit right with Ernie. He might have gotten on board if the bus was headed for Baton Rouge. But to sit out the hurricane in the Dome? He might as well be comfortable at home. Besides, there was no one else to keep an eye on his neighbor, Miss Mable, an eighty-year-old homebound widow with no family, nowhere to go, and no way to get there. So he stayed.

He hadn't gotten much sleep as the wind and rain lashed the house. Now, at half past seven in the morning, Ernie was half asleep in his easy chair, staring at his blank TV. The power had been off since late the night before. He didn't own a radio, but he figured he could see what was going on by taking a look out the window.

What he didn't know was that, for the last thirty minutes, the water had overtopped the storm walls of the Industrial Canal. Water seeping into the neighborhood was bad enough, but the storm walls weren't designed to take that kind of stress. It was only a matter of time before there was a breech, and it finally occurred at 0730 CDT, threatening the Upper Ninth Ward as well as the Bywater and Treme neighborhoods.

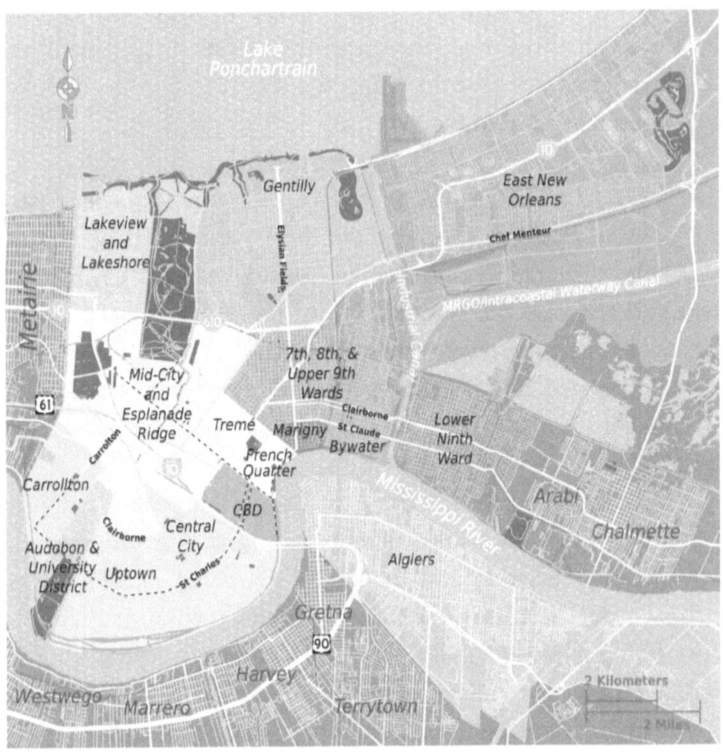

But even this break in the levee wasn't enough to relieve the enormous pressure of the storm surge slamming against the storm walls. Fifteen minutes later, the water won in spectacular fashion as the storm walls on the eastern side disappeared under the torrent, flooding the Lower Ninth.

Ernie, dozing in his chair, was startled by a loud boom. He struggled to his feet and shuffled to the window. What he saw made his mouth drop open: a neighbor's car smashed into the house next door, pushed by a great, gray force.

His house then began to shake. At first, Ernie believed it was from the wind, but then he noticed water was coming in under his front door. Looking out the window again, he realized with horror that gray water was rushing around the house, getting deeper every second. He jumped as he felt water on his ankles.

Ernie ran as fast as he could to the back room of his shotgun and climbed on his bed. As the water in the house climbed higher, he remembered the only other time he had ever disappointed his momma, besides the day he dropped out of school. As a child, he had refused to learn to swim.

The catastrophic failure on the east side of the Industrial Canal would do more than drown the Lower Ninth Ward and flood the St. Bernard Parish communities of Arabi and Chalmette. It would also trap the National Guard pre-positioned at Jackson Barracks. The troops were safe in buildings on high ground next to the river levee, but the parking lots and garages were vulnerable. All the equipment the Guard owned would soon be useless junk under eight to ten feet of water.

While the Lower Ninth died, St. Bernard's agonies were just beginning. The flow from the Industrial Canal was bad enough, but when the seven- to nine-foot-high 40 Arpent Canal levee was overtopped, "Da Parish" was doomed. Twenty thousand structures, almost all habitable buildings in the parish, were destroyed. The tanks of the big local oil refinery—the pride of the local economy—were damaged, and they leaked crude oil for blocks. An entire parish, home to over sixty thousand people, was obliterated.

Things were not much better in neighboring Plaquemines Parish. While Belle Chase escaped the brunt of the catastrophe, the same couldn't be said for the southern half of the parish. For decades, the people of Plaquemines debated relocating the courthouse and parish seat from Pointe a la Hache to Belle Chasse. A 2002 fire in the courthouse forced a temporary move.

Now, the monster might have made the move permanent. Almost all of Plaquemines south of Belle Chasse was flooded, and much of it was wiped out, some of the land returned to the sea.

Meanwhile, the choice to consolidate telephone-switching equipment for New Orleans and Slidell was proving unwise. Power failed for the equipment on the South Shore while floodwaters soon inundated the concrete structure in Slidell. Backup equipment elsewhere could not take the additional traffic, and like a house of cards, telephone service started going out, not only in the affected areas but all over southern Louisiana and Mississippi. Without power and switching equipment, cellular systems could not operate, either.

A communications blackout fell over the central Gulf States.

Gulf of Mexico

THE MONSTER, FORTY MILES SOUTHEAST OF THE CITY OVER BRETON Sound, was moving northwards at fifteen miles per hour. It was damaged by its short trip over the Mississippi River Delta. The internal pressure rose another ten millibars, and the winds dropped to 127 mph.

Shockingly, this was bad news.

The low pressure in the eye had sucked up billions of tons of seawater. As the pressure dropped, the eye expanded like an ice skater extending her arms to slow her spin. Hurricane force winds now extended one hundred twenty miles out, and the surge spread out, too, far wider than forecast.

This was no compact horror like Camille. This was now a gargantuan four hundred fifty-mile wide creature set on laying waste to everything before it.

K minus two hours: Downtown

THINGS WERE NOT GOING WELL IN THE MAYOR'S HEADQUARTERS at the Hyatt. They had power, thanks to generators, but laptops and phones, both land-based and cellular, were useless. Internet and television were down. The satellite phones were unreliable. The mayor and his staff were blind and deaf.

Anna Elliot realized it was a mistake not to be at the Emergency Center at City Hall. But they were trapped for the time being. With hurricane winds blowing outside, nobody was going to travel even the half block. Fortunately, they weren't completely out of touch. Two-way radio with the Office of Emergency Preparedness hadn't failed, and someone brought a hand-cranked transistor radio.

Anna glanced at the windows overlooking the Superdome. The winds and rain, coming out of the north, lashed the side of the building full on. She forced herself to ignore the frightening roar. The Hyatt was built soon after the Superdome, and it had survived hurricanes before. Surely, it could stand up to the storm. She once again tried to reach Baton Rouge on the satellite phone.

Suddenly, glass and rain flew everywhere amidst a great explosion of noise. It was as though a bomb had gone off. Anna found herself screaming on the carpeted floor, gray rain and clouds where a pane of glass once stood. The storm had blown out the windows.

Once the initial shock had subsided, Anna took in her surroundings. Those who could move rushed to the door as a staffer struggled with it. Anna saw a young lady curled up on the floor in terror. She crawled to her, grasped the woman's ankle, and pulled her co-worker towards the door. Her actions got the panicked woman's attention, and the two crawled out of the devastated room.

Once they reached the corridor between the rooms and the atrium, they were caught up in the crowd of staffers and guests of the hotel. Many were in shock; apparently, windows were failing all over the place.

"Oh, my God!" screamed the woman she had helped. "You're covered in blood! Help! Help!"

Feeling wetness, Anna touched her face. Sure enough, there

was blood on her fingers. Nausea gripped Anna, and she fell to her knees. The police guard with a first aid kit was there in a moment. Sitting on the carpet, back against the wall, she looked around as the guard treated her. Other people had been cut by flying glass too. The injured and uninjured alike were wandering the halls, moaning and muttering and crying, unsure of what to do.

The government of the City of New Orleans had been completely knocked out.

IT WAS DIFFICULT TRYING TO KEEP UP WITH THE HURRICANE COVerage at Dansereau Plantation. The local cable gave up the ghost during the night, and the spotty DIRECTV dish provided only national coverage when it worked at all. Elizabeth and William watched the TV with the sound off and listened to the local radio on the coffee table.

In Baton Rouge, the cable *was* working, but without electricity, it was useless. The same could be said for Chackbay.

In Lafayette and Lake Charles, things were more normal—if one could say that watching a major storm come ashore live on television was normal. The Breauxes in Lafayette were glued to the coverage, as were Emma and Cathy in Lake Charles. In Emma's case, her grief for her father was compounded with fears for her husband.

Not that the coverage said a whole lot. Radar and satellite images clearly showed the slightly weaker storm marching inexorably towards the Mississippi Gulf Coast. But besides the occasional live reports from Mobile, Hattiesburg, or the French Quarter, no one *really* knew what was going on.

K minus one hour: Superdome

BUFORD WAS BESIDE THE SUPERDOME MANAGEMENT OFFICES, THE howling of the winds outside a steady background noise. But it wasn't the gale that sent a chill down his spine—it was the sound of thousands of voices screaming in fear along with the terrifying reverberation of metal being torn away.

"What the hell? Come on!" he cried.

Fighting his way through the panicked crowd, Buford and others finally reached the arena, only to stop short. Rain and light were pouring into the building. Looking up, they could see two huge holes torn into the ceiling of the Superdome.

For the first time since Afghanistan, fear choked any words Buford could utter.

Oh, my God! Is the Dome collapsing?

Orleans/Jefferson line

THE MONSTER'S STORM SURGE WAS MUCH LARGER THAN IT SHOULD have been. Twenty-five feet of surge flowed into Lake Pontchartrain, overwhelming the I-10 Bridge. Like Pensacola during Ivan, the incredible pressure of the water pushed at the trapped air beneath the bridge sections. The half-floating concrete sections slid off the supports and sank to the bottom of the lake.

The surge didn't have the same effect on the old US 11 bridge that ran parallel to the shattered Interstate span. Built in an earlier time, the two-lane bridge was considered a relic with its unreliable drawbridge. But it survived the onslaught without damage, leaving one thin, precious link to the city from the east.

The water moved in all directions. By the time the surge reached the North Shore, it was fifteen feet, enough to easily put much of the coastal areas of St. Tammany Parish under water. Slidell's city hall, over four miles inland, was flooded, as was half the city. The surge was not high enough to damage the roadbed of the Causeway bridge, but it was enough to rip apart the old nine-mile turnaround.

A ten-foot surge of water flowed backwards into the drainage canals in Orleans and Jefferson parishes. At the end of the Orleans Avenue Canal, the embankment was six feet lower than the flood wall. Water from the lake streamed into City Park, endangering the Museum of Art.

This was not the worst problem.

The surge exerted enormous pressure onto the banks of the drainage canals. The Corps of Engineers had taken this into consideration with the design of the storm walls, and while they knew the half-levee, half-storm wall design would not hold up to an overtopping—a fact not revealed to local officials—the water was still far from the top.

The strength of the design depended on the rigidity of the walls. The small, earthen levee would not be sufficient to contain the water. The design called for pilings of long, corrugated steel sheets to be driven deep into the ground. Like a corrugated box, as long as the sheets remained rigid, the structure would succeed.

It came down to money. The Corps had to design the levee using the bare minimum amount of materials because funding from Congress was never sufficient. Ten feet of sheeting was deemed enough, as long as the soil was the famous rock-hard Louisiana clay. But once again, budgetary limitations intruded. There was not enough money to do all the test borings called for by the original specifications. Pressured to complete the job, the Corps reduced the number of borings to the bare minimum. It was one of a series of decisions that would kill thousands.

The canals were dug where they were because the land was cheap—low and swampy. Underneath a portion of the land were old filled-in swamps. The buried reeds and other vegetation had turned into peat moss, notorious for its jelly-like consistency. Without the borings, the Corps did not know peat moss was there. Ten feet of sheet piling would prove completely inadequate.

Another decision played a role. To improve drainage, the Corps had the canals dredged over the years. Therefore, there was less earth between the canal sides and the sheet pilings than the specifications required. This weakened the entire structure.

So it was at 0930 CDT on August 29, 2005, tons of water exerted enough pressure against the bottom of the half-filled London Avenue Canal to cause the underground sheet pilings, encased in peat moss, to begin to move inward. Any bend in the sheeting would compromise the internal structure of the levee. The water pushed on both sides—towards Gentilly to the east and Lakeview to the west—and one or both of the levees were in danger of failure. Finally, the Gentilly side gave way first. Without the underground support from the sheeting, the concrete storm wall fell inwards. The storm surge of the monster began to flow into the City of New Orleans.

Fifteen minutes later, the 17th Street Canal failed on the Orleans Parish side near the 17th Street Bridge, and water poured into Lakeview.

There were only a few people in the area, and they had no way of reporting the disaster even if they were aware of what was happening.

The Crescent City began to die, and hardly anyone knew it.

Chapter 8

K-hour: Louisiana/Mississippi Line

At 0945 CDT, the monster made its third and final landfall six miles south of a small, wide place in the road, deep in the delta of the Pearl River, called Pearlington, Mississippi. Back in 1969, Pearlington had survived Hurricane Camille, the last monster to come calling. Katrina was far less kind. The hamlet was simply annihilated.

By this time, her winds were down to 125 mph, which the experts call a Category 3. Hurricane force winds covered an area from Mobile to Baton Rouge.

As destructive as the winds were, the major problem for over one hundred miles of coast was the twenty-eight to thirty-foot storm surge. Louisiana's St. Bernard and Plaquemines parishes were already smashed and flooded. Now, the fury of the monster was concentrated on the counties of the Mississippi Gulf Coast.

Gulfport

John Waguespack opened his eyes, having the strangest feeling his world was moving. *What the hell was that?*

The first thing he realized, as he fought through the haze of alcohol and cocaine that still wrapped his brain, was the howling whine of winds buffeting the building. He threw his feet to the floor and sat on the edge of his bed, rubbing his face with his hands.

He glanced behind him. Lucy was lying face-down, nude, and

completely passed out. He was surprised at the amount of blow and booze she consumed last night. After the power failed, they spent the early hours of the morning trying to set a new record for fucking each other's brains out. At the time, the sound of the winds had only spurred them on.

Now, the wailing excited him in a far different and unpleasant way.

Waguespack pulled on his navy shorts and padded into the den, tugging on a black Southern Miss T-shirt as he approached the window. At first, all he saw was gray rain. He couldn't tell the sky from the land.

He blinked. *Was the land moving?*

The fog from last night washed away as an icy feeling took hold in his gut. *Where the hell is the highway?*

There was movement—something big and dark. Waguespack peered through the rain-swept window, focusing. It was a floating car. Waguespack's eyes snapped wide open.

The storm surge is here. Holy shit, there's no land! The surge is already over Highway 90, and it's deep enough to float cars!

He had paid big bucks to get a condo with Gulf-facing windows. He had to go to the front door to see the parking lot. As he reached it, a massive shudder almost caused him to fall. With horror, he realized his building was moving. He pulled open the door, fighting the suction of the winds, and staggered to the breezeway. Looking down through the sideways-moving torrent, he saw waves.

The cars in the parking lot were already deep underwater. The Gulf of Mexico, driven by winds in excess of one hundred twenty miles an hour, was trying its best to tear down the condo complex. Already, the waves had reached the bottom of the second story, water going through holes gouged into the bricks.

Panic gripped Waguespack as he tried to process what was before his eyes. The storm was destroying his home. Katrina was trying to kill him.

Lucy! I gotta get Lucy!

Just then, he was thrown to the concrete floor of the breezeway. The whole building was shaking violently, tilting. The condo was collapsing. He had no time left.

He half-ran, half-crawled to the stairwell. Gusts tore at his body as he descended, needle-sharp rain stinging his skin. Pieces of roofing and the tops of trees became deadly missiles. He got halfway down when the building trembled again. Without another thought, Waguespack threw himself into the turbulent water.

Striking out with his arms, he swam towards a nearby tree, trying to get far away from the building as quickly as possible. The warm salt water drew him inland, waves crashed over his face, and the sea filled his mouth. Blindly, he reached out, stretching for all he was worth. At the last instant, his fingers touched the branches.

Waguespack, gasping and coughing, pulled himself into the limbs before he looked back at his condo. At first, he wondered whether he had been wrong—that the place might survive after all. Suddenly, the building shuddered and slowly collapsed into the maelstrom. Horrified, he knew he had just seen Lucy die.

He held on to the tree limb with an iron grip, thinking of his next move. The rain was agonizing. He feared the tree could fall victim to the waves at any time.

He thought back to what he knew about hurricanes. The storm pulled in the surge as it came ashore, but the waters would eventually recede. If he were going to live through the next few hours, he would have to get inland. The land rose, so it would be shallower. If he swam a couple of blocks, he would be able to walk onto dry land.

Should he wait for the calm of the eye? He peered at the other trees. No, the winds were straight out of the south. The winds of a hurricane are counter-clockwise. If the winds were from the south, the eye would pass to the west. No calm time for him. He would have to leave then if he was going to leave at all.

Waguespack took a few deep breaths and pushed himself out of the tree. As he hoped, the waves pushed him inland. At first, he tried to lower his legs, but after hitting his knee against something hard—a sunken car, maybe—he attempted a breaststroke as he moved with the gray waves.

Just keep going—focus on going on. The further I go, the shallower it will get. Just keep going.

THE FAILURE OF THE EAST STORM WALL OF THE LONDON AVENUE canal wasn't enough to relieve the pressure on the rest of the levees. A half hour after the storm came ashore, the west levee collapsed. Now water was pouring into Lakeview from two directions. It only sped up the unavoidable annihilation of the neighborhood.

In Jefferson Parish, the price to pay for the decision to evacuate the pumping station operators was coming due. The surge forced water up the wrong way into the pumping stations. There was no one to shut off the valves, so the flood backed up into the drainage system. Already suffering from six inches of rainfall, Metairie and Kenner now had water coming out of the storm drains. The East Bank of Jefferson Parish was slowly flooding.

K plus one hour: Covington

CHUCK'S BATTERY-POWERED RADIO, TUNED IN TO THE HURRICANE coverage, was the only sound to compete with the howling winds outside. He heard the drama of the announcer taking shelter in a closet as the window of the studio imploded, all reported live as it happened.

The radio station is in the Dominion Tower next to the Dome! How can the winds be that strong down there? I'm closer to the storm than they are.

What Chuck didn't know was that the gusts were much stronger the higher up they were. Trees, structures, even the ground effect, all reduced the power of the winds. A tall glass office building was the *last* place anyone should be during a hurricane. That was why the idea of vertical evacuation—seeking shelter in high-rise office buildings—was rejected by the experts.

Chuck, having nothing else to do, watched the storm as if it was a reality show on TV. The sideways-moving rain wasn't heavy enough to obscure what was happening. It was fascinating, in a car-wreck kind of way. The northerly winds weren't steady. They came in gusts, and that was when things got interesting. Every time the winds increased in power, down would come another of the tall pine trees.

The process was a lot slower than Chuck expected. The trees seemed to fall in slow motion. Only the floor-shaking thud vibrating through his feet proved that what he was seeing was not a dream.

When a tree struck a building, like his neighbor's detached garage, it didn't slice right through it. At first, the trunk buried itself into the roof. Over time it would make its way through the framing and sheetrock, until, an hour later, the tree was lying flat on the ground, cutting the structure in half.

He had been fortunate. He had a lot of trees down, but all missed the house. His fence wasn't so lucky. He could see at least five trees on it, and there were probably more he couldn't see. He was relieved Rufus was in Baton Rouge. Otherwise, he would have to walk him on a leash rather than just let him run wild in the backyard. The rain wasn't heavy or consistent, but it had been going on for hours. He estimated about six inches had fallen so far.

Chuck rested his eyes for a moment as the radio droned on. It sounded as though the storm had made landfall. Damage to New Orleans seemed to be minor. It appeared the city had survived another storm. There were no reports about the Mississippi coast, and he expected it got hit hard. There would be plenty of work making reconstruction loans.

A change in the howling outside caught his attention. The winds, steadily out of the north for hours, shifted to the northwest. Even through the gray rain, the sky was lighter than before. Chuck tried to picture what was happening.

Winds move in a counter-clockwise direction around the eye of the hurricane. North means the eye is due east. The storm itself is moving north. So, if the winds shift to a more westerly direction, then that means the hurricane is well inland. The eye is northeast of here and moving away. The storm's almost over, thank God!

The tree canopy's destroyed. Hundreds of tress must have come down around here. All the beautiful pines around the neighborhood—gone.

It will never be the same.

The room darkened suddenly. It took Chuck an instant to register what he was seeing.

A shadow grew from the northwest. *What? Oh, shit—a tree!*

This time the rumble was in conjunction with a crash. A loud, close, and sickening crash. The whole house shuddered. Chuck's stomach dropped to his knees. He knew his beloved house had taken a hit.

He dashed up the stairs to his daughter's room. Sure enough, the sounds of the storm grew much louder after he opened Hailey's door. A tangle of wood, glass, sheetrock, and pine tree were where a window used to be. Rain was blowing into the house from a gap between the trunk and the remnants of the window frame.

Chuck stripped the bed and used the mattress as a plug. He jammed pillows and sheets around the mattress to hold it in firmly. He knew he had to stop the rain from coming in. The water would rot the drywall, carpet, and floors.

Once the hole was filled, Chuck collapsed to the floor. It was a surreal experience, sitting with his back against his daughter's dresser as he surveyed the damage. A long branch stuck out, knocking the ceiling fan sideways before burying itself into the wall on the far side of the room. Pine needles were all over the carpet.

He watched the tree closely. It didn't seem to move. Might this be the extent of the hit? Was the tree close enough to the house that it would remain in its current position?

Another thought occurred to him: *How the hell am I going to get it out of here? How do I fix this?*

K plus two hours: French Quarter

THE WINDS WERE BEGINNING TO DIE DOWN IN THE QUARTER, which gave the media the chance to do their stand-ups in the street.

"...and as you can see behind me, except for a little water and minor debris in the street, it looks like New Orleans was spared the knock-out blow so many feared. Earlier, this scene wasn't so benign."

"And...cut!" said Middleton. "Good take, Bryan."

Thorpe nodded as he ran his hand through his hair.

Middleton checked his notes. "We'll run Sam's footage now. Are you ready for the close? Good. On my mark: five, four, three—" He counted down the last silently and pointed at the reporter.

Thorpe gave the camera his best sincere look. "It's much more peaceful now as Katrina races northward. I can safely say that the Big Easy dodged the Big One this time. This is Bryan Thorpe for Action NOW News."

St. Charles Parish

Elizabeth and William joined Mrs. Reynolds in the kitchen and discussed the storm while they fixed sandwiches.

"A lot of water in the yard," William reported as he looked out of the small window over the sink. "Sugarcane doesn't look good."

"Do you think the farmers will get any of it out?" asked Mrs. Reynolds as she sliced tomatoes.

William rubbed his head. "Well, it's the end of August. Harvest doesn't start until October. That's a month for the cane to recover. If it stays dry, it ought to straighten up a bit, and the new chopper harvesters are real good at getting out flattened cane."

"Not like it was during Hurricane Andrew," said Elizabeth, placing three cans of Coke on the counter. "The farmers lost a lot of cane that year."

"I remember. Even with the new machines, the farmers are going to hurt some this season."

"I wonder who else got hurt," said Elizabeth. "You've got to know the coast got hit hard. Do you think the reports are right, that the city was spared?"

"Don't know. If the reporters would get their asses out of the Quarter, we might find out."

"Be nice of them to work for a change," Mrs. Reynolds observed. "Do you want any cheese on your sandwich, Miss Lizzy?"

Lake Charles

"It's not in here! It's not in here!" Emma cried.

Cathy watched as Emma knelt in the parking lot of the hospital, franticly going through Abe's suitcase. "What are you looking for?"

"Papa's *kittel.* It's a special white robe. It's very important." She sat back on her heels, and Cathy knelt beside her.

"Why?"

Emma's expression was numb. "It's our tradition. Jewish men are buried in their *kittel* or *tahrihim,* a burial shroud. Whenever we go on long trips, the men are supposed to take it with them. Papa must have left his in New Orleans."

"Can we get it later?"

"No. You see, we…we bury our dead as soon as possible. No embalming. We don't have time to get his *kittel.*"

"You mean, you have to bury him here? In Lake Charles?"

"If we can't get him back to New Orleans very soon—yes."

"I am so sorry, Emma." Cathy took her hand.

Emma nodded. The two women closed up Abe's suitcase, placed it back in the trunk of the car, and returned to the hospital. The emergency nurse informed Emma she had visitors. In the waiting room, they found two elderly gentlemen who rose from their seats as they entered the room.

"Shalom," greeted the shorter of the two. "I'm Daniel Copeland, a member of the local *chevra kaddisha.* This is Leonard Rosen. Is one of you Mrs. Katz?"

Emma stepped forward. "I am."

He took her hand. "Mrs. Katz, please accept our condolences."

"Thank you. How—"

"The hospital left a message for us after your father passed."

Emma's legs began to give out. She excused herself and sat down. "That was very kind of them."

Mr. Copeland smiled. "We have a good relationship with Memorial. The Jewish population in Lake Charles may be small, but we take care of our own. We'll see to everything."

"Thank you."

Cathy shook their hands and introduced herself. "I'm sorry, but I'm not Jewish. What is it you do?"

"We care for the body, Mrs. Tilney," Mr. Rosen said. "We prepare it for burial, watch over it, and pray until the funeral. It's our way."

"We don't have Papa's *kittel,*" Emma said.

Mr. Copeland nodded. "Don't worry. All will be as it should be. We have *tahrihim*. Whatever's missing, we will provide."

"I…I don't know when we can have the funeral. My husband's in New Orleans, and my sister is in Washington, D.C. She can't get here until tomorrow."

"I understand. Is your husband all right?"

Emma shook her head in frustration. "I don't know. The phone system's out."

"It's bad even here," Mr. Copeland remarked. "Well, nothing can be decided until tomorrow. Do you have a place to stay?"

Emma shook her head, and Cathy said, "I thought she might come back with me to Baytown for the night."

Emma looked at her friend. "Cathy, that's too generous—"

"No, it's not. Come with me. Didn't you say your sister's flying into Houston?" At Emma's nod, she continued. "Well, then, she can pick you up on her way to Lake Charles. Come on, Emma, let me do this for you."

Exhausted and dispirited, Emma agreed.

K plus three hours:
Third District Headquarters

Fitzwilliam had his patrol cars out during the storm. While the cell phones were shot to hell, and the computers in the cars were inoperable, at least the radios still worked. The reports up to now were uneventful—just the usual damage.

Suddenly everything changed.

"Say again," Fitzwilliam ordered into the microphone as he leaned over the dispatcher.

"Lots of water in the streets around Lakeview and Carrolton. It's starting to get deep. And it's moving."

Fitzwilliam glanced at the dispatcher. "Moving? Is it the wind?"

"No, it doesn't seem—hold on."

The Third District held its breath as they awaited the response from the patrol.

"District, we have an eyewitness here who says there's a breech in the 17th Street Canal. Repeat—a report of a breech in the 17th Street Canal."

Fitzwilliam cursed. "Can you verify?"

"We'll try to, but the water's getting high."

"Do your best, but be careful. We'd rather you come home than not."

"Roger that. Out."

Fitzwilliam turned to the district commander. "I know this report's unconfirmed, but I think we ought to pass it on downtown."

"Agreed," his boss said. "See to it."

Within a few minutes, it and other reports that flowed to the command center were compelling enough for the mayor to report a break in the 17th Street Canal. No one yet knew the scale of the trouble, so the comment was rather low key.

The helicopters were in the air again.

The US Coast Guard knew they had to get ships and aircraft back to New Orleans and the coast as soon as possible. So, even while the monster was moving inland, now something between a Cat 2 and Cat 1, the Dolphins and Jayhawks were launched and headed back to their forward bases in Mississippi and Belle Chasse. They were coming from all directions—Lake Charles, Alexandria, Shreveport, Houston, Tampa, and other bases. It would take hours, but that's what the crews were paid to do.

All over the country, National Guard troops were on alert, awaiting activation orders. In Georgia, the Army's famous 82nd Airborne, just back from the wars, prepared to go in.

From the sea, Coast Guard and Navy ships that had been prepositioned to ride out the storm steamed through mountainous seas towards the mouth of the river. There, they would stand by until the channel was clear of sunken boats.

Chapter 9

K plus four hours: Covington

Chuck shut off his generator to save fuel and walked out of his garage into the misting rain and still-gusty winds. He had cracked open the garage door to prevent any carbon monoxide buildup. He needed to survey the damage to the house and see whether any potential danger still threatened.

He knew things were bad but had no idea they were *this* bad. Trees were down everywhere; he lost count after twenty. He couldn't see the grass for the limbs, leaves, and water—water all over the place. He tried to get to the street, but it was covered with water. The debris in the ditches had limited the drainage.

But the worst sight was the power poles. They had fared no better than the trees. Chuck knew it took hours for the utility company to replace a single pole taken out by a thunderstorm or a drunk driver. How much longer would it take after a hurricane? On his street alone, dozens of poles were down, mixed with large trees. How big an area did Katrina hit? How many *hundreds* of square miles? How many *thousands* of poles? It could take weeks to fix.

Hell, it could take months!

The rain returned, chasing Chuck back indoors. He got a tumbler from the cabinet and tried to get water from the kitchen faucet—and failed. The water was out.

Of course. There's no power for the pumps at the water utility.

Things had just gotten worse.

Baton Rouge

CARRIE WAS WORRIED AS SHE PREPARED TO CHECK IN AT THE capital. Her first concern was for John; reports had come in about damage to the Superdome. But, except for talking about downtown New Orleans, it was as though the rest of the area had ceased to exist. Jane was doing her best to be calm, but there was hardly anything out of the North Shore. No calls and few reports except for one lunatic from a cable outfit who thought it was a great idea to stand in the wind and rain outside of Covington. The tone of the reports around the region varied from cataclysmic to hopeful and back again.

And there was Catherine. Carrie knew her mother could be difficult, even at the best of times. Now, in the face of this calamity, the woman had lost all sense of proportion. She sat on the couch, listening to the radio and engaging in catastrophic event fantasies.

"I hope Chuck's all right, dear," she told Jane, "but with all this damage, well…I just hope he's all right."

"Mother, please!" Carrie hissed.

Jane got to her feet. "Excuse me, but I'd better walk Rufus now the rain has stopped." The others remained quiet until the back door closed. Once it did, Carrie began.

"I wish you wouldn't say such things in front of Jane. She's worried enough about Chuck as it is, but in her condition…well, you ought to have more tact."

"Tact? This is *my* house, and I will say what I please!" Catherine snarled.

"And what about Jane's feelings?"

"I know Jane's feelings very well. That's why I haven't said what needs to be said!"

"What are you talking about?"

Catherine sat up straight, her voice with a tone of finality. "If Charles is killed and she and the children move in with me, I will *not* have that dog in my house!"

Carrie looked towards the stairs. "Mother, the children! Lower your voice!" After a pause, she continued. "Why are you even talking about that? Chuck's fine, I'm sure."

"We have to be prepared for any eventuality."

"That's ridiculous! Why would you even *think* that, much less drop hints in front of Jane? Have you lost your mind?"

"Don't take that tone of voice with me!" Catherine cried. "If Charles had done what he should have and evacuated, we wouldn't be having this conversation. He should be taking care of his family instead of imposing his responsibility on others. But I shouldn't be surprised. He's just like his father. And now I'll probably have to raise his family in his stead!"

Carrie knew her mother's behavior was only a response to her own worries and fears. She wasn't really serious, but it was potentially damaging to Jane in any case.

"Mother, it's no good talking about things like that while Jane is so worried. You wouldn't want anything to happen to the baby, would you?"

"Of course not!"

"Then, please, try to keep your conjectures to yourself. You know Chuck as well as I do. He loves Jane and the kids more than life itself. He'll call us as soon as he can find a working phone—you'll see."

Catherine shook her head. "Is this our lot in life—to be abandoned by our men just when we need them most?"

"Mother, please." She tried to tell herself Catherine's jab wasn't aimed at John, too.

"All right! I'll keep my thoughts to myself just as I always do! If people would just listen to me sometimes—" She saw Carrie's glare. "I said I'll keep this all to myself, and I meant it!"

"Thank you. I have to report in now. I'll be back as soon as I can." She leaned down and kissed Catherine.

"At least John has a gun," Catherine mumbled.

Carrie smiled. "Yes, at least there's that."

She walked outside to have a quick word with her sister-in-law before she drove to work. She found an aggravated Jane in the backyard, tugging at Rufus's leash.

"C'mon, c'mon, do something," she urged through gritted teeth.

She noticed Carrie approaching. "Rufus just won't go while he's on a leash, Carrie! It's so frustrating!"

Carrie stood next to Jane in the soggy yard as Rufus continued to sniff the grass. "I'm sure he's not the only reason you feel stressed, Janie."

Jane closed her eyes, and her free hand touched her abdomen. "Catherine's been very kind in allowing us to stay here. I should be more grateful—have more patience."

"Oh, bullshit!" Carrie cried. "She's your mother-in-law; it's the least she can do." Jane glanced at her before returning her attention to the dog, and Carrie continued. "I've talked with Mother. Hopefully, she'll curb her tongue, at least for a little while. If she gets to be too much, go to your room. I've got to check in at work. I'll be back as soon as I can."

"I was planning to spend some time with the kids after I finished with Rufus. Shall I walk Max too?"

"Only if you have Hailey help you," she replied as she gave Jane's midsection a look. "You've got to take care of yourself."

"You, too."

Carrie laughed as she rubbed her own pregnant belly. "That's why I know you're stressed." She kissed her sister-in-law's cheek. "Don't worry, Janie. Chuck can take care of himself."

Jane smirked. "Shall I tell you not to worry about John?"

"You can try."

"Will it work?"

"No." They hugged each other. "I'll be back soon. Hang in there."

Superdome

Buford had helped oversee the movement of the people off the field of the Superdome into the stands. The surface of the field was soaked. To save power, the air conditioning was off. More refugees were showing up every minute. The air was humid and close, and the folks were getting restless.

The neighborhoods of New Orleans were territorial, especially those that contained public housing projects. Gentilly did not get along with Iberville, which didn't get along with Algiers, which didn't get along with St. Claude, which didn't get along with New Orleans East. At first, the groups tended to congregate in different parts of the Dome. But as the hours passed and more and more people streamed in, the young men from the 'hood reverted to type and began arguing over turf.

The National Guard was stretched thin, trying to control and patrol, much less feed the mass of humanity. For not the first time, Buford missed the feel of his sidearm against his hip.

Another twenty-four hours. Just hang in there for one more day, and we can send these people home.

Tulane Medical Center

A few blocks away, George Katz walked outside of the main building of Tulane Hospital, taking a break from moving the emergency room back down to the first floor. The storm hadn't been too bad for the doctors and patients. The only exciting incident happened when a crew from one of the cable networks, who had ridden out Katrina with them, tried to do a stand-up outside during the worst of the winds and caused rain to be blown all over the lobby.

George stretched his aching muscles—medical equipment was heavy—trying to get his mind off of Emma and Abe and his failure. Emma had called early in the morning with the bad news just before most of the phones failed. George wrestled with his sorrow and guilt.

In the last few months, things had been going really well. Not only had he and Emma turned a corner in their relationship, but so had Abe. He was again the friend George had known most of his life.

Now that things were finally looking up, Abe was gone. And Emma had to handle it by herself.

It was irrational to feel guilty about that, but he did. He felt he, somehow, should have been with them. Maybe he could have saved his father-in-law. As he paced, he glanced down the street at the nearby Park Plaza Hotel.

I screwed up. I should have made Em and Abe stay in town with the other dependents. Maybe he wouldn't have had his heart attack.

Or, if he did, I would have been there. I would have saved him. Abe would be alive right now if I had just gotten my head out of my ass!

George's self-incrimination was interrupted as he was jostled by a passer-by. "Hey, man, watch it, will ya?" the young black man advised as he steadied the shaken doctor. "Ya almost ran me down."

"Oh! Excuse me," George offered.

"S'okay, dude," the young man waved as he strolled along in the middle of the street.

At first, George was struck by the fact that Tulane Avenue, usually one of the busiest streets in the city, was almost deserted. Except for the staffers of the hospital and the occasional NOPD squad car, the only person George had seen was that man, and he was in the middle of the street. It was strange.

George then noticed something else. The man's pants were soaking wet about halfway up his thighs.

Street flooding must be bad, he reasoned. *I hope they got the pumps going.*

A call from the door told George his break was over. Time to bring some more equipment down.

K plus six hours: St. Bernard Parish

CAJUN 101 WAS IN THE AIR AGAIN AFTER REFUELING AT NAS JOINT Reserve Base Belle Chasse. The old naval air station was fully functional, having taken only minor damage from the storm. This was good news, for it was about to be one of the busiest airports in the world.

Lt. Commander Fredrick Wentworth turned his Dolphin due north and flew towards St. Bernard, beginning initialization of search and rescue operations. This was what Wentworth and his people had trained for years to do, and they would be called on to use all their experience, talent, and endurance in the days to come.

The team was larger this time out. Besides co-pilot LTJG Jeremy Price and PO3 Donald Lauck serving as AST, they were joined by Airman Marcus Randle. Randle was the rescue swimmer, the man lowered out of the aircraft by the AST to assist people in distress.

His was the most dangerous job but not the most difficult. That fell to the pilot who had to fly the aircraft, taking acceptable risks in order to save people while not killing the crew.

The winds were still gusty as the Dolphin crossed the Mississippi River into Chalmette. The flight down prepared them for the sight of an entire parish underwater, but it was still disquieting. Fighting the gnawing horror in their guts, the crew scanned the scene below, looking for survivors. It took only a couple of minutes before Price sang out.

Wentworth dove towards the contact, the winds buffeting the helo. He made a slow pass over two people—a man and a woman, waving frantically on the roof of a flooded house—looking for trees, power lines, and other dangerous obstacles. He gained a bit of altitude while considering his approach. Only after Price agreed to his plan did Wentworth bring the copter around, pointing her into the wind.

Cajun 101 was placed into a hover before Randle, two life preservers hanging from his gear, leaned out of the door. Lauck checked his teammate's harness one last time before slapping his crewmate on the back. He then lowered the rescue swimmer by a cable to the house below. He had stopped just above the roof when the male victim a made a move towards Randle. Randle shouted at the man, he backed off, and the airman gave the signal to continue. Once down, Randle immediately freed himself from the cable, and Lauck quickly retrieved it.

The winds were too much to hold position, and Wentworth was forced to go around. By then, Randle had life preservers on the civilians and cleared the way for the basket. Lauck lowered the basket by the cable, and once it was on the roof, Randle helped the woman into it. Safety line attached, he called the all clear, and Lauck raised it.

Wentworth was drifting again, so he pulled the Dolphin up. A minute later, Lauck got the frightened woman out of the basket. He waited for the helo to get in position again before lowering it to retrieve the man. Once the male survivor was secured in the aircraft, Lauck dropped the basketless cable to his teammate. Moments later, Cajun 101 was cleared to leave.

Wentworth made a beeline to New Orleans Armstrong International Airport and triage. On the way, the crew could not help but notice that there was water in more areas than just St. Bernard.

"Holy crap, skipper!" cried Price. "The whole fuckin' city is flooding!"

Wentworth glanced at his right-seater. He knew Price owned a house in New Orleans East.

"Price!" Once he got the man's attention, he barked, "Are you up for this? Are you in the game? *Are. You. In. The. Game?*"

Price paused a moment. "Yeah. Yeah, I am."

"Hang in there, Jeremy. I need you. We all need you."

Price's expression grew stony. "I'm good, skipper. Let's get to work."

Lauck patted the officer on the shoulder. "Fuckin'A, sir."

K plus seven hours: Convention Center

NO ONE YET KNEW THE SCALE OF THE IMPENDING DISASTER, BUT the people of the Ninth Ward, Gentilly, and Carrolton could see the water rising. It was time to get to shelter. Mostly on foot, they made their way downtown. The vast majority went to the Superdome, the "shelter of last resort." Others, for reasons known only to them, went towards the river and the Ernest N. Morial Convention Center.

The largest building downtown at over one million square feet, the Convention Center was the real centerpiece of New Orleans tourism. It was big enough to hold huge national conventions. It was a massive structure, but it wasn't intended to be a shelter. Built at ground level, it didn't have the Dome's electrical generators. No one was supposed to gather there. But gather there they did.

By 5:00 p.m., about a thousand refugees milled about the locked doors. They were but the vanguard.

Chapter 10

K plus eight hours: Gentilly

The inhabitants of the Johnson household relaxed in the front room, after having undergone a harrowing day, and listened to the wind and rain beat against the walls as they tried to get the radio to work. Unfortunately, the batteries gave out by mid-morning, so the only sounds were the slowly dying winds. It was quiet enough for the last couple of hours for Kaywanda to nap against Scott while Mrs. Johnson rested in her easy chair. The room was warm but not unpleasantly so. A movement disturbed Kaywanda's catnap.

"Don't move," she mumbled, eyes resolutely closed.

Scott's hand returned to her shoulder. "It's gettin' dark, Kay. I just wanna take a quick look outside."

"Okay," she said as he slowed disentangled himself from her. Kaywanda fell full on the couch, half listening to her boyfriend as he moved towards the door.

"Shit!"

Kaywanda opened her eyes. "What's wrong, baby?"

"There's a hell of a lot of water in the street! Come see."

Groaning, she got up and joined Scott, standing in the open doorway. The flowing water caused her to become fully awake. "Scott! I've never seen it this high!"

A trash can floated by. Scott turned to her. "Is it just me, or is the water flowing against the wind?"

Mrs. Johnson called out from her chair, "What's up, babygirl?

Whatcha lookin' at?"

Kaywanda ran over to her, eyes wide in fear. "Momma, come quick! We got trouble!" Kaywanda half dragged her mother to the door.

"Lord Almighty!" Mrs. Johnson cried. "The water's rising!"

Scott's face was pale. "It's risen an inch just since I've been standing here."

Kaywanda grasped his arm. "Oh, God! One of the levees must have broken! We've got to get outta here!"

"But, it's already too high for the car," Scott protested.

"Then we'll walk!"

Mrs. Johnson fell back. "Walk in that? I can't do it! I can't swim! I'll drown!"

Scott seemed to get hold of his emotions. "Don't worry, Miz Johnson, Kay and I'll help you."

"No. No, I'm not going—"

"*Momma!*" Kaywanda screamed. "We're leavin' *now*, goddammit!" She pulled her mother into the bedroom. "Get what you need, Your medicines, money, stuff like that. We can't carry much. Only the important stuff, okay?" Satisfied her mother understood, Kaywanda left and gathered her own belongings from her room.

Scott knelt and threw gear out of his duffle. "We'll put everything into this bag."

"Good idea." Kaywanda and Scott repacked the duffle, then moved to Mrs. Johnson's room and added her necessities.

The trio stood in the living room, thinking about what else to bring.

"Let's see." Scott counted his fingers. "Money, checkbooks, wallets, medicines, personal items, cell phones—"

"My Bible!" cried Mrs. Johnson.

Kaywanda dashed to retrieve it. As she returned, Scott was packing his iPod. Zipping up the bag, Scott looked Kaywanda in the eye.

"Okay," she said, "let's go."

The late afternoon sun was hazy behind the remaining clouds as the group set out. The thigh-high water was brown with a slight smell of the sea. They could feel it push against them as they shuffled in the middle of what used to be the street and was now a canal.

Scott and Kaywanda were on either side of Mrs. Johnson, helping her along, the duffle slung against Scott's back.

"Where do we go?" asked Scott.

Kaywanda tried to get her bearings. "Downtown's high land. It's, uhh...that-a-way." She pointed, and they moved off in that direction.

The journey was a nightmare. New Orleans was not a level city, and as they walked on, the water's depth varied, from knee-deep to up past their waists. They had to walk slowly and carefully, so as not to trip over some unseen obstacle. The smell of the water changed as sewers and underground tanks added their contents to the deluge. Mrs. Johnson wanted to stop and quit several times, but once the party caught up with other refugees, she stopped complaining. They all sloshed towards what they hoped was the French Quarter and safety.

Looting was widespread as victims sought food and criminals collected electronics. Mrs. Johnson was scared, and Kaywanda was disgusted. Hopes rose as they came across a NOPD officer. To their astonishment, instead of stopping the looting, he was engaging in it.

Scott looked over at his girlfriend, a sick expression on his face. "Kay, we're on our own."

Things were not going well for G-Daddy—not at all. Wickham had waited until the winds died down before driving his black Camaro to a place in Gentilly where he suspected a rival gang hid their supplies. The sight of the guard was both rewarding and disappointing. It proved his intelligence was accurate, but it made his task more difficult. He hoped he brought enough ammo for his Glock.

He sat low in the car for hours, waiting until sundown before beginning his assault. A couple of blocks away, he knew he couldn't be seen. Aggressiveness was always an advantage in an attack, as he recalled from the incident in the Gulf so many months ago. All he needed was the cover of darkness.

He must have napped because he didn't know he was in trouble until his feet were wet. Wickham woke up to find water in the passenger compartment of his car. Cursing, he jumped out into the flood, shocked at how fast the water was rising. He jumped back in and tried the ignition, desperate to save his car, but it was too late. The storm had drowned it.

There was nothing to do but walk back to his crib in the Upper Ninth; the assault was pointless without a getaway vehicle. And the way the water was rising, nothing less than a boat would work.

G-Daddy was wading through the stink towards his house when he came across a group of people. Most of them were black, but there was one white Goth dude with a hot-looking chocolate babe helping an old black lady. The babe's momma, maybe? The nose ring-wearing man waved at him.

"Hey, dude! Is that the way downtown?"

G-Daddy didn't have time for this. "Fuck if I know."

Goth Boy shifted the duffle bag on his shoulder, and Wickham wondered whether there was something worthwhile in it. But there were seven of them and one of him, so he dismissed the thought of taking the bag.

The white guy was still talking. "Come with us, man. The city's flooding."

Wickham blinked. *Flooding? Did the levees go?*

The pretty girl grabbed the guy's arm. "Uhh, Scott, let's just go."

Wickham scowled. He wouldn't mind a little jungle fever with Miss Hottie.

"In a second, Kay. C'mon, mister—you can help," Goth Boy said as he approached him.

Wickham decided to end things right then and there and raised his shirt, displaying the Glock in his waistband. "Fuck off, loser. You go your way, an' I'll go mine."

The guy backed off, his hands raised and his eyes wide open. "Sure, man, sure. It's cool."

Wickham stood his ground as the group moved off rapidly.

The city's flooding. His mind wrestled with the implications. Might this be the way to re-establish his empire? By staying while the competition fled? Or was he just shitting himself?

He couldn't make up his mind. There was only one thing to do: secure his merchandise and then think. After some blow, of course.

Wickham continued the trek to his house.

SEVERAL BLOCKS LATER, KAYWANDA, SCOTT, AND THE OTHERS found dry land. They didn't tarry; the constant current during their walk was proof they were only ahead of the water, not out of it. Besides, they wanted to get as far away as possible from the spiky-haired lunatic with the gun. They found themselves close to Esplanade, and they held a short council to decide their destination.

"Do we go to the Dome?" Scott asked.

"No, man," responded one of the people they had met along the way. "I heard it was full-up."

"Then where?"

"Me, I'm going to the Convention Center. They gotta have stuff there." The others agreed.

"Whatcha think, Kay?" Scott asked.

Kaywanda was tired and confused. "It sounds good, Scott. Let's go with them."

Lower Ninth Ward

THE HIGHER-UPS IN BATON ROUGE SCREWED THINGS UP BY POSI-tioning the National Guard at Jackson Barracks. They were trapped with their trucks underwater, but they would not wait for orders or rescue. The Guard was not an outfit to sit on their hands. There were civilians out there who needed their help, dammit, and the Guard had boats chained up somewhere.

The troops found bolt cutters. The Louisiana Army National Guard had become a navy.

THE NATIONAL GUARD WASN'T THE ONLY GROUP OF FIRST RE-sponders flooded. NOPD Third District remained at its post on Moss Street, between the Fair Grounds and City Park, for as long as they could before the floodwaters drove them out. Captain Fitz-william found himself on a boat heading Downtown.

Of the eight NOPD district offices, only two—the Second in Uptown and the Eighth in the French Quarter—did not suffer flooding. Communications breakdowns cut the Second off completely, and the First District refused to abandon their headquarters on North Rampart Street, even though it had water in it.

The NOPD was scrambling to recover and regroup.

Baton Rouge

CARRIE FOUND THE LOUISIANA OFFICE OF HOMELAND SECURITY in complete chaos. Communications had utterly failed, so everyone was responding to rumors spawned by the radio and TV.

Things were great—things weren't great. The city had dodged the Big One—the city was doomed. Rioting and looting had broken out at the Dome.

The last rumor was the worst because that was where John was.

Nobody knew who was in charge. The state said it was the governor. FEMA said *it* was. But, where was FEMA? Except for the FEMA director and his personal staff, the rest of the federal response was scattered all over the place or was still at the pre-positioning areas, waiting to move in.

How to move in became a major question. The state knew that the I-10 Bridge between New Orleans and Slidell was gone. Reports from the Causeway Commission were confusing. Was the Causeway smashed or not? Was the longest bridge in the world destroyed, or did it survive with only minor damage? The rest of the bridges needed to be inspected, so all of them south of Baton Rouge were closed except to emergency vehicles.

The reports from New Orleans, such as they were, became increasingly desperate. The state had to assume there was at least water overtopping the levees. But had they been totally breached? If so, how many? No one could say for sure.

Everyone expected St. Bernard was underwater, and Plaquemines would be almost as bad. But what about the bayou parishes of Terrebonne, Lafourche, and St. Mary? The North Shore? Reports were incomplete, and there was nothing on the news.

All Carrie could do was to focus on her job and try to put John out of her mind. She was not successful.

Covington

It was weird, standing outside, barbecuing a steak on the gas grill while there was a tree in his daughter's window. Chuck didn't want the food in the fridge to go bad, so he decided to eat the cold stuff first and save the canned food in the pantry for later. He was going to need it.

Chuck knew he was in trouble. Once the rain stopped for good, he tried and failed to walk out. Between the water and the fallen trees, he was trapped but good. His little chain saw was no match for all that timber. And if it was this bad on his little street, how much worse were the highways? St. Tammany Parish loved its piney woods, but that love had come back to bite it in the ass.

In the gathering darkness, Chuck realized that he had traveled back in time. Twenty-four hours ago, he was secure in the twenty-first century. Now, one Katrina later, he had lost a hundred years of technological advancement. No electrical power, no TV, no phones, no Internet, and with the roads blocked, no cars. Only his little-bitty generator kept the refrigerator going. And how long would that last? Running constantly—less than two more days. There was no way all this stuff would be cleared out by then.

The steak done, Chuck shut off the gas to the grill—natural gas was the only utility still working. He'd have hot water, because he had gas water heaters. That is, if he had water pressure. It had come and gone all day, and Chuck realized that power to the water towers had been cut. They had generators, but if the workers couldn't get to the generators to start them or get diesel to fuel them, Chuck wouldn't have water.

No showers for ol' Chuckie. Best save the water for the toilets—and don't flush them until I really need to.

Chuck ate his meal and drank a beer, the darkness of his house interrupted by the candles placed about the room. It would have been romantic if Jane had been there and the world hadn't just come to an end.

He was glad that she and the kids didn't have to share his misery, but he missed them dearly. He desperately wanted to call them to let them know he was safe, but for the time being, it was impossible. He was left alone to his thoughts in the silence.

He couldn't believe how *quiet* it was. If he turned off the radio, all he could hear were the bugs, broken up by the soft hum of distant generators.

And it was dark, *really* dark. He hadn't realized how used he had become to streetlights and lamps. Now there was nothing except starlight. Without a flashlight, he was blind.

Chuck finished his meal and blew out the candle. There was nothing else to do but go to sleep.

Was this how it was back in the day before power and radio? Did people on the farm just live their lives according to the sun—rising with the sunrise and sleeping when it got dark?

It was something to think about—something more interesting than worrying about how to get out of this disaster.

In Baton Rouge, the power was still out, so the only information available was from the radio, and they only had reports about the city and Jefferson Parish. The lack of news about the North Shore was galling to Jane Bingley, so she stayed away from the radio and kept the children occupied.

On the outskirts of the area, things were incredibly frustrating. All the Breauxes in Lafayette could do was to watch the confusing news coverage. Joy that the city was spared a direct hit gave way to concern—and then finally horror—as reports of flooding kept coming in. The local news channels knew nothing, and the national outfits were inconclusive. All they talked about was Downtown or the Quarter except for the odd report from coastal Mississippi.

Worse was the collapse of the telephone system. Even as far away as Lafayette, service on landlines and cell phones was spotty. Chris couldn't check on work, and Marianne couldn't reach her mother.

K plus ten hours: central Mississippi

By now, the monster was well inland. Without the warm waters of the Gulf to sustain her, Katrina began to fall apart. Her highest winds were now below sixty miles per hour. But she still had rain—tons of it. The mortally wounded beast pelted northern Mississippi and the central Southern states with inches of rain and spawned hundreds of tornados as she continued to move northwest. The rainwater collected in the ditches and storm sewers, which flowed into the rivers and bayous. They all flowed south, and the floodwaters headed right toward the already devastated counties of southern Mississippi, right as the storm surge was receding. A new surge was coming, this time from the north.

MOST OF THE TELEPHONE LINES WERE DOWN IN THE NEW ORLEANS region, but enough information filtered back to Baton Rouge to convince the government that an unprecedented disaster was occurring eighty miles away. The governor made many decisions that night, but three would weigh heaviest in the days to come.

The first decision was to get boats to the flooded streets of New Orleans. There was no agency in Louisiana that owned more watercraft than the Department of Wildlife and Fisheries. LDWF was best known as the bane to hunters and fishers who dared violate the state's laws and regulations. The agents were hardworking and dedicated. Therefore, when the call went out for help in search and rescue operations, hundreds of agents responded. They would be instrumental in saving countless lives.

The second decision was to get a *lot* more help. The governor sent a plea for additional aid from Washington. She literally asked for "everything you've got."

It was not the *request* that would prove controversial. Washington was becoming aware of the scope of the catastrophe and expected the appeal. The controversy was the *manner* of the request.

For good or ill, government is run by a peculiar category of humanity know as bureaucrats. Owning all the usual virtues and vices as the rest of civilization, they are particularly fond of rules and regulations, for they satisfy their deep need for order and predictably. Bureaucrats claim they wish to be of help to their fellow citizens, and many truly mean it, but their one great fear is the loss of their career.

It is very hard for bureaucrats to lose their jobs, for the law is designed to protect them. Except for elimination of positions by budget cuts, the only other way of getting fired is not to follow the rules. As long as a government staffer put in the hours and followed all policies and procedures, nothing could stop them from collecting their sizable government pension in twenty years. The great nightmare of any bureaucrat is to be brought before a government committee investigating mismanagement. It was a direct route to being shuttled to counting moose in Alaska, if not outright termination.

To keep their jobs secure, bureaucrats did *nothing* if a request was not in the proper form. Every "i" must be dotted and each "t" must be crossed, or the request was sent back for "clarification."

Governments were well aware of this. All levels of government had staff whose only job was to review inter-governmental requests and reports, making sure the local bureaucrats were speaking the same exotic language as their state or federal brethren and vice versa.

Therefore, when the governor's panic-stricken cry for "everything you've got" was received in Washington, it generated a great deal of sympathy but no action. Bureaucrats had no idea what to do. Exactly what kind of "everything" was Louisiana asking for? The box requesting additional help for debris removal was checked, but what else was needed? How much aid? How many personnel? Where should it be brought? Who would be responsible for it? Must watch out for government waste, you know. Were grants or loans needed?

Exactly, what is it you want?

It would take days to get answers out of Baton Rouge.

The third decision would put people's lives at risk.

Baytown, Texas

BY 8:00 P.M., EMMA WAS CURLED UP ON THE SECTIONAL IN THE Tilney's living room. She had talked to her sister and brother-in-law on the phone when not watching the coverage. Emma was running on fumes. Her grief over her father and her worry over her husband drained her reserves of energy. The Tilneys did what they could, but only one voice could give her comfort, and he was trapped in the communications blackout in New Orleans.

Cathy and Henry had gone to bed, and Emma knew she should do the same, but she couldn't rest. She sat in the den, hugging a pillow and numbly watching the muted TV. It took her a moment to realize her cell phone was ringing.

She pounced on it. "Hello?"

"Emma, can you hear me? It's George."

"George! Oh my God, George! I've been so worried! How are you?" Her heart was beating a mile a minute.

"I'm fine, Em. We're all safe and fine." He sounded exhausted.

"Thank God…thank God," she murmured before she remembered the reports. "George, the TV says the city might be flooding. Do you have any water in the hospital?"

"No. Flooding, you say? Do they say how bad it is?"

"Not really, but some say one of the levees has failed, or overtopped, or something."

"I hope that's wrong. Emma, I only have a couple of minutes. We're taking turns using this phone. It's the only one working. Tell me how you're doing. How are you holding up?"

She gave him a quick recap of what had happened since their last phone call almost eighteen hours before: the local temple in Lake Charles was seeing to all the details for Abe, her family was flying down to Houston the next day, the funeral would take place on Wednesday, and she was spending the night with the Tilneys in Baytown.

"Thank you, baby, thank you for calling Henry and Cathy. They've been so kind. I can't tell you what a comfort they've been."

She heard something that sounded like a sob on the other end. "It should have been me, Emma. I should have been there for you. I should have made you and Abe stay in the hotel. Maybe he would have—"

"No! Don't say that! I don't know why it happened, why Papa had to go, but…but maybe it was his time. Please, George, don't tear yourself up over this! Be strong! Be strong for yourself; be strong for *me*. Save your people, and come home to me!"

"I will, come hell or high water."

She snorted in pain and humor, grateful he could still joke at a time like that. "You're all that's important to me. *You're* the only thing that's irreplaceable. I love you so much."

"I love you, too." There was a pause, and she could hear her husband talk to someone else. "Honey, my time's up. I've got to go. I'll call again as soon as I can."

"Oh, George, don't worry about that! Take care of your people so you can get out of there."

"I can't wait. Love you."

"I love you, too." She hung up the cell and fell back into the cushions of the couch, relived beyond measure. She was asleep within moments.

K plus eleven hours: St. Charles Parish

WILLIAM LEFT ELIZABETH AND MRS. REYNOLDS AND RETREATED to his study to use his satellite phone. Unlike the first three times, he got through to Houston.

"Leon? It's Will."

"Hey, boss. How're you doing?"

"We're okay. No power, but we've got a generator. Lost a couple trees, but no damage."

"We've been trying to call, but we couldn't get through."

"Yeah, phones are out all over. How's everything at your end?"

"All inbound traffic has been rerouted to Houston or Miami. Once they get to port, that's another problem. It's been hell trying to get berths. Both ports are full. We're gonna lose big money, Will."

"Can't be helped. That's why I stayed here. I'm going to try to reopen operations at New Orleans soonest. Look, this satellite phone is unreliable. Please stay in touch with me via e-mail, okay?"

"Sure thing. How come that fancy gadget ain't working? The storm can't bother something in space, can it?"

"I don't know for sure. Maybe the system is overloaded."

"Right, that makes sense. Umm, any word about Algiers?"

William had expected the question since Leon's house was in

Lakewood Golf Club off General de Gaulle. "No, nothing. Hell, I'm in St. Charles, and I don't know what's going on a mile down the road."

"I hear you. Anything else?"

"No. I'm patched into DGS via my dish. I can't send out e-mails, but I can receive them. Follow the emergency plan. You guys are in charge until they restore communications here. Don't worry about checking with me. You know your stuff. Just do what needs to be done. We'll clean up everything later."

K plus thirteen hours:
Tulane Medical Center

George Katz was confused. "Water in the streets? I was outside at sundown, and it was dry!"

"It isn't now. Things just went to hell," his boss advised him.

"Damn, Emma was right. We've got to move everything up from the ground floor again."

"Right, but we've got a bigger problem. We've got to get these patients out of New Orleans."

"How do we do that? High-water trucks like the Army has?"

"If we can get them. We're talking to HCA now."

Convention Center

Kaywanda, Scott, and Mrs. Johnson knew that, although they were dry, they were still in trouble. A crowd had grown around the Convention Center even though there was no food, water, or bathroom facilities. Most milled around or dozed, having nothing else to do.

Not all of the throng were sheep. There were those, mostly young males, who didn't have much respect for society's rules. They lived outside of the dominant culture, and they prized only strength. If they wanted something, they took it. People wanted lavatories. People wanted food and water and shelter. These individuals weren't going to let a few locked glass doors stand in their way.

By midnight, the crowd had forced its way into the Convention Center.

Chapter 11

Tuesday, August 30
K plus fourteen hours:
Superdome

Right after midnight, the first of the FEMA disaster medical assistance teams arrived to set up operations in the New Orleans Arena, the "small Dome" next to the Superdome. During the night, special needs patients would be transferred out of the chaotic larger stadium to the relative comfort of the home of the New Orleans Hornets NBA basketball franchise. The floodwaters had not reached Downtown yet.

Tulane Medical Center

The staff at Tulane Medical Center now knew they were in enormous trouble. The water was rising and would soon kill the generators. They had to evacuate patients, and they had no way to do it by land. So the staff and the corporate parent, HCA, came up with an audacious plan. They would evacuate by air.

What made it bold and daring was the fact that TMC had no heliport. They would have to make one.

The maintenance people spent most of the early hours of Tuesday removing the light poles from the top of the five-floor-high parking garage. They had to move quickly. Corporate contacted private providers of MEDIVAC helicopters, arranging for pickups. The first copter was due to arrive at dawn.

HCA wasn't the only private corporation to shine during the crisis. Countless trucks from major retailers, such as Wal-Mart and Home Depot, were already on their way filled with food, building supplies, and medicines. Most importantly, they brought water—thousands of cases of water—to be given away to the people of Louisiana and Mississippi.

Banks across the region immediately waved all fees for their ATMs, a policy that would remain in effect for months. Utility crews were on the job as soon as the winds receded sufficiently to begin the laborious job of rebuilding the electrical and communication network in the central Gulf States. Airlines stood ready to fly back into New Orleans to help in the evacuation.

There were two groups *not* coming: the American Red Cross and the Salvation Army. They wanted to. The Red Cross had already set up shelters in cities outside the affected area, and the Salvation Army was positioned to move into the stricken city. However, they were forbidden to enter New Orleans by the Governor's Office of Homeland Security and Emergency Preparedness. This was the governor's third decision.

The reason given was that the state was concerned over the levee breaches and wanted to get people out of the Crescent City. If either charity moved in, it might encourage people to stay. So the state had decided to force the matter by not permitting the establishment of relief centers anywhere on the South Shore, be it Orleans, St. Bernard, Plaquemines, or Jefferson.

So it was, as tens of thousands of people were stranded at the Superdome, the Convention Center, and on highway overpasses all over the state's largest city, America's two greatest charities, organizations specially designed to help refugees, were ordered by the State of Louisiana to stay out.

K plus twenty hours: Superdome

By now, it was painfully obvious that the city of New Orleans was going underwater. The flood had reached Downtown. People streamed out of the affected areas all night.

At the Superdome, Buford joined other officers leaning over the railing of the plaza and down at the street in the early dawn light. Where it had been bone-dry, it was now covered by two to three feet of water.

"Shit," breathed one of the officers, "the levees did break."

"Katrina's killed us," groaned Buford. "That fuckin' bitch has killed the city."

The top officer in command, a major, brought everyone back to the problem at hand. "How much time do we have before the water drowns the generators?" Told it depended on how fast the waters rose, he continued. "Okay, people, let's work the problem. Sooner or later, we're going to lose power. Without those generators, we have no lights, no toilets, no running water—nothing. We've got thousands of refugees to take care of, and more coming every minute.

"Brief your people and prepare for the worst. Food and drink will be MREs and canned water. Conditions are going to deteriorate. It could take days to get these people out of here. Tempers are going to get short. Get ready. There will be no riots on my watch. Is that clear?"

The officers nodded.

"Get going. I'm going to try to contact Baton Rouge again and advise them as to our situation. Dismissed."

The men returned inside as dawn broke over a dying city.

Covington

THE RAYS OF THE RISING SUN WOKE CHUCK BINGLEY. STUMBLING out of bed and into the bathroom, he discovered to his relief that the water was back on although the pressure was low. He dressed quickly and went downstairs to eat breakfast.

As the gas was still working, he brewed coffee in an old percolator he found in back of the cabinet and fired up the generator as he considered his options. By the time he poured his first cup, he knew planning was useless until he determined the extent of the blockage on the streets and roads. Having used up the last of the milk the day before, he ate a bowl of Cheerios dry. He then put on a ball cap and went outside.

The sight awaiting him was amazing. For one thing, it was hard to tell where the street was. With the fallen trees and leaves, it looked like a primeval forest in sections. At least the storm water had drained away. Chuck had to climb over the trunks lying on the road as he moved towards the highway.

If anything, the damage there was more extensive than he'd thought. Massive trees were down everywhere. Power poles were shattered, their cables hanging uselessly. Some of his neighbors had two or more trees on their houses. There was little sign of life except for the soft hum of generators.

Chuck became more depressed as he moved forward. Logic told him it had to be this bad all over St. Tammany. How long would it take for the roads to be cleared? How long would it be before he could get out? When would he see his family again?

"Hello!"

The sound of the greeting pulled Chuck from his musings. One of his neighbors was waving from his open garage door. *What was his name? Prechter—that's it!* Chuck climbed over a tree trunk, joined Mr. Prechter, and shared survival stories.

"Got a chain saw?" Prechter asked him.

"Yeah, sure." Chuck owned a small, fifteen-inch model he used to clear brush.

"Good. I'm supposed to meet up with some of the others in an hour and start clearing all this crap. Be a long time before the parish can get to us. Can you join us? We gotta take care of ourselves now."

Chuck looked back at the street in disbelief. The pines Katrina blew down were massive—some of the trunks were five feet in diameter or more. "How the hell are we going to do that with a few chain saws?"

Prechter pointed up the street. "One of the guys is a contractor, and he's got a bobcat and some other heavy equipment."

Hope flared in Chuck's chest. "All right, I'll go get my gear, and I'll be back as soon as I can."

K plus twenty-two hours:
Pope, Tennessee

At 0800 CDT, with the center of the system located at 35.6°N by 88.0°W, about halfway between Memphis and Nashville, the National Weather Service determined the monster had weakened so much it was no longer a tropical storm. With winds of thirty-five miles per hour, it was just a large mass of thunderstorms. Katrina was almost gone, and the scientists would follow it until no remnant remained.

In its wake, hundreds of people had died. All that remained in the coastal areas was to recover the bodies, clean up the debris, and add up the cost.

Except in New Orleans. The dying had just begun.

Tulane Medical Center

The first helicopter landed at the makeshift pad on the top of the parking garage at 8:00 a.m. Everyone held their breath, hoping the structure could take the weight. It did, and staffers moved the first of the critical patients into the waiting aircraft. A few minutes later, the MEDIVAC gently lifted off and headed towards the airport.

This was no panicked evacuation. Once it had been decided to fly the patients out, HCA had burned up the phone lines to find receiving hospitals, mostly in their own system. The law said a patient could not be discharged unless a receiving medical facility was identified, and HCA was going to do everything by the book. They were not going to lose track of any of their patients if they could help it. The helicopters would refuel at Louis Armstrong Airport before continuing to the receiving hospitals.

George worked to make sure the proper identification and papers went with each patient. The most difficult were the children. They had to make sure they couldn't be misplaced. Paper and tags could be lost, and George and the staff wanted to make sure the young charges would not be misplaced in the chaos. They wrote the children's names and that they belonged to TMC on their arms or backs with indelible markers. Parents' names and addresses were useless, because those addresses might be under ten feet of water, and the parents could be anywhere.

Within minutes, the second helicopter arrived.

Lafayette

CHRIS PULLED OUT OF THE BREAUXES' DRIVEWAY AT EIGHT O'CLOCK on his way to Jackson. It had been over twenty-four hours since they had last heard from Mrs. Dashwood, and both Marianne and Chris were worried. There was absolutely no word on conditions in Mississippi. While the decision to drive to Jackson was easily made, convincing Marianne to stay behind was not. The newlyweds fell into the first argument of their married life. Eventually, Marianne capitulated, Chris convincing her it was best to drive alone and light, in case he needed to transport her mother and sister back to Lafayette.

Chris felt no sense of victory, and he promised himself he would not throw his weight around again once the initial emergency was over. *We'll work together later*, he swore, *but things are so bad now we can't take unnecessary chances.*

He now hoped, as he drove through the city to the interstate, that Marianne's comment about driving all the way from Lafayette to Jackson being the very definition of taking unnecessary chances did not prove to be a prophecy.

K plus twenty-four hours:
Superdome

THE DOME MAY HAVE BEEN SURROUNDED BY WATER, BUT IT DIDN'T stop helicopters from using the landing pad on top of the parking structure. And it was an important helicopter that landed at 1000 CDT, one day after Katrina's landfall. Under heavy security, the governor of the State of Louisiana arrived, accompanied by the state's two US senators and the FEMA director.

The dignitaries were briefed about conditions in the structure as more refugees streamed in. The governor declared she would have buses there the next day. The group then left the city without ever meeting with the mayor, whose offices were just across the street.

EXCEPT FOR A FEW NEWS OUTLETS, THE MEDIA IN general had blown the Hurricane Katrina story. Rather than the Big Easy having dodged the Big One, America's most unique city was flooding, and thousands of her people were trapped.

The communications breakdown affected the news media just as severely as it had the government and first responders. Nobody *really* knew what was going on. The big picture was way too large for a thirty-second sound bite. All the reporters could see was what was right before their eyes.

Rumor had replaced reliable information. No story was deemed too unbelievable to be reported. If a half-drowned alcoholic on Bourbon Street claimed he saw a corpse floating up Canal Street, it went out over the airwaves as "witnesses assert seeing hundreds of bodies." If a cop said he heard from a friend there might have been gunfire in the Superdome, it was "officials report rioting and murder of children." Claims of rapes and shootings and bombings were sent up the satellite link unfiltered and unsubstantiated.

This affected the government response. Contrary to snide asides made by self-righteous correspondents, local, state, and federal government officials *were* monitoring the media reports. That was part of the trouble. With the near-breakdown in communications and command-and-control in the city, the mayor and police chief took the reports as gospel and repeated them, giving an official credence to misinformation that the media later would use to justify their performance during the crisis. Instead of rushing in personnel to help, officials now had to wait for more and more armed security before moving in.

Worst of all was the myopic obsession with the Lower Ninth Ward. The pictures beamed all around the globe gave the impression that only the poorest of the poor African Americans of New Orleans were suffering. The devastation in that neighborhood was almost total, but it was just as bad almost everywhere in the city. The much larger, affluent, and mostly white Lakeview area was actually under deeper water. Gentilly, Mid-City, and Metairie were flooded, too. The entire New Orleans East—half of the city—had water. St. Bernard Parish was *gone*—simply gone. There were no reports at all about Plaquemines or the West Bank or the North Shore.

As for Mississippi, ground zero of the storm, the coverage was spotty and incomplete at best. Alabama was not mentioned at all.

How this contributed to the wretchedness cannot be determined nor underestimated.

St. Charles Parish

THINGS WERE FRUSTRATING AS HELL AT DANSEREAU PLANTATION for the two techno-nerds. Even with state-of-the-art computers, satellite dishes, BlackBerries, and high-def TVs, all powered by a natural gas generator, neither William nor Elizabeth knew what exactly was happening in the city. The telephone system, both landline and cellular, was out. The satellite phone proved to be unreliable. Without cable, they couldn't send an e-mail.

"We might as well be living in 1905." William was slumped on the couch. "There just isn't any way of talking to anybody!"

Elizabeth wasn't in any better mood, but complaining wasn't going to help matters. She crossed behind the couch and reached over, embracing William while kissing the top of his head.

"Poor, poor baby. None of your toys work."

"You think that's funny?" he said without anger.

"No. I think your reaction to something you can't change is though." She pulled at his hand. "Come on, let's go outside." A few minutes later, the two were walking hand in hand along the river levee.

"Damn, it's high." William watched the swiftly flowing muddy water.

"Will, what's that boat over there?" She pointed at a cabin cruiser secured to a small dock on the river.

"That's my boat. We had her brought up from Venice before the storm." He reached back to rub his neck.

Elizabeth knew he only did that when he was considering something. "What are you thinking about?"

William explained his surprising plan.

"They'll let you do that?"

"Only one way to find out. We'll try it in a day or two."

Downtown

An hour earlier, the mayor announced the initial efforts to repair the 17th Street Canal breech had failed. A shell-shocked administration was being bombarded with reports from all over. They became fixated on four issues: the levee breaks, the people in the Superdome, tourists trapped in the hotels, and the looting throughout the city. The pressure was becoming unendurable.

Finally, the mayor ordered the mandatory evacuation of New Orleans. It was all well and good, but how were people supposed to get out? The city was practically underwater.

Meanwhile, the city, the NOPD, the state, and FEMA all were completely unaware of what was happening at the Convention Center. It was only a dozen city blocks from the city's command center, but without modern communications, it may as well have been on the dark side of the moon. Due to all the tall, modern office buildings between Loyola Avenue and Convention Center Boulevard, no one could see the people milling inside and around the vast building. Literally, it was out of sight, out of mind.

K plus twenty-eight hours:
Las Vegas, Nevada

The casino industry knew they had taken an enormous hit from Katrina. Conditions at their location in New Orleans were surprisingly good. The big, land-based facility was on high land and undamaged._Since it would be some time before gambling resumed, the owners made provisions to feed first responders and other emergency personnel for the duration of the initial recovery.

But the news from Mississippi was terrible. Damage ranged from missing roofs to missing casinos. Some were washed ashore by the storm surge. Some simply sank. Those were total losses.

Assets were important, but their most important asset was their employees. The workers were well trained and loyal, invaluable if operations were ever to resume. The casinos would be loyal to their people, promising to keep as many of the staff on salary as possible until facilities could be repaired or replaced.

The suits in Vegas did not want to pull out of the lucrative Mississippi market, but they could not stand a hit of this magnitude ever again. The industry wanted changes made.

It was a coincidence that an industry-wide meeting had been scheduled in Las Vegas that week. Discussions were held between companies and a joint decision made. Twenty-eight hours after the storm of the century came ashore, the State of Mississippi received an ultimatum: Change the rules mandating floating casinos on the Gulf Coast or the casino industry would abandon Mississippi.

Superdome

The mayor made his first visit to the Superdome over four hours after the governor left. His outlook was decidedly bleak, his depression a stark contrast to the overly optimistic governor.

The mayor warned the officials to prepare to remain at the Dome for another six days.

Shit, Captain Buford thought. *We don't have six days' worth of MREs. What the hell are we supposed to do for food and water?*

Baytown, Texas

A very drawn Emma Weinberg made plans over the phone with her sister, Irene, as she sat across the Tilney's kitchen table from Cathy.

"Give me tomorrow's flight schedule. We'll meet you at the baggage claim. … Don't worry about a hotel. We'll take care of that from here." Cathy nodded. "No, I'm fine. I'll talk to George tonight. It seems he can get through at night. … No. Irene, I don't know when he can get out. They've got to see to the patients first. … I know. I worry about him, too. I'll see you tomorrow. All my love to Tyler. Bye."

"You okay?" Cathy asked.

"No, not really," she admitted, "but it would be a lot worse if it weren't for y'all."

Cathy patted her hand. There wasn't anything else to say.

Jackson, Mississippi

Chris made good time through Lafayette to I-49. The interstate took him to Alexandria, where he picked up US 167. Normally, he would have struck out eastward on LA 28 to catch US 61 at Natchez, but he had no idea of the conditions there. By eleven, he was eastbound on I-20 out of Monroe, headed for the bridge at Vicksburg. While the traffic wasn't too bad in Mississippi, there were enough trees down to slow things up occasionally while the crews worked hard on the side of the road. Some places looked fine while others were torn up. Some stands of pine trees looked as though a buzz saw had cut the tops off halfway up the trunks.

Chris made it to Jackson at about two in the afternoon and finished his three hundred-mile journey a half hour later, pulling into the Dashwood driveway. The neighborhood looked normal except for the opened widows, a sure sign of power outage. Mrs. Dashwood opened the door to her darkened house to her new son-in-law.

"Chris! Oh, honey, you didn't need to drive all the way up here!" she cried as she hugged him. "Excuse me, I'm all sweaty."

"Had to come," he said as he hugged Marianne's sister, Margaret.

"How long has the power been out?"

"Over a day," Margaret replied. "And we can't get through on the phones to Louisiana—landlines or cellular. A recording keeps saying the circuits are busy."

"We think the whole phone system in South Louisiana has collapsed."

"Oh, my God."

Mrs. Dashwood looked at Chris. "What time did you leave this morning?"

"About eight."

"Did you have anything to eat? Come into the kitchen so I can fix up something for you."

"I don't want to put you to any trouble."

"It's no trouble," Mrs. Dashwood assured him. "All the food will go bad anyway if we don't eat it. Ham and cheese okay?"

AS MORE AND MORE WATER FLOWED INTO THE CITY, THE ENGINEERS fought over the best way to stop it. The large sandbags the military helicopters dropped didn't work, so even bigger ones were being made.

Some experts said flying sandbags in was a waste of time. Heavy ground equipment was needed to to do the job right. That would take too long, others claimed.

The only point agreed on by all was that they needed help. All equipment from the Corps of Engineers and the Orleans Levee District that was not underwater was already in use. So the team tasked with saving the city asked their neighbors for assistance.

The West Jefferson Levee District responded immediately and put all available assets at New Orleans' disposal.

The East Jefferson Levee District's flat refusal to lend equipment shocked everyone. When challenged, East Jeff claimed they didn't have enough. They made their decision clear: We're here for us, and the hell with everyone else.

This would not be the last instance of selfishness between government bodies.

Chapter 12

K plus twenty-nine hours:
Upper Ninth Ward

Wickham sloshed out of his neighborhood though the flood, but he wasn't evacuating. He had way too much product and equipment in his crib to abandon it, but he needed food.

The first couple of stores were completely cleaned out, but there was some stuff in the third. He loaded up a shopping cart with as much canned spaghetti and fruit as he could. It sucked that all the beer was gone, but he scored a couple bottles of wine. He also grabbed a couple of plastic storage boxes.

During the return, the water got too high for the cart a block away from his house. He transferred his booty to the boxes. As he hoped, they floated well enough for him to continue. Wickham figured he had enough food to last a few more days. As for blow, he had plenty.

His new plan was to wait out the competition. Give 'em a couple days to pull out, and he would collect their product. It made perfect sense to his increasingly delusional mind.

The elevated intersection of I-10 and I-610 sat right over the 17th Street Canal. The roadbed was high and dry, but both highways were cut off heading east where they dropped down to ground level, which was now under several feet of water. A few of the city's famous cemeteries were close by the intersection, and the very tops of the aboveground tombs could be seen as they poked through the dirty water.

The Louisiana Wildlife & Fisheries agents used this as their improvised boat launch and dock. In shallow-bottomed craft, they motored over the sunken streets, looking for survivors. A flotilla of watercraft from the W&F, Coast Guard, LA National Guard, and boats commandeered by the NOPD crisscrossed the deluge like mosquitoes across a pond.

Civilian volunteers tried to join the effort, but the bureaucratic nature of FEMA recoiled. The First Responders had papers and orders, but citizens? Who was responsible for them? Who was in charge?

FEMA got very little leadership out of Baton Rouge. The governor's office stood paralyzed. Only the FEMA director could short-circuit calls up the time-consuming ladder to Washington, but he was out of pocket, flying around with the governor.

FEMA reacted instinctively. Until a proper chain of command was established, volunteers were not welcome.

K plus thirty-three hours: Covington

It had been a long, hot, hard day, but as he sat on Prechter's driveway in a lawn chair, watching the sun dip beneath what was left of the trees and sipping the best-tasting beer of his life, Chuck reflected that it had been a very rewarding one. To his surprise, the neighborhood crew had been able to clear all of the timber and wires covering the streets and had time to open up blocked driveways.

While they worked, they learned that the firefighters down the road had been working since mid-day yesterday to clear the main highway from Covington to Bogalusa. They still had miles to go, but at least the residents in Chuck's neighborhood could get to Covington. Already, people were out looking for supplies.

Chuck had completed an on-the-job graduate course in the use of a chainsaw. With a fifteen-inch blade, he was assigned to branches and small trees, leaving the big trunks to the guys with eighteen-inch saws. He learned that sharp chains and heavy equipment made all the difference in the world. He was taught how to maintain the tension on the chain and how to replace it—which reminded him he owed Prechter a new chain.

He felt distant aches and pains, which would make themselves better known the next day, but he didn't care. Sitting, covered in sawdust and sweat, Chuck felt he earned his stripes. He missed his family terribly, but he was too tired to try to drive to Baton Rouge now that he could get out. His plans were an early shower, bed, and to try to drive out in the morning.

"You okay there, Chuck? Need another cold one?" Prechter inquired.

He assured his neighbor he didn't before turning his attention to a sign Mrs. Prechter was painting.

YOU LOOT—WE SHOOT

"You think that's necessary?"

Prechter nodded. "If there's one thing storms bring out, it's the looters. I've had my .357 loaded since the storm and my shotgun too. I ain't taking any chances, and you shouldn't either."

Chuck grinned as he took a drink. "I don't know—"

He would have continued his thought, but Prechter interrupted, gesturing at the street.

Rolling slowly down the street was a pick-up truck with four men. Two in the cab and two riding outside in the bed. They were looking at the houses as they passed. Chuck was familiar with all the cars in his small neighborhood. He had never seen this truck before or its occupants. There was no through street; the subdivision had a single entrance.

"Guests of somebody?" Chuck suggested hopefully.

"Let's find out." Prechter stood up, walked a few steps towards the street, and called out, "Hey! How're you guys doing? How did y'all make out?"

Instead of answering, the driver hit the gas, and the truck sped away.

"Out-of-state plates," Chuck observed, a chill going down his back. "You don't think—?"

Prechter turned to him. "In times like this, shoot first and ask questions later, Chuck."

Chuck took a big swallow of his beer, dearly wishing he owned a gun.

Las Vegas, Nevada

"HEY, LYDDIE, YOU READY YET?" ANNE BETTENCOURT ASKED FROM the bathroom. "We gotta get to the club in an hour." Hearing no answer, she found her glued to the TV. "Honey, we gotta go."

Lydia Boudreaux nervously wrung her hands. "I'm trying to find out what's happened back home. The TV's only talkin' about New Orleans. They haven't said anything about Covington, or Chackbay, or nothing." She bit her lip. "I tried to call, but I can't get through. I don't know what's happened to my parents or any of my sisters."

The long-legged exotic dancer sat down and took her girlfriend into her arms. "I know, baby, but there's nothing we can do from here in Vegas." She dried Lydia's eyes with her hands. "Look, the only flooding they talked about is in New Orleans, right? So, everybody else must be okay."

"But...but Lizzy lives in Metairie, an' Mr. Will's place is in New Orleans."

"C'mon, baby, Mr. Will can take care of himself and your sister too. Worrying about them ain't gonna do them any good."

Lydia smiled weakly. "Yeah, you're right. Mr. Will's smart. He'll take care of Lizzy."

Anne hugged her. "'Course he will."

"Annie?" Lydia said into her shoulder. "How's about we start a relief fund at the club? You know, to help out."

Anne looked at her lover with newfound respect. "Lyddie, that's a *wonderful* idea. But we gotta get ready quick so's we can talk to the manager."

Lydia smiled as she jumped up from the couch. "Okay. I'll just be a couple minutes!"

Anne watched Lydia dash into the bedroom before she let her face fall. She said what she did to her girlfriend to keep her spirits up, but it was all bravado. She turned her attention and troubled thoughts to the TV.

Oh Lyddie, I hope Mr. Darcy's as smart as we think he is. I surely hope so.

K plus thirty-six hours: Superdome

BY 10:00 P.M., THE GUARD ESTIMATED TWENTY-FOUR THOUSAND people had taken refuge in the Superdome. Things were rapidly going downhill. Not only were there fifty hungry, tired, angry, and frightened survivors for each security person available, the water pressure had fallen so much that the toilets had failed. They had enough food for the next few days, but what would happen after that?

Meanwhile, a dozen blocks away, thousands were trying to find a quiet corner in the Convention Center to pass the steaming night.

Lafayette

CHRIS HAD BEEN ABLE TO TALK TO MARIANNE A COUPLE OF TIMES during the day. She knew her mother and sister were safe and had refused to evacuate to Lafayette, so she wasn't completely out of her skin with worry about her new husband while he gallivanted around two states, just anxious and irritated at being left behind. Her relief was total as the familiar lights of his truck lit up the windows of the Breauxes' house from the driveway. Marianne had his door open just as Chris switched off the engine.

"Miss me?" he joked as she pulled at him.

"No," she lied as she led him inside the house, "but your mother did."

He laughed. "Good. Glad to see that some things haven't changed."

Her only answer was to kiss him breathless. "So, how was it? How much damage is there?"

"Awful. Your mom's okay. As for the rest, I'll tell you inside."

She bit her lip. "Should I get you a beer?"

"Oh, yeah."

K plus thirty-seven hours:
Tulane Medical Center

It was 11:00 p.m., and the last, most important helicopter evacuation had yet to occur. A young heart-transplant candidate was to be sent by MEDIVAC to Lafayette and then flown by fixed-wing aircraft to Houston's Texas Children's Hospital. It was the most nerve-racking evacuation of them all, for the boy was kept alive solely by a large cardiac-assist machine.

It took eleven Tulane personnel, including George, to manhandle the wheeled machine up two flights of stairs and across to the parking lot roof, all in pitch darkness. The generators had failed at eight that evening, and the patient had been kept alive by a nurse operating a hand-pump mechanism for the last three hours. Both nurse and boy soon joined the unwieldy machine on the improvised helipad.

Headlights from parked cars marked the landing area, and the pilot brought the craft right in. The teenaged patient and his nurse were loaded first then the huge life-sustaining machine. At first, it wouldn't fit, but after the wheels were removed, it slid right in. The copter took off to the cheers of the staff standing by.

"Damn, George, we did it!" cried one of George's fellow doctors as he slapped him on the back. "Wait—what's that?"

The echoing sound of gunfire could be heard.

The other doctor was shocked. "Shooting? Somebody's *shooting* at a time like this?"

George looked around in the darkness. Tall hotels and office buildings were all around. Were the shots coming from one of them? Were they in danger?

"Let's just get inside," he suggested. "There won't be any more flights until dawn anyway."

Chapter 13

Wednesday, August 31
K plus thirty-eight hours

Not all of New Orleans was underwater. Uptown, the Garden District, the Warehouse District, the French Quarter, and most of Downtown were high and dry. The commercial heart of the Crescent City—the home of the port, the financial district, and most of the tourist assets—had survived.

But, for the residential and local retail areas, it was a different story. Water had invaded the medical district and surrounded the Superdome. Neighborhoods like Bywater, Gentilly, Mid-City, Carrolton, Upper Ninth, St. Claude, and the vast New Orleans East had between one and five feet of water. Hardest hit were the poor Lower Ninth and the wealthy Lakeview, both under as much as ten feet.

Jefferson Parish suffered. Water had flowed into Old Metairie. Parts of the areas near the Lake had received two feet of water or more. On the West Bank, trees were down everywhere.

In St. Bernard Parish, both Arabi and Chalmette were drowned. Not a single inhabitable building remained. Plaquemines, except for Belle Chasse, was in a similar state. Half of Slidell in St. Tammany Parish was underwater.

In Mississippi, the horror was different but no less complete. From the Louisiana border on the west to the Alabama line in the east, it was as if the hand of God had wiped everything away from a few hundred yards from the shore to two miles inland. Houses, buildings, and floating casinos were all gone. The three coastal counties of Mississippi, the powerhouses of the economy in the southern part of the state, were flat on their backs. Alabama's coast had received damage, as well.

The storm effects weren't limited to the coast. Inland, from Louisiana to Alabama, wiped out were over five million acres of pines trees grown for the lumber and paper industries. Katrina didn't care whether the stands were owned by giant timber companies or were living retirement accounts for families. All of it was now worthless. There was no way on earth to get all the downed timber out and processed before it rotted. An enormous crop, some twenty to thirty years old, was garbage.

From space, the extent of the devastation could be seen as equal to the land mass of Great Britain. Katrina was the greatest natural disaster in the history of the United States.

K plus forty-four hours:
St. Charles Parish

Elizabeth left Mrs. Reynolds in the kitchen fixing breakfast and walked to William's office with two mugs of coffee. As she expected, he was seated at his desk, checking e-mail via the satellite dish, hurricane coverage on the TV.

"Anything?" She set down a mug for him.

"DGS is still with us. Our people have been doing a great job rerouting our traffic. Thanks, sweetie." William took a sip as Elizabeth perched herself on the arm of his chair. "Still missing a lot of people from New Orleans though."

"They have no way of checking in, Will."

"Those in the strike zone, yeah." He rubbed his face. "The others? The procedure is to phone into the automated system and let us know where you are. But a quarter of our New Orleans staff hasn't phoned in yet. It's been almost two days."

"You're worried," she said as she ran a hand through his hair.

"Those are my people. How many are trapped in the city? How can we help them?"

She kissed his head. "Honey, there's nothing you can do right now."

He sighed. "Might as well check my personal e-mail." He typed on the keys.

Elizabeth leaned in to get a better look at the screen. "Can I check mine with this thing?"

"Sure—I'll show you how in a minute. Hey! An e-mail from Henry Tilney. Let's see…" The e-mail popped up on the screen.

Elizabeth set her coffee down abruptly as she stood up. "Oh, no! Not Mr. Abe!"

"Aww, crap," William moaned. He reached for the satellite phone.

"Can you send e-mail back?"

"No, it's not set up for that. I can only check web mail. Full-blown satellite broadband is as slow as frozen molasses. Wish I had it now, though. Until Cajun Net comes back on-line, it's the satellite phone or find a place where our cell phones still work. Do you have Emma's cell number?"

Elizabeth retrieved her BlackBerry and got the number from her directory. William was in luck and got through right away on the satellite system.

"Will?" Emma's voice sounded stressed. "Oh, Will, are you all right? Where are you?"

William held the phone so Elizabeth could hear. "We're both

fine. Lizzy's right here. We're both at Dansereau. But, how are *you*? We just heard about your father."

Elizabeth leaned in. "Emma, we're so sorry."

"Thank you so much for calling." She spent the next few minutes recounting the last three days. "Irene and Tyler are flying in this morning, and Cathy and I are going to pick them up. The Tilneys insist they stay at their house. It's hard to get a hotel room in Houston anyway. The funeral is tomorrow."

William glanced at Elizabeth. "Tomorrow? How—"

"It's going to be in Lake Charles." Emma explained the Jewish custom of quick burials. "It's going to be very small. Please, I would feel better if you don't trouble yourselves about it. Stay home."

Elizabeth felt terrible for Emma, knowing she would have to lay her father to rest in a strange place instead of in the family plot next to her mother.

Emma changed the subject. "Have you heard from George?"

"No. Have you?" Elizabeth suspected George was trapped in the city.

"Late Monday night. He's all right, but I don't know how long it will be before he can get out. He said they were evacuating the patients first."

"I see," said William. "What are your plans?"

"I'm not sure. I haven't thought much past tomorrow."

"Look, I've a proposition for you." He explained his idea, Elizabeth looking on in approval. It took a minute to convince Emma, but in the end, she accepted. Once they ended the call, Elizabeth gave William a big kiss.

"What was *that* for?" he asked.

"I'm so proud of you." She slid down into his lap and proceeded to show just how proud she was of his generosity when Mrs. Reynolds poked her head through the door.

"Sorry to interrupt—again—but there's a truck pulling up in the driveway."

Elizabeth and William untangled themselves before following Mrs. Reynolds to the front window. The gate was not part of the grid handled by the generator, so it had been left open. Elizabeth recognized the truck.

"Daddy!"

K plus forty-five hours

LITTLE NOTICED BY THE PEOPLE MOST AFFECTED, THE REMNANTS of the monster merged with a storm front at 0700 CDT over the eastern part of the United States. After one hundred eighty-six hours of life, Katrina was finally gone.

AS AIR FORCE ONE WAS ON ITS WAY FOR A CONTROversial flyby of the devastation, the governor formally requested the aid of forty thousand regular duty troops to help in the recovery, a number she would later admit she pulled out of thin air. She also demanded the immediate return of all Louisiana National Guard personnel and their equipment from the Middle East. She pointedly ignored the offers of National Guard troops from neighboring states.

This puzzling message caused the administration in Washington to think there was something critically wrong in Baton Rouge. The president's staff suggested he seriously consider federalizing the National Guard.

This was not a decision to be made lightly. According to law, the National Guard answered to the governor of the state in which it was located. They were to be used in times of natural disasters, providing help in recovery or law enforcement. If a state needed more help, it would formally request other states send in their Guard units. Nonfederalized troops could not enter a state without permission.

In times of war, the president had the power to nationalize the National Guard, placing them under the command and control of the Pentagon. The president had done a limited form of that when Guard troops were called up to serve in Afghanistan and Iraq.

The administration staff was now considering doing the same for Guard troops in the Katrina recovery. They would fall under the direct command of Joint Task Force Katrina, the Department of Defense's hurricane recovery efforts, but there was a potential legal issue.

In the aftermath of atrocities committed by Federal troops during Reconstruction after the Civil War, Congress passed the Posse Comitatus Act of 1878. It forbade military personnel from participating in arrests, searches, seizure of evidence, and other police-type activity on United States soil. The Coast Guard and National Guard, under the control of state governors, were excluded from the act. Therefore, some advisors claimed that, if the Guard was nationalized, they could not be used to supplement local police, a primary function of the Guard in natural disasters.

Another law, the Insurrection Act of 1807, gave the president the authority to deploy troops within the country to put down "lawlessness, insurrection, and rebellion." In other words, he could declare martial law. No president wanted to issue *that* executive order unless there was no other choice. This was America for goodness sake! Besides, by doing so without the direct request of local government, the locals' competence would be called into question. It just wasn't done.

The president was, in the end, a politician. As such, his first instinct was to defer to his fellow politician in the governor's seat in Baton Rouge. Nationalization was a sledgehammer, one that he would not use unless absolutely necessary.

K plus forty-six hours: Covington

CHUCK BINGLEY WOKE UP LATER THAN HE HAD INTENDED, unsurprising due to exhaustion from cutting trees the day before. After dressing, he walked around the house, taking pictures of the damage with a digital camera while munching on a granola bar. It would be important for the insurance claim, and Jane had all the household files with her. They could make a claim from Baton Rouge.

He was in his daughter's room, photographing the damage, when he heard voices—voices of people coming into his house!

Terrified, Chuck almost dropped the camera. He thought hard, wondering what he could use as a weapon, before he recognized a voice. He moved carefully to the head of the stairs.

"T.B.? Is that you?"

"Chuck!" his father-in-law answered. "Are you all right?"

Chuck ran down to the first floor. "Dammit, T.B.! You almost gave me a heart attack!" Without another thought, the two men embraced in a bear hug. "Where the hell did you come from?"

T.B. Boudreaux grinned. "Chackbay. Me an' Bubba come up here to check up on you. We picked up some help, too."

Chuck raised his head and saw two big figures standing just inside the front door. William Darcy was dwarfed by Bubba Teresina, Mary Boudreaux's fiancé. Everyone exchanged hugs, and the four men quickly shared their experiences from the storm.

"Really, not too bad back home," T.B. claimed. "Some trees down, an' the power's still out. Bubba made out good, too."

"How about phones?" asked Chuck.

"Nah, nothing. So, let's see this tree."

Chuck showed them the damage from outside before leading them upstairs. They stood silently in the room, all thinking of what could have been: Hailey's bed, right beside the window, had a large tree branch across it.

T.B. looked closely at the busted window. "It's not too bad. The window took most of it. I think the studs are okay. What'cha think, Bubba?"

"Hard to tell till we get that tree outta there."

Chuck had his hands on his hips. "How are we gonna do that?"

T.B. grinned. "Come on down to the truck."

A minute later, Chuck saw that the bed of the pick-up was jammed with tools, saws, and gasoline—even another generator.

"I didn't know if you had one," T.B. explained. "But it'll come in handy to run more stuff."

"I… This is great, T.B.! But, are you sure you can spare it?"

T.B. slapped Chuck on the back. "Don't worry 'bout that."

"I don't need three chainsaws, though."

"Those ain't for you," Bubba piped in. "Those are ours."

Chuck turned to the other men, confused.

"We're here to help," Bubba continued. "Spend a few days cleanin' up. We brought sleeping bags and chow. Beer, too."

"It's the least we can do, Chuck," said his father-in-law.

Chuck gaped a bit before embracing T.B. again. He then turned to William. "You, too?"

"I can give you a few hours, but I have to get back to Dansereau." He gestured to his car parked behind the truck. "T.B. and Bubba stopped by this morning to check on us, and they recruited me."

Chuck thought that over. "Look, Will, there's something else you can do for me. With T.B. and Bubba's help, I can clear up some of this mess and get the house weather-tight. Would you please drive over to Baton Rouge later and let Jane know I'm all right? She must be worried sick." His voice caught. He coughed and spoke again. "Tell her I'll see her and the kids in a couple of days, okay?"

William placed a hand on his shoulder. "No trouble, buddy. I'll put in a couple hours, and then head to Tiger Town. Be happy to do it."

"We're burnin' daylight, dammit," T.B. declared. "Let's get this truck unloaded an' get to work."

K plus forty-eight hours: Baton Rouge

THE GOVERNOR AND FEMA FINALLY ANNOUNCED A PLAN TO GET the people out of the Superdome. They claimed that five hundred buses had been secured to shuttle people to a refugee center set up in Houston's Astrodome. The impressive estimate was the operation would take less than two days.

Tulane Medical Center

The helicopters returned to Tulane Medical Center at daylight, and the staff worked calmly to get the remaining patients evacuated. Things were not so calm at the Park Plaza Hotel, where many of the families and dependents had ridden out the storm. By now, the blacked-out building was filled with not only guests but also refugees from the flooded neighborhood, and conditions had deteriorated. Fights had broken out over food and water. Roving gangs controlled the hallways, some brandishing guns. The families, especially the children, were terrified.

When word got back to the hospital, staffers set out to rescue their relatives. They waded through chest-high water and confronted angry armed people, but they brought their people back to TMC without serious incident. Some heard gunshots as they left the hotel-turned-hellhole.

Now Tulane had scores more people to evacuate, and the MEDIVAC choppers weren't large enough. HCA needed something else.

THE WATER HAD POURED IN FROM MULTIPLE BREECHES in the levees, but it still took days to fill the city. Finally, at 1200 CDT, a little over two days after landfall, the experts declared the City of New Orleans had achieved equalization with swollen Lake Pontchartrain.

The initial deluge had drowned hundreds of people in New Orleans, St. Bernard, and Plaquemines. Nothing could be done for them except collect their bodies for proper burial. The rescuers in the air and in the boats grieved for them but had to focus on a different task. They knew hundreds of people in the flooded areas had taken refuge in their attics, and many of the attics didn't have windows for the people to escape to roofs or boats. They were trapped. The lucky ones had tools to break a hole in their roof, but not everyone had the means or the presence of mind to do that. The survivors were sitting in the stifling, stinking darkness waiting for deliverance without water or food.

The rescuers worked at a feverish pace as time and numbers worked against them. With scores of helicopters and hundreds of boats, there were still thousands and thousands of buildings to check, crowded into more than two hundred square miles—houses enough for half a million people. That took time, and time was running out. The rescuers came to the realization, buried deep in the back of their minds, that it would be impossible to save everyone.

For hundreds of victims, a combination of exposure, shock, and dehydration would kill them before they starved to death.

Chapter 14

K plus fifty hours:
Warehouse District

The story about New Orleans had changed overnight, and Bryan Thorpe was afraid of being left out. How was he going to impress the networks if he missed the story of the century? A quick meeting was held in the hotel room with his producer and cameraman, and Justin Middleton soon found himself looking for a car. It took him an hour before he could return to the room with a scraggly-haired busboy.

"This is Carlos. Carlos, this is Sam and Bryan. Bryan is a famous reporter."

"Yeah, yeah," Carlos said as he gave the others a halfhearted handshake. "You got my money?"

Justin handed him some cash. "Fifty more after we get back. Now, where's your car?"

Minutes later, the four men were crammed into Carlos's ten-year-old Dodge Intrepid. Carlos insisted on driving rather than just renting the car to Justin. He claimed he was afraid the others might run his car into the floodwaters by accident. As he turned the ignition, he informed his passengers he had to be back at work in the kitchen in three hours.

Thorpe, sitting in the front passenger seat, gave the busboy his patented TV smile. "By this time tomorrow, *hombre*, you're going to be the most famous busboy in New Orleans."

The busboy rolled his eyes. "Yeah, yeah."

After leaving Downtown, they drove down St. Charles Avenue. Sam half hung out of the rear passenger window, filming the damage. They saw a few bedraggled survivors walking down the middle of the empty streetcar tracks and evidence of a stores having been broken into but nothing exciting. Thorpe grew impatient.

"Look, Paco, we want some footage. Where's the looting?"

"The name's Carlos, asshole!" the driver shot back.

Justin laid a reassuring hand on the busboy's shoulder. "Carlos my man, Bryan don't mean nothing. We're just trying to tell the story of what's happening here. We've got to tell it with the camera, you understand?"

Carlos growled. "I gotcha covered, dude. Just a little respect from hair-guy here, okay? We'll go up a little ways an' turn towards Magazine Street. You ought to get all your pictures there."

Carlos was as good as his word. The car pulled up to a convenience store ransacked by a dozen people. The TV people, in their excitement, stumbled out to film as Carlos nervously kept the engine running. Thorpe set up for a stand-up.

"This is Bryan Thorpe, reporting from a city where Katrina has not only broken its buildings and levees, but also any sense of law and order. You can see behind me dozens of people just helping themselves to an abandoned shop. No police, no one to stop it. Believe me, this scene is taking place throughout this broken and flooded city. Let me try to talk to this man." Thorpe walked a couple of steps to intercept one of the looters. "Hey, mister. What do you have there?"

The man looked at Thorpe if he had lost his mind. "I gotta get me something to eat," his tone clearly patronizing.

"So, you think you can just help yourself?"

The man was outraged. "I ain't no thief! I come here all the time. I'd pay for it, but there ain't nobody here! 'Sides, everybody else is doing it." He held up cans of evaporated milk. "I've got a baby at home."

Thorpe gestured to two men carrying armfuls of cartons of cigarettes. "What about them?"

The man shrugged. "What about 'em? I don't know 'em. Go ask 'em." With that, the man trotted away.

The other two looters seemed to be a rougher type than the man Thorpe had just interviewed. He turned to the camera. "And this is the new normal in New Orleans. Things aren't so easy in the Big Easy. For Action NOW News, this is Bryan Thorpe."

The entire time, looters moved in and out of the store.

"Okay, that was good," Justin declared. "Let's go find some more footage for Sam."

The Intrepid drove slowly around the Garden District for the next hour, stopping every so often for Sam to get a good shot of a tree on a house. Many streets were blocked, so there was almost as much backtracking as progress. They did see some city crews trying to clear things. Sam filmed them, but they were too busy to give an interview.

Carlos made his way down Tchoupitoulas next to the river as he headed back towards the Quarter. He uttered a curse as he grew close to the Convention Center.

"What's up?" Thorpe demanded as Carlos tried to turn off Tchoupitoulas. "The hotel's that way. I can see the skyscrapers."

"Tryin' to avoid that crowd by the Convention Center."

For the first time, the others saw the throng. "No! Head that way!"

"No way, dude."

Justine leaned in. "Another hundred if you take us over to the Convention Center."

Carlos thought for a moment. "Fuck it. All right—it's on you, though." The busboy wheeled the Intrepid towards the structure with what looked like hundreds of people milling along its half-mile-long façade. Sam and Justin had switched places, and the cameraman filmed the incredible sight of thousands of Americans in abject misery.

"Shit, this looks like something out of a movie," Justin muttered.

"Slow down, not too fast," Thorpe demanded. "You getting this, Sam?"

"Oh, yeah," he responded before adding under his breath, "Oh, my fucking God."

The car rolled slowly up Convention Center Boulevard, Sam

recording the wretchedness for posterity. The faces—mostly black, some angry, and all exhausted and miserable—were enough to give nightmares. The cameraman and the driver, far more sensitive than the other two, had the same thought: *There, but for the Grace of God, go I.*

They were almost at the end of the building when Thorpe yelled, "Stop the car!"

"What?" Carlos turned to the reporter. "Are you crazy?"

"Stop the damn car! I saw something!" Thorpe jerked at the door handle. "C'mon, Sam!"

Having no choice, Sam and Justin followed Thorpe. He had only walked a few steps. "Look over there! Is that what I think it is?"

He pointed at a blanket-covered figure in a wheelchair.

"Oh, my God. Is that a dead body?" Justin managed.

"Sam, shoot it," Thorpe whispered, a strange excitement in his voice.

A figure in the crowd shouted, "Yeah, let everybody see that! She died a little while ago. Are you here to help? Are you gonna get us some help?"

"We're trying to," Thorpe told him. "Our footage will be shown all over the world. We'll let everybody know what's going on."

"You gonna get us some buses?" another man yelled.

"Yeah, you gonna get us some help to get outta here?" came a third voice, this one a woman, pointing back at the Convention Center. "That place is full of dead people!"

"We'll do what we can," Thorpe promised as he made a gesture, indicating for Justin to turn on the tape. "How long have you folks been here?"

"Too long!" cried the second man. "You got room in that car?"

Control of the situation was slipping. "Uhh, no, just room for us. We'll, uhh, go get some help, won't we, guys?" he said to his companions.

"Aww, c'mon, you can get two or three more people in that thing," the man said as he walked towards them, a few others following.

"Shit!" Justin hissed. "Bryan, let's get outta here!"

A terrified Thorpe didn't argue but scampered back into the car.

"Pop open the trunk. C'mon, don't leave us here!" the man demanded as he pounded on the car's roof.

"Gun it!" Thorpe cried unnecessarily, as Carlos had already floored the accelerator. The Intrepid shot up the boulevard towards Poydras Street, the refugees cursing and gesturing at them.

"Fuck—that was close!" Sam cried.

Thorpe turned with a wolf's gleam in his eye. "The hell with that! You got the footage, Sam? Hot damn, we'll be the lead on every newscast in the country!"

Carlos shared a look with the others.

K plus fifty-two hours: Baton Rouge

The telephones had started working again in Baton Rouge, and Jane Bingley burned up the lines, talking to family and friends. She was relieved to hear that not only was the family in Chackbay safe and sound, but her father was trying to get to Covington to check on Charles. She was delighted to receive a call from Elizabeth, who had driven a little upriver to find a cellular signal for her BlackBerry. She learned William had joined T.B. and Bubba's mission to the North Shore. She also found out about Mr. Weinberg's passing.

But she couldn't get through to the one person to whom she most wanted to speak. Jane was not one to let her emotions show, but since Sunday night, she had heard nothing from her husband, and the suspense was agonizing. Carrie tried to console her, but it did little to offset Catherine's constant bitching. Jane was a nervous wreck.

She didn't want to watch the storm coverage, but she did in the forlorn hope there would be *some* news about the North Shore. Unfortunately, if the reporters weren't talking about the Superdome or the newly discovered crisis at the Convention Center, they were replaying looting footage from downtown. The rest of the area just didn't exist in the media's eyes.

"Dammit," she muttered half to herself, "more than New Orleans got hit."

"Do you think they care, Jane?" Catherine may have agreed to stop sharing her expectations of Jane's impending widowhood, but she felt completely free to bloviate about all other topics.

The doorbell rang. Jane, weary of the sound of Catherine's voice, rose to answer. She opened the door to a tall, dirty man on her mother-in-law's front porch. He was not the man she most wanted to see, but he was a decent second place.

"Will!" She embraced her sister's fiancé without hesitation. "Oh, come in! Did you see Charles? How is he?"

Arm in arm, the two old friends walked into the den. "Yes, I did, Janie. He's fine."

Jane covered her mouth in relief. "Oh, thank God."

William nodded at the other woman in the room. "Hello, Mrs. Bingley."

Catherine Bingley was frozen in place, her mouth working a little. She shut her eyes and took a breath before rising to her feet. "Excuse me, William, but did you say you saw Charles?"

Leaving Jane's side, he took Catherine's hand. "Yes, ma'am. He's absolutely fine."

The other two could have sworn Mrs. Bingley whispered a prayer of thanks. She then scowled. "Then, where is he?" she demanded.

"Catherine! Can't you see Will's exhausted? Let him sit down before the interrogation, please!" Jane's sharp tone took the others by surprise. When she directed William to a chair, Catherine remembered her manners and offered to fix him a drink. Water was all he wanted, and after she left for the kitchen, he turned to Jane.

"Chuck is fine, but there's some damage to the house," he warned her.

Jane smiled a little. "As long as Chuck is safe, that's all that matters. What happened?" Told a tree had come through her daughter's bedroom window, she gasped and closed her eyes. "Chuck must be upset. He loves the house so."

"You wouldn't have known that if you had heard him today. All he talked about was you and the kids, and how thankful he is y'all were safe in Baton Rouge instead of Covington. He'll see you in a couple of days."

"Thank you, William," She wiped away a tear. "What is he doing?"

"Trying to fix things. Your dad and Bubba are helping."

"Chuck and *Daddy?* Are you sure?"

William grinned. "You ought to see them, Janie." By then, Catherine had returned with a glass of water, which he accepted thankfully. "Blazing away with their chain saws, side-by-side, cracking jokes. They would be having a ball if it wasn't for the tree in the house."

"Tree in the house?" Catherine screeched. "*What* tree in the house?"

"There's a tree in our house, Mommy?" Hailey had just walked into the room.

Even though he was covered in grime, William picked up the little girl and assured her that her daddy was working hard to repair their house. Told that her Grandfather Boudreaux was helping, she brightened.

"Paw-Paw can fix *anything,*" she explained to Mrs. Bingley.

"I'm sure." At least Catherine didn't roll her eyes.

William spent another half hour taking his leave. Jane walked him to his car. "William, thank you so much for coming by. You've been a blessing. We're so relieved. Did Chuck say when he was coming?"

"No, but I think it'll be soon. Oh, before I forget, I better give you this." He reached in for Chuck's digital camera. "Chuck took some shots of the damage."

"This will help for the insurance claim. Thank you, Will. Say hello to Lizzy for us."

K plus fifty-three hours: Houston, Texas

Emma found it surreal to stand in the terminal of the airport, waiting for her sister and brother-in-law as if it was any other visit. For one thing, she was in Houston, not New Orleans. It was Henry and Cathy Tilney standing next to her, not her husband, George. George was trapped in a flooded hospital hundreds of miles away. And her dear father was in a refrigerated morgue in Lake Charles.

She couldn't help but resent the others walking past—ordinary folks living their regular lives. Did they know of her grief? That within twenty-four hours she had lost both her father and her home?

How dare they act so...so...normal!

"Emma? Are you all right?"

Emma rubbed her forehead. "I'm fine, Cathy. I'm fine."

A few minutes later, Irene and Tyler Parker arrived. The two sisters simply embraced in the middle of the terminal, sharing their grief and tears while the Tilneys introduced themselves to Emma's brother-in-law. Tyler renewed his protest about staying with the Tilneys.

"I really hate putting you out."

"Hey," Henry said, "the hotels are all booked up. We've got room at our place. Let's get your stuff, and after you get a rental car, you can follow us to Baytown."

Irene frowned. "You sure about this?"

"Of course," said Cathy. "The kids love to sleep in the den. They'll think they're camping out."

Three hours earlier, the governor received a request from Louisiana's junior senator. He had forwarded a White House suggestion that the state request federalization of both the Guard and the evacuation efforts. Finally, her office responded. The governor flatly rejected the proposal. She instead renewed her demand for the return of the Louisiana National Guard from the Middle East. There was no mention of Guard troops from other states.

Meanwhile, thirty thousand additional National Guard troops were mobilized across the nation. They sat on their collective asses, awaiting orders.

K plus fifty-five hours: Covington

As the sun dropped low in the west, Chuck grilled pork chops on his barbeque pit while warming up a can of red beans. Dinner was served on plastic plates *al fresco*. Chuck, T.B., and Bubba, covered in sawdust, sat on a pile of logs they had spent the day cutting.

"These are real good," Bubba declared as he took another mouthful.

T.B. slapped his son-in-law on the back. "Damn, Chuck, cookin' like this, I'd marry you myself, 'cept for Miz Francis."

The men ate in companionable silence, drinking beer amidst the result of their labors. About half the fallen trees were now cords of timber. The going was slow; the soft pinewood, green and full of sap, ate up the chains. The trio had gone through two chains each.

Chuck eyed the big tree still leaning into his daughter's window. "T.B., how're we gonna get that thing off the house?"

"It's too big for just us to handle. I've got me a portable crane we use in the business to move drilling pipe. That might do the job."

"When can you bring it up here?"

"Not 'til next week. Got to see if it's needed at work. We'll need more men too." He sighed. "Shoot, we've done a day's work, I'll tell you that." He glanced at Chuck. "About as tired as you've ever been, eh?"

"Nah, that was yesterday after we got finished clearing the road."

T.B. nodded. "That was a good job."

"Yeah," added Bubba, "those were some big trees, huh?"

"Big enough," Chuck agreed. "The bobcat helped a lot."

"Yeah," T.B. considered. "Got one of those too. I'll bring it with the crane."

"Sheesh, that's gonna cost some money, T.B." Bubba observed.

"Whatever it costs, I'll cover it," Chuck declared.

T.B. shook his head. "Don't you worry 'bout that."

"Thanks, but this is my house, my responsibility! I can't take your charity!"

The two men argued over the issue while Bubba looked on uncomfortably. Finally, T.B. relented to Chuck's offer to cover the fuel costs. Father and son-in-law shook hands over the deal as Bubba left to refill his plate.

T.B. sat back and looked around. They cut up most of the trees that had fallen except those that landed on the chain-link fence. They decided to leave them until some temporary barrier was erected to keep the Bingley's dog in the yard when the family returned. They did not expect to find a fence contractor anytime soon.

"Chuck, there ain't a whole lot more we can do 'round here. We can't move these logs, an' the wood's too green to burn. How 'bout we take a break 'til I can get back here next week with more equipment, eh? Get a good night's sleep and leave in the morning. You too. Get yourself to Baton Rouge and see the family."

Chuck eyed the torn-up fence. "You think it's safe to leave this place for a few days?"

The older man shrugged. "Either it will be or it won't. You don't have a gun, do you? If somebody really wanted in, you couldn't stop 'em. Get your neighbors to watch the place and get outta here. 'Sides, ain't nothing 'round here worth losing your life for."

Bubba sat down with a plate of beans. "Well, whatever you decide, I've got dibs on the shower."

The other two men laughed. "You?" snorted Chuck. "No way, partner. We'd like some hot water left."

"There ain't enough water in Lake Pontchartrain to wash that body," observed T.B.

Chuck lost his smile. "There is now."

A grim Mr. Boudreaux nodded. "Got that right."

K plus fifty-nine hours

For all the promises, by 9:00 p.m., only six buses had moved seven hundred people out of the Superdome to Baton Rouge, and those were special-needs patients. Now, late in the evening, large numbers of buses appeared before the damaged Hyatt Hotel to begin the evacuation in earnest.

Later, it was determined that the Guard distributed 70,000 MREs and 120,000 bottles of water since operations began.

The mayor had enough of the news reports claiming widespread looting, shootings, rapes, and other atrocities. He declared martial law and changed the NOPD's mission. Search and Rescue operations were suspended. It was time to take back the streets. Police fanned out to stop the looting of stores and homes.

As for the Convention Center, they would move in the next day.

Part Two: September

Times are not good here. The city is crumbling into ashes. It has been buried under taxes and frauds and maladministrations so that it has become a study for archaeologists ... but it is better to live here in sackcloth and ashes than to own the whole state of Ohio.

– Lafcadio Hearn, letter to a friend, 1879

Chapter 15

September was about two hours old when the first buses carrying refugees pulled up at the Houston Astrodome. The world's first domed stadium, once declared the Eighth Wonder of the World, the Astrodome had fallen on hard times. Abandoned by the professional sports teams for which it had been built, the place was now used for tractor pulls and trade shows. Now, it was to serve the greatest purpose in its existence. It would ultimately house over eleven thousand souls.

It was a fraction of the refugees Texas took in. It was said everything was bigger in the Lone Star State. Over the next few weeks, the world saw the size of Texas's heart.

Thursday, September 1
K plus seventy hours: Superdome

The evacuation had started, but it would take days to empty the Superdome. People were still trying to get in, and everyone had to be fed. Additional supplies had come in by truck and helicopter. Food and water would not be a problem for most people.

"What *is* this crap?" screamed a tall, heavy-set woman in line for breakfast. She tossed the MRE right back at the soldier handing it out. "I ain't eating this no more! I want me some real food!"

Buford, observing the operation, stepped in to intervene. "Ma'am, what's the problem?"

She ranted and raved at the captain. "You can't treat us like this! I want me some *hot food*—not this shit!"

"Ma'am, please, we're doing the best we can. We're all eating the same thing. These MREs are very nutritious—"

"Nutritious, hell! I can't eat this no more! It tastes like the plastic it comes in!"

Buford worked overtime to hold his temper, frayed by tension and exhaustion to the breaking point. "Perhaps something else? The chicken a la king is tasty." He exchanged the brown plastic envelopes. "There's a heating element in this package. It's pretty amazing. Can I have one of my people to show you how it works?"

The woman yanked the MRE out of his hand. "Goddamn government! Can't feed people right! Just get away from me!" She stalked off, cursing up a storm.

"Thanks, Captain," said the private who had been her original target. "I was about to lose it."

Buford felt a touch on his arm. Looking down, he saw a disheveled, elderly black woman with a cane, escorted by a young man in a long, white T-shirt, stained with God-knows-what.

"Sir," she said in a trembling but strong voice, "you pay no mind to that person. I just want to tell you you're doing a marvelous job helpin' us folks out, and I surely appreciate it. It's very kind of you to leave your families at a time like this to help us. God bless you, son. God bless you."

Buford heard the rest of the crowd murmuring agreement with the woman.

"Do you need any assistance, ma'am?"

She turned to the young man next to her. "Thank you kindly, but I have my grandbaby right here. He's been helpin' me out. We'll be fine."

Before Buford could continue the conversation, his walkie-talkie squawked. "Pardon me, ma'am," he excused himself as he stepped away to hear the message. A moment later, he turned to his sergeant. "Mack, we're needed at the VIP level."

The Guardsmen dashed up the ramps and stairs, dodging people and trash. The place was festooned with discarded MRE wrappers, drinking water cans, used diapers, and trash of every sort. They had to use their flashlights in the dark passages. The two were escorted by two armed soldiers, M-16s at the ready. It took them a few minutes to reach the hallway outside the skyboxes.

"Report," Buford panted as he came upon more Guardsmen.

The corporal offered a quick salute. "We came upon some looters in the VIP section. However, they were able to successfully elude capture."

Buford nodded, knowing it was closer to the truth that his men had allowed the perpetrators to escape. The NOPD already had many vandals in custody, and they were running out of room.

"They tore this place up pretty bad," the corporal continued.

Buford peeked into the suite. Unsurprisingly, the cabinets had been broken into, probably in search of alcohol. What was shocking was the rest of the damage. The vandals had destroyed anything and everything they could, including the replay TV mounted above the seats.

"And, you're not gonna believe this..." The soldier pointed at one of the seats, which had a familiar brown substance on it.

"Aw, shit!" cried Mack.

"Yep, that's what it seems to be," Buford remarked.

"Damn animals," muttered one of the troopers.

"Stifle that, private!" barked Mack. "We have to keep our heads, so keep your comments to yourself! Now, fan out and keep the people where they belong." After the patrol walked off, he turned to Buford. "Ain't no way we can stop this, sir. There are five hundred of us and twenty thousand of them."

"I know. Our job is to do the best we can to keep everybody alive. Private property comes in second."

"At least there's been no real trouble 'cept for the suicide." Earlier a young man had jumped off the terrace level to his death. There had been reports of two other deaths from natural causes.

Buford wiped his sweating forehead. "Thank God for that. Let's get out of here." As they were leaving, he glanced at the logo and words on the nameplate next to the door: DELTA GLOBAL SHIPPING, INC.

Baton Rouge

It was time to walk Rufus again, and Jane's patience was wearing thin.

"C'mon, c'mon, you stupid dog. Take a pee already!"

Suddenly, Rufus barked.

"Well, I guess he told you."

Jane whirled around and saw an unshaven Chuck by the corner of the garage. Rufus wanted to see Chuck as much as Jane, and she dropped the leash in her rush to embrace her husband. Chuck stopped kissing his wife long enough to retrieve the dog's lead.

K plus seventy-one hours:
St. Charles Parish

"Are you ready back there?" the skipper of the motor vessel *Dreamboat* called out.

His first mate responded. "I have the line loose, Will."

"Good. Just hang on until I tell you to release it." William applied power to the twin screws of the cabin cruiser and turned the wheel out towards the middle of the channel. "All right, Liz, let her go!"

Elizabeth pulled the rope aboard the Bertram 570. She then joined her fiancé at the fly bridge of the yacht as William piloted through the quickly moving current. It was vital to move faster than the water to maintain control, but with twin engines generating 1,300 horsepower each, it was not an issue.

Dreamboat was nearly sixty feet of blue-water fishing machine. All exterior surfaces were gleaming white fiberglass and aluminum, a strip of marine teak lining the cockpit. Rising high over the fly bridge was the "tuna tower," a second outside helm used to control the boat when hunting the giants of the sea. It also supported the radar and radio masts. With its deep V-hull and massive engines, *Dreamboat* was fast and dry. But speed was not needed on this voyage.

The pilot's position was along the centerline, so Elizabeth sat in the seat to the right of William. The boat cruised at a relaxed pace along the river in the cloudless morning sun, William watching for what little traffic there was ahead.

"Spooky, seeing the river this empty. Usually, there's ship and barge traffic all around."

Elizabeth watched in silence for the next half-hour as they passed moored ships and push boats with their barges. Except for debris in the current, one would never know a hurricane had passed that way.

A NEW CAJUN NAVY HAD BEEN FORMED OF BOATS, SKIFFS, PIROGUES, jet skis, and airboats, and the watercraft scurried like water bugs down the flooded streets too deep for National Guard trucks. Some were LANG or W&F, some were Coast Guard or NOPD, and some were civilians determined to help their fellow citizens—no matter what anybody said. They ferried thousands to overpasses and drop-off spots, working around the clock.

High above it all was the Cajun Air Force—hundreds of helicopters from the Coast Guard, National Guard, Navy, Marines, and civilian MEDIVAC companies, plucking survivors off rooftops and overpasses, or ferrying medical patients from Tulane Medical Center and other hospitals. With so many aircraft crisscrossing the skies, it wasn't long before one saw the incredulous sight of a cabin cruiser motoring down the Mississippi River. Calls were placed to the proper authorities within minutes.

THE BOAT'S RADIO, SET TO THE EMERGENCY CHANNEL, BARKED out, "Unidentified pleasure boat, this is the United States Coast Guard. You are entering a restricted area. You are requested to come about and leave the area. Unidentified pleasure boat, respond."

William glanced at Elizabeth as he picked up the microphone. "Well, here we go." He depressed the switch. "Coast Guard, Coast Guard, this is Motor Vessel *Dreamboat* of Venice, Louisiana, master and owner William Darcy aboard. I am president of Delta Global Shipping of New Orleans. We are heading for the DGS headquarters at the Julia Street Wharf. Request permission to continue downriver."

"*MV Dreamboat*, state your purpose."

"Coast Guard, I am attempting to do a damage survey of the port and our facility."

"*MV Dreamboat*, things are really hairy right now. Request you delay your survey."

"Coast Guard, I understand. However, I am trying to reestablish operations as soon as possible. Our intention is to bring in relief supplies. I need to put my eyes on the situation. Please pass my request to your superiors." William turned to Elizabeth. "Let's see if that works."

"*MV Dreamboat*, hold your position and stand by."

William turned *Dreamboat* into the current and applied only enough power to the screws to maintain his position. As the minutes ticked by, William grew increasingly concerned.

"This is taking too long. I don't know if they're going to go for it."

The radio came on again. "Mr. Darcy, you have been granted permission to continue to your destination. You are requested to hold your position until a Coast Guard vessel can escort you to the Julia Street Wharf."

William breathed a sigh of relief. "Coast Guard, thank you very much for your cooperation. *MV Dreamboat* standing by."

"*MV Dreamboat*, you're welcome. My boss said for you to get those supplies you talked about here soonest. Coast Guard out."

Elizabeth smirked at her fiancé. "It's good to be the king."

Warehouse District

Captain Richard Fitzwilliam held his head in his hands, a headache caused by stress and lack of sleep pounding in his skull, as he listened to an after-action report of the attempt by the NOPD to re-establish control at the Convention Center. The operation had been a fiasco. The NOPD could only round up eighty-eight officers, a number completely inadequate for the job. The crowd of nearly twenty thousand became so unruly the police had to retreat.

All right, so it's back to patrolling the area and trying to stem the looting until we can get some reinforcements. We can't start evacuating until we get some order around here. We need National Guard troops.

A police officer tapped Fitzwilliam on the shoulder. "Captain, I got a strange radio call."

"Since when have the radio calls *not* been strange?" Fitzwilliam sighed. He got up from the table and moved away to talk. "What's up?"

"We got a report of a cabin cruiser tying up at the Julia Street Wharf."

Fitzwilliam blinked. "Okay, you win. That's about the strangest thing I've heard all day. Julia Street Wharf? Where, by the Port Offices?"

"No, by DGS."

Fitzwilliam narrowed his eyes. "Oh, you've *got* to be kidding me. If that son of a bitch is behind this… Of course, he would be. Shit!"

"Sir?"

"Get me a car. We're going to check this out."

Minutes later, the squad car pulled up outside of the offices of Delta Global Shipping. Fitzwilliam, walking toward the riverside, saw a tall man with a backpack reaching down to assist someone climbing up the dock.

"Goddammit, Will! Don't you have a brain in your head?" Fitzwilliam shouted.

William pulled Elizabeth up beside him and turned to his cousin with a grin. "Nice to see you, too, Fitz. You remember my fiancée, Elizabeth?"

"I do. Lizzy, hello. I thought you'd be smarter than this idiot here." Still, Fitzwilliam hugged them both. "Shit, I'm glad to see you. You doing all right?"

"Yeah, we're fine. Just checking on my building." William frowned. "Fitz, you look like hell."

"Well, that happens when you've gone through hell." He pointed at the Convention Center behind the storm wall from them. "Do you have any idea what it's like over there?"

"We've seen some stuff on TV," Elizabeth said.

"Then you know this is no place you wanna be. Can I convince you to get back on your boat and get the hell outta here?" He looked out and saw a Coast Guard cutter pull away. "Fuck! You've got the *feds* on your side?"

William put a hand on his cousin's shoulder. "Fitz, let me check out my building real quick, and I'll get out of your hair. I promise."

"What's so goddamn important about your building?"

"I'm trying to reestablish operations here at the port. If everything's okay, I can try to get a ship in here with recovery supplies."

Fitzwilliam looked up at the heavens. "I can't argue with that. C'mon, let's get it done."

He introduced his driver to the two civilians, and the four of them moved towards the empty corporate offices. William extracted two flashlights from his backpack, handing one to Elizabeth, before unlocking a service door in the back. The policemen used their own flashlights as they followed the others in. They climbed up the internal staircase four flights to the top floor.

They walked through the warm, unlit offices in silence. There was enough light streaming from the windows for them to extinguish the flashlights. Still, it was an unreal experience. Where there should have been the hustle and bustle of a worldwide corporation going about its business, there was only the sound of their own breathing. Tiny particles of dust floated in the sunbeams, lending a ghostly air to their inspection. Papers, pens, and coffee cups sat on desks as if they had just been abandoned, their owners disappearing from where they sat. Trash baskets sat un-emptied. Computer screens sat dead on the desktops.

Elizabeth followed William into his corner office. He stood and stared at his desktop, papers neatly stacked in piles, the phone quietly sitting on one corner of the credenza.

"So quiet," she breathed.

"Yeah," he said. "It's never this quiet. Even at two in the morning, the European office is sending stuff to us, the night crew handling it. I miss the hum of the air conditioning." He brushed his hand across a memo. "My meetings for the week. My travel plans. A week ago, this was my whole life. But now..." His voice trailed off.

Elizabeth took his hand.

"It doesn't matter. None of *this* matters." He gestured at a pile of paper. "What matters is bringing all this alive again. Bringing the city alive again." He stared out the window at the skyline.

"Can you help do that?" Fitzwilliam asked from the doorway.

William's lips were set in a grim line. "If I fail, it won't be through lack of trying." He turned and walked out of the office, the others hurrying to keep up. "C'mon, let's check the rest of the building. So far, it looks like there haven't been any break-ins or water damage. That's good. We get my people back, and DGS is back in business. We can route traffic in, get ships in. Got to get my people back, though. And generators."

It took another fifteen minutes to see William's initial estimate was correct. The building was undamaged. All it needed was electricity and people. Both would take time to restore. The four stood outside as William relocked the building. He then turned to his cousin.

"Fitz, do you think it would be okay if I check out my condo up the street?"

Fitzwilliam's face darkened. "No, it would *not* be okay! We're in a controlled riot situation here, and I'm not going to nursemaid you through it so you can check on your poor little house! I've bent enough rules allowing this little jaunt." He pointed at the boat tied up alongside the dock. "You get yourself and Lizzy right back on board your floating palace and get the hell home, or I'll run you in for disorderly conduct. I mean it!"

"We're sorry, Richard. Thank you for all your help." Elizabeth tugged at William's hand. "C'mon, hero, we've got to get ready for our guest."

"Sorry, Fitz, I wasn't thinking." His cousin was clearly mortified. "I'm sorry, I really am, about your...about everything."

Fitzwilliam understood what was left unsaid, and he appreciated it. "It's okay, Will. Just get that ship here that you promised."

"I will." William joined Elizabeth in *Dreamboat*. "Take care of yourself, Fitz!"

"You bet!" Fitzwilliam waved as the yacht pulled away and began to make its way upriver. He got back into the squad car and began to issue orders to the driver as he wrote in a small notepad he had pulled from his shirt pocket. "Make sure all the patrols for the Port Offices include this place as well." He ripped off a note from the pad. "And have a squad pass by this address. Personal request from me."

The driver squinted at Fitzwilliam's scrawl. "This is a residential address."

"Yeah," spat Fitzwilliam, before adding *sotto voce*, "Damn that Darcy."

K plus seventy-four hours: Lake Charles

The LORD is my shepherd; I lack nothing.
He makes me lie down in green pastures;
He leads me to water in places of repose;
He renews my life;
He guides me in right paths as befits His name.

The small party stood in the harsh noonday sun around the newly dug grave in the Jewish Cemetery of Lake Charles. A cantor from the local synagogue led the service, for there was no available rabbi within a hundred miles. Emma stood beside her sister Irene, holding hands, both too overwhelmed to speak. Her brother-in-law, Tyler, read a short eulogy for the family. The Tilneys were there in support of Emma, along with the members of the *chevra kaddisha,* who had served as pallbearers.

Though I walk through a valley of deepest darkness, I fear no harm, for You are with me;
Your rod and Your staff—they comfort me.

Emma listened to the service, a torn silk scarf, her *keriah*, about her neck fluttering in the breeze. She looked down at the plain wooden casket with pain, knowing her father was being laid to rest in a purchased shroud instead of his *kittel* far from the side of her mother.

You spread a table for me in full view of my enemies;
You anoint my head with oil; my drink is abundant.

At least George was safe, if still trapped. The brief phone call the day before was the most wonderful, most heartbreaking event of her life. He was determined the patients and dependents get out before he did. She didn't know when George would be airlifted out of the flooded city, but she knew where *she* would be.

Only goodness and steadfast love shall pursue me all the days of my life, and I shall dwell in the house of the LORD for many long years.[2]

The prayers done, the men began filling in the grave. The hollow *clomp* of earth falling on the casket chilled Emma to her bones. She could hear Irene softly sob in Tyler's arms. As for herself, Emma was too numb to cry.

The *Tziduk Hadin* and 49th Psalm were recited at the end of the service. After thanking the men from the synagogue, the party gathered in the parking lot, and Irene begged her sister once again to come with them to Maryland. Once again, Emma refused.

"Reenie, I have to stay here until George is rescued. Surely, you can see that."

"I do, but we don't know how long that will be. Where will you stay?"

"I'm going to Will Darcy's place in St. Charles." Emma hugged her sister. "Don't worry, I'll be fine."

"Once George gets out, Tyler and I want you both to come up to D.C."

"Yeah," added Tyler, "we've got an extra bedroom you can use,

2 The 23rd Psalm: The Tanakh English Translation (1985), Jewish Publication Society.

just waiting for you."

"I'll remember that." She then turned to her long-lost friends. "Cathy, I don't know what to say." She hugged them both. "Thank you for everything, Henry."

"I'm sorry it took a hurricane to bring us together again," said Cathy. "Please let us know where you end up."

"I will, I promise." She gave them both a kiss, and then kissed her sister and brother-in-law one more time before climbing into her car.

"You have that map I made for you?" asked Henry.

She held it up. "Thank you, Henry."

"Drive safe," cried Cathy.

Waving, Emma pulled out of the parking lot as the rest of the group returned to their cars to begin their journey westward, the Tilneys for Baytown and the Parkers for Houston International Airport.

Chapter 16

At a White House ceremony, the president appointed his two most recent predecessors to head Katrina fundraising efforts. The former presidents had proven to be an effective team raising donations after 9/11, and it was hoped their bipartisan good will would be successful during this crisis.

Meanwhile, the mayor was not concerned with what was to come in the future, but what was required now. Interviewed on television, he begged for massive amounts of assistance immediately. His outcry was understandable given the situation, but it was unfortunate that he used the opportunity to repeat rumors of atrocities in the Superdome and the Convention Center.

Already spread nationwide by panicked and gullible press, the stories now developed a life of their own. The mayor and the police chief would later repeat these stories again to the press—stories they heard from other press reports. This circular exercise gave authenticity to these terrible tales. The world wondered what kind of despicable people populated New Orleans. Rapes of children? Rioting in the streets? People murdered for MREs? Snipers shooting at rescue helicopters?

It did not matter that the reports were totally

without merit—in other words, completely untrue. No one meant anything bad by passing along false rumors. There was no grand conspiracy to denigrate the city. But in their efforts to emphasize the magnitude of the disaster, politicians and press alike planted seeds of disgust in the minds of countless viewers, including policy makers.

If New Orleans and New Orleanians are so appalling, is the city worth rebuilding?

K plus seventy-six hours: Convention Center

Scott Davis had done many things in his life, few of which he was proud. Bright and clever, he should have been among the academic leaders in his Michigan high school. But he was bored with rules and requirements, especially from people he considered his intellectual inferiors. He spent more than his share of time in the principal's office, but he vowed that all the detentions in the world would not break his will. Certainly, he was proud of the time he and a buddy had hacked into the school's computer and posted a semester's worth of tests, but he still felt bad that his friend had taken the rap without ratting him out.

He rebelled against his parents' suffocating authority. Each tattoo on his body was a declaration of independence. Scott refused to attend his grandparents' fiftieth wedding anniversary because his mother had demanded he shave his goatee. Instead, he went to a Marilyn Manson concert. How was he to know his grandfather would die of a stroke the following week?

He left home after that, tired of the condemnation and nagging. He would make his own way in the world, away from his idiot of a father, who spent his days working as little as possible at General Motors and his nights drinking as much as possible in O'Malley's Pub. Scott rejected the knee-jerk racism of his family. He would work for the people in the South, where they needed him the most. Here was one white man who would not judge others by their skin color.

He dismissed working-class values. He sought to toil for a

non-profit, for capitalism was the root of all evil. Yet, he learned as he sweated in the southern sun that, if you wanted that non-profit to pay its employees, it had better make money.

Was he a traitor to his beliefs, or had his thinking matured? He didn't know. His professors said one thing, his co-workers something else. And he was reluctant to challenge either. Scott knew he was a coward. He stepped up to help neighborhood children repair broken bicycles but witnessed muggings in silence.

But never before had he intentionally stolen something. What else could he do? Mrs. Johnson needed food and water. All he had in his duffle were some granola bars of indeterminate age, and those had been consumed the night before. There was nothing in the Convention Center. Some gang members had broken into the kitchen, ransacked it for food and booze, and carried it all away. The water fountains didn't work. His family needed food, and a man had to do what a man had to do.

Scott made his way through the stench and misery to the spot Kaywanda and her mother claimed, clutching a plastic bag close to his chest, terrified the envious eyes following him were the precursor to violence against his person.

There were occasional patrols of NOPD, but Scott didn't put much faith in what a couple of cops, even armed, could do to help. The police certainly didn't stop the hoodlums from hot-wiring forklift trucks and using them as battering rams to break into other parts of the building.

"Here." He unceremoniously thrust the bag into his girlfriend's hands before he sat on the floor beside them. "Sorry, but the store was pretty cleaned out. I got as much as I could."

Kaywanda peered into the precious bundle. A box of crackers, some tins of tuna fish, beef jerky, and five bottles of water. "Oh, baby, you did good. Look, Momma, Scott got us somethin' to eat."

Mrs. Johnson sighed. "Never thought I would be happy to see tuna fish. Can't stand it, but I'm so hungry, I could eat my shoe."

"Here's some water, Miz Johnson," Scott said as he handed her a bottle. She sipped as Kaywanda opened a tin and used her fingers to spread some of the tuna onto crackers.

The trio was exhausted. Scott doubted they had slept more than a couple hours at a stretch since the three of them walked out of Gentilly. There was always noise, and a few times they were startled by gunfire. Their bellies were empty and their throats parched. The building provided shelter from the unforgiving Louisiana sun but not the stifling heat. The bathrooms were useless, covered with filth. The smell defied description. While some of their fellow refugees spent their time walking around and talking, many simply lay still where they had collapsed. Unless they moved, Scott had no idea whether they were alive or dead.

The three munched their meager meal in silence until Scott was jostled by a passerby.

"Hey, man, where'd you score that shit?" a young, thin black man demanded.

"Store about a mile away upriver. You can try, but it was really picked over, dude." Scott steeled himself for an assault, but it turned out the youth was only hungry and curious.

"Shit. I ain't had me nothing since yesterday. Upriver, you said?"

Scott was giving the man directions when there was another disruption, this one different. Both men watched apprehensively as a large group of people made their way in through the doors, shouting and crying.

"They turned us back! Those sons of bitches turned us back!"

"What's going on? What're you talkin' 'bout?" another person cried.

"The police! They're blocking the bridge!"

Scott, Kaywanda, her mother, and the young man listened in amazement as the story came out. A large group of refugees, about two hundred in all, had decided to walk out of the city by crossing the Crescent City Connection bridge to the West Bank of Jefferson Parish. The group had made it most of the way across when they were stopped by a roadblock manned by the Gretna Police Department. Through loudspeakers, the police announced there was no food, water, or any other relief in Gretna. Only those with an operating vehicle could pass. No foot traffic was allowed. The refugees were ordered to return to New Orleans.

"They shot at us, man!" one man cried.

Another explained. "This one cop shot in the air, like to scare us."

"Fuck, no, man!" the first shouted. "He was shootin' at me! They wanna kill us, the motherfuckers!"

Scott huddled down next to Kaywanda and Mrs. Johnson to become more inconspicuous. He was not the only white face in the Convention Center, but he was nervous regardless. He could not miss the open hostility erupting all around, and he was afraid some in the crowd would take out their frustration and anger on him.

"They all wanna kill us!" another voice insisted. "Where's the government? Where's Bush? Where's Nagin? Where's Blanco?"

The voices rose to a deafening level. Only phrases could be made out over the cries of children, the screams of women, and the rage of men.

"They blew up the levees, you know, to get rid of the black people!"

"That's crazy talk! Fuckin' storm took out the levees!"

"Where's my sister? Josephine! Where are you, Josephine?"

"It was the terrorists!"

"Fuck them! Fuck everybody! I'm gonna get mine! This is our time!"

"That ain't right! Just calm down, brother; you scarin' the children."

Finally, the angry and terrified people shouted themselves out. The black youth next to Scott shook his head.

"This shit's all fucked up. Thanks for telling me 'bout that store." He patted Scott on the shoulder and made his way to the doors.

The situation in the Convection Center was back to quiet horror. A sense of total despair descended on the people, alone and abandoned. For not the first time since the storm, Scott Davis wondered whether he and his family would die where they sat.

K plus sixty hours: St. Charles Parish

It was late afternoon before Emma's Volvo turned into Dansereau's driveway. By the time she stepped out of her car,

Elizabeth was upon her. William and Mrs. Reynolds stood silent witnesses as the two old friends hugged and cried together. It was then William's turn to greet her, and he renewed his offer for Emma to consider Dansereau her home for as long as she wished—and George, too, after his evacuation from the city.

William asked Mrs. Reynolds to show Emma to the guest room prepared for her. After the two left, he took Elizabeth's hand.

"Honey, I've been on the horn with Houston. There isn't much more I can do from here, now that I've seen the building. It's going to be a while before the city lets us back in."

"I know. The mayor's just called for a forced evacuation." She frowned. "Are you going to Houston?"

"I think I have to. Our board, our customers, they're getting antsy. I have to be there to handle that kind of stuff." he paused. "There's rumors going around that DGS may transfer permanently to Houston."

"But DGS is *your* company. You're not moving it, are you?"

"Lizzy, it's not so simple. *I* have no intention of moving, but the board may have other ideas. I might have a fight on my hands. I need to be there to run the company and strengthen my position against relocation."

Elizabeth's heart sank. "How long will you be gone?"

"Until we can move back, I think I need to be in Texas almost full time. I can come back on weekends—drive in Monday mornings and come back Friday afternoons. Or take the jet if we house it at Baton Rouge and I cover a portion of the operating cost." He squeezed her hand. "At least we'll have the weekends."

Elizabeth mentally shoved aside her personal disappointment that William was leaving and put on her economic developer's hat. "Is there any way EDNO or I can help?"

He thought for a moment. "For us to come back to the city after it reopens, we need power, telecommunications, an operating port, and most importantly, workers. We can't have workers without housing. Do you think EDNO can get housing for my people?"

She held up her BlackBerry, now operating since cellular service had been restored in St. Charles Parish. "Carl Eden's called an all-hands meeting at Louisiana Department of Economic Development in Baton Rouge Saturday morning. LDED has offered EDNO office space and phones. We can start to find housing then. FEMA's going to buy trailers. Why not have them where people work?" She warmed to her idea. "You're going to need them and so will the Port. NASA, Avondale Shipyards—all of the big employers will need them. We can make that priority one."

William smiled. "That's good thinking."

"Besides, the sooner I get your workers back, the sooner I get you back." She caressed his face as he leaned down to kiss her. "When do you leave?"

"I've got to check with Houston, but I'm thinking of driving in tomorrow."

THE ASTRODOME MAY HAVE BEEN THE LARGEST BUILDing in the world at one time, but even it had its limits. By 11:00 p.m., the City of Houston declared the building full after admitting 11,400 men, women, and children in less than a day. City and state officials immediately turned to the Reliant Center, but it would be hours before it could be prepared.

So the endless line of buses filled with refugees were rerouted to drive another two hundred miles through the Texas night to San Antonio and the Alamo Dome.

Chapter 17

Friday, September 2
K plus ninety hours:
Tulane Medical Center

Things were moving much more quickly at TMC. Late the day before, National Guard CH-47 Chinook helicopters had joined in the airlift. Unlike the MEDIVAC copters, which could only manage between two and six evacuees each, these twin-rotor behemoths were designed to carry as many as sixty people. As they were the property of the US Government, HCA could not hire them as they hired the MEDIVAC helos. They could only request the Guard's help.

The Guard came out in force. One after another, the Chinooks and smaller Black Hawks shuttled the staffers, their dependents, and the others still trapped at TMC. It wasn't a moment too soon. Things were getting worse each day. They could not guarantee the security of the building, and after the last of the patients was flown out on Thursday, the decision was made to abandon the hospital and move the remaining people to the parking garage.

George and the others spent their last night sleeping on the bare concrete of the parking structure with only blankets and pillows for comfort. It was dark and smelly and noisy, but the worst was a rumble at 4:30 a.m. George and the others looked out to the east to see it glowing red.

"Fuck!" cried one voice in the darkness. "Is it a terrorist attack?"

"Something blew up or maybe a plane crashed," said another.

There was little sleep after that.

K plus ninety-five hours:
Convention Center

AT 0900 SHARP, ONE THOUSAND ARMY NATIONAL GUARD TROOPS stormed the Convention Center. Dressed in camouflage and armed with M-16s, they completely intimidated anyone even thinking about causing trouble. The operation went like clockwork, and while it would take hours to completely search the huge building, the Guard was in situational control of the facility within fifteen minutes.

Like Scott, Kaywanda, and her mother, the vast majority of the refugees were overjoyed to see the federal troops. They had little trust left in the NOPD. Then they became ecstatic when they saw what the Guard brought with them—two hundred thousand MREs and all the water twenty thousand people could ever want.

St. Charles Parish

WILL DARCY THREW THE LAST OF HIS SUITCASES INTO THE BACK of his BMW while Elizabeth watched.

"Okay, that's it," he said as he slammed the trunk. He turned to take Elizabeth into his arms. "I'll call as soon as I know where I'll be staying in Houston," he said after a kiss.

"When are you coming back?" Elizabeth played with his collar.

"Probably not until next weekend. I'll call you when I know."

"Are you driving or flying?"

"If we can get a place to store the jet in Baton Rouge, I'll fly."

They shared kisses and whispered endearments before Will reluctantly pulled away. Elizabeth stood outside sometime after the BMW drove out the front gate.

"Lizzy!" cried Emma from the kitchen door, holding up a telephone. "Come quick!"

Tulane Medical Center

AS THE LAST FOUR HUNDRED PEOPLE WERE BEING AIRLIFTED,

George and the others spent their time cleaning up the parking garage. Asked about it later, all George could say was that Tulane was their place and they wanted to leave it clean for their return.

George remembered little of the flight. One minute he was being hustled into the Chinook, and the next thing he knew he was on the tarmac of Louis Armstrong Airport. He was handed a cold bottle of water and a granola bar and escorted to a waiting air-conditioned bus. He was in the seat before his tired mind could function well enough to ask where they were going.

"Southwest Medical Center, Lafayette," he was told.

"But...but my wife's in St. Charles Parish," George protested as the bus began to move.

"Call her and have her meet you," he was advised. "That's what everyone else is doing. We can't stop. Does your phone work?"

And so a couple of hours later, George climbed off the bus to see Emma and his friends waiting for him. He didn't say a word; he trotted in his fifthly scrubs to meet her halfway in an emotional embrace.

Elizabeth, holding hands with Marianne Breaux, hung back with Chris, allowing the couple this moment of relative privacy. Theirs was not the only happy reunion. The others exiting the bus moved into the hospital, shyly glancing at the celebrations occurring about them.

Elizabeth was close enough to hear George sobbing into Emma's shoulder, his hands tangled in her hair.

"Emma, Emma, I'm so sorry... I'm so sorry."

Emma's eyes were shut, her mouth firm, as she clutched her husband tightly to her. "Hush, baby... It's all right. We're going to be all right."

"I should have been there for you."

The three others backed away, embarrassed to overhear such a private, heartrending moment. They kept a respectful distance and waited until the couple was ready to join them. George wiped tears away with the sleeve of his scrubs and grinned.

"You better not touch me, Lizzy. I stink like hell."

"Get over here, big guy," she ordered. They embraced, and Marianne demanded a hug, as did Chris.

"You okay, buddy?" Chris stared hard into George's face.

"I will be now." His smile did not reach his watery eyes.

"You need to talk, call me. All right?"

George did not answer. Instead, he draped an arm around Emma's shoulder.

"You sure you don't wanna come to the house with us?" asked Marianne. "Miz Breaux said it was no bother."

"Thanks again, Mari, but I just want a shower and a soft bed." He kissed the top of Emma's head; she was clinging to her husband as if her life depended on it. "We'll stick to the original plan."

Elizabeth pointed across the parking lot. "Your ride to Dansereau is right over there."

The Katzes and Marianne strolled towards the Honda, but Chris held Elizabeth back. "I don't like the look in his eye," he whispered, his gaze not leaving George's back. "Let me know if things get rough."

Elizabeth bit her lip, worried. "What do you think? PTSD?"

"After what he's gone through, it would be amazing if he didn't have it."

"I'll keep you advised" She kissed his cheek. "You two come see us once Will gets back."

He assured her they would. Once they reached the car, farewells were exchanged, and Elizabeth and the Katzes began the drive to Dansereau Plantation.

AN EVENT OF SOME SIGNIFICANCE TOOK PLACE AT HIGH noon. Louisiana native Lieutenant General Russel L. Honoré stepped off a US Army Black Hawk helicopter at Louis Armstrong International Airport as the commander of Joint Task Force Katrina. An officer described by the mayor as "one John Wayne dude," he was in command of an estimated hundred thousand troops, FEMA representatives, and other US government personnel, including two US Navy amphibious assault ships (*USS Iwo Jima* and *USS Bataan*), that had poured into the region in the greatest governmental response to a natural disaster ever.

Immediately upon hitting the ground, the general began barking orders. He was not one to find out whether he had authority before acting; he simply assumed it until informed otherwise. To most, it seemed the best thing to do was cooperate with this brash soldier with an oversized personality. For the first time since landfall, order had come to the recovery.

Meanwhile, the US House of Representatives passed HR 3645, the first of the Katrina relief bills, authorizing $10.5 billion in help. The Senate passed the same bill the night before, so it went straight to the president's desk for his signature.

That would happen the next day because the president was finally on the ground in the strike area, touring the devastated Mississippi Gulf Coast.

K plus ninety-eight hours: Gulfport

Sergeant Danielson had been a member of the Ohio National Guard since high school, and he had worked natural disasters before. But never had he seen anything like the devastated Mississippi Gulf Coast.

Depending on the topography, the storm surge had come onshore anywhere from one-half to two miles, wiping out everything in its path. Brick buildings fared little better than wooden ones, slabs the only evidence they had ever existed. Huge trees were torn from their roots and tossed about like matchsticks. Most horrifyingly impressive was the sight of the massive floating casinos stranded hundreds of yards inland. Danielson could not imagine mere water could have the power to cause such desolation.

His squad was working a mixed detail with the Mississippi Highway Patrol and the Gulfport Police, searching for bodies. It was a grim, depressing, and necessary job, made all the more unpleasant by the scorching sun reflecting off the sand. The Army had made many improvements to the camouflage BDU, but it was stifling in the late summer heat.

"Sergeant!" cried a private at the point.

"What do you have?"

"I smell something...yeah! Got one right over here."

The detail made its way over to a clump of vegetation tangled with an uprooted tree. "It's right under there. You can see a bare foot." A flash of pale flesh stood out from the debris.

The stench of decomposition filled the air, and the detail put on their medical masks. They worked quickly with limb cutters, clearing the branches away from the body. It was that of a white male, dressed in a black T-shirt and navy shorts. A police officer took photos, and a trooper called in the truck.

As the Guardsmen pulled on latex gloves, the police officer examined the body, reciting into a small tape recorder. "Body appears to be Caucasian, young, somewhere in his twenties or thirties. State of decomposition suggests the body has been here for more than four days. Some post-mortem damage to the body, probably from the vegetation he was found tangled in. Preliminary cause of death appears to be drowning." He stopped and withdrew a brown object from the victim's back pocket.

"I've extracted a wallet from the body." He opened it and removed a card from it. "Mississippi driver's license in the name of John Lewis Waguespack." He rattled off the address, one that sounded familiar to Danielson.

"Hey, isn't that the address of the condo torn up a couple of blocks from here? Where we found the woman?"

"Yeah, it is. I passed by it often enough before." The cop didn't finish because he didn't need to. *Before the storm.* Before Katrina tore the hell out of Gulfport.

"Think there's a connection?"

"Don't know if we'll ever know." He rifled through the wallet. "ID from the Jean Lafitte Resort & Casino in the same name." No one was stupid enough to ask whether the photos matched the body. He had been out in the sun for more than four days. "Maybe there's a connection after all. We can check with the casino owners if they had a young blonde woman working there. Someone connected with Mr. Waguespack. Might get a name. It's worth a shot."

The detail took great care to remove the body from where it lay and placed it into a heavy black plastic zippered bag. The recovery vehicle rumbled up, an Army M939A2, 6-by-6, five-ton cargo truck in desert brown. The police officer put the wallet in a small, clear, plastic envelope and inserted it in the body bag before it was closed. The detail then gently lifted the body into the bed.

As the truck drove off with its macabre cargo, the team renewed its patrol, glancing at a massive dark object only a quarter mile away. The barge sat on the beach as though it had been placed there, its phony castle superstructure in tatters.

Ironic, isn't it? thought Danielson. *Mr. Waguespack and his place of work died only a few blocks from each other.*

After a flyover of the city, the president spent an hour touring the flooding with the governor and the mayor. The three then retired to Air Force One to begin a momentous meeting, coordinating the relief.

The mayor was angry and made no bones about hiding it from the governor or the president. He demanded help—a lot more help—though he did show appreciation for the general's arrival.

The president agreed more personnel were needed and pledged to do whatever he could to get them to the city. The president then turned to the governor and talked about how things could be better.

The governor repeated her insistence for the immediate return of all Louisiana Army National Guard personnel, and their equipment, from Iraq and Afghanistan. According to witnesses, the demand stunned both the president and the mayor.

The president told the governor that help needed to be brought in as soon as possible. Returning the LANG would take too long and make little practical sense, as there were Guard troops in other states ready to be deployed. More troops would be needed, he agreed, and he stressed the need for a unified command. He brought up federalization for the first time.

The governor balked at federalization and requested time to fully consider the matter. The president did not push the idea and moved on to a joint statement to be issued before he left New Orleans.

The governor's actions dumbfounded those who witnessed the exchange. The President of the United States had flown in with an offer of help to handle the disaster, and she held to her pipe dream of bringing home the LANG. More than one witness wondered whether the woman had lost her mind.

K plus 102 hours:
St. Charles Parish

ELIZABETH LISTENED TO THE RADIO IN THE KITCHEN AT Dansereau, catching up with the news. Apparently, a warehouse in New Orleans East had blown up spectacularly early that morning, alarming most of the city. A natural gas leak was suspected to be the cause. Emma walked in, combing her hair.

"Where's George?" Elizabeth asked as she turned down the radio.

"He took a shower and then climbed in bed. The poor dear is exhausted."

Elizabeth noted that Emma's hair was damp, but she let it go without comment. The two moved towards the den, Emma looking all round.

"Lizzy, I don't think I've ever told you just how beautiful Dansereau is."

"I know. It's hard to believe this will be my home."

"Here? Not the condo in New Orleans?"

"Will prefers to commute into the city, and I'm happy to agree! I grew up in the country, and the city never really felt like home. We both love it here."

"It's like a fairy tale. Did you ever think you'd be living in an antebellum plantation house?"

Elizabeth laughed. "I dreamed about it, but I never thought it would come true. But Em, Dansereau's not an antebellum house."

"Really? It looks like it. When was it built?"

"This one—1930."

Emma stopped short. "This one? How many Dansereaus have there been?"

Elizabeth suggested they sit down. "Now, I'm trying to remember everything Will told me about this place, so I hope I get it right. This is the third house on this site if you don't include the shack that was the first farmhouse. The first house was built by the Dansereau family before the Louisiana Purchase. They were Acadians who immigrated to Louisiana after their expulsion from Canada. Have you ever seen Destrehan Plantation?"

Emma nodded. "Yes, it's close to the I-310 Bridge."

"Well, I'm told the original house was much like that—a two-story house with open galleries on three sides. It didn't have the flanking two-story wings like Destrehan has. It was entirely made of wood.

"Will's family is originally from Maryland. An ancestor came down, fought in the Battle of New Orleans, and married into the Dansereau family. That's how the Darcys came to Louisiana.

"A couple of generations later in 1862—after the Union captured New Orleans—northern gunboats patrolled the river, looking for rebels. But there weren't any; most of the Louisiana Confederate soldiers were in the northern part of the state or scattered throughout the South. The boat crews got bored and took cannon practice on the plantation houses lining the river, the ones that refused to fly the Union flag. One day they fired upon Dansereau House, and it caught fire. The slaves by then had already fled, so the family could do nothing but watch it burn."

Emma shook her head. "How sad!"

Elizabeth warmed into her favorite part of the story. "The Widow Darcy refused to leave Dansereau and moved into one of the old slave quarters. One maid, a former slave, stayed with her. The two sons were away, fighting in the war. Mrs. Darcy sent her daughter to the Ursuline Convent in New Orleans—not to be a nun but to be educated and safe."

"Oh, yes, I remember," cried Emma. "That was in the days of the notorious General 'Spoons' Butler."

Elizabeth nodded. "What a terrible man! Anyway, when the war ended, only one son survived, a lieutenant in the Confederate navy. He promised his mother he would rebuild Dansereau House, but he had to raise the money first. He also brought home a friend, a Lt. Fitzwilliam. They had served together on a commerce raider and learned a lot about sailing. They decided to start a shipping company."

Emma gasped. "That was the start of Delta Global Shipping?"

"Yes, although it was called Darcy & Fitzwilliam Shipping at the time. Lt. Fitzwilliam became more than a partner—he married Lt. Darcy's sister. So that also was the start of the family connection between the Darcys and the Fitzwilliams.

"The shipping business did well, and after a few years, construction began on a new Dansereau. Unfortunately, the Widow Darcy died in one of the yellow fever epidemics, so she never saw the new house.

"The Darcys didn't suffer too much during Reconstruction, unlike other families. Things proceeded without incident, the house passing from son to grandson, until it was badly damaged in a hurricane during the 1920s.

"The stock market crash of 1929 hurt a lot of people, but it gave an opportunity to the then-owner of Dansereau Plantation, Edward Darcy. Labor was cheap, and the Depression didn't hurt the sugar business too much, so he decided to raze the house completely and rebuild her in the Greek Revival style, all in brick and plaster this time. He put in modern plumbing and wiring, too. That's the house you see today. Will's father, George Darcy, commissioned a major renovation of the place during the 1990s." Elizabeth waved her hand about the room.

Emma nodded. "So, this place is a reconstruction. They did a wonderful job, Lizzy."

The phone rang, and Elizabeth checked the caller ID. "It's Gina. She's been calling every day since the phones came back. I have to take this. Please excuse me."

"No, go ahead. Tell Gina 'hello' for me."

K plus 106 hours: Lafayette

A disaster in America had occurred, and the entertainment industry stepped forward as it always did: it put on a show. In the tradition of the Concert for Bangladesh and all the ones that followed—Live Aid, Farm Aid, and the 9/11 Concert for New York City—singers performed acoustic versions of ballads, and actors read from badly written scripts on teleprompters, urging their fellow citizens to call a toll-free number and donate to a charity: in this case, the American Red Cross.

Of course, the people on whose behalf they were performing couldn't hear or see the concert; they had no power for their TVs.

Chris and Marianne enjoyed Aaron Neville's soulful performance of Randy Newman's "Louisiana 1927," Marianne wiping tears from her eyes. Chris was hoping the scandals that engulfed the Red Cross back in 2001 wouldn't erupt again when he sat straight up. A well-known comedian had just finished his solemn pitch for donations when his partner, a rapper, began to speak.

"*What* did he say?" Chris turned to Marianne.

Marianne blinked. "Something about soldiers shooting black people in New Orleans."

"That's bullshit! Where the hell does he get off— *What*? 'The President doesn't care about black people?' My God, people are dying down here, and this lying asshole wants to make a political statement? Where did they get this clown?"

Marianne shook her head. "He's a popular rapper, but that's no excuse to say those things on national television." Chris jumped up from the couch and paced, working off his frustration. Marianne tried to console him. "Baby, please calm down. Look, I'll turn off the set."

"No, Mari, leave it on," he fumed. "I know I shouldn't let it get to me, but this jerk just kicked us in the shorts!"

"I know. Right now, everybody feels sorry for us. But if this disaster turns political—turns black vs. white—the region is going to lose a lot of support. People will be pointing fingers instead of helping. We've got to stick together."

Chris sat back down on the couch, wrapping his arm around his wife, as the performers all sang "When the Saints Go Marching In" to close the hour-long broadcast.

After the screen went black, Chris asked, "Heard from Kyle yet?"

Marianne frowned as she shook her head. She had gotten e-mails or phone calls from all of the members of her combo except the guitarist. "No, and I'm really worried about him. What could have happened to him?"

"I don't know. Maybe he's caught up in the evacuation and can't get to a phone."

"I hope so, but I keep worrying he's trapped somewhere and—"

"Babe, it does no good to think about what might be."

"You're right." She was quiet for a minute. "Baby, what are we going to do if LSU can't reopen Charity anytime soon?"

Chris ran his hand though his hair. "We'll have to go elsewhere."

"Leave the state?"

"It's not like there are a lot of positions for psychiatrists in Louisiana. Guys with seniority, like Dr. Segura, will get positions somewhere, but for newbies like me…"

Marianne steeled herself. "Okay. First thing tomorrow we start looking for a new position for you."

"Honey, I'm sorry. Your music—"

She slid into his embrace. "Look, we know my singing is secondary right now. It was barely paying the bills before the storm. With my insurance background, I should be able to get a job anywhere."

"I don't want to leave New Orleans."

"Neither do I, but we have to be practical. We need to find a position for you. I can continue my music anywhere. When the city recovers and there's a job for you, we can come back home."

Chris looked her in the eye. "Mari, if we have to leave, we *will* come back someday. I promise. We will come back home."

"I know… I know. As long as we're together, we'll be okay. 'For better or for worse,' remember?"

He enfolded his wife into his arms. "I don't know how much worse it can get."

Convention Center

The people the celebrities were most concerned about never saw the broadcast. They were either in the Superdome or in the Convention Center.

Since the National Guard assumed control, conditions had improved for Scott and the Johnsons. Truckloads of water and MREs were on hand. The floor was still hard, the heat was still stifling, and the stench had only grown worse, but their throats weren't parched, and their bellies were filled.

For the first time since the flooding began, Kaywanda had hope this torturous existence she and her family had endured was coming to an end.

The midnight oil was burning in Washington and Baton Rouge. Even though the governor had declined the president's offer to federalize the National Guard, the White House was still concerned over the evacuation efforts. The governor's continued insistence of the return of the LANG from the Middle East was worrisome, and aides wondered whether state officials realized the impracticality of the governor's scheme.

Late that night, right before midnight, Washington offered one last time to place the National Guard under command of JTF Katrina and General Honoré. Surely, Baton Rouge would see the advantage in consolidating command and control during this crisis. They couldn't object to a Louisiana native being in command.

Baton Rouge promised a quick response.

Chapter 18

Saturday, September 3, K plus 112 hours: Superdome

It was two in the morning when Captain Buford was released from supervising the evacuation. Handing over command to his relief with a quick exchange of salutes, Buford made his way from Loyola Avenue back to the Dome.

New Orleans is not flat, despite its appearance. Poydras Street slopes gradually downhill from the Mississippi River levee, running past the Superdome towards the Lake. While the Dome was surrounded by filthy, stinking floodwaters, Loyola Avenue in front of the Hyatt Regency was dry. The refugees had been gathered in the huge plaza outside the Dome, herded to the overpass into what was left of the New Orleans Centre shopping mall and the atrium of the Hyatt, to the street and the waiting buses.

Louisiana and FEMA had secured hundreds of buses, but there were twenty thousand refugees, and that didn't include the hundreds of people who were trapped in the downtown hotels. There were also fifteen thousand at the Convention Center. At fifty people per bus, the evacuation took hours. The crowd was manageable as long as progress was made, but the Guardsmen and police were nervous during the time between bus arrivals. The refugees' patience had just about run out, and there was a real concern that some might try to rush the transport, forcing the armed NOPD to draw their weapons.

Fortunately, the wait between buses was relatively short. Buford saw,many fewer people along his trek than he expected, and the stadium itself was almost empty. As Buford crawled into his sleeping bag, he hoped the long nightmare was almost over.

By now, thirteen thousand National Guard troops had poured into New Orleans, and the president, after signing the emergency funding bill, announced they would soon be supplemented by seven thousand active duty soldiers and Marines. In total, nearly one hundred thousand active duty, Guard, and Reserve troops had been sent or called up for deployment to the Gulf Coast region.

The governor had declarations of her own. She had finally responded that morning to the White House's offer of federalization, faxing her refusal. She publicly announced a "new attitude" in New Orleans, and promised that the evacuation of the Convention Center would begin within three hours. Abandoning her quest for the return of LANG troops from overseas, she accepted the offer of National Guard from other states.

Meanwhile, her office was negotiating the hiring of a state director to manage Louisiana's response. While no one at the time criticized the ability and good reputation of the pick, James Lee Witt, who served as FEMA director in the Clinton administration, many wondered whether there wasn't just a bit of partisan politics in the governor's choice.

K plus 119 hours: Baton Rouge

The guard manning the security desk at the Louisiana Department of Economic Development directed Elizabeth to the conference room set aside for the meeting. The first co-worker from EDNO she saw as she entered the room was Jan Hill, and in a gesture that would be repeated all over Louisiana and Mississippi for the next year, they greeted each other by hugging.

"Oh, it's good to see you," the older woman said.

"You too, Jan. How'd you make out?"

"Okay. Our house was on the West Bank. We're staying with relatives in Donaldsonville until we get power back. And you?"

"I don't know. I think there's flooding on my street in Metairie, but I live in a second-story apartment. I'm staying at Will Darcy's place in St. Charles Parish."

After a little more catching up, Elizabeth repeated the same conversation with everyone assembled. This was the new normal for a post-Katrina world. Her boss, Carl Eden, was in Baton Rouge. Eddie Masters had ridden out the storm in a casino resort in Tunica, Mississippi. Charlotte Lucas had just returned from Shreveport.

It was Charlotte who briefed her on who was still missing. Coworkers were scattered all over: Atlanta, New York, Dallas, and Cincinnati. She paused. "No one's heard from Kaywanda."

Elizabeth turned to Jan, her heart sinking. "Doesn't she live in Gentilly with her mother?"

Jan nodded. "I'm scared to death about her."

Carl Eden called the meeting to order. "I know we were waiting for a couple of folks to drive in, but we've got a lot of ground to cover, and we can bring them up to speed later.

"First thing on the table is: the business community got hit hard. Our lobbying team's already in Washington, working with our congressional delegation and federal officials. For them to do their job, we need to learn exactly what our big employers need.

"I know everybody got hit, but we can do our best work by seeing that large employers, like the Port, the shipyard, NASA, and the petrochemicals get up and running as soon as possible. If the foundations of our economy aren't working and paying wages to their employees, the retailers and other service industries will die.

"DED has generously offered office space, technical support, and telephones for our use. Our tech guys are standing by. We're trying to get approval to get back into the city and get our server and PCs out of our office. Until then, we can use state computers, and DED has set up for us a virtual drive on their server. Until further notice, we're going to set up shop right in this room."

Eddie Masters spoke next. "Our first job is to contact the big outfits and find out what they need. On my team will be Sarah and James, when he gets back. Steve will call people from Ohio and stay in touch via e-mail until he can return."

Carl turned to Charlotte. "We anticipate the biggest issue will be worker housing. I want you to get in touch with FEMA and try to get trailers here ASAP. Bonita will work with you. Lizzy will be working with me, dealing with the state and federal bureaucracy and coordinating with our people in Washington."

Carl looked around the table. "There's one other issue you should all know. Our finances are tight. Of our major contributors, the electrical utility, Entergy, is the only one standing by their commitment. The others, especially the banks, are baulking at continuing their contributions." There were groans across the room with not a few angry remarks tossed in. "You know we get a quarterly distribution from the state. Unfortunately, it's a reimbursement contribution, and we've already received the latest one. The next payment isn't due for three more months. It will be difficult for us to meet all the contractual agreements laid out in the memorandum of understanding we have with the state, but the governor's office has pledged to work with us.

"I'm working hard to see if it's possible for the state to up-front its contribution. The attorney general's office is looking into the legality of that. While we're okay financially for now, we still have to pay the lease on our offices. The building owners are not cutting us a break. So, between that and salaries and benefits, we're going to eat through our reserves fairly quickly if I can't convince our private investors to back us."

He grimaced. "I'm not saying it's going to happen, but please be prepared that we might have to institute a temporary salary cut."

The room was completely silent at that pronouncement.

"Well, come on, we've got some phone calls to make!" Eddie cried as he stood up. The three teams gathered in separate corners of the room, setting up workstations. Carl motioned Elizabeth over.

"How bleak is the money situation, Carl?"

"Unless we change some minds or get funding from FEMA, pretty bad."

"Great. Just when New Orleans needs us the most, our investors walk away."

He patted her on the back. "So we start thinking outside the box."

Elizabeth glanced at the rest of the team. "That just might have to be our new slogan, boss."

Insult turned to injury as looting continued throughout the area. The looters became more and more vicious. It seemed they were no longer bent on enriching themselves, but rather intent on partaking in an orgy of destruction.

First Oakwood Mall on the West Bank burned on Wednesday, only hours before the incident on the Crescent City Connection bridge, and now smoke was seen coming out of the Shops of Canal Place in the heart of Downtown. What fire departments remained managed to save the building that housed Saks Fifth Avenue and other upscale stores, but the damage was heavy.

The National Guard reinforcements could not come fast enough, and the people on the ground were overwhelmed.

These events were broadcast on news channels across the nation.

K plus 122 hours: Hattiesburg, Mississippi

A Penske rental truck made good time on this, its second day out of Charlotte, NC. It was part of a caravan heading for a relief center in Hattiesburg. Three people sat on the bench seat, two men and a woman, the lady with one hand on the driver's thigh.

"Careful, Nick," she told her husband, "the Mississippi Highway Patrol is notorious for stopping out-of-state speeders."

"I'm just keeping up with the group. Call your dad on the cell and tell *him* to slow down."

"Rachel," said her brother, "I don't think the cops are going to give tickets to relief trucks. Besides, we're not that much over the limit."

"Well, I hope you're right."

"It's okay," Nick Patel said to his wife, "we'll be in Hattiesburg soon."

"That's right, you used to drive this way when you were going to Tulane," she remarked.

Nick nodded, not happy to have that memory reemerge.

The spring of 1999 was the worst of Nikhil "Nick" Patel's life. He had no idea the panicked phone call to his family in the wake of the incident on Mardi Gras night would begin such an awful series of events. His domineering father took charge. An attorney was retained to instruct Nick on what to say and do. Mr. Patel demanded Nick turn over the stained sheets to the lawyer. Both insured he would tell nothing to the authorities by frightening him with the possible penalties for evidence tampering. It was Mr. Patel's decision for Nick to transfer to Duke, leaving all his friends behind.

His father's reasoning chilled Nick. It was not out of love or concern for his son that the man acted the way he did. No, it was so that no son of his would be anything less than rich and successful in business and life. Nothing would prevent Nick from getting into a top graduate school, even if it meant participating in illegal activities. It only mattered that the money invested in Nick's education would pay off.

Nick, molded by a lifetime of submission, obeyed the directives without complaint. He transferred to the business school like a good little Patel, keeping his qualms and guilt to himself.

For months, while his doubts grew, he did nothing. Forbidden by his father from joining any more fraternities, Nick took to hanging around the Duke library. He made the acquaintance of a pretty student worker by the name of Rachel Robinson. The two had common interests in technology and philosophy, a unique mixture that bound them in friendship.

They were only buddies until Rachel, a minister's daughter, took him to her father's church for Sunday services. Having grown up in an agnostic family—Patel's parents left their Hindu tradition behind in India—Nick had no opinion one way or another when it came to religion. He went only to please his friend. To his surprise, he found the congregation diverse, friendly, and accepting. It was startling to an occasional victim of prejudice. He was invited afterwards to Sunday dinner and football on TV.

One Sunday turned into another, and before he knew it, he was a regular at services. His relationship with Rachel changed too. Somehow friendship had grown to something more. Nick's life was thrilling and frightening. He was falling in love with Rachel, and he had found a home in her church, but neither would be acceptable to his family. As Americanized as the Patels believed they were, for any of their children to marry a person not of Indian descent, much less become a born-again Christian, was unthinkable.

Therefore, Nick lived a double life, keeping the Robinsons secret from his family. But finally the day came when he stepped out of the shadows. He stood before the congregation, accepted Jesus Christ as his personal Lord and Savior, and submitted to baptism. He was the only Patel there. After counsel and prayer with the Robinsons, he told his family of his intended conversion, which resulted in outrage. In a heated phone conversation, Mr. Patel learned of his son's engagement to Rachel and vowed to cut him off if he went through with the marriage. But Nick had matured, and his father's threats held no power over him. Nikhil Patel walked into the church alone and crossed the Rubicon, disavowed by those who had raised him but left with a new faith and family.

Without financial support from the Patels, a combination of scholarships, loans, and an after-school job paid the bills for Nick's final year at Duke. The work was hard but liberating, and he learned he could live on his own, support himself, and not have to compromise his principles. Encouraged by Rachel, he kept in contact with his mother and siblings. While Nick's integrity would never be enough to soften his father's heart, his mother, sisters, and brother attended his wedding to Rachel on a beautiful July afternoon.

Nick found work as the CFO of a small technology firm in Charlotte—the owner, a member of the congregation. Between his job and Rachel's, they were able to buy a small house a half mile from their house of worship. This was important as the church became central to their lives. Nick became a church deacon and head of the building and finance committee while Rachel taught Sunday school. Nick found peace and joy in his new life. His family noted it, and his sisters had recently joined the church.

While watching the reports of Katrina's devastation, Nick and Rachel decided to do whatever they could. A team was assembled, and a truck was rented. Nick worked hard to raise contributions for the mission of mercy. Church members filled boxes with clothes, food, water, and bedding. The toy donations were left behind.

They left late on Friday. As Charlotte was closer to the Gulf Coast than to New Orleans, Mississippi was their destination, and they expected to pull into the relief center at noon on Saturday.

Theirs was not the only house of worship pitching in. They had come across many similar convoys along the highway or at rest stops, the names of their churches emblazoned on their vehicles. Cars, vans, buses, and trucks of all sizes were on the road to do the Lord's work and help their unfortunate countrymen. They joined the steady stream of eighteen-wheelers and military convoys rolling through what was left of the Southern pine forests of Mississippi. Trees were down all over, some snapped right in half.

At the relief center, officials had to direct the enormous traffic. When they stopped, the people from Charlotte rolled up the door on the panel truck and distributed their goods from the tailgate to people of all colors and creeds, a chorus of "thank you" and "God bless you" their only reward.

During a break, Rachel watched her husband and father speak earnestly to a refugee for a few minutes before they returned to the truck.

"Who was that gentleman?" Rachel asked them as she handed them cold drinks.

"A preacher from Gulfport," answered her father. "His church was only a few blocks from the ocean. Now it's nothing but a slab."

"That's terrible!"

Nick lowered his drink can. "He says it was a real inspiring place, lots of programs for the kids and underprivileged, a center for the neighborhood."

"Losing something like that can kill a community," added Rachel's father.

"I'm thinking we can do something," Nick said. "Not now, because everything's so messed up. But maybe we can raise a team to come back and help them rebuild." He warmed to the idea. "We've got members who know how to swing a hammer. We'll have to raise money to buy the building materials, but we can do it if we put our minds to it."

Rachel's brother took up the idea, claiming he knew of some supply companies that might donate the lumber. The others joined in, a jumble of voices as a plan came together. It wasn't long before they sought out the Gulfport preacher to discuss their proposal.

"Lord Jesus! Praise God! Praise God!" the exhausted man cried before breaking down in tears, crying on Nick's shoulder while Nick's father-in-law lead them all in a prayer.

K plus 123 hours: Baton Rouge

Chuck had spent one full day at his mother's house, and it was more than enough. After greeting him upon his arrival from Covington, Catherine Bingley waited only until he was finished with his shower before starting to list her complaints. The kids were too noisy. The dog was whining. Why hadn't they heard more from John Buford? His mother refused to allow Jane to help in the kitchen yet bitched she had to wait on everyone.

Catherine stood outside, arms crossed, as Chuck loaded the last of the suitcases into his wife's van. "I don't think this is a good idea, Chuck. Carrie's house isn't as large as mine."

"Mom, don't worry," he said as he shut the tailgate. "Carrie and I talked about this last night, and we've decided it'll be better this way. We'll be out of your hair, the kids can all bunk together, and Rufus will have a fenced yard to run in. I've got to go back to Covington early Monday to meet up with T.B. and his crew anyway."

"Well, I hope you know you weren't any trouble at all," she simpered.

Chuck somehow caught himself from laughing in her face. Jane and the children came out to say their good-byes, and Chuck went to retrieve his Great Dane from a now-empty washroom. He walked the lumbering puppy to his mother to take his leave.

"Bye, Mom, thanks for everything," he said as he kissed her cheek.

Catherine, in a moment of kindness, patted Rufus's head. That was all the invitation the puppy required. The dog jumped up on his back feet, threw his front paws on Catherine's shoulders, and gave the protesting matron a sloppy lick directly on the mouth. Catherine spurted in indignation while a mortified Chuck pulled Rufus down and hustled him into the van, his children giggling and Jane clamping her hand across her mouth. He tried to apologize, but Catherine only waved him off.

"Get that creature out of here!" she demanded.

Nodding, he hustled to his car as Jane pulled the van out of the driveway, beginning the short trip to the Bufords' house.

K plus 125 hours: Convention Center

At noon, the rumors and promises came true as the first buses pulled up in front of the Convention Center. The refugees immediately broke into three groups. The first were the most desperate to leave, and they would have rushed and overwhelmed the transportation had it not been for the presence of the troops and police. A second tiny group did nothing, the shock of the entire experience having plunged them into a pit of apathy. Kaywanda, Scott, and Mrs. Johnson were in the third and largest group. Salvation was at hand and would soon be theirs after a bit of patience.

For three hours, the impromptu family stood with the jostling multitude in the broiling September sun, moving ever so slowly towards the front for their turn to board a bus. The worst moments were when there were no buses in the queue and some in the crowd began to panic. People began to complain, and children cried. Then another four or five buses would show up, and the loading continued. It was not organized in lines like at the Superdome; it was a mass of humanity, smelling to high heaven, straining to reach the safety promised by big, rolling, diesel-powered magic carpets.

When it seemed to Kaywanda she would spend the rest of her life in this crowd, there suddenly wasn't any—only a big, white wall before her.

Scott took her arm. "Babe, c'mon, let's get on board."

It took her a moment to believe it was their turn. They were instructed to move to the back and to sit in the next available seat. She maneuvered her mother next to the window before sitting on the aisle while Scott placed their precious duffle bag, containing all that was left of their world, into the upper rack and sat opposite her. Kaywanda held her mother's hand while reaching across the aisle for Scott's as a woman behind them recited a prayer of thanksgiving. Moments later, the group cheered as the squeal of the air breaks heralded their imminent departure, the cheer turning into applause as the bus began to roll.

"We did it, Kay," Scott babbled as he squeezed her hand, "we did it."

Kaywanda couldn't respond, except to squeeze back in return.

An official on the bus announced on the P.A. that information cards for the refugees were being passed out. He was in the middle of instructions when he was interrupted.

"Hey, man, where are you taking us?" a voice cried out.

The official conferred with the driver. "San Antonio, Texas. You'll be staying in the Alamo Dome for now. We have plenty of food and water on board, and there's a restroom in the back of the bus." As a few people got up to rush to the back, he continued, "Hey, take it easy. We're going to be together for at least ten hours yet."

"Ten hours!" whispered a woman behind Kaywanda, but it was Mrs. Johnson who responded.

"Well, I don't know about you, but I'm in a soft chair an' in air conditioning for the first time this week, an' my baby an' her man are right here next to me. They can drive for three days for all I care!"

The first man cried out again. "So, when are we gonna get there?"

"Some time after midnight Sunday," the official answered. At the puzzled faces, he added, "That's tomorrow. Didn't you know today is Saturday?"

"*No!*" the rest of the bus returned.

K plus 127 hours: St. Charles Parish

ELIZABETH SAT AT WILLIAM'S DESK IN HIS STUDY, READING AND

responding to e-mails from her fiancé. Somehow, the company had found a hotel that could squeeze him in, but the room was not to his liking.

```
You wouldn't believe the size of this place. I'd bet
I could park both our cars in here and still not
feel crowded. A suite is nice for an extended stay,
but this room is ridiculous. It would be too big
even if you were here. I'd have to chase you too far
to corner you and have my dastardly way with you.

Did I mention I miss you?
```

Meanwhile, George Katz had spent most of the day sleeping in a guest room at Dansereau Plantation, and Emma had joined him for an afternoon nap. He woke up around five in the afternoon, rubbing his hand along his jaw, shaven for the first time in a week, watching his wife sleep. Emma stirred and opened her eyes to gaze at his unreadable expression.

"What's wrong?" she asked.

George reached over and touched her cheek. "Just making sure this isn't a dream."

Emma clasped her hand over his and kissed his palm. "You've come back to me," she said. "I say that's a dream come true."

George took her into his arms and the two of them lay in the bed for a while, silent, quietly grieving, and gathering strength from each other's embrace.

K plus 128 hours: Superdome

The last few hours of the evacuation from the Dome were the worst, Buford considered. Just when there was light at the end of the proverbial tunnel, the buses stopped coming. Later Buford would learn that the governor, responding to press reports, ordered busses diverted from the Superdome to the I-10 overpass at Causeway Boulevard in Metairie. While those people deserved to be evacuated, for the remainders at the Dome, the delay was cruel. The crowd was always unruly, but this was the first time Buford feared things would get out of hand. His relief at the return of the buses could not be measured.

Finally, at six o'clock in the long shadows of the evening, the Louisiana National Guard could report the Superdome was empty and secured. Captain Buford's weeklong mission was done.

Katrina was not yet done with John Buford, however—not by a long shot.

K plus 130 hours: Baton Rouge

CARRIE HAD RETURNED HOME WITH TREY AFTER POWER HAD BEEN restored, and she was happy to have her brother and his family move in until they could return to Covington. She found Jane, Chuck, and Hailey sitting at the patio table, the young girl in her father's lap, keeping watchful eyes on Rufus and Max as the two dogs romped happily and barked up a storm in the Buford's fenced-in backyard.

"What's so interesting?" Carrie asked as she joined them.

"Just allowing the dogs out before we put them in their boxes for the night," Jane replied.

"You haven't seen that before?" Carrie teased. She noted Jane was holding Chuck's hand.

She snorted. "Rufus has done his business twice without my begging. I'll settle for that after the week I've had."

"I'm just enjoying a bit of normalcy," Chuck said as he hugged his daughter, causing her to giggle.

"Daddy, you look like a big old 'grizzy' bear," Hailey said as she pulled her face away from his week-old beard.

"That's *grizzly*, sweetie-pie." Chuck nuzzled Hailey again, causing another eruption of giggles.

Carrie eyed her brother. "*I* think it looks ridiculous, but"—she turned to Jane—"I guess it's *your* opinion that counts."

Chuck laughed. "She thinks it gives me a rugged, outdoor look." He mouthed, *"It makes her hot,"* with a waggle of eyebrows.

Carrie looked incredulously at Jane, but she simply smiled serenely.

Chuck kissed the top of Hailey's head. "I'll never take moments like these for granted ever again. The boys are inside?"

Carrie nodded. "Yes, watching TV. It's time to put them to bed."

Chuck pulled a face. "Aw, let them stay up a bit longer."

"Please, Aunt Carrie, *pleeeease*?" begged Hailey.

Jane sighed. "Normalcy is good, Chuck, and that means sticking with our regular bedtimes." She stood and took a protesting Hailey from her father. "We'll take care of the kids if you handle the dogs."

Dogs boxed and children tucked in with kisses and prayers, the grown-ups assembled in the Bufords' den.

"Are you *sure* you won't sleep in the master bedroom rather than the couch, Chuck?" Carrie asked her brother for the fourth time that evening.

"Yes, yes. I'm not kicking a pregnant lady out of her bed. Besides, if John ever found out I made you sleep on the sofa, he'd beat my ass, and I'd let him do it. You and Jane share your king-sized bed, and I'll be fine right here for two nights."

"John wouldn't do that, and you know it. So, you're still planning to go back to Covington?"

"Have to, Carrie. T.B.'s meeting me Monday morning with a crew from B&B to get the tree off the house."

Jane spoke up. "I've put in a claim with our insurance company, and I'm going to start contacting all of our creditors next week. With both of us out of work, we're going to have to arrange things with the utilities, mortgage company, and credit cards."

"Are you going to file for unemployment?"

Jane shook her head. "I hope we don't have to. I'm waiting for the doctors' group I work for to get back up and running, and we have to see what Gallic National Bank is planning."

"Jane's already called in on the recorded line to let 'em know I'm okay," Chuck said. "But it's going to be a long time before anybody's working in downtown New Orleans. Gallic's got to be planning something. I just don't know what it is."

"Are you still on the payroll?"

"As far as I know."

"Chuck's last paycheck was credited to our account," Jane added.

"What about all the hurricane assistance programs?"

"I've already applied for FEMA assistance. They'll direct deposit two thousand into our bank account, but as for the Red Cross—" Jane made a rude sound.

"Can't you go online and apply?"

"No. You have to call this 1-800 line, and it's always busy."

"I've heard the Red Cross people on the radio," Chuck chimed in. "They said to have patience and keep trying. They recommend late at night."

Jane frowned, a very rare occurrence. "I've tried at two in the morning for two days, and I still get a busy signal!"

Carrie tried to sound helpful. It was not like sweet Jane to be so riled up. "Maybe they'll add more operators soon. How much financial assistance are they promising?"

"Four of us—something over twelve hundred dollars," Chuck said.

"I feel funny asking for the money, but a promise is a promise. And we can use the money with things being so unsettled," Jane admitted before stifling a yawn.

That was as good a signal as any to begin closing things down. Carrie went first into the bedroom to give Jane and Chuck a little privacy. She wasn't surprised that it was almost a half hour later before her pregnant sister-in-law joined her.

AT 10:00 P.M., 132 HOURS AFTER THE MONSTER'S LANDFALL, THE Morial Convention Center was empty, and all the people who had taken shelter there were on their way to refugee centers inside and outside the state. The calamity was finally over.

It was not to say the rescue effort was done. There were still uncounted numbers of people trapped in their homes and others who had so far refused to leave. There was no power or drinkable water. Looting and lawlessness was rampant.

The mayor's office decided that the only way to get control of the situation was to completely evacuate the city. While the USCG and others continued their search and rescue efforts, the new mission of the NOPD and National Guard was to get everybody else out.

The Crescent City was to be emptied.

Chapter 19

Monday, September 5
K plus seven days

By Monday, the exhausted Corps of Engineers finished the temporarily patch of the breached 17th Street Canal. However, pumping out the stinking floodwaters would be a long process. Not only was there a massive amount of water to pump, but many of the city's pumping stations were still inoperable. Complicating matters, the water in Lake Pontchartrain was very high.

As the rescue phase of the recovery wound down, FEMA concentrated on its primary task: coordinate federal aid to state and local governments. The agency quickly activated its plans on setting up shop in the affected region.

FEMA was small for a federal agency and needed to call on its sister agencies to participate. HUD, Social Security, and other social services were always needed. In the case of Katrina, almost every agency in the government was involved, even the Department of Agriculture.

Still, they would not be enough. Outside contractors were hired to do much of the work

Space was needed for a headquarters to manage the thousands of government workers and contractors. Since three states were affected, three headquarters had to be set up. FEMA requested space in Montgomery, Alabama; Jackson, Mississippi; and Baton Rouge, Louisiana.

Congress had authorized massive amounts of aid. Most of the immediate aid was to pay for the workers, clean up the debris, and begin to fund the reconstruction of government buildings, such as city halls, fire and police stations, schools, hospitals, and other public infrastructure. The need was colossal, time was short, and the staffers on the ground knew it, and tried to show initiative.

The Louisiana-based FEMA director of recovery command sent out a memo on September 6, notifying all that, once local and regional officials approved of a project, the money to fund it would be released within three days.

Once the senior bureaucrats up the line heard about her directive, they balked. There were *rules* to follow! Anyone who could read the Stafford Act could see that! Government had a duty to make sure the government's money was spent wisely. The order was immediately countermanded. All requests for money would go through the usual channels.

The result of this reversal was to delay needed projects for months while staffers checked and doubled-checked requests, looking for graft. It would be telling that *not one single project was rejected or even sent back for further information.*

The money would eventually be paid out, but the fears that were the basis of the delays would prove to be groundless.

IN 70 AD, THE CITY OF JERUSALEM FELL TO A SIEGE waged by Titus Flavius, son of the Roman emperor, and the holy Second Temple was razed. Thus began what many Jews call the Diaspora, the scattering of God's people throughout the world, wandering until the Hebrews returned to build the Third Temple.

The word *diaspora* has entered into the language to describe wholesale displacement of large populations, defined by race, religion, or region. Diasporas have occurred all over the world to many people: Stalin's purge of the Kulaks, the Armenians from the Ottoman Empire, the Kurds, the Vietnamese, and many others.

Louisiana was created by a diaspora. *Le Grand Dérangement*, the Great Expulsion, occurred between 1755 and 1764. The British expelled ten thousand Acadians, over three-fourths of the Acadian population of Nova Scotia, because they feared they would not accept their new English overlords. Most eventually settled in the plains and swamps of Louisiana, their name corrupted to Cajuns.

Now a state built by a diaspora was the victim of an even greater one. Over one million people were scattered across every state in the nation, almost four hundred thousand in shelters or hotels. Almost every county in the lower forty-eight states had at least one refugee from the Gulf area.

They all wanted to come home. But without housing, come home to what?

Friday, September 9
K plus eleven days: Washington, DC

POLITICS RAISED ITS UGLY HEAD. THE SECOND OF THE KATRINA relief bills authorized an additional $51.8 billion to pay for the Defense Department's response, the Corps of Engineers' emergency levee repairs, and to fund FEMA's Disaster Relief Account. This seeming bipartisanship was already falling apart. Congress was looking for someone to blame for the slow response to the disaster. The Republicans pointed at the local officials—all Democrats—while the Democrats went after the Republican White House.

It didn't help matters that the FEMA administrator didn't seem to be doing anything. Even while the president was patting him on the back, thanking him for his "heck of a job," stories about his preening for the cameras and his detachment from the real efforts on the ground came out. When reports surfaced that his résumé had been padded, the administration reacted quickly. The administrator was relieved from his duties on September 9 and resigned three days later.

This wasn't enough for some in Congress. They were smarting from the president's attempt to suspend the Davis-Bacon Act in the affected region, preventing politically connected building trade unions from profiting from the massive rebuilding of public structures. Davis-Bacon was saved, and revenge was needed. The cry went out for investigations into FEMA. The search and rescue operation was mismanaged, it was claimed, and the government needed to get to the bottom of it. It didn't matter that FEMA had responded to the disaster exactly the way Congress designed it to do.

In every government-mandated emergency preparedness plan across the country designed since 9/11, it is stated that communities must not expect aid from FEMA for the first seventy-two hours. It would take that long for the federal response to ramp up. In other words, *for the first three days, communities will be on their own and should plan accordingly.*

The basic fact of the matter was that FEMA was not a search and rescue organization. During the first days of Katrina, the organization was involved in matters and issues that were essentially beyond its purview. It wasn't ineffectual because it was staffed by incompetents. It was ineffectual because it was rushed in to do things it didn't know how to do, and it was trying to learn on the fly.

Congress knew this because it was in the Stafford Act, but it kept the fact quiet lest it got tarred by the same brush being using on the White House, Louisiana, and New Orleans.

FEMA staffers fumed and stewed in silent indignation over the unwarranted criticism. They did not challenge their political masters and so saved their jobs and pensions. They shed no tears over the fall of the FEMA administrator, as he was only a politically appointed fool anyway. They sat and nodded and promised to do better before the cameras and public hearings.

They knew their time was at hand as Congress handed over $60 billion dollars for FEMA to manage. If there was one thing FEMA knew how to do, it was how to spend money. Now FEMA would show the nation how it was designed to operate.

Baton Rouge

ELIZABETH AND CHARLOTTE MADE THEIR WAY TO THE MEETING room at the Department of Administration for a ten-thirty update meeting on housing. Upon entering the room, Elizabeth saw Carrie Buford in an embrace with a slim black woman.

"Lizzy!" Carrie cried. Elizabeth had no choice but to greet her with the now-standard hug. "How'd you make out?" The two quickly shared their stories before turning to the others. "Lizzy, I don't know if you remember my friend from school, Anna Elliot. She works for the mayor."

The two shared a half hug, Elizabeth trying not to stare at the small bandages on the woman's face. She then introduced Charlotte, and they all got into a general discussion of the storm. The foursome broke up as others came in and began taking their seats. A short, heavy-set man bustled in, his government-issued ID swinging from a lanyard around his neck.

"Ah! Everyone here? Wonderful. Let's get started, shall we? I don't know if everyone is acquainted with each other, so let's go around the room and introduce ourselves. I'm Bill Collins, field officer with FEMA, assigned to short-term recovery."

The rest of the people in the room followed suit, even though they each had table tents before them inscribed with their names and organizations. The City of New Orleans and almost all of the surrounding parishes had sent representatives to the quickly called meeting; only Washington Parish was absent.

Collins continued. "I have some good news. According to information I've received from Washington, FEMA has begun taking delivery of about 145,000 mobile homes and travel trailers. Also, we've made an agreement with Carnival Cruise Lines to take the cruise ships we originally had docked at Galveston for refugees and move those ships to New Orleans. They'll be used for housing police, firefighters, municipal workers, and their spouses. They will also be available for FEMA workers and other recovery personnel not housed in hotels."

"The city thanks you, Mr. Collins, for responding to our suggestion," said Anna dryly.

"You're welcome, Ms. Elliot. Remember, we're FEMA-flexible here!" Collins checked his notes. "Oh, we're also ready to ramp up Operation Blue Roof. We've hired contractors to put blue plastic tarps over damaged roofs at no cost to homeowners. We've already been in contact with the local governments about this, but those of you who want more information, please see me afterwards.

"The reason I've called you all in today is to continue to find locations to establish refugee housing. We know it's important to bring people and workers back to the affected areas. That is our priority here.

"Not that we aren't looking for housing for displaced people! We certainly are, but other teams are working that issue, preparing vouchers for apartments and other rental property, so that will not be part of our discussion today. Those programs will be offered directly to the people in the evacuation centers, so they will have a place to live until we can get housing back in Southeast Louisiana.

"We need to get a list from all of you of acceptable property that can be used by the mobile homes and travel trailers. The locations should be a minimum of six acres. Ten would be optimal. The lots must be flat, free of trees, and have available power. There must be municipal water and sewer, or have some sort of sewage-treatment plant brought in, as I know there is a lot of well water around here."

He pointed to a map taped on the wall. "As you can see here, we've already identified two locations in East Baton Rouge Parish, here and— Yes?"

The representative from Jefferson Parish had raised his hand. "Mr. Collins, those locations are several miles outside of Baker. They're nowhere near Metairie or New Orleans!"

"Uhh, that's true," Collins admitted.

"They're not near anything!" cried the St. Tammany rep.

Charlotte spoke up. "My friend from Mandeville is right, Mr. Collins. We need these FEMA cities you're building to be closer to the city, closer to the jobs."

"I wish you wouldn't use the term *FEMA cities*." Collins requested.

"All right—trailer parks!" Anna snapped. "Excuse my bluntness, Mr. Collins."

"No, that's fine, Ms. Elliot. Candor is good." The fake smile on his face belied his good humor.

"Thank you. Sir, you're forgetting many of the people who will be housed will be poor African Americans from the inner city. They're used to having shops within walking distance of their homes. You're taking these people to trailers in farm fields, miles from stores and jobs. They don't own cars."

Collins interrupted her. "We're planning to provide shuttle service to local markets and to bus transfer stations."

"Oh, come on!" Anna cried. "These are people who are used to walking! You're going to put them in the middle of the country!"

"It's the most efficient way," Collins explained. "We're tied by the Stafford Act to use government property and assistance in the most efficient and cost-effective way possible. Now, if you can find locations in the city when water and sewer is restored, we can certainly look to establishing parks there."

Anna waved her hand in disgust, and Elizabeth used it as an opportunity to change the subject. "Mr. Collins, how large are these mobile homes and travel trailers?"

Collins rifled through his notes. "I'm sorry, Ms. Boudreaux, but I don't have the exact figures. Umm, the mobile homes are about forty feet long. While we're ordering about fifty thousand of them, we've learned from our experiences in Florida that many people don't need something that big. Also, a large grouping of forty-foot trailers takes up lots of space. That's why we're also ordering thousands of travel trailers. They'll sleep between two-to-six people and they're around twenty-three feet long if I remember correctly."

"A camping trailer."

"Yes, that's what they are."

Anna jumped back in. "Why put them in trailer parks? Why not park them in people's driveways?"

Collins blinked. "You mean, individually?"

The St. Tammany representative spoke up again. "Yes, that's exactly what my parish president has been asking for!"

"Jefferson, too!" The other parishes's representatives voiced their agreement with the concept.

"Let me tell you, partner," drawled the man from St. Bernard, "my people got nothin' left o' their houses but slabs, but they ain't gonna live in no FEMA cities, no matter what you call 'em. Let a man park one o' those trailers in his front yard while he fixes up his place is what you oughta do."

Collins held up his hands. "Hold it, hold it! We've heard your requests for individual deployment of the travel trailers, and those requests have been passed on to our superiors for review. That's all I can say for now."

Carrie, sitting next to Elizabeth, leaned over. "So much for being FEMA-flexible," she whispered.

Elizabeth bit back a laugh. Carrie had reflected her own thoughts on the matter. She cleared her throat.

"Mr. Collins, I have another issue to bring up, and that is worker housing. Our large employers, like the Port, NASA, and the shipyards are virtually undamaged, and Entergy has done a magnificent job of restoring power to these locations. But they can't resume operations until they can get their workers back, and the workers need housing."

"That's certainly true, Ms. Boudreaux," Collins conceded.

"The obvious solution is to provide housing on site. When we asked before about providing trailers to the shipyard, FEMA said the mobile homes were too large to park in the parking lots. But these travel trailers sound like the answer."

"Yes," said Charlotte, "they're small enough to be transported by train, or even by barge."

"Bringing them in by barge makes sense," added the Jefferson representative. "All the employers we mentioned are on the river or the Intracoastal Canal."

"I can safely say the city would back this idea," Anna stated.

"So would the state," added Carrie.

Collins looked around the room. He resembled a rabbit trapped in a corner. "Very well, I'll send the request to Washington." He made a note. "Meanwhile, we need to return to the subject of park locations. Uhh, Tangipahoa Parish, do you have any locations available?"

Elizabeth received a lunch invitation from Carrie and surprised herself by accepting. Both Anna and Charlotte had to beg off, so the two of them sat in a downtown café, perusing menus while the waitress took their drink orders.

"Just water for me," Carrie said with a sigh after Elizabeth asked for iced tea. "Two more months—the doctor wants me to stay off caffeine."

"Two months? You and Jane are due about the same time," Elizabeth observed. *I don't even want to know what was going on around Mardi Gras!* "I have to thank you for taking care of Janie for the last couple of weeks. She's told me all about it."

Carrie waved that off. "What's family for? I'm only sorry things weren't as pleasant at my mother's house as they should have been. It's been nice having Jane around while John's been gone."

Elizabeth couldn't miss the wistful tone in her companion's voice. "Have you heard much from him?"

"He tries to call once a day as his schedule allows…" Her voice trailed off, and Elizabeth was struck by the painful expression on her face. "And Will? How is he? I know you must miss him."

"Of course, I miss him, but Carrie, Will's safe in Houston while John's been stuck in New Orleans. It's hardly the same thing. I haven't gone through anything like you have."

"Houston, New Orleans—it's the same thing when your man's gone."

There was only sincere concern on Carrie's face, the anxiety of a woman who shared her pain. Elizabeth admitted she did not know Jane's sister-in-law as well as she should, and it was her own fault.

They had socialized at family events, mostly hosted by Chuck and Jane, but Elizabeth never took the opportunity to spend much time with her. There was still a tiny bit of resentment in Elizabeth's heart over Carrie's pursuit of William during their college years, and she was jealous of Carrie's close friendship with Jane. She felt the woman was forever intruding into her territory—first her boyfriend, then her sister.

But now she had to reevaluate Carrie Buford. There was no doubt of the devotion between Carrie and her husband. Jane had shared her difficulties with Catherine Bingley and Carrie's attempt to help. Elizabeth never dreamed Carrie would defend Jane against her mother, and she was thankful that she did.

Looking back at their history, Elizabeth had to admit that Carrie had changed. She had never been anything less than polite to her, and many times, she had been welcoming. She realized she had allowed her prejudice against her one-time rival to color her opinion of the woman's character. She had never allowed her to become her friend.

I've been so wrong about you. Elizabeth reached out and briefly grabbed Carrie's hand in thanks.

As they ate, Elizabeth found they had many opinions in common. She wasn't surprised that neither of them was impressed with either Bill Collins or FEMA.

"Sending our request for trailers up the line!" Carrie snidely recalled. "It'll take weeks to get through the bureaucracy. I hope you've got your lobbyists working on this."

"It's on the top of their list along with funding for the region. The Port doesn't have much pull in Washington, but the shipyards with Navy contracts certainly do."

"Good," Carrie said as she munched on her salad. "I've been talking to other communities that have had to deal with FEMA in the past—New York, south Florida, Oklahoma City, South Carolina, San Francisco. They've all said the same thing. If we wait for the federal government to pull us out of this, we'll be waiting for a *long* time. Most of the recovery needs to start with us."

"Our congressional delegation seems to be doing a good job."

"That's one bright spot." The Louisiana delegation wasted no time coming together across party divides and reaching out to their counterparts from Mississippi and Alabama. Together, the three states were leading the way, pushing for assistance for the Gulf region. "Baton Rouge could learn a lot from them."

"Oh, really?" It seemed to her that Carrie wasn't blindly loyal to Louisiana's government.

Carrie looked around, making sure they couldn't be overheard. "You know what I've heard out of Jackson? The governor there is looking to call a special session of the Mississippi state legislature before the end of the month."

"As he should. Isn't Louisiana doing the same?"

Carrie smirked. "When the going gets tough, Big Momma calls for a conference," she said in a low voice. "There are no plans for a special session anytime soon."

Elizabeth's mouth dropped open. "You're kidding!"

"Shush, not so loud!"

"But what is she waiting for?"

"She and the rest of her inner circle want to plan everything down to the last detail. Then they'll call the lawmakers to Baton Rouge and present them with a near fait accompli—in effect, approve whatever Big Momma's staffers dream up. Otherwise, there's no telling what the legislature would do as far as they're concerned."

"Carrie, some of the legislators are extremely bright! Why not use them? Use the committees to hold hearings and formulate plans with the administration."

"I know. I've dealt with them for years. But remember the governor's background. She was a schoolteacher and marketing consultant. She was a Public Service Commissioner and Lieutenant Governor under the previous administration, dealing with tourism. She's served only four years in the Louisiana House, and that was like twenty years ago. She's not used to the give-and-take of politics. She wants to plan everything and then reach consensus with the legislature. We don't have time for that now, but she can't see it."

Carrie lowered her voice again. "Also, she carries grudges. Don't think for a minute that she's forgotten the mayor endorsed her opponent in the last governor's race. Surely you've noticed how tough it was for New Orleans to get anything through the governor's office *before* the storm, right?"

Elizabeth looked horrified. "You're not saying she's going to abandon the city, are you?"

"No! Absolutely not! But, whatever she does, you watch—she'll make damned sure the mayor gets no credit or as little credit as possible."

"Great, she's playing politics with this."

"It's who she is, Lizzy. We permanent employees in the Office of Administration will do what we can, but we have to be careful. We're protected by civil service, but if we make too many waves, we can be transferred to another post or even have our position eliminated. They're the only ways they can use to get rid of us, other than an accusation of malfeasance and a civil service hearing, and they hardly ever win one of those."

"Why do you put up with it?"

Carrie shrugged. "I try to make a difference. I'm good at what I do. Besides, the retirement and health benefits are great."

The ladies talked of other things as they finished their lunch, during which Elizabeth learned that she and Carrie shared a similar, slightly sardonic view of the world. The real difference between them was that Carrie was more willing to voice what Elizabeth generally kept to herself. After settling the bill, Carrie expressed a desire to have lunch again while Elizabeth was posted to Baton Rouge. Elizabeth happily agreed.

"Maybe one night, while Jane's still here, you can come over to the house for dinner on your way home," Carrie offered. "I know you want to see her and the kids."

"I'd love to, Carrie, and to see Trey, too. I'll bet he's grown a bunch since the last time I saw him."

Carrie smiled widely. "You don't know the half of it! He takes after his father. C'mon, let's get back to work."

Chapter 20

TIME LOST ALL MEANING IN THE AFTERMATH OF KAtrina. There were no clocks, no television, nothing to give a sense of which day of the week it was. There were no appointments to make, no places to be. The weather was unvaryingly hot and muggy. One day was like another, dragging on and on, with nothing to distinguish any of them. Time had stopped on Monday, August 29 in Katrina-land.

More and more assistance flowed into the affected areas. Regular Army troops joined the National Guard. The Navy sent in two amphibious assault ships, *USS Bataan* to the Gulf Coast and *USS Iwo Jima* to New Orleans. Resembling small aircraft carriers, the LHDs housed troops and fueled helicopters. Utility trucks re-hung power lines. The Red Cross, the Salvation Army, and other charities inched their way into the devastation, reaching out to the thousands in need. Trucks poured into the Gulf Coast to replenish the retail and grocery stores.

Except for New Orleans. Under a mandatory evacuation order, the job of the NOPD, the Guard, Coast Guard, and other military units was to get people out of the stricken Crescent City, whether they wanted to leave or not. Meanwhile, helicopters continued their increasingly futile mission to rescue stranded people.

In the months afterward, it was documented the USCG had rescued thirty-three thousand people throughout the Gulf Coast region. The National Guard saved seventeen thousand, and the "Cajun Navy" was responsible for another twenty thousand lives. It was the greatest rescue in American history.

Upper Ninth Ward

LT. COMMANDER WENTWORTH AND HIS TEAM WERE DOG TIRED. Cajun 101 had been in almost constant operation since the storm, standing down on Sunday only due to a direct order from the commander. Now they were in the air yet again, looking for people. Some were stranded on elevated roadways, others on roofs. A couple of people were found trying to walk out on the Bayou Savage levee. They lost count of the number of people saved.

Cajun 101 had to stay in the game, not only for the sake of those who were in need, but to get their minds off of what each of the crew had personally lost. It was never far from their minds—they had flown over their houses and apartments for days.

Wentworth was flying over the Upper Ninth Ward, close to the Bywater, when LTJG Price sang out. Glancing over, Wentworth saw nothing at first, and then PO3 Lauck took up the cry. There—a thin, dark arm extending from a tiny attic window, weakly waving a bed sheet.

"Got it, skipper?" asked Price.

"Yeah." He switched his intercom to Airman Randle. "You're gonna need the axe again, Randy." This wasn't the first roof the airman needed to hack through.

"Yes, sir—got it already," the rescue swimmer replied as he and Lauck again went through the preparations to be lowered out of the aircraft.

"You see an approach, Jeremy?" Wentworth asked his right-seater.

"Not yet, skipper. How about from the north?"

Wentworth shook his head. He didn't like how close that billboard was to the house. He orbited, trying to decide.

Prince Gregory of Orléans sat in his throne room as his favorite concubine presented him with a tray of fruit and cheese. He sipped his tankard of beer, his eyes greedily caressing the wench's neckline. It was his order that all women in his kingdom display their bounty for the perusal of their prince, and it was not unusual for a comely maiden to occasionally fall out of her top. He idly considered ordering her to the royal bedchamber for a bit of ravishing, a command she appeared to expect with some anticipation, when his chamberlain came running into the room.

"What is this?" roared the prince. "You approach your monarch without being summoned? We can have you killed for this!"

"Forgive me, my prince!" the terrified old man begged, throwing himself to his knees before the throne. "All compliments, mighty sovereign, but the dragon approaches yet again!"

"Why do you bother us with this? Do we not have guards? They certainly cost us enough."

The chamberlain set his forehead upon the floor in trepidation. "A thousand pardons, my liege, but the guards have all fled in fear. Only your Power can save the castle."

"What, again?" Gregory asked in a bored tone. The councilor said nothing as he trembled at his feet. The prince turned to his companion. "Well? What say you, my pet?"

"Oh, please, sire, save us, and I shall serve you in any manner you require!" Her bosom heaved quite nicely in her agitation.

"Any way?" Gregory inquired with a leer.

"Yes," the concubine returned, her eyes flashing, her voice full of dark desire.

"Very well. Prepare for us our Royal Magic Powder, and after we dispatch this creature, meet us in the royal bedchamber—with your sister."

"Your wish is my craving, oh prince," she said as she fulfilled her task. Gregory fortified himself, and after a quick grope of the buxom girl, he strode through the open window to the battlements.

The moat was nothing but an open sewer, the stench overpowering, and it served its use of keeping enemies at bay. But dragons were a different problem. They had the power of flight, and no earthly defense could stop them.

Then again, Gregory had the Power of the Magic Powder, which gave him command of lightning and thunder. He would see to this menace. He contemplated the various different combinations he would employ later with the sisters as he awaited the dragon to come within range.

And there it was—a vast, ugly, orange beast, screeching in its characteristically low voice. The air itself trembled at the monster's approach. Gregory stood silently, unaffected, his Power in his hand. He waited until the beast was almost upon him before raising his arm.

"Begone, fell creature!" he bellowed. "I send you back into the hell from which you were spawned!"

Lightning flew from his Power and thunder split the air. The dragon came to a dead stop, frightened by the incredible forces deployed against it. Wings flapping too fast to see, it began backing up.

"Flee, you thing of the dark! Flee from Gregory of Orléans! Flee from our sight!" Power flowed out yet again as the creature retreated.

"WHAT THE FUCK?" WENTWORTH CRIED AS A ROUND CRACK APpeared high in the windshield right between Price and himself. "Price, do you see where that came from?"

"No, not— Yeah! There he is! Shit, it's some nut with a gun! Pull up, pull up! Hold on, guys!" he warned his teammates in the rear.

Wentworth didn't wait to respond, working the throttle and collective to first stop his forward momentum, then pull away, and down. Once they were dashing away at rooftop level, he called for damages.

Price looked around. "Everybody's okay, skipper. No damage to the aircraft, except for the windshield. What the hell was that all about?" he asked as he reached for the radio.

"Hell if I know. They must be going insane down there." Wentworth had heard the rumors of sniper fire at helos, but except for one confirmed report, most of the shooting turned out to be people trying to shoot holes through their roofs and escape their flooded houses. This was the first crazy Cajun 101 had come across.

"Command, this is Cajun 101," Price reported on the joint distress channel. "We are under fire. Repeat, we are under fire. We have received minor damage to the aircraft. Suspect is on the balcony of a house in the Upper Ninth Ward, near St. Claude Avenue. Repeat, Cajun 101 has received fire and sustained minor damage. We have taken evasive action and are now in a wide orbit around the area. Come in, Command."

"Cajun 101, this is Command. Request your coordinates."

WITH THE EMPTYING OF THE CONVENTION CENTER, NOPD THIRD District was redeployed to the Central City area. Today, Captain Richard Fitzwilliam worked a mixed detail of NOPD and National Guard along St. Claude Avenue, enforcing the anti-looting and forced evacuation orders from City Hall. It was the first time such an order had ever been issued by any mayor of the city. With no power, water, or sewerage, New Orleans was a disease outbreak waiting to happen. The evacuation order was understandable. What made it controversial was the additional order to confiscate all firearms found.

Fitzwilliam was of two minds about the command. There were still too many looters in the city, and that fact kept the police and Guardsmen on edge. They were jumpy because anyone they saw could be a potential bad guy, including people who were trying to help. Yesterday, his people damn near shot two animal rescue fanatics breaking into a residence. Until order was restored, somebody was likely to get hurt. Certainly, the streets would be safer if there were fewer guns.

On the other hand, there was that pesky thing called the Second Amendment to the US Constitution as well as safeguards in the Louisiana Constitution. The NOPD was shorthanded, and even with thousands of National Guardsmen and other law enforcement personnel supplementing them, they couldn't be everywhere to protect lives and property.

Fitzwilliam decided to do as he was told and to leave the legal arguments to the lawyers. They had just loaded into the back of a Guard truck a short, half-crazed, middle-aged white man who kept screaming, "I can't leave! Don't you know who I am? I'm Reginald de Courcy, and I must save the theatre!" over and over again when the call came in about shots fired on a USCG helicopter. Fitzwilliam's team was the closest detail to the area, so it was the first responder.

The water in the streets in this part of town, close to the Quarter, varied from almost dry to three feet deep. Fitzwilliam established a command post two blocks away, looking towards the Lake at the house where the suspect was alleged to be holding up. Thanks to high-water trucks from the National Guard, Fitzwilliam was able to surround the area with officers and troops.

The standard procedure was to reconnoiter the vicinity and wait for the arrival of a Special Operations Division SWAT unit to initiate operations against the building. With the city gone to hell, it might take hours for the SWAT unit to arrive. Fitzwilliam pulled out his binoculars, propped his arms on the roof of his un-marked squad car, and scanned the two-story house.

"Suspect has just left the interior of the house and is on the second-floor balcony," his radio blared in his ear.

Fitzwilliam moved his binoculars, refocused, and damn near dropped them. The man was pacing from one end of the balcony to the other, looking up into the sky, occasionally shouting and waving a black handgun in the air. It had been over five years, he couldn't hear the suspect's voice, and the man had lost a lot of weight, but it was the face that had haunted Fitzwilliam's dreams.

"*Wickham*," he breathed.

Greg Wickham was deep into his drug- and hunger-induced, sword-and-sorcery fantasy. Since the deluge began, he had consumed more and more of his product. He no longer knew where reality ended and his dreams began. Sometimes, he was a 1970s mob boss in the Bronx. Other times, he was an eighteenth century pirate on the high seas. The Gregory of Orléans hallucination was a favorite.

Wickham forgot he was trapped in a half-flooded house in the Upper Ninth Ward. He was the Prince of Orléans with women at his beck and call, protecting his castle from the dragons of his enemies.

In his mind, Gregory strode up and down the battlement high on top of his keep, screaming for the dragon to return to face its ultimate destruction. He gestured in his anger and impatience, brandishing his instrument of Power above his head.

"*Wickham*." Without moving his attention from the spiky-haired drug dealer, Fitzwilliam toggled his radio. "Attention all units—weapons free. I repeat, weapons free."

"Sir?"

Fitzwilliam turned to the patrolman behind a squad car parked next to him, a scoped M-16 in his arms.

"Aren't we to wait for the SWAT team?"

"The suspect is armed and dangerous," Fitzwilliam returned. "He has fired upon a Coast Guard helicopter engaged in search and rescue. We can't wait hours for a tactical team." He activated his radio again. "All units. We cannot wait for backup. The sniper is a danger to us and to rescue personnel. It is incumbent to neutralize this situation in quick order. We are acting on my authority. Take your positions and stand by." Fitzwilliam turned to the officer with the M-16. "Can you take him from here?"

"I've had sharpshooter training." The patrolman had sunglasses on, so Fitzwilliam could not make out his expression, but his voice was confident. He turned his ball cap backwards, raised the rifle to his shoulder, and sighted the target in the scope. "He's within range, sir. Am I clear to shoot?"

Fitzwilliam returned to his binoculars. Wickham was walking back towards the near side of the balcony.

"You are clear to shoot," he croaked, his mouth dry. He waited intently, following every move of his nemesis.

Now! Shoot him now! Kill him now!

"Send it!" he hissed through his teeth.

So absorbed with his quarry's every movement, the report of

the gunshot startled Fitzwilliam, jerking the binoculars from the lock he had on the house. He tried to reacquire his target, but the balcony was now empty.

No! Did he get away? Did he escape again?

"Suspect is down, suspect is down," he heard the sharpshooter report. "Torso shot—upper chest."

Fitzwilliam turned to the officer, trying to believe the words. After a moment, which seemed to stretch for hours, he radioed his men.

"All units, suspect down. The suspect is down. We do not know his condition. Begin moving in. Follow standard procedures. Repeat, the suspect is down, and his condition is unknown. Move in following standard procedures."

It took almost twenty minutes for the first officers to reach the building. Standard procedures were designed to maximize the safety of police and EMT personnel, not the wounded suspect. They determined the suspect was lying motionless on the balcony, so a National Guard truck was brought in to use as a platform for ladders. The first police in the house were surprised to see their assistant precinct captain right on their heels. Fitzwilliam hauled himself over the railing and stepped onto the balcony. There, five feet from him, lay Wickham, surrounded by the initial assault team.

One of them looked up. "He's dead, Captain."

"Dead," Fitzwilliam repeated in a voice devoid of emotion.

The officer glanced at the trail of blood at Wickham's feet. "Suspect appears to have dragged himself to this spot after being shot, and then expired. Not long—he's still a bit warm." He sighed. "Maybe ten minutes, sir."

Fitzwilliam nodded as more police climbed over the railing behind him. While the others fanned out to search and secure the premises, Fitzwilliam squatted next to the filthy body of his opponent. His mind was filled with incomplete thoughts as he wrestled with the concept that his long odyssey was over. The fog of hate that clouded his thoughts was gone, and he could see the obvious. Death could not hide the fact that life for Gregory "G-Daddy" Wickham had not been good. The wretched man's limbs were basically skin and bones. Wickham appeared as malnourished as any survivor of the Holocaust or Darfur.

Was this someone to fear? he considered. Wickham had been a walking dead man. The sniper's bullet had ended his existence only a few days before starvation would have killed him. Fitzwilliam glanced back at the Glock, still lying where Wickham had dropped it after being hit.

How many rounds were left in that thing? For the first time he considered whether there might have been another way.

"Captain!"

Fitzwilliam looked up.

"There's a methamphetamine lab in one of the bedrooms, and we just found a cache of hand grenades in the closet!"

Fitzwilliam leapt to his feet, back in command. "All right, everyone out! Now! Nobody touches this place until the bomb squad clears it. Now, move it!" A cop started towards the body. "No. Leave Wickham where he is."

The officer started. "You know him, sir?"

Fitzwilliam exhaled noisily. "Yeah, I knew him."

Less than five minutes later, the police were gathered around the impromptu command post. Downtown had been alerted, and the bomb squad and a medical examiner were requested. Fitzwilliam set his people to work. He would take command of the crime scene with a small deployment and wait the hours it would take before being relieved while the rest of the team went to rescue the people the Coast Guard had spotted. The police sniper, as per regulations, stayed behind with Fitzwilliam to await transfer back downtown and desk duty until cleared by PID. Fitzwilliam hated to have one less man on the street, but he had broken enough rules today.

It was a clean shooting, he told himself. *That officer will be back on the streets in no time. I must not do anything to jeopardize that. We need him. We need all of my people. We've got to save the city—my city. We've got to save it, so we can rebuild it.*

Captain Richard Fitzwilliam had found his new obsession.

Chapter 21

THE EFFECTS OF KATRINA'S DESTRUCTION WERE FELT across the nation. Before the storm, one-tenth of the crude oil consumed and a quarter of the natural gas supply came from the region. Half of the gasoline produced in the country came from refineries in the states along the Gulf of Mexico. The majority of all this was now shut-in.

The USCG reported at least twenty offshore oil platforms were adrift, sunk, or had simply disappeared. The Louisiana Offshore Oil Port, responsible for eleven percent of US consumption, was out of commission for lack of electrical power to run it. But even with electricity, the crude oil had nowhere to go. Ten refineries were shut down, four of them damaged or destroyed. The rest worked at reduced capacity. Supply and demand pushed oil prices to over seventy dollars a barrel.

Gasoline prices spiked to six dollars a gallon in isolated locations. Long lines materialized at the pumps, something not seen since the oil crisis of the 1970s. Prices finally stabilized at a nationwide average of over three dollars a gallon, the first time in history.

With the largest bulk port in the country out of action, corn, wheat, and other commodities could

> not be exported overseas. The economic impact from that was not immediately felt by consumers. Suddenly spending twenty percent more to fill up the car *was* noticed. It hurt and got people's attention.

Saturday, September 10
K plus twelve days: Madison, Wisconsin

Conditions in the evacuation centers were unpleasant despite the best efforts of local officials and Red Cross personnel. Things were hot and humid, close and loud, with no privacy whatsoever. Inevitably, fights broke out, sometimes over the smallest and silliest of issues. The small number of thieves filled the centers with a sense of mistrust.

At least the evacuees had working bathrooms and, occasionally, showers. Charities donated welcomed clothing because the rags on the refugees' backs were fit only for the trashcan. Best of all, hot food broke the monotony of MREs and canned drinking water. Things were far better than in the Superdome or the horror of the Convention Center.

Relief officials huddled to decide what to do with the multitude. The football stadiums in Houston and San Antonio had to be emptied for upcoming games. There was no New Orleans or Gulfport or Chalmette for the people to return to, so long-term housing became the priority. Teams interviewed the refugees, their plans and skills checked against a list of placement offers flooding in from all over the country. Skilled workers and college students were the easiest to place.

So it was with thankful hearts and confused minds that Scott Davis, Kaywanda Johnson, and her mother walked off an airliner at General Mitchell International Airport in Milwaukee, Wisconsin, with nothing but Scott's duffle bag and the clothes on their backs.

Met by a welcoming committee from Lutheran Social Services, the little family was soon whisked to a waiting van and headed out of the city. They passed signs emblazoned with strange names, like Waukesha, Pewaukee, and Oconomowoc, as they motored westward along Interstate 94. The driver, a man named Kruepke, kept up a monologue about the passing countryside and the rolling hills of southern Wisconsin. Scott and the Johnsons watched as the built-up area gave way to vast acres of corn and soybeans broken by tall, wooded hills and dairy farms.

After about an hour, civilization reappeared as they approached the state's second-largest city. Turning off the interstate, the straight main drag into Madison reminded the refugees of Jefferson Highway on a bad day. But in the distance, at the end of the road, was an unusual sight. Soon, they were upon it: the Wisconsin State Capital building, centered on a thin isthmus between the twin lakes that defined the city. It had four wings set at right angles to each other at the points of the compass, like a large plus sign lying on its side. Soaring above the axis was a familiar looking dome.

"Looks like the US Capitol, doesn't it?" Mr. Kruepke said as he drove around the square surrounding the building. "It's two hundred sixty-five feet tall, about three feet shorter than the one in Washington. On top is a statue of a woman with a helmet with a badger on top. It's really something, isn't it?"

"Badger, huh?" Scott asked politely, while Kaywanda and her mother sat back, trying to recover from culture shock. They hadn't seen a black face since they left the airplane.

"Oh, yes," said Kruepke in that slight, hard-to-place Wisconsin twang which sounded vaguely Scandinavian. "Lots of things in Wisconsin are tied somehow to badgers—that's the UW mascot, you know. Badger this, or Badgerland that. We love our badgers."

Scott rolled his eyes. He was originally from Michigan and knew the ways of Big Ten country. "Yeah, it's the same way with Baton Rouge and the LSU Tigers," he politely pointed out.

"Really? I suppose so. Never been to New Orleans, myself. Guess it's too late now. Oh! And the Packers. Packer football is just about the state religion."

"Of course," Scott replied, flashing a smirk at a bewildered Kaywanda. "I'll explain later, babe," he whispered.

The van continued out of downtown Madison a short ways into the University section. "This is the University of Wisconsin,"

Kruepke said. "Which one of you is enrolling?"

"That would be me," Scott answered.

Wisconsin, like many universities across the nation, had reached out to the student victims from Tulane, UNO, and the other colleges in New Orleans. Tuition waivers were common, and in some cases, board and books were covered as well. Lutheran Social Services had found housing near the UW campus and had arranged for transportation from Texas. There was an opening at UW Madison for Social Work, and the Johnsons and Scott had decided to take advantage of it, knowing the rental house in New Orleans was a total loss.

Minutes later, they walked into a small, two-bedroom apartment. "It's got a good location. It's only a few blocks from the campus, and there's a bus stop right in front," Kruepke said. "It might get a little noisy on Saturdays! You know, from Camp Randall."

Kaywanda turned to him. "Camp Randall? There's a military base around here?"

"Oh, no!" Kruepke laughed. "Camp Randall is the name of the football stadium where the Badgers play!"

"Oh," said Mrs. Johnson. "And where do the Packers play?"

"At Lambeau Field in Green Bay," he responded as if Mrs. Johnson had grown a third eye.

Kaywanda saw Scott hiding a smile and almost swatted him.

Kruepke pulled out a folder from his briefcase. "We have papers for you to sign. Your rent and utilities will be covered for at least six months through FEMA, though we think it will be extended up to a year. If not, Lutheran Social Services will cover it. You'll have to pay for phone service and any cable or internet. A social worker will meet with you in the next few days to explain all the assistance programs. FEMA will be either issuing debit cards or transferring money into your bank account. It will be two thousand each. If you don't have a bank here in Madison, we can help get one for you.

"Kaywanda, you said you have a background in secretarial work. We'll arrange for some interviews with local firms who are hiring. Mrs. Johnson, I believe you're on disability. The social worker will help you with that, including medical care and prescriptions. Scott, you're to meet with the Dean of Social Work on Friday."

"Uh," Scott interrupted, "we really don't know what day it is. What's today, again?"

Kruepke nodded. "I understand. You've had a lot thrown at you. Today's Wednesday. We'll have people meet with you about clothing and other necessities." He looked down at his paper. "Oh, and there's lots of nice restaurants nearby for Friday Fish Fry." He pointed to one. "I really like the perch at this place, and most times they get walleye. Good potato pancakes, too."

Scott nodded, but Mrs. Johnson and Kaywanda looked at each other. *Friday Fish Fry? Walleye? Potato pancakes?*

Kaywanda leaned close to her mother. "Momma, I don't think we're in Louisiana anymore."

Sunday, September 11
K plus thirteen days: Downtown

CAPTAIN BUFORD AND SERGEANT MACK PARKED THE HUMVEE next to the burned-out Shops at Canal Place and walked across Canal Boulevard to Harrah's Casino. The owners had set up a kitchen for the soldiers, police officers, and others involved in the city's recovery area. The food was good and plentiful, and the air conditioning was working, so they tried to eat at Harrah's every chance they got.

Buford was comforted by the weight of his government-issued M9 Beretta pistol nestled in its holster at his hip. With the change in orders from search and rescue to law enforcement, his unit was cleared to carry firearms. A detail was sent to the armory in Baton Rouge to fetch their weapons, and Mack was pleased to get his hands on his trusty M4 assault carbine. While the governor talked tough about "shooting looters on sight," the actual orders were far more benign. The presence of armed National Guardsmen was thought beneficial in keeping the peace.

As he and his sergeant got their food, Buford noticed a familiar face sitting alone. Mack joined some fellow LANG NCOs in the room while Buford walked over to the NOPD officer.

"Fitzwilliam? That you?"

Richard Fitzwilliam looked up. "Buford! Well, I guess it was only a matter of time before I ran into you around here. Sit down and tell me how you've been."

Buford sat across the table. "Tired as hell but okay. You?"

"Fine, fine." The haunted look in the back of Fitzwilliam's eyes told Buford a different story. "How did you make out?"

"I live in Baton Rouge, you know. Except for the power going out, no problems. You live in Mid-City, right?"

"Yeah, I did."

Buford winced. "Aw, jezze, I'm sorry. Is your family okay?"

"Yeah, they're in Atlanta. But I've got four feet of water in my house."

"That's tough."

Fitzwilliam shook his head. "Some people got it a lot worse. Have you been able to talk to your family?"

"Yeah, I call home every night." His eyes grew a little misty as he recalled the conversation from the night before.

Fitzwilliam's attention seemed to be on his food. "Yeah, I try to call every day, too. Olivia's staying with family."

"My brother-in-law's wife and kids are staying with us. You know Chuck and Jane Bingley, right?"

"Oh, yeah. Will told me what happened to Chuck's house. He's still working on his place?"

Buford confirmed it, and the two ate for a bit.

"So, were you stuck at Jackson Barracks when the levees went?" Fitzwilliam asked.

"Nope, I was at the Superdome."

"Crap! No kidding?"

"I was there for a solid week. Don't wanna go through *that* again."

"I hear ya." Fitzwilliam paused. "It was real bad, right?"

"Bad enough, but not as bad as the Convention Center."

Fitzwilliam grunted. "You know, I was at the Convention Center."

Buford gaped. "Really? Shit! I heard it was like a Wild West rodeo in there."

Fitzwilliam chuckled without humor and spent the next couple of minutes telling the soldier about his experiences. At the end, Buford was confused.

"Wait a sec, Fitz. I heard you had a hundred dead bodies in there."

Fitzwilliam rolled his eyes. "I've been hearing that story ever since we cleared the place. There was one fatality from stab wounds. We've no idea if the victim was attacked in the building, or it happened somewhere else, and he got to the Convention Center before he expired. The other three were from natural causes." He looked down. "Four dead is bad enough without exaggerating it."

Buford couldn't believe what he was hearing. "I heard this report from the Chief of Police."

"Who didn't know shit!" Fitzwilliam angrily spat. "They say two hundred people died from gunshot wounds at the Dome. Is that true?"

"No. One suicide, one suspected overdose, and four from natural causes. The only person shot was a Guardsman, and he wounded himself in the leg by accident."

Fitzwilliam leaned back. "See? Six dead at the Dome, and four at the Convention Center. But according to the mayor on Oprah, we might as well be in Baghdad. Shit." The two sat in contemplation of the misinformation being broadcast across the country.

Fitzwilliam broke the silence again. "You getting any leave soon?"

"Maybe next weekend. How about you?"

"No, nothing. We're too shorthanded." Fitzwilliam grinned. "But, you know FEMA's bringing in some cruise ships for housing."

"I heard something about that. We're bunking on *Iwo Jima*."

"Yeah, I saw that big sucker docked over there." He gestured at the river with his thumb. "Well, about those cruise ships, they're for police and firefighters—*and* their families."

"Really? That's cool."

"You said it. As soon as those puppies get here, I'm gonna get Olivia to come back and stay on board with me."

Buford smiled. "That's great. You guys have really had it tough. You need something nice to happen."

Fitzwilliam took a sip of his water. "Yeah. After this last couple of weeks, things can only get better, right?"

Chapter 22

Monday, September 12
K plus fourteen days: Lafayette

Chris Breaux set down the telephone with a stunned expression. "Well, that's it."

His wife and mother exchanged glances. "Bad news, baby?" asked Marianne.

He ran a hand through his hair. "Yeah. LSU has absolutely no idea when—or if—they're going to reopen University Hospital. Charity Hospital is gone."

Mrs. Breaux blinked. "Does that mean you've lost your job?"

"For now, they're still paying me, but long-term doesn't look good. LSU is setting up an emergency clinic at the New Orleans Centre next to the Dome, but that's for triage and serious injuries."

Marianne sat next to her husband and took his hand. "What do we do?"

"I don't know, honey. I just don't know."

Houston

William Darcy sat back in his chair and surveyed the group assembled around the conference table, mentally noting his allies and enemies. A special meeting of the DGS board of directors had been called, ostensibly to review conditions in the wake of Katrina. But neither he nor his uncle was fooled. The future of Delta Global Shipping was to be debated.

As Leon Anderson droned on about the last quarter's numbers, William took the opportunity to weigh the strength of his position with the people in the hotel conference room. He knew the board was happy with his performance during the *Edmund Fitzwilliam* incident six months ago. Profits were good and tonnage was up.

However, a few board members were unhappy with the infrastructure in New Orleans. The Port of New Orleans was dragging its feet, they said, in making needed improvements for handling cargo containers. The city wasn't an airline hub, so travel to meetings was inconvenient. They desired to move the corporate headquarters to a larger city, such as Houston.

These issues existed before Katrina. Previously, the majority of the board was satisfied with New Orleans and stopped cold any relocation talk. But the storm had changed the equation. William knew he had to act and act now, or things could get out of hand.

"Thank you, Leon," said DGS Chairman F. Edward Fitzwilliam at the end of the presentation. "Let me congratulate the operations division's performance during this difficult time. You've had to think on your feet and react quickly to a very fluid situation, and you've done marvelously." The rest of the board gave Anderson a polite round of applause as Ed gave William an encouraging glance. William knew his uncle was hoping to get out of this meeting without a confrontation. William did not share that hope.

Ed tried to bring the meeting to a close when a hand went up. It was Phil Osborne, the representative of an investment group that had taken a five percent stake in DGS two years ago. Ed blanched, and William sighed, knowing what was coming. Osborne had been the most vocal about the headquarters issue.

"Ed, there are a couple of things I believe I should bring to the board's attention. One is to congratulate William and Leon on their hard work during this crisis. Let's give them another hand, shall we?" Osborne began clapping and the rest joined in.

Slick bastard, thought William.

"I also think Will's plan to bring the new *George Darcy* to New Orleans with relief supplies is a noble thing to do, even though we could have waited for a contract from FEMA first." He chuckled. "Hell, the way they're throwing money around, I wonder if we did the right thing by our shareholders by not waiting, but that's beside the point."

Asshole.

Osborne sobered. "What's not beside the point is the future of this company and whether we can afford the luxury of maintaining our corporate headquarters in a city that's so vulnerable to natural disasters."

William listened as Osborne laid out the advantages of transferring the corporate offices to somewhere with a higher global identity, such as Houston or Miami, rather than remaining in a "ruined city."

First time he's mentioned Miami. Good move, Osborne. You're trying to drive a wedge between Uncle Ed and me, knowing Ed has a house in Fort Lauderdale. But that's not going to work.

Osborne finished his presentation and sat down without making a motion. William knew the game the man was playing. It wouldn't do for Osborne to make the motion to move DGS. Instead, the venture capitalist pretended his argument spurred someone else to do it. He certainly had an ally in place to make the motion. They were waiting a minute, letting Osborne's arguments sink in, before acting.

You're not going to get that time, thought William. Instead, he put into action his contingency plan to cut Osborne off at the knees. He glanced at Anthony Markunas, who then raised his hand.

"Yes, Tony?" said Ed.

"Ed, I'd like to make a motion that this board pass a resolution stating that an undeniable and unbreakable connection exists between Delta Global Shipping and the City of New Orleans, and that this board pledges to reestablish operations of its corporate headquarters there as soon as possible."

"Second!" cried the other plant, David Delacroix.

Osborne immediately saw the ploy for what it was and began to shout it down, but William got to his feet.

"The chair recognizes Will Darcy," Ed said quickly.

"Thank you, Mr. Chairman," William said formally. He took a breath to collect his thoughts. He had authority to vote his family's shares, and he had the support of a large block on the board, but Osborne had the ear of a large number too. Neither had a majority of the board under control, and the vote could go either way. William had to shore up his votes and sway the undecided to his side. Two votes could make all the difference.

"I rise in support of Tony Markunas's motion. Delta Global Shipping has been a Louisiana company under various names for 140 years. This company is part of Louisiana and part of my family. Our roots run deep. Our homes are—"

"This is about more than *your* family's homes, Will," injected Osborne.

Darcy smiled because the obnoxious Osborne had fallen right into his trap. "True, Phil, but it's also home to almost half of our employees, including the entire executive team, and they've been with us a long time." He gestured to the man beside him. "Leon, here, has worked for this company for over twenty years." He turned his attention back to the people assembled around the table. "The executive team has well over a hundred years of combined experience in shipping. They're smart, hardworking, and loyal. They have roots in the New Orleans metro area too. They serve on numerous boards, they volunteer at their children's schools and in their churches, and they coach their neighborhood athletic teams." He flashed a smile at Osborne.

"And what of our other headquarters employees? Finance, HR, secretarial, scheduling, IT, training? They are the heart and soul of this company. They have their homes in New Orleans. Some have been flooded out; others are in need of repair. It's not that easy to sell a house in these conditions. I don't see the value of uprooting and moving anyone, much less an entire company, for someone else's *convenience*."

Osborne paled as the verbal slap sunk in. Darcy had Osborne on the ropes. Now, he had to finish him off.

"Let's face it. We're in Louisiana for a reason. While container traffic is the growth area for the company, the majority of our traffic is steel, dry bulk, and break-bulk cargo. We ship in coffee and ship out corn and wheat. *This*," he pointed to a map of the Mississippi River which was taped on the wall, "is where our cargo is. Not Miami, not Houston. Our goods are *here*. The railroads and barges are *here*. And *here* is where DGS should be." He turned to the table again.

"If the majority of our business and profits are here, why the heck move our headquarters somewhere else? Why spend the money? Who is best served by this? Not our staff, not our workers, not our shareholders." He stared at Osborne. "I ask again—who is served?"

William sat down. "For the sake of our workers and our shareholders, the Darcy and Fitzwilliam families as well as the Darcy Charitable Trust will vote in favor of the resolution on the table."

Ed Fitzwilliam looked around the silent table. "Is there any other discussion on the motion, or shall I call for a vote?"

"Now, *THAT* WAS A BUTT-KICKING! YOUR DADDY COULDN'T HAVE done it better, Will!" Leon Anderson laughed as he sipped a scotch in Darcy's Houston office.

"If Dad was still here, Osborne never would have opened his mouth," said William grimly.

Leon and Ed Fitzwilliam shared a look.

"Maybe, or maybe not, Will," Ed stated. "George was a good man in the board room, but you did just fine. Unanimous, with Osborne abstaining. Even his plant voted for us, whoever that was. You set him down firmly but fairly. The board's solidly on your side."

Leon leaned forward. "Look, Will, I'm not saying this because you're my boss or the son of my friend. I've never seen someone come along and get up to speed as fast as you. You've got that special something that makes you a leader. This company could not be in better hands than yours."

"Amen," agreed Ed.

William scowled over his bourbon. "Thanks, but don't think this is over. Osborne won't go away. This vote gives me maybe a year to get us up and running again, that's all."

Ed shifted in his chair. "I agree, and that's why I've reconsidered my intention of stepping down this year. You've got enough to do without the mantle of chairman hanging around your neck."

"Thanks, Uncle Ed. I can use you in there."

"How's the trailer proposal going?" asked Leon. "Any movement?"

"Elizabeth's working on it. With the others putting pressure on the government, we ought to get them."

"Good." Leon threw back the last of his drink. "Let me get back to work."

Ed got to his feet. "I'm flying out this afternoon to Fort Lauderdale. Why don't you hitch a ride, Will? We can drop you off in Baton Rouge. Go spend some time with Elizabeth. Maybe get that smile back on your face."

William glanced at Leon.

"Go on, boss," said the VP. "You can do more there than here right now. Go get us up and running again so we all can go home."

"All right, you've talked me into it. Give me some time to talk to my secretary and run back to the hotel to pack a bag. Maybe an hour?"

Ed waved. "Take all the time you need. I can hang around here and make a nuisance of myself."

Leon laughed. "Just like old times, eh, Ed?" The two left the office while William dialed Elizabeth's cell.

St. Charles Parish

THAT EVENING AFTER WILLIAM CLIMBED OFF THE DGS CITATION and into Elizabeth's loving arms, he was drafted to grill steaks for dinner. A quick drive to Dansereau later, he and George Katz shared a beer on the back patio while the filets cooked.

"How's it feel to be back, Will?"

"After living in a hotel? So good I can't tell you."

George looked around the backyard, the sky a darkening gray with streaks of red. "Thanks for putting Emma and me up for the last couple of weeks. We can never repay you and Lizzy."

"Aw, knock it off. We're glad to have you here. To be honest, I like having someone to keep Lizzy company. You're doing us both a favor. Consider the place yours for as long as you need." William turned back to the steaks.

"About that..."

Something in George's voice—a finality—caught William's attention. He turned. "You're leaving?"

"Yeah. Emma and I have talked it over, and we can't impose on y'all any longer. It's time to move on."

William stared into his fraternity brother's eyes. "You haven't imposed."

"It's time. Emma's talking to Lizzy right now."

"Where are you going?"

"We've decided to go up to Maryland and stay with Emma's sister for a while until we get back on our feet."

William nodded. "You coming back?"

George looked out at the distance. "I don't know. We both grew up here, but with losing both Abe and the house and everything, there are too many memories here. Bad memories." He sighed. "Emma can't go back. Not now. It's too soon, too raw."

William wasn't surprised. "When?"

"We're booking the airline tickets now. In a few days."

"Is there anything we can do?"

George looked at his feet. "Yeah, there is one thing if it's not too much trouble. If you can get me back to the hospital to pick up my car, I'd appreciate it. It's still in the Medical Center parking garage. We'll park it and Emma's Volvo at some storage facility until we decide what to do with them."

William flipped the meat. "We'll take my pick-up and go tomorrow. I've got a pass that'll get us in the city. And don't worry about any storage place. You can keep the cars here at Dansereau until you need them." He chuckled. "We've certainly got the room."

"Thanks, buddy. We'll probably sell them—the Volvo, certainly. I don't think Emma can drive that car again."

"I can understand it. Think you'll miss this place?"

George took a deep breath. "No. Maybe later, but I think we both need a fresh start. It's way too soon to get sentimental over this town." He turned to William. "But we will miss our friends. You and Lizzy, Chris and Mari, Ch-Chuck and…and…"

To William's surprise, his big, strong friend began sobbing. "It's okay, George, it's okay."

Tears flowed down George's face. "I know, it's…it's like I can't stop. I don't know what's wrong with me."

He broke down, and William, without another thought, pulled him into a hug. George wept on his shoulder, and William looked helplessly into the house, only to see Elizabeth staring at him in pain, Emma crying in her arms.

Chapter 23

Whether from seeing the logic of the proposal or bowing to political pressure, FEMA allowed the positioning of the small travel trailers for workers at large employers deemed important to the national economy. That meant oil and gas refineries, shipyards engaged in military construction, and ports. DGS parked theirs on a barge docked near its headquarters, using the huge hollow platform as a wastewater-holding tank for the dozen travel trailers. There was one frustrating requirement from FEMA, however—only workers could use the trailers. Spouses and dependents were forbidden from even stepping into them.

Still, it was better than nothing. DGS contacted its workers, promising food and water, and a goodly number showed up to work.

For all his efforts, William Darcy could not completely keep his promise. On Tuesday, September 13, around 7:15 p.m., the *Lykes Flyer*, operated by CP Ships, docked at the Napoleon Avenue Container Terminal, marking the return of commercial shipping to New Orleans.

The brand new container ship, the *George Darcy*, filled with relief supplies, arrived two days later.

Wednesday, September 14
K plus sixteen days: Baton Rouge

Carrie was already in bed when Jane came into the room to

undress. She could tell her sister-in-law was unhappy. "What's wrong, Jane? Are the kids still up?"

"No, they're asleep. I just got off the phone with the mortgage company," she said as she took a maternity nightgown out of a drawer. She wore the thing as a courtesy to Carrie. If she had been at home, she would have slept in the nude as usual.

"Again?" Carrie exclaimed to Jane's back, as the other woman moved into the bathroom.

"Oh! They're so hard to work with! You know I've been calling all of our credit and gas card companies, explaining the situation down here. We're not asking for much—just a little more time on the payments until the worst of the emergency is over without running up any late fees or interest rate hikes. Almost all of the companies have been completely cooperative. Some had already placed holds on accounts from our zip codes, even before we called. They all understand we have a historic disaster down here, and they're willing to help. No payments until January, a freeze on interest costs, things like that. The banks are even letting us use whatever ATM is nearby without fees." She stuck her head out of the bathroom. "All except for Acme National Mortgage!"

Jane brushed her hair so hard Carrie was afraid she would pull it out.

Jane continued to rant. "I call up, and after I finally get through to a live person—and that was wasn't easy, let me tell you—the first thing they want to do is put me through to the re-work department, like we're somebody with bad credit issues. I explain again to them that no, I don't want to do that, that we've had a hurricane, and no, I don't want to suspend payment to our loan, which would go onto the back end and cost us more interest! I would like to spend our money on *food*, now that Katrina has put us temporarily out of our jobs! I explain to them—again—what our other creditors have done and ask them what Acme National's plan is. Now, they tell me they don't have a plan for Katrina victims yet!"

Carrie frowned. "Jane, they're the country's biggest mortgage company. How can they *not* have a plan?"

Jane held her head. "They can't tell me. I don't know why Gallic sold our home mortgage to Acme National, but they've been trouble since day one. Until they tell me they have a plan that will not cost us more money or ruin our credit, I'll just have to continue making our mortgage payments." She sat on the bed.

"Can you afford that?"

"We have some money in our savings."

"Oh, Janie, I'm so sorry."

Jane sighed and lay down next to Carrie. "At least Standard Insurance has been great. They're supposed to send an adjuster out next week to the house."

"Wow, that's fast. Good thing you got your claim in early."

"I imagine they're getting overwhelmed by calls now. I've seen insurance claim centers spring up all over the place in the last week." Jane smoothed down the sheets. "Charles is going to stay in Covington, cleaning up, until the adjuster arrives."

"How are things there?"

"Better. They've restored power along US 190 from I-12 into Covington, so Chuck doesn't have to drive to Hammond for gas. He says the stores are trying to restock but have limited hours because they have no workers." She turned over on her side. "What is it with men?"

Carrie laughed at her *non sequitur.* "Now, *that's* a loaded question. What's Chuck done now?"

Jane pursed her lips. "He won't leave the house! He's over there with no power or air conditioning, running the refrigerator with a generator, cleaning up the yard, and trying to fix Hailey's window. He's not a carpenter, for heaven's sake. We're going to hire a contractor once the insurance settlement comes through. But he's still putzing around."

Carrie snorted. "Men! Always showing off!"

Jane played with the sheets. "Well, it's partly my fault."

"How is that?"

"Back in February, Chuck was using a chainsaw to clear some brush in the yard, and I mentioned to him it made him look real *manly*, if you know what I mean."

Carrie pointedly eyed her sister-in-law's midsection. "Is that the reason for *that*?"

"*Carrie*!" Jane blushed and added, "Maybe."

THANKS TO A MIGHTY EFFORT, THE CORPS OF ENGINEERS, THE levee districts, and their contractors had sealed, albeit temporarily, the breaches in the canals. The Corps brought in huge pumps to augment the Sewerage & Water Board's equipment. To everyone's relief, the city's pumps worked once the level of water was lowered enough to restore power. By the middle of the month, over half the floodwaters were gone, enough for the mayor to plan for the repopulation of the Crescent City.

The president returned on September 15 to speak to the nation from Jackson Square. He encouraged tourists to return to the Big Easy, to enjoy its hotels and sights and restaurants. Pundits said the president's remarks were at best overly optimistic, but it was exactly the message the city wanted to get out. The Port and the shipyards would come back, and oil was always needed, but the third leg of the economy needed the shot in the arm. The grim truth was, without tourists and the convention trade, New Orleans would never recover.

Many thought the mayor's plan was too much too soon. The local electric utility had worked hard, but vast areas of the city were still without power. With the utility bleeding money, it would be months before even half the city was inhabitable. Without power, there would be no phone or cable service except for cell phones. The Sewerage & Water Board had restored much of the water in the dry central part of the city, but it was unsafe to drink.

The tourism trade needed a jump start, and that meant people to work in the lodging and entertainment industries. The mayor knew his citizens. Most were straining at the bit to return, and with an election next spring, he wasn't going to get in the way. The return would start next week.

Unfortunately, Mother Nature had other plans.

The monster wasn't the end of the 2005 Hurricane Season. The people in K-land were unaware that five named tropical systems had developed and faded in the last three weeks. Tropical Storm Lee and Hurricanes Maria, Nate, and Philippe formed, grew, and dissipated in the expanse of the Atlantic Ocean. Only Ophelia, a minimal hurricane, threatened inhabitable areas. The storm danced off the Carolina coastline from September 13 to 15 before dashing off to fall apart in the chilly waters off Newfoundland.

On the day Ophelia was declared to be no more, a sister was born north of Hispaniola.

Sunday, September 18
K plus twenty days: Baton Rouge

Jane sat in front of Carrie's computer, holding her head after another frustrating day. The mortgage company had finally admitted management had not come up with a plan to help, but they promised they were working on it. Meanwhile, Gallic National Bank moved forward with reopening their branch offices in the surrounding parishes, but made no announcement about the future of the main offices in downtown New Orleans. As for the Red Cross, it was a joke. Jane still couldn't get in via the phone to register for the financial relief. The spokespeople on the radio continued to deny any plans for setting up local service centers to handle the program face-to-face. Instead, they patronizingly insisted people continue to call the always-busy, toll-free telephone line.

Added to that was the anticipation of going home. The electrical utilities had set up web sites where customers could see the restoration progress. Covington had power for government buildings, hospitals, schools, and other facilities. Service was slowly fanning out along the major thoroughfares, restoring power to residential and commercial buildings.

It was agonizingly slow. While clearing the roads after the storm, all downed cables had been cut up for safety. It wasn't a matter of re-hanging cables and drops. The utilities had to rebuild entire networks, often setting new power poles.

Today's progress report showed they were a mile from the house. How much longer it would take for them to get there, she didn't know. Jane was antsy to leave. Carrie had been loving and gracious during their stay, but Jane ached to be in her own house, especially with the schools reopening that week.

The telephone interrupted her thoughts. "Hello, Buford residence."

"Hey, babe. How's everything?"

"Chuck? Oh, hi. We're fine over here. Just a little stir-crazy. How are you?"

"Oh, good. Listen up. I want you to hear something."

Jane frowned, wondering what her husband was about. In the background, she heard noises. "Honey, what are you talking about?"

"You didn't hear it?"

"Hear what?" There was the sound of a motor followed by a familiar ding.

"The microwave."

"Oh, that's what that—the microwave!" Jane shouted with joy. "Chuck, is the power back on?"

He heard her husband laugh. "It sure is!"

"Mommy?" Jane turned to Hailey, standing in the doorway of the Buford's home office. "Why are you yelling?"

Jane's grin threatened to split her face wide open. "It's Daddy! He says the power is back on at home!"

Hailey clapped her hands while jumping in place. "Yay! Yay, Daddy! Can we go home now?"

"We sure can, sweetie! As soon as we can pack!"

The Bingleys' twenty-two day exile had ended.

Rockville, Maryland

EMMA NEVER THOUGHT SHE WOULD WALK INTO HER SISTER'S HOUSE in Rockville with almost nothing but the clothes on her back. Yet, all of her and her husband's worldly goods were contained in the two suitcases George and Tyler pulled out of the Parker's trunk. Almost everything they owned remained in their still-inundated house back in Lakeview.

Emma and Irene took the opportunity to play with the Parker's daughter as Tyler showed George the spare bedroom that would be the Katzes' home for the foreseeable future.

"Irene? Is there a chapter of NCJW near here?"

"Yes. They meet at the Jewish Community Center on Montrose Road."

"Can we go by there soon? I'd like to start getting involved."

THE TROPICAL DISTURBANCE QUICKLY BUILT UP TO TROPICAL STORM status, earning the next name on the 2005 list. As the letter Q was never used, the seventeenth named storm would be named Rita. She was still a tropical storm as her wind lashed southern Florida, the Keys, and Cuba, but the models forecasted a rapid strengthening in the coming days.

Chapter 24

Tuesday, September 20
K plus twenty-two days: Convention Center

New Orleans was in danger again. The city called a press conference with Joint Task Force Katrina and the state at the Convention Center.

The models all said Hurricane Rita would gain strength as it entered the Gulf of Mexico. The scientists predicted a major storm by the time it made landfall somewhere near Houston, Texas. The storm surge would affect a broad area. As shaky as the levees were, New Orleans had to abandon its resettlement plans and re-evacuate the city. Thus, the officials laid their plans to get people out of the Crescent City.

The press conference wasn't going well, Anna Elliot could tell. The reporters ignored the officials' proclamations. Instead, they demanded the city justify its actions during Katrina. It was turning into an interrogation.

Bryan Thorpe of Action NOW News had talked his station into extending his stay in New Orleans. With another storm in the Gulf, management gave approval, as long as the crew beamed back film equivalent to the footage they had shot the last time they were by the Convention Center.

General Honoré politely took over the microphone from an increasingly frustrated mayor. In beret and sunglasses, he projected power and confidence. He reminded the assembled that the purpose of the press conference was to explain the plan to evacuate the remaining people out of the area. As he revealed that buses were going to be at the Convention Center, several reporters broke in. A reporter overrode Thorpe.

"But, General, that didn't work the first time—"

"Wait a minute," the general shot back. "It didn't work the first time. This ain't the first time. Okay?"

Anna almost laughed. She had been in a few meetings with the general, and his gruff, take-no-prisoners manner of speaking had won her over.

"You got good public servants working through it," the general continued. "Let's get a little trust here because you're starting to act like this is *your* problem. You are *carrying the message*, okay?" He repeated the details of the plan to the assembled press, reemphasizing the importance of getting this information out. He then asked for questions.

Another reporter asked about a rumor of a staging area on the West Bank, which the general repudiated. Once again, he explained the plan, and Anna thought he was showing incredible patience with the mostly hostile reporters.

The general then added, "Let's not get stuck on the last storm. You're asking *last* storm questions for people who are concerned about the *future* storm. Don't get stuck on stupid, reporters. We are moving forward. And don't confuse the people, please. You are part of the public message."

The same reporter then asked a follow-up. "General, a little bit more about why that's happening this time, though, and did not have that last time—"

The general, his patience exhausted, exploded. "*You are stuck on stupid!* I'm not going to answer that question! We are going to deal with *Rita!* This is public information that people are depending on the government to put out! This is the way we've got to do it!"

Thorpe and the other reporters seemed taken aback at the set-down. Anna tried to contain the grin on her face, something the mayor made no attempt to do.

The general pulled back a bit. "So, please, I apologize to you, but let's talk about the future. Rita is happening, and right now we need to get good, clean information out to the people that they can use. And we can have a conversation on the side about the past in a couple of months."

The press conference continued, and the needed information was relayed to the locals. However, the general's comments made the national news and cable outlets that night. Within days, General Honoré would become a nationwide folk hero.

Covington

THE CABLE WASN'T WORKING IN COVINGTON, BUT CHUCK HAD found an old set of rabbit ears for the TV. He, Jane, and the kids watched the news about the new monster.

"Are we going to evacuate, Chuck?"

Chuck thought for a moment. "I'd rather not. It looks like Rita's heading for Houston, anyway. But it's up to you, honey. Whatever you want."

"We stay," she said firmly without hesitation. "I'd rather be in my own house without power than go through another three weeks like we've just had."

"Mommy, are we going to lose 'lectricity?" asked Hailey.

Her father answered. "We probably will, sweetie. After the last storm, there're a lot of weak limbs and trees. But don't worry," he quickly reassured her. "With all the crews around, it won't be long before we get power back. That's not what worries me."

"What's wrong?" asked Jane.

Chuck gestured at the set. "Look, you know me. I've never wished a hurricane on anybody. The worst thing that can happen is we get hit again. But if Houston takes a hit from a storm like Rita, it's almost as bad. It's the fourth largest city in the country, and it can flood. Remember Allison in 2001? If Houston gets clobbered, who's gonna care about us?"

LIKE HER SISTER, RITA KEPT SURPRISING THE EXPERTS. ASTONISHingly, the storm intensified from Category 3 to Category 5 in just a couple of hours. The internal pressure reached an incredible 897 mb, one of the lowest ever recorded. Winds of 175 mph made it stronger than the monster that wrecked the Central Gulf three weeks before. If the storm and its surge ran up the Houston Ship Canal, unbelievable damage and flooding would devastate Texas's largest city.

Rita moved rapidly, and that usually meant it would keep its heading constant. It was now due south of New Orleans, and the Crescent City could breathe a little easier. But storms had been known before to stop and turn. From central Louisiana to Corpus Christi, Texas, all eyes were glued to the weather forecasts.

Wednesday, September 21
K plus twenty-three days: Lafayette

Henry and Cathy Tilney could appreciate the irony. Only a few weeks before, they had housed Emma Katz during the evacuation from Hurricane Katrina. Now, with Hurricane Rita bearing down on Texas, it was their turn to get out of Dodge.

Texas ordered a mandatory phased evacuation from the coastal areas on Wednesday, September 21. One of the last scenes the Tilneys saw on TV before they left the house was a stream of school buses heading towards Galveston, commandeered to move people without vehicles from the seaside city.

Henry had originally planned to head north, but after receiving a quick call from Chris Breaux, they decided to make a dash eastward to Lafayette, skirting before and beyond the expected track. The traffic was bad but not impossible, especially after they hit Louisiana. While the southwestern part of the state was evacuating, the traffic flowed relatively smoothly, as it seemed the locals had things well in hand. After all, the Louisiana officials had plenty of practice. The Tilney family reached the Breaux homestead before nightfall, and they were greeted with hugs from Marianne Breaux.

"Mari," Cathy managed, "thank you so very much. We really don't deserve this kindness."

Marianne faced her in a perfectly collected manner. "What's done is done, and what's in the past stays there, Cathy. We're happy to have you for as long as you need. May I introduce you to my in-laws?"

Thursday, September 22
K plus twenty-four days: Houston

THE LIMO PULLED UP TO THE DGS CITATION JET PARKED AT Houston's William P. Hobby Airport in the early hours of the morning, discharging the dozen Delta Global executives right at the air-stair door. Leon Anderson talked to William on the cell phone as he helped his wife aboard.

"Is there anyone left downtown?"

Leon shook his head. "Anyone who wanted to save their car got out yesterday. Your car should be safe in the parking garage. What about New Orleans?"

"Evacuating now. I'll be all right here at Dansereau."

"Okay. We'll be in Miami in a few hours. How did the handoff to London go?"

"Smooth as silk. Ed's in the Miami office, now."

"Good. Hey, I just thought of something. I don't think Osborne is gonna give us any more grief about relocating to Houston."

"You're probably right. Call me when you land."

THE GENEROSITY OF TEXAS CAN NEVER BE DOUBTED. During the early weeks of the Katrina evacuation, up to two hundred thousand were sheltered for some time in the Lone Star State. However, with that big heart came a big ego. Texans watched the chaos of the Louisiana flight from Katina with a mixture of sympathy for the victims' situation and smugness that such a confounded mess could not happen there.

The forecasters' models indicated Houston was still in the crosshairs as dawn arose on Thursday. Heeding the entreaties of the mayor, the governor, and the sensational warnings of disaster from the newscasters, the nation's fourth largest city began to empty. Three million people, twice the number that had fled from Katrina, moved inland. Unlike the Crescent City, the residents of the Bayou City had no large bodies of water in the way and could go in three directions: north, east, or west. Yet, the carefully laid out evacuation routes were quickly overwhelmed, and the governor called for the implementation of their own Contraflow plan.

To their consternation, they learned Contraflow was not easy to implement. The state was woefully unprepared. It took hours to coordinate various law enforcement entities to close and reverse traffic on the southbound lanes of I-45, the eastbound lanes of I-10 from San Antonio, and the southeastern lanes of US 290 from Austin. Half of Texas was in gridlock as traffic collapsed to a crawl. Trips out of the strike zone were taking ten to thirty-six hours, depending on the destination.

It was more than inconvenience. Cars ran out of gas. Scores of people, the very young and the very old, died from dehydration in the hundred-degree heat. Early that day, a charter bus carrying elderly residents of a retirement home caught fire in the bumper-to-bumper traffic on I-45 south of Dallas. It exploded before it could be evacuated, killing twenty-three. The earlier satisfaction of the phased migration from the coast faded in the face of the horror on the highways.

Friday, September 23
K plus twenty-five days: New Orleans

As the hours moved on, Rita's track moved ever eastward. Fading from its Category 5 peak, it was still a dangerous Cat 4 with an enormous storm surge. She moved across the Gulf, forcing water towards the Louisiana coast. From the Texas line to the mouth of the Mississippi, the tide rose and rose. The flooding in St. Mary, Terrebonne, and Lafourche parishes was worse than during Katrina, and many levees were breached. One thousand people had to be rescued from flooding in Vermillion Parish. As the surge moved into the Barataria Bay estuary, it overcame the inadequate levees, which the Corps of Engineers had long neglected. Lafitte and the southern parts of the West Bank of Jefferson Parish, which had escaped Katrina's fury, now flooded.

Worse, the pressure placed upon the temporary repairs in the Industrial and London Avenue canals was more than the patches could stand. With their failures, the city began to re-flood. By Friday night, parts of the Crescent City were once again under as much as eight feet of water.

The Corps of Engineers and the levee boards had to start all over again.

LOST IN THE SUFFERING WAS A BIT OF NEWS FROM federal court.

In 1922, the City of New Orleans chartered a new company called New Orleans Public Service Inc. to take over the struggling, competing companies that provided electricity, gas, and transit to the city. By 1926, it was known as NOPSI. This company would be a subsidiary of a larger holding company eventually known as Middle South Utilities. However, the citizens of the city did not trust state regulators to set utility prices and demanded power remain with New Orleans government. Therefore, NOPSI and MSU's other Louisiana operations, LP&L, would be run as separate companies.

In 1979, the transit operations were transferred to the Regional Transit Authority, and ten years later, MSU changed its name to Energy Corporation. LP&L and NOPSI became Entergy Louisiana and Entergy New Orleans, with separate boards and operations. By this time, Entergy New Orleans could not generate its own power and had to purchase most of its electrical and gas needs from its sister Entergy companies in Louisiana, Mississippi, and Arkansas. Still, rate regulation stayed with the New Orleans City Council.

Because of the set-up, the finances of Entergy Louisiana and Entergy New Orleans were separate. In the wake of the storm, Energy New Orleans ran through its cash reserves quickly. Every erg of power, every cubic foot of gas, and every foot of electrical cable had to be bought from Entergy Louisiana, and Entergy New Orleans was broke.

On September 23, as the city flooded again, Entergy New Orleans filed for reorganization under Chapter 11 of the US Bankruptcy Code. New Orleans's insistence on a separate utility had borne the inevitable fruit.

Saturday, September 24
K plus twenty-six days: Texas/Louisiana line

Hurricane Rita continued to fade and made landfall between Sabine Pass, Texas, and Johnson Bayou, Louisiana at 02:38 a.m. CDT as a 115 mph Cat 3 storm. Cameron Parish, south of Lake Charles, took the brunt of the hit. Like St. Bernard Parish almost a month before, it was completely wiped out by a twenty-foot storm surge. Calcasieu and Beauregard parishes received heavy damage from wind and rain.

On the Texas side of the strike, communities in the so-called Golden Triangle of Beaumont, Port Arthur, and Orange sustained enormous wind damage. Thanks to onshore winds, the surge was far less there than in Louisiana. Thousands of acres of trees were felled, a major part of the East Texas economy, and two million people lost power.

Of Rita's one hundred thirteen victims in Texas, only about nine were directly caused by the storm. Many of the rest died during the evacuation, something that would haunt state officials for years.

The effects on the oil industry were greater than during Katrina. More offshore oil rigs were damaged or sunk, and the rest of the refineries in the central Gulf were shut down. Twenty percent of the US capacity was out of service. Between the two storms, over one hundred oil platforms were destroyed, and more than four hundred fifty pipelines were damaged.

Tuesday, September 27
K plus twenty-nine days: Downtown

AT A HASTILY CALLED NEWS CONFERENCE, THE NOPD SUPERINTENDENT stunned the assembled press by announcing his retirement. Everyone knew the enormous pressure the superintendent had been under since the storm. Officer suicides and alleged desertions devastated morale. The courts overturned the mandatory confiscation of firearms. Exaggerated stories and false rumors were run by the press with little attempt at verification. The worst lie was that the superintendent had driven his family to Texas during the crisis. Actually, his eight-months-pregnant wife and their daughter were in Denham Springs—twenty-five miles east of Baton Rouge—while the superintendent remained at his post.

Still, no one expected this resignation. The mayor, present at the event, claimed he did not force the superintendent out and thanked him for his service. He placed the assistant superintendent in control during a 45-day transition period.

A grim Captain Richard Fitzwilliam wasn't buying the mayor's story. He had already heard rumors of an angry confrontation between the mayor and the superintendent early that morning. The word in the department was that he had been effectively pushed out. The new boss was a good, solid cop. Richard had no worries there.

Still, the old police chief was a guy who had risen through the ranks to become superintendent, and that counted for a lot with the men and women in blue. Yes, the superintendent became emotional during many of his press conferences and passed along bad intel, but who didn't panic during the worse of the emergency? The nagging fear was the unknown effect of politics. Was the chief let go for the good of the NOPD or to serve as a scapegoat for the mayor? Fitzwilliam could not say for certain.

Part Three: RENEWAL

Through pestilence, hurricanes, and conflagrations the people continued to sing. They sang through the long oppressive years of conquering the swampland and fortifying the town against the ever-threatening Mississippi. They are singing today. An irrepressible joie de vivre maintains the unbroken thread of music through the air. Yet, on occasion, if you ask an overburdened citizen why he is singing so gaily, he will give the time-honored reason, "Why, to keep from crying, of course!"

– Lura Robinson, *It's an Old New Orleans Custom*, 1948

Chapter 25

Saturday, October 1
K plus four weeks: St. Charles Parish

For the first time in a very long time, the joyful shouts of children were heard at Dansereau Plantation. William and Elizabeth had invited the Boudreaux clan for a relaxing afternoon, a chance to unwind from the agonies of the storms, and a last chance to refresh themselves before the mid-October wedding of Mary Boudreaux and Bubba Teresina. The weather since Katrina had been dry, except for some rain from Rita. It was a fine day to dash about the yard as Hailey and Brett Bingley were doing. At least, Brett was trying to dash.

"Hailey!" cried her mother from her chair on the patio. "Be careful with your brother! Don't let him fall and hurt himself!"

"Kit, why don't you go keep an eye on them?" suggested Mrs. Boudreaux.

"Aww, Mom! Why me?" her daughter complained.

"Because Jane is eight months pregnant, that's why! Now, go on!" Mrs. Boudreaux shook her head as Kit stalked off. "That girl will be the death of me."

"Now, Franny, don't you get all wound up again," mumbled T.B. Boudreaux while he sipped his beer.

She glared without rancor at her husband. "My nerves wouldn't get all wound up if people around here would mind what I say!"

T.B. grinned. "See how it is, Bubba? You know what they say,

'Know the Momma, know the daughter.' You sure you wanna go through with this?"

"T.B.!" growled Mrs. Boudreaux.

Bubba grinned good-naturedly as he hugged his intended. "More than ever, T.B."

"William!" cried Mrs. Boudreaux. "Did I tell you how lovely your family home is?"

"Five times already," said Elizabeth under her breath.

"Yes, thank you," said William.

T.B. snorted. "Franny, stop droolin' all over Will's house. You're embarrassin' the boy."

Elizabeth could tell an argument was about to break out, so she turned to Bubba. "I suppose you're pretty happy about last night's football game?"

"Oh, yeah," chuckled the assistant coach. "Anytime we beat our rival, it's a good night. What makes it better is we're 3-and-1 going into conference ball."

"No problems about taking time off during the season?" asked William.

"Nah, I'm an assistant after all. The AD cleared it."

"The storm messed up everybody's life," added Mary. "The school administration is being very accommodating."

Bubba shook his big head. "Shoot, we're not as messed up as the New Orleans schools. Kids are scattered all over the place. It's tough on the kids graduating this year, especially the ones looking to play football. Their seasons got canceled, so they can't show the college scouts what they can do. I feel for them."

Chuck piped in. "Those storms tore up everybody's football season. LSU had to move all those games around, and the Saints home games are going to be split between the Alamo Dome in San Antonio and Tiger Stadium in Baton Rouge. Tulane's got it the worst. They haven't *got* a home. Their entire season will be on the road."

William sighed. "It was going to be a good year, too. They'll be lucky to win a game now."

Mrs. Boudreaux got out of her chair. "Football, football, football! If you're going to do nothing but talk sports, I'll go inside to the kitchen and start warming up the appetizers I brought. Kit! Come inside and help me!"

Kit, sitting on the grass playing with the children, looked up. "Aw, Mom! Why me?"

"Because I said so, that's why! Now, come on!" As the two disappeared into the house, T.B. finished his beer. After taking requests, he followed the women to get refills.

"So, how are you two holding up?" Elizabeth asked Mary and Bubba.

"Okay, but Mom's been a bit of a pain."

"I can't complain. Mary's been doing most of the work," Bubba said, earning a look from his intended. "Hey, you told me to stay out of the way!"

"And *now* you listen? Men!" She would have protested more, but Bubba picked her up and kissed her. "No fair!"

Bubba laughed. "Hey, Will, when are ya'll gonna go through this? When are you gonna get hitched to Lizzy?"

William blinked and turned to Elizabeth. "To be honest, we haven't given it much thought lately."

"We've been so busy just putting one foot in front of the other," Elizabeth explained.

Bubba sobered. "Heard that. Why don't you just run off to Vegas or something? It's what we should've done."

"Bubba!" cried Mary.

"Aww, I'm just kidding, Mary, you know that."

Mary grunted, pretending to be offended, and missed the horrified look William and Elizabeth shared with the Bingleys.

"Umm, no, I don't think we'll be going to Vegas," Elizabeth said. *Not while Lydia's there.*

Chuck had a suggestion. "If not Vegas, how about the islands? Aruba or Barbados or someplace like that?"

"I think Lizzy wants a church wedding," William answered, and Elizabeth nodded.

Mary screwed up her face with a thought. "Church wedding, hmm? Well, how about—"

"Come and get it!" cried T.B. from the kitchen door. "It's your Momma's oyster dip! Hurry up, I'm starved!"

"We'll talk later," Mary told Elizabeth as they left to gather the children. Chuck helped Jane out of her chair.

"Hey, T.B.! Is the LSU/Florida game on, yet?" Bubba turned to William. "Can't wait to watch that one on your big screen TV, Will."

William smiled. "That's what it's for, big guy."

The group went into the house for a few hours of normalcy.

Louisiana and Texas were reeling from the effects of Hurricane Rita, so it was understandable that attention was not on the neighbors to the south. Hurricane Stan only lived five days, from October 1–5, and its winds hardly exceeded 80 mph. But Stan slowly crossed the Bay of Campeche, dumping tons of rain onto unstable hillsides all over Central America. Sixteen hundred people lost their lives from floods and mudslides in Guatemala, Mexico, and El Salvador, proving even a minimal Category 1 storm could be monstrous.

Chapter 26

Wednesday, October 5
K plus five weeks: New Orleans

There was no doubt about it. The Crescent City was broke. Cash reserves were gone. Without business, commerce, and the sales taxes they generated, there was no hope of quickly restoring the city to fiscal health.

On October 5, the mayor announced that, due to lack of funds, New Orleans would lay off three thousand nonessential employees from the city's payroll—about half its workforce—over the next two weeks.

He also said residents from all parts of the city, with the exception of the Lower Ninth Ward, would be allowed to return to their homes. He warned, however, that many houses were damaged to the point of being uninhabitable, there was little chance of restoration of power soon, and the boil water order remained in effect.

Friday, October 7: Mandeville

THE LINE OUTSIDE MANDEVILLE'S PELICAN PARK ATHLETIC CENTER advanced a bit, and like the hundreds of others in the queue, Chuck Bingley dutifully moved his folding chair.

It was a strange experience for the former corporate lender. A little over a month ago, he sat in an air conditioned downtown New Orleans office, working on deals worth millions of dollars. Today, he sat on a beat-up folding chair in line for hours in the late morning sun, waiting for his turn to apply for $1,265 from the Red Cross, and he had hours yet to go.

Ever since the storm, the American Red Cross offered cash assistance to those affected. All one had to do was call a toll-free phone number and the money would be transferred into their bank account. For those who did not use banks, a pre-loaded debit card would be issued.

The problem was that the phone line was always busy, no matter the time of day. Chuck heard horror stories of those who got into the phone queue, only to wait for hours and hours for a human voice. Those with cell phones were cut off when the batteries died. One family talked of being on hold for thirteen hours before their call was handled.

The Red Cross spokespeople on the radio acknowledged the problem but claimed they had "hundreds of operators, working around the clock" to handle the thousands of calls. They promised to put more on the lines and asked for patience. The charity would not allow people to apply via the Internet and denied time and again persistent rumors that they were going to set up local relief centers. The mantra remained: just be patient and call us.

Though twelve hundred dollars would not solve all of the Bingleys' problems, hearing about it day after day wore on them. It was their money, they deserved it, and the Red Cross was being unreasonable and cruel to offer money that was impossible to collect.

Without warning, the Red Cross breathlessly announced in late September the establishment of a drive-up relief center in Slidell within forty-eight hours. They warned it would only be in operation for a few weeks, and they would only take about seven hundred applications per day. People were urged to arrive early, and police would turn cars away when they reached their daily quota.

Arriving before five in the morning and sitting in one's car for up to seven hours was not Chuck's idea of a good time. He had waited a week until the walk-up center at Pelican Park opened.

Now he was sitting on a lawn chair, wearing a ball cap, and waiting in line with hundreds of others. He had been there before

5:00 a.m. and had been in line for five hours. He figured he had at least two hours to go.

Everyone was good-natured about the whole thing. Red Cross volunteers constantly handed out bottles of water, and those in line who brought food shared with those who didn't. There were a bank of portable toilets set up, and people were happy to hold places in line for those who had to use them. It was a socially mixed bag of mostly North Shore residents: workers, doctors, professionals, teachers, housewives, poor people, young people, and elderly. Most were white and had never stood in a line for anything except at the DMV. People told jokes, shared storm experiences, and asked for advice from those who had sought assistance in the past. Chuck found it fascinating to listen to a single mother on TANF[3] explain the expected procedures to an accountant.

While people were appreciative of the local personnel, they weren't as kind to the national Red Cross office. They knew the Red Cross had planned for weeks to put in these relief centers. It took time to pull together the logistics of such an effort. But the spokespeople said over and over there would be no centers until the centers were going up. Why did the institution lie for over a month? Why such cruelty?

Chuck sat contemplating the spitefulness of the few. The American Red Cross wasn't the only entity acting in a way that could only be described as wrong. Gallic National Bank mailed politely phrased ultimatums to their workers. His boss, Manwarring, had decided to move Corporate Lending out of Louisiana to the Dallas regional office. All lenders were expected to transfer to Dallas or they would be placed on unpaid leave until the Louisiana office reopened—if it ever did.

He and Jane talked it over. Even with house prices jumping twenty-five percent in the wake of the storm, only undamaged homes were selling. The Bingleys could not sell their house until it

3 TANF - Temporary Assistance for Needy Families, which replaced what was commonly known as welfare: Aid to Families with Dependent Children (AFDC) and the Job Opportunities and Basic Skills Training (JOBS) programs.

was repaired. Only the Good Lord knew when that would happen.

At least Standard Insurance had come through. The same day the hated letter arrived from Gallic, their settlement check from their home insurance came in. The settlement was fair, but the check was made out to both the Bingleys and Acme National Mortgage Company. A young man named Karl assured Chuck the company would simply co-sign the check and the $25,000 would soon be in his bank account. In a week or so, Chuck could start looking for a contractor to fix Hailey's window. The trick was to find one. It was a moot point, however, since they did not want to sell.

What was unfair was that the Prechters down the street were also Standard Insurance customers. They put in their claim at about the same time, but they had seen neither hide nor hair of an adjustor. Chuck's adjustor explained that no insurance company had enough people to work a major event like a hurricane. Most of the adjustors were contract employees who worked a set area: a county or parish. To make sure the adjustors' recommendations were fair, different adjustors worked each neighborhood. Assignments were random and results were compared. The problem with that approach was that it slowed everything down. It was only luck that the Bingleys were on the beginning of the list while the Prechters were apparently on the end.

So Charles Bingley sat in a folding chair without a job, waiting to apply for free money. He had signed up for unemployment—on the Internet, ironically—and a woman in line just told him of the emergency food stamp program available across town. Chuck had no false pride left, and if he finished soon enough, he would go and get in another line. FEMA, Red Cross, insurance, trees falling on houses—everything was a crapshoot.

The line moved, and Chuck moved his chair up again.

Tuesday, October 11
K plus six weeks: Lower Ninth Ward

THE ARMY CORPS OF ENGINEERS, THE LEVEE BOARDS, AND THEIR contactors worked like demons and repaired the new breaches in the levees. They got the pumps operating again, and the waters receded. Two weeks later, the Corps declared New Orleans dry.

Meanwhile, those National Guardsmen not involved in assisting the police were occupied in a grim and necessary task: the recovery of the bodies. It was a time consuming, dirty, hot, terrible job. Each and every structure in Orleans and St. Bernard parishes in Louisiana—and Harrison, Hancock, and Jackson counties in Mississippi—was painstakingly searched for human remains. Damaged areas in Slidell and Plaquemines underwent the same process.

Captain Buford sat in his Humvee watching a squad from New Mexico go through the procedure. A detail of two or three Guardsmen would enter a structure, breaking in if necessary, and search each room. Knowing strange things happened in a flood, they looked in closets and behind furniture. Most bodies were found in bedrooms or attics. The stench was unmistakable, so using one's sense of smell was often the best method to accomplish the gruesome mission.

Once the house was cleared, a large *X* was spray painted on or near the front door, indicating it had been searched. In the top quadrant, they put the date, and in the left quadrant, they marked some indication of who searched it—in this case, "NMNG" and their unit number. The right quadrant indicated any hazards future teams should be aware of such as unstable stairwells or missing floors. If any bodies were found, the information about their location was put in the bottom quadrant.

The searchers did not remove the bodies; that was left to the DMART teams.

Some houses had numerous markings. Animal rescue teams adopted the same system, so there were *X*s marked as "SPCA," and the bottom quadrant might say "1 dead dog" or "1 cat under house, left food 9/18." It led to confusion, so close attention was required.

A loud shout came from the house, followed by cursing. Buford unfastened his service pistol just in case, although he had a fair idea what had happened.

Sure enough, two guardsmen stumbled out the front door, one of them falling to his knees and vomiting in the gray-brown grass.

Buford slipped on the surgical mask hung around his neck as the telltale, god-awful stench followed the men outside.

"All right," cried the leader of the detail, "who opened the refrigerator?"

The men at first claimed it was an accident. Under the glare of their commanding sergeant, they admitted they had opened the appliance on a beer bet of who could take the stink the longest. They had no idea what food locked in a sealed container in ninety-degree heat for two months would turn into, and through their stupidity, they found out.

No sympathy was felt for the retching privates. The sergeant ordered them to complete the inspection. The two sad sacks trudged back into the foul structure. Buford grinned from behind his mask.

At least it wasn't a body, he thought.

"Whoa!" cried Mack from behind him. "Are you through here, sir?"

"Yeah. Let's get back to the staging area." He climbed back in the Humvee.

"Two more days and we're outta here."

"Can't be too soon for me, Mack."

Carrie, I'm coming home!

Thursday, October 13: Lafayette

"NEW YORK."

"New York City? You must be crazy-out-your-mind, woman. I'm not having any daughter-in-law of mine livin' in New York City."

"Watch your lip, old man."

"I'd rather watch yours. Heeheehee."

"Knock it off, Dad. Don't worry; we're not going to New York City or Los Angeles. Too big. Too much competition."

"Well, where then? Mari, what's on the list so far?"

Chris and Marianne sat in the living room with Mr. and Mrs. Breaux, discussing the younger couple's future. "All right, we've got Atlanta, Chicago, Memphis, San Francisco, Miami, Dallas, and Denver."

"What about Branson?" Mr. Breaux asked.

"Dad," said Chris, "Mari's a little young for the Branson crowd. We want to build up her career not bury it."

Mrs. Breaux put up a finger. "Well, in that case, there's Orlando. Lots of young people go to Orlando."

Marianne shook her head. "People don't go to Disney World to hear a blues singer."

"Maybe you should change genres, *chere*," advised Mr. Breaux. "How about Nashville? Country music's hot nowadays."

"I know, and they're doing some great stuff, but it's not me."

Chris cleared his throat. "We also need to find a place where I can get a job. A university-run hospital or mental health facility would be ideal."

"Austin?"

Marianne nodded. "Small, but…yeah."

Mr. Breaux glanced over. "I think we've got enough for now. Let's talk this over. Y'all need a place where Chris can work and grow in his profession while Marianne builds her singing career. Looks to me we've got us some good places. Anything stands out good or bad, Mari?"

Marianne thought about it. "Memphis is known for the blues. Chicago, too."

"Both of them are airline hubs. We can get out of there for gigs easy," Chris noted.

"What about you, Chris?" asked his mother.

"Well, my specialty is not children's care, but St. Jude Children's Research Hospital is in Memphis. Really great behavioral medicine department. As for Chicago, there's the University of Chicago Medical Center and Northwestern Memorial. My friend Dr. Segura has some contacts in the field. He can see if there are any openings." He turned to Marianne. "What about you, Mari? What's best for your career?"

She bit her lip as she took her husband's hand. "I can get restarted in either place—whichever has an opening."

"Okay, I'll call Segura in the morning."

Chapter 27

Saturday, October 15
K plus six weeks: Chackbay

The congregation crowded into the pews on a fine, dry October day at Our Lady of Prompt Succor Catholic Church in Chackbay. Adam "Bubba" Teresina, uncomfortable in a rented tuxedo, and Mary Boudreaux, properly resplendent in her white wedding gown, stood before the altar, their attendants on either side, the bridesmaids in silver and crimson, as the priest recited the Liturgy of the Sacrament of Marriage.

Mary handed her flowers to Elizabeth as the priest turned to Bubba and had him repeat the words of the vows.

"I, Adam, take you, Mary, for my lawful wife…"

Elizabeth saw William smile as Bubba stumbled over the familiar phrases. It was then Mary's turn to recite the vows, and she did so in a clear, strong voice. Never had she seen Mary so aglow.

The priest raised his hands in benediction. "You have declared your consent before the Church. May the Lord in His goodness strengthen your consent and fill you both with His blessings. What God has joined, no one must now divide." He accepted two rings from Bubba's brother, his best man. "Lord, bless and consecrate Adam and Mary in their love for each other. May these rings be a symbol of true faith in each other and always remind them of their love. We ask this through Christ our Lord."

The congregation all responded with "Amen" as the couple placed the rings upon each other's hand. Mary reclaimed her flowers from Elizabeth.

The priest then moved to his right, to stand before the *other* couple before him. "William and Elizabeth, have you come here freely and without reservation to give yourselves to each other in marriage?"

"I have," they said together.

William and Elizabeth calmly recited their commitment to each other, both pleased and surprised to be there. When they mentioned their desire to have as short an engagement as possible in the wake of the storm, it was Mary's suggestion to share her wedding day. She and Bubba were able to convince an initially unwilling Elizabeth and William that they did not look upon the participation of another couple on their special day as anything other than an exercise in family affection and Christian love.

The two weeks following the decision had been a firestorm of work. The cooperation from the local parish priest had been secured after a special dispensation was granted from the bishop in Houma. Family and friends were contacted. Gina Darcy was able to drive in from Auburn, and Richard Fitzwilliam got a day off from work, but the still-grieving Katzes sent their regrets from Maryland.

Elizabeth's bone-white dress was pretty and flattering even though it was off the rack from a Baton Rouge shop. It was certainly not the handmade extravaganza most people would expect the bride of William Darcy to wear. The florist was able, at the last minute, to make a second bouquet to match Mary's. William wore his tuxedo.

The statement of intention completed, the priest said, "Since it is your intention to enter into marriage, join your right hands and declare your consent before God and His Church." It was Mary's turn to hold Elizabeth's flowers.

William hardly needed the prompting as his dark eyes were fixed upon Elizabeth. "I, William, take you, Elizabeth, for my lawful wife, to have and to hold, from this day forward, for better, for worse, for richer, for poorer, in sickness and in health, until death do us part."

Elizabeth's smile could have lit up all of Chackbay. "I, Elizabeth, take you, William, for my lawful husband, to have and to hold, from this day forward, for better, for worse, for richer, for poorer, in sickness and in health, until death do us part."

There was a slight pause as Marianne Breaux cried out in joy, unable to resist celebrating this final stage of her dear friend's odyssey.

The priest continued, accepting rings from Chris Breaux, who was standing for William. "Lord, bless and consecrate William and Elizabeth in their love for each other. May these rings be a symbol of true faith in each other and always remind them of their love. We ask this through Christ our Lord."

If anything, the "Amen" was louder than before.

The nearby fire station housed the reception, and William found it amusing that the Fitzwilliam family was sitting on metal folding chairs, nibbling on finger sandwiches. Jane Bingley and Carrie Buford, both too far along in their pregnancies to take part in the dancing, sat in a corner, keeping an eye on their children and talking up a storm, thick as thieves. John Buford, back from New Orleans, talked at the bar with Chuck Bingley and a few of the locals. Mr. and Mrs. Boudreaux were on the dance floor with a group that included Chris, Marianne, and the Breauxes, shaking it to an Elvis Presley song. Kit Boudreaux loudly begged the DJ to play some Gwen Stefani. Bubba and Mary, hand in hand, made the rounds while Elizabeth introduced Gina to some of her old school friends.

For his part, William, his back against the wall and a glass of champagne in hand, talked to his Uncle Edward as he surreptitiously watched another relative.

"Fitz looks bad, Ed."

Richard Fitzwilliam, sitting at a table with his parents and aunt, indeed looked like the world had punched him in the stomach.

Ed glanced at his other nephew. "This thing with Olivia is tearing him up. But what did he expect? Did he really think she was going to leave their daughter with her folks in Atlanta and come back to live on a boat with him in New Orleans? Her job is gone, the schools are closed, the city is just now crawling back onto its feet, and their house is trashed. Richard's being unrealistically stubborn."

"She still wants him to move to Atlanta?"

"She's suggested he do that and get a law-enforcement job there or take a position with DGS outside of Louisiana. The bottom line is she wants him out of the NOPD and out of the city."

"And he says no."

Ed frowned. "He says he'll think about it, which is the same thing."

William sighed. "Want me to talk to him again?"

Ed put a hand on his shoulder. "No, this is your wedding day. Richard and Olivia have to solve their own problems. Your attention should be on more pleasant subjects." He took a sip of his scotch and soda. "You sure you don't want to use the jet for you and Elizabeth to go somewhere?"

He smiled. "We both have work on Monday. Lizzy and I have talked about it. We've got the rest of our lives to travel."

At that moment, the subject of their conversation approached. "Hey, handsome. Buy a girl a drink?" Elizabeth asked as she slid an arm around her husband. William handed his wife his glass as Gina hugged her uncle. They talked for a few minutes until the music changed to Roy Orbison's version of "Pretty Woman." That brought Kit over in a huff.

"Gina, come with me," she demanded as he took the coed's hand in hers. "We've got to talk this guy into playing some real music!" William grinned as the two young ladies made their way through the dancers to berate the DJ.

"Care to dance, Mrs. Darcy?" he whispered.

Elizabeth looked at him coquettishly. "Why, Mr. Darcy! How is it I always seem to be dancing with you?"

As he pulled her onto the dance floor, he answered. "If I have my way, you'll be dancing with me for the rest of your life."

"I'm counting on it."

The two couples adjourned to separate rooms in the back of the hall and changed into their going-away clothes. William and Elizabeth were quick and intercepted Bubba and Mary before they reentered the hall.

William offered an envelope. "Lizzy and I want you to have this. It's our wedding gift to you."

"What?" cried Mary. "You already gave us those lovely crystal candleholders."

Elizabeth smiled. "This is a thank you for today. Open it."

Bubba was confused as he handed the paper from the envelope to Mary. "What is this?"

William and Elizabeth grinned as Mary stared at the paper. A bit quicker on the uptake, she cried out, "This is a credit notice from the resort in Gatlinburg! They've refunded our deposit!"

"What? Did they cancel our reservation?" Bubba took the paper back as Mary stared at the other couple. "Paid in full? What do they mean by paid in full?"

Mary stared at her sister. "You *didn't*!"

Elizabeth laughed. "We did."

William put an arm around Elizabeth's shoulders. "Your honeymoon trip to Gatlinburg is all paid for—room, meals, everything. You just go and have a great time."

Bubba spurted, "This is too much! We can't accept this!"

Elizabeth took Mary's hand in hers. "Please let us do this. We can never thank you enough for sharing today with us."

William nodded. "Use your money towards the down payment on your first house."

Realization struck Mary and Bubba. They had decided to put off starting a family until they could afford a house. This gift just moved that dream a lot closer.

"You make it impossible to say no," Mary said.

"Good, then you won't." William's laughter turned into a grunt as Bubba pulled him into a bear hug. Mary and Elizabeth were tearing up in each other's arms.

"Look what you two did to my make-up." Mary giggled as she wiped the tears from her face after she kissed William. "Lizzy, help me repair this damage."

St. Charles Parish

BACK AT DANSEREAU PLANTATION THAT EVENING, ELIZABETH AND William lay intertwined, their bedroom lit by a dozen candles, their skin glistening from the delightful labor of consummating their vows.

"So long," William murmured, propped on one arm. "So long we've been on this journey. Seven years. Over seven years since I first saw you at that smoker at the Alpha Iota House. Seven years since I fell in love with you."

Elizabeth's eyes went wide. "You fell in love with me at first sight?"

He gently brushed back the hair from her face. "I didn't know it at the time. Heck," he chuckled," I fell in lust with you at Fat Harry's a few weeks before, watching you eat those cheese fries."

She gently slapped his chest. She had heard this part before. "You and cheese fries. Besides, I thought it was my great rack."

He laughed. "I forgot about that remark! And, yes, you do have a magnificent rack." He showed his appreciation by kissing each nipple.

Elizabeth grew thoughtful, her eyes falling to the plain platinum band next to her engagement ring. "I had no idea. I was so hateful to you at school."

"Shush. We've already gone over that. Besides, how were you to know? I fought my attraction to you all semester, thinking you were too young for me. I was a moron." He caressed her face. "You are everything I have ever wanted."

She took his hand and kissed the palm. "It's terrifying in a way, isn't it? This needing, this requirement of another person's presence to assure your own happiness? William, never leave me. Never."

"Don't worry, Mrs. Darcy. Riptide and I will always be watching out for you. You'll never get rid of us."

She followed his eyes to the Beanie Baby of the Tulane mascot, the first gift she received from William so many years ago. As usual, it stood sentinel over her jewelry box. "Well then, if Riptide's here, I've got nothing to worry about!" She drew a fingertip provocatively down his chest. "Though he does a lousy job of protecting me from being ravished by a certain insatiable beast."

"You've any complaints?"

She gave him a slow, sexy smile. "Not if he does it right—and right now!"

William's grin widened. "I think I can handle that." He took his beloved bride into his arms, and the two of them made love again.

As they lost themselves in a tempest of feelings and desire, a completely different sort of tempest was brewing in the Caribbean Sea south of Cuba.

Chapter 28

Sunday, October 16
K plus six weeks: Covington

The Bingleys had a surprise awaiting their return from Chackbay. After almost two months, cable television and Internet service had been restored. The return of Internet was the more welcomed. Chuck could job search, and Jane could e-mail without having to wait in line for a computer at the parish library. Hailey was overjoyed at the return of Nickelodeon, Cartoon Network, and Sesame Street, but her parents' joy at the return of television was muted.

During their forced withdrawal from the boob tube, The Bingleys grew used to quiet conversation or silent reading. Occasionally, they played a favorite DVD, but the only other times they used the TV after Chuck hooked up the rabbit ears was to watch the local news and weather, barely visible on the snowy screen.

Watching the news clearly for the first time that night, they learned of Tropical Storm Wilma.

THE RULE OF THREE IS A PRINCIPLE IN WRITING AND suggests things that come in threes are inherently funnier, more satisfying, or more effective than other numbers of things. There was nothing funny or satisfying about the 2005 hurricane season. Never before had there been three major hurricanes in the Gulf of Mexico in a single year.

Wilma grew at an astonishing rate as it moved northwesterly towards Mexico's Yucatan Peninsula. It almost exploded with power, moving quickly from a tropical storm to a Category 5 horror. The central pressure dropped in thirty hours to 882 mb, the lowest of any Atlantic storm in recorded history. By October 19, sustained winds were clocked at 185 mph.

Somewhat fortunate for the people of Cozumel and Cancun, the inner eye dissipated and underwent an eyewall replacement cycle just before it made landfall on the twenty-first. The Cat 4 monster's 150 mile per hour winds still caused considerable damage. It slowed down significantly and wrecked the coast for nearly two days. Amazingly, there was only one confirmed death.

The people of the Gulf Coast, still reeling from the one-two punch of Katrina and Rita, worried about their neighbors. But truth be told, they were even more concerned about what Wilma would do once it entered the Gulf.

Thanks to an upper level trough high in the atmosphere and shearing winds closer to the surface, the storm stabilized at Cat 3, 125 mph strength as it dashed across the Gulf at over twenty-five knots. It slammed into Cape Romano, Florida, twenty miles south of Naples, at 0630 EDT on October 24 with an eight-foot storm surge. Wilma crossed the state in less than five hours, dumping as much as nine inches of rain and killing thirty-six people. It entered the Atlantic Ocean near Jupiter, still generating winds in excess of 110 mph. Wilma raced off to the northeast, transitioned into an extra-tropical cyclone, and its remnants were absorbed by another storm off Canada on October 27.

The government moved as quickly as it could to help those affected by the latest calamity to strike the United States. Resources, already stretched to meet the needs of Katrina and Rita, were brought to the breaking point.

Every year, the hurricane forecasters have a roster of twenty-one names ready for the season. They almost never use the last few, so there are no names past "W." But 2005 was not like any other year. Vince and Wilma were the first named "V" and "W" storms ever in the Atlantic basin. When a twenty-second tropical storm developed on October 22, it was named Alpha. Four days later, Hurricane Beta formed near Nicaragua.

Saturday, October 29
K plus eight weeks: Baton Rouge

NOW THAT WILLIAM WAS PERMANENTLY BACK IN NEW ORLEANS, Elizabeth was assured of seeing him every night, which was about the only time she could see him. EDNO continued their work, but the cash reserves of the non-profit were draining fast. Expenses had to be reduced, and the staff took a healthy pay cut.

It wasn't enough. Elizabeth and Carl Eden talked it over and together decided that Elizabeth would take unpaid leave from EDNO to sign up as a contractor for FEMA. Firms like Fluor, CDM, and others secured enormous federal contracts and paid outrageous sums—fifty dollars an hour or more, depending on experience. Contractors were expected to work sixty hours a week during their contracted period, lasting from sixty to ninety days.

The rules were strange. Elizabeth received fifty dollars an hour for the first fifty hours, but overtime was eighty percent of pay, or forty dollars an hour. An average week was $2,900 before taxes. She was to work exactly sixty hours—no less and no more unless authorized. They did not want to pay for the use of a personal car but insisted one was to be rented because it was easier to keep track of expenses. FEMA offered no benefits, but Elizabeth was now covered under William's health insurance policy with DGS.

On her two-week anniversary, Elizabeth maneuvered her rented Hyundai Sonata around the jammed parking lot of the FEMA Joint Field Office in Baton Rouge. Located in the old Goudchaux's Department Store, a massive building taking up most of a city block, the JFO housed over nineteen hundred government employees. That many hands caused a lot of confusion, and it was up to contractors to make sense out of it.

Elizabeth showed her photo ID to the security guard. With a government-issued laptop in her briefcase and a government-issued cell phone clipped to her waist, she made her way to her cubical. It wasn't long before Charlotte came by. Her former EDNO co-worker had accepted the same deal as Elizabeth.

"Guess what I just heard, Lizzy?" she said in a loud whisper. "You know all those mobile homes FEMA has in Arkansas? Well, the agency won't place them in New Orleans."

"Why not?"

Charlotte made herself comfortable in a side chair. "You're gonna *love* this. The Stafford Act forbids any permanent government property to be placed in a flood zone. Those mobile homes are considered unmovable, permanent government property according to federal regulations. So because of federal law, no government-paid-for mobile homes will be placed in New Orleans or almost anywhere in South Louisiana!"

Elizabeth thought she had grown impervious to the inanities of the federal government, but she was wrong. "Oh, my God. I can't believe it. Wait! What about all those travel trailers?"

"That's the best part. Those are *movable*, according to the regs. Apparently, if they're twenty-three feet long, they're movable, but if they're forty feet long, they're 'immovable,' even though they're both on wheels!"

Elizabeth put her head into her hands. "Great. The government spends millions to buy housing for people who need it and then won't use it. What a country!"

Charlotte got back on her feet. "Every time we try to do

something, that damn Stafford Act gets thrown in our face! Why doesn't anybody do something about it? You know, suspend it or something!"

Elizabeth sat back. "That's a good question. I have no idea. I wish Carrie Buford were here. She might have a clue."

"Her baby's about due, isn't it?"

"Yes, just like Jane."

Some in Congress saw the insanity of the Stafford Act. They tried to suspend all or part of it, but they got nowhere with their colleagues.

The unions got much better service. Congress forced the president to rescind his suspension of the Davis-Bacon Act, assuring the rebuilding of public property would be done at *prevailing wages*, which was government gobbledygook for union wages. The rebuilding would cost far more, true, but it was most important to keep priorities straight. An election year was coming, and the politicians' war chests needed donations from the building trades.

Chapter 29

Monday, November 7
K plus two months: Covington

Chuck replaced the phone gently into its cradle, careful not to dash it into a hundred pieces. *Damn that mortgage company!*

The Bingleys were fortunate that their insurance company had processed their claim and delivered a check into their hands. Many of their friends and neighbors were still fighting with their insurers, and the stories they had heard on TV about insurance companies denying claims wholesale were beyond shocking.

The Bingley's problem was their mortgage company, Acme National. The $25,000 insurance settlement check was made out to both the homeowner and the mortgage holder, and all parties needed to sign it. Chuck and Jane had signed the check, as instructed, and overnighted it to Acme National. They were told Acme National would endorse and return it.

They had not. Chuck was furious. He had been misled if not outright lied to.

Instead, he learned the money had been placed in an escrow account, and paperwork had to be completed before the money would be released. In effect, Acme National turned the Bingley's money into a reimbursement account. Once Chuck could prove he made repairs on the house and submitted the invoices and forms, a draw on the account would be done. The company maintained the $25,000 belonged to the Bingleys, not Acme National, and this system was for their benefit.

How was Chuck supposed to get a contractor to fix his daughter's window if he had nothing to pay him? Acme National claimed he should have received an information packet as well as an initial reimbursement check for five thousand. After repeated telephone calls, Acme National admitted indeed nothing had been mailed. They blamed an overwhelmed mailroom. When suggested they direct deposit the funds into the Bingley's bank account, Acme National said they would once the proper forms were filed.

They had promised to fax those forms to Chuck three days ago. So far, nothing. Chuck had just gotten off the phone with yet *another* supervisor, who apologized for the inconvenience and promised to make things right.

Acme National made it clear they needed receipts for *all* work, but T.B. and his people from B&B had removed the tree and cleared the timber in Chuck's yard for only fuel costs. To get the fair portion of the settlement for the house and tree damage, Chuck needed a receipt from T.B. He knew his father-in-law would draw one up at his request, but it was just one more pain-in-the-ass thing that needed to be done.

Chuck sat with his head resting in one hand. At least Acme National had suspended payments on the mortgage until February. It was a help but not enough. Money was tight, the job search had little to show for it, the mortgage company was being difficult, and Jane was on maternity leave, the baby due at any time. The same couldn't be said for his sister.

Carrie had her baby last night. I wonder if we can run over to Baton Rouge and see her and—

"CHUCK!"

Chuck jumped to his feet. He had heard *that* cry from Jane twice before. Any time was *now.*

Tuesday, November 8

"HI, JANIE, IT'S CARRIE."

"Carrie! How're you feeling?"

"Fine, just settling in. They released us from the hospital yesterday."

"Chuck told me. So...how's the baby?"

"Beautiful. John's right here, holding our little Mackenzie. She already has her daddy wrapped around her finger."

"Aww, I'll bet."

"So, how're you doing?"

"Tired."

"And the baby? Does she have a name yet?"

"She does. Miss Joanne Caroline Bingley."

"Caroline? Oh, Jane, you didn't have to do that!"

"Yes, I did. Remember 'Mackenzie Jane'?"

There was a laugh on the other end. "Tell me what she looks like."

"Well, she's seven pounds, eight ounces, and nineteen and a half inches long. She has a full head of hair, and she's very pretty."

"How long were you in labor?"

"Seven hours—about the same as you."

"Was Chuck there?"

"The whole time, just like the first two."

"I'm so happy John was here for Mackenzie. It meant so much to both of us. When are they sending you home?"

"Tomorrow." Jane looked up as the door to the room opened. "Carrie, they're bringing in Joanne now for a feeding."

"I'll let you go. Call me as soon as you get home, okay?"

"I will. Bye."

CHUCK BINGLEY PUNCHED THE BUTTON ON THE COFFEE VENDING machine, thinking about his new daughter and hoping Brett wouldn't be too disappointed that the new baby wasn't a boy.

"Chuck? That you?"

"Tim! How're you doing?" Chuck recognized Tim Lefoy, an acquaintance from the banking industry. The two men shook hands. "What are you doing here?"

"My dad's in for some tests. I just finished visiting. And you?

Jane have the baby?"

"Yeah, a little girl."

"Congratulations." The two talked for a minute about their maternity experiences until Lefoy changed the subject.

"Look, Chuck, it's good I ran into you. You know my dad retired from Bayou State Bank, and I got kicked upstairs."

"Yeah, I heard about that." Bayou State was a fast-growing local bank on the North Shore.

"Well, I can't run the bank *and* the lending department as fast as we're growing—especially since we're trying to do more corporate lending. I heard you were available."

"Who told you?"

"Tom Bennett. Are you available?"

"Yeah, I am."

"Great!" Lefoy handed Chuck one of his business cards. "I know you've got stuff to do. Give me a call in a couple of days, and we'll get together to talk about it."

Chuck could hardly speak. "Thanks, Tim. I… Thanks, buddy."

"Don't mention it. Gallic's a bunch of assholes. You're well outta there. I gotta run. See you."

"Right. I'll call you." He pocketed the card.

"Good. Maybe we can do Friday?" Lefoy said as he backed out of the waiting room.

"Sure." Chuck waved as Lefoy turned the corner and then he collapsed into a chair. He pulled the card out again and stared at it.

We came in the hospital to have a baby, and we might be leaving it with a job offer.

The receptionist at the front desk looked up at his "*YESS*!"

Monday, November 21: Faubourg Marigny

"Do you want to pack this, dear?" asked Mrs. Dashwood.

Marianne looked over from the cabinet. Her mother was holding up some strange kitchen implement. "I don't know, Mom. What is it?"

"Don't you know? It was in your drawer."

"I think it came with the house. The previous owners didn't clean out everything. Just throw it out."

The unusual-looking device was tossed into the trashcan with a clunk, and Mrs. Dashwood went back to work. She had come down to New Orleans with Margaret during the Thanksgiving holiday to help Marianne pack for the move to Chicago. Chris was there now, working in the psychiatric department of Northwestern Memorial Hospital, a job secured through the efforts of Dr. Segura. He was planning to return to New Orleans the day after tomorrow to help complete the packing. The moving truck was due on the Saturday after Thanksgiving.

Marianne was busy trying to put her life in the Crescent City into as few boxes as possible. The apartment in Chicago, which cost them an arm and a leg, was a lot smaller than the shotgun house Marianne was leaving behind.

At least it had sold. An institutional broker, looking for a place close to Downtown, had bought it. The real estate market in the city was generally non-existent except for very particular properties. That Marianne's little six-room house had survived the flood and the looting without a scratch made the place worth its weight in gold. She was embarrassed to be making a profit on the deal with the hospital covering all of their moving expenses.

Marianne focused on the job at hand, trying not to think too much. It was exciting in a way to move to a new place, especially somewhere as different as Chicago. America's Second City was a thriving center of music and arts with a public transportation network that placed the whole city at their fingertips. She was pleased that one of her bandmates agreed to move to the Windy City too. He had friends there, and together with Chris, they would rebuild the combo. Her husband had agreed to join the band.

Marianne was leaving behind an entire way of life. She dearly loved her little house, so close to the French Quarter. It was the place she and Chris had decided to live before the storm, so the living room was filled with boxes from Chris's apartment as well, all set to be shipped up north.

Chris had promised they would move back south as soon as they practically could, and Marianne knew he had every intention of keeping his word. The painful part was that, when they did come home, it wouldn't be to this one.

That pain was nothing like leaving their friends, especially Elizabeth and William. What made it bearable was that the separation was only temporary. One day she and Chris would be back to stay.

"Hey, Mari," Margaret called out from the bedroom, "are you taking these shoes?"

Marianne set down the drinking glass she had been wrapping in newspaper. "What do you mean, am I taking my shoes? Of course, I'm taking my shoes."

"Oh! Well, I thought with all the snow up in Chicago, you wouldn't need these open-toe heels."

"Open-toe heels? Are you talking about my four-inch red pumps?" She gave her mother a look as she began to make her way around the boxes to the bedroom. "Margaret, get your cotton-picking hands off my Stuart Weitzmans!"

Thursday, November 24: St. Charles Parish

USUALLY, WHEN TWO FAMILIES IN SOUTH LOUISIANA MERGE DUE to a wedding, one side of the family is at war with the other as to where the holiday dinners would be held. There wasn't a mother who didn't want Thanksgiving, Christmas, and Easter at their house and not at the in-laws. Such was the constant stress under which the Charles Bingley family often found themselves.

When Lizzy Boudreaux became Elizabeth Darcy, no one realized it would be Chuck and Jane's salvation. William and Elizabeth simply made it clear that, since Dansereau Plantation was the largest and most centrally located of the houses in the Darcy/Boudreaux/Bingley/Buford families, there would be an open invitation to hold all family dinners at the Darcy estate. A huge dining room, an enormous back yard, a state-of-the-art kitchen, and the talents of Mrs. Reynolds to assist in the cooking effectively eliminated all but the most intrinsic arguments. Catherine Bingley didn't like the idea of being out of control, but at least she wouldn't have to journey down to the wilds of Chackbay and *that woman's* house.

The downside: this first Thanksgiving turned into perhaps the biggest potluck meal in St. Charles Parish history. It didn't matter that William and T.B. were frying a twenty-pound turkey; as far as the Bufords were concerned, it wasn't the holidays without one of John Buford's smoked masterpieces. Bubba and Mary brought a ham, and among the families, there were four styles of stuffing. Sweet potatoes with pecans, Spinach Madeline, corn on the cob, and green bean casserole. Crescent rolls and garlic French bread. Gumbo and rice and salad. Gravy and cranberry and pepper jelly. Cases of wine. There was enough food to feed the 82nd Airborne.

After a scrumptious Thanksgiving meal, the survivors staggered out of their chairs to find a place to collapse. If overeating was a sign of success, this meal had been a triumph. No one was ready to take on the three pumpkin pies, two pecan pies, and one red velvet cake waiting on the sideboard. Gina and Kit disappeared upstairs to burn up the Internet chat lines while the ladies brewed coffee and talked. The men sat in brotherly discomfort before William's big screen TV to watch the Denver Broncos beat the Dallas Cowboys in overtime.

Tropical activity decelerated slowly during the record-setting year of 2005. Gamma was born on November 15 and Delta on the twenty-third. Epsilon became a hurricane on December 2, two days after the official close of the season.

Everyone thought it was over, but Mother Nature had one more surprise. Tropical Storm Zeta became the final storm of the season when it formed on December 30, six hours short of tying the record set in 1954 by Hurricane Alice as the latest-forming named storm in a season. Zeta dissipated on January 6, 2006, the longest-lived January tropical cyclone in Atlantic basin history.

The meteorologists and climatologists immediately began arguing about what it all meant. The meteorological community claimed tropical activity occurred in cycles. They predicted there would be more named storms in the years to come than had been the norm over the last few decades. The climatologists were more alarmist. They pointed to the record-making activity as proof that global warming was changing the climate forever. Man's foolishness was to blame for New Orleans' destruction, and it was only a matter of time before Miami, Houston, and New York suffered the same fate. Meteorologists weren't prepared to go that far, which caused the other side to accuse their brethren of being "global warming deniers," and therefore, unworthy of being regarded as scientists.

New Orleanians could not have cared less about the scientific catfight. They were too busy trying to rebuild their city and too worried about the slow pace of the repairs to the levees. After all, the Corps of Engineers was in change, and they did *such* a good job before.

No one was sorry to see the end of 2005.

Chapter 30

Friday, January 6, 2006
K plus four months

New Orleans started the New Year striving for normalcy as much as possible. With the damage to the tourist infrastructure, the Sugar Bowl could not be played in the Superdome, and the game was moved to Atlanta. Still, certain things were going to happen, come hell, high water, or FEMA.

To the shock of almost everyone outside of Louisiana, the city announced a Mardi Gras schedule. It was abbreviated: ten days of parades to end on Carnival Day, February 28. The rest of the country thought the Crescent City had gone mad. Perhaps it had, but it was a unique insanity that made perfect sense to the locals, who didn't care what people said on CNN.

Monday, January 16: Downtown

LIKE MOST CITIES, IT WAS A TRADITION IN NEW ORLEANS FOR THE mayor to give a speech on Martin Luther King, Jr. Day. Anna Elliot knew this speech was important to her boss. There was an election coming up later that spring, and the mayor need to reenergize his black constituents, reaffirming the poor and black would not be left behind in the *Come Back Home* recovery program.

Anna was troubled by the erratic behavior recently displayed by her boss. Just when he had settled ruffled feathers through long and blunt-talking private meetings with allies and the business community, he would stir things up again with strange, off-the-cuff remarks to reporters. The staff would have to do damage control time and again.

The mayor had not let any of his inner circle see the draft of this speech. That was not unusual, but today Anna was uneasy.

He moved to the microphone at City Hall and began by welcoming everyone in a spirit of love and unity.

Love and unity. Good, thought Anna as she began to relax. *A nice, boring speech, filled with platitudes would just be the—*

What?

"You know, when I woke up early this morning and I was reflecting upon what I could say that could be meaningful for this grand occasion," the mayor said. "And then I decided to talk directly to Dr. King. Now, you might think that's one Katrina post-stress disorder. But I was talking to him, and I just wanted to know what would he think if he looked down today at this celebration."

To Anna's increasing horror, the mayor continued his bizarre recanting of a conversation with a man long dead, putting words in Reverend King's mouth. It wasn't hyperbole; he was talking as if he had *actually* had this conversation.

"And as we think about rebuilding New Orleans, surely God is mad at America. He's sending hurricane after hurricane after hurricane, and it's destroying and putting stress on this country. Surely, he's not approving of us being in Iraq under false pretense. But surely, he's upset at black America, also."

"God is mad at America"? Oh no, boss, oh no!

Then, he spoke words that would flash across the country. "We ask black people: It's time. It's time for us to come together. It's time for us to rebuild a New Orleans, the one that should be a chocolate New Orleans. And I don't care what people are saying Uptown, or wherever they are. This city will be chocolate at the end of the day. This city will be a majority African-American city. It's the way God wants it to be. You can't have New Orleans any other way; it wouldn't be New Orleans."

Anna's brain would hardly register the mayor's call for the end of the renewed violence in the poorer sections of the city. She could focus on only one thought.

Oh, my God! You just insulted half of the population of the city. You just told the white folks to go to hell. You're calling to rebuild black New Orleans, not all *of New Orleans. Oh, my God!*

It would be days before Anna recognized the resolution she made at that moment. By the end of the week, her résumé would be in the hands of a recruiter. Anna Elliot had had enough. It was time to leave the madhouse.

Monday, February 6
K plus five months: Baton Rouge

There might have been billions of dollars appropriated for the rebuilding of the Gulf States, but the US Government wasn't releasing a penny until there were plans in place. It needed to know who would spend the money, on what, and who would be accountable. No plan, no check.

Mississippi had gotten the message long ago. Since the storm, its governor had called two special sessions of the Mississippi legislature before the regular session on January 3. Their plans either were in place or were being drawn up. The Mississippi federal delegation used this to their advantage, securing allocations for funding.

Louisiana cried foul, claiming theirs was the bigger disaster. The state was right, but it was also far behind their neighbors in planning. It wasn't until February 6 that the governor finally felt ready to call her own special session, the first since Katrina and Rita. Federal aid had to wait until Louisiana got its act together.

Downtown

"Welcome back, Lizzy!" cried Jan Hill.

The two shared hugs in the lobby of the EDNO offices. Elizabeth's FEMA deployment was over, and thanks to Carl Eden's non-stop fundraising, she was able to return to her communications job. Elizabeth was accosted by several of her co-workers as she made her way to her office.

Not all of the team was back. The new tighter budget meant positions would be eliminated or left unfilled. The woman who ran international business was let go. However, Louisiana DED hired her for a similar position with their international department, and the state pledged to work closely with EDNO on projects. A developer left to take a position with an outfit in Texas. Kaywanda Johnson was now living in Madison, Wisconsin.

With the storm came more shake-ups. EDNO suspended the rule on family members on the board of directors. No one pretended the move was for anything other than keeping William Darcy on the board. With the city's economic development department in shambles, EDNO moved forward independently, working even closer with the other EDOs in the region. Identifying and writing grants became the major effort of the organization, which meant the research arm worked overtime.

As Elizabeth sat in the familiar comfort offered by her office chair, she breathed a sigh of relief that her time inside of FEMA was done. While there, she put in sixty intense hours a week and more and had little to show for it. It wasn't as though the workers weren't trying. They stayed in constant contact with local officials, searching for funding, debris removal, and public infrastructure repair.

The fault lay in FEMA's structure. There was constant turnover in FEMA contractors; everyone's contract ended at different times, and replacements had to be brought up to speed. This wasted time. Responsibilities kept changing, but locals had no authority, and one couldn't get a straight answer out of anyone. Everything had to be "kicked upstairs."

Worse were the government employees borrowed from other agencies. Each government department had its own way of doing things, and each ingrained a particular bureaucratic culture into its employees' souls. These loaners knew they were short-timers, so there was little motivation to think outside the box. No FEMA-flexibility there.

FEMA proved more and less helpful than advertised. They threw around enormous amounts of money, but much of it came with a tangled web of strings attached. Elizabeth had never seen red tape like it. To receive assistance, governments—towns, cities, parishes, counties, and states—had to provide matching funds or, in the case of reimbursement, front the expense. Both rules were horrendous for locals. Everyone was broke, so even raising a modest 10% match was often out of the question. And with tax coffers dry, how could governments pay the bills, even if they were to be reimbursed? The money had to be borrowed, and the indebtedness would be a sword hanging over the heads of taxpayers who already had their world torn asunder.

Elizabeth could not handle talking to another distressed mayor about the red tape. She was happy to be out of FEMA.

There was a stack of calls for Elizabeth to return. As she reached for the first of the messages, the phone rang.

"Hey, honey, how's the first day back at work?"

Elizabeth smiled at the warm tones of her husband's voice. "Great. I've got a stack of calls to make, and I couldn't be happier."

"Okay, I won't keep you, but I just got off the phone with Gina. How're you for a half-dozen guests over Easter?"

"Half a dozen? Is Gina in a basketball team?"

"Gina's organizing a group of friends from Auburn to come down here over Spring Break and work for Habitat for Humanity. She volunteered Dansereau as a place to bunk."

"That's wonderful, Will! You won't mind having a house full of college students for a week?"

"Nah, we'll put them in another wing. We'll hardly know they're there. You okay with this?"

"Honey, it's your house—"

"It's our house, Elizabeth, and you're the boss of me, so it's your call."

Elizabeth laughed over the thought of anyone being the "boss of" William Darcy. "I'd be happy and proud to host Gina's friends. My folks are supposed to come over Easter Day, but we've got plenty of room."

"Okay. I'll let Gina know it's a go. Want me to pick up something for dinner?"

"What's open?"

"I don't know. There's got to be a po'boy shop open around here someplace."

"Mother's is open."

"Roast beef or Ferdi?"

"You know what I like."

"Yeah, plenty of gravy. See you tonight, honey."

Wednesday, March 8
K plus six months: Baltimore, Maryland

IF EMMA GLANCED OUT OF THE HIGH-RISE OFFICE WINDOW, SHE could have seen a bit of Baltimore's famed Inner Harbor. Instead, she sat quietly in the armchair before the desk, her sister, Irene, beside her, as their attorney finished her long-distance telephone call.

The woman made a few more notes before ending the call. "Thank you for your patience. That was my colleague in Louisiana, giving me an update on how things are moving under probate."

She glanced at her notes. "To recap, your late father had a last will and testament drawn up by his lawyer, now deceased. We know Mr. Weinberg's copy was in a file in the house and was destroyed in the flood. Apparently, the lawyer's copy was stored with the rest of his papers in a warehouse in New Orleans East, which also flooded.

"Therefore, we are moving forward settling your father's estate as though he died *intestate*, without a will, under Louisiana law. Mr. Weinberg's life insurance policy named Emma Katz and Irene Parker as beneficiaries, and that has been settled. What is not settled are the investments, bank accounts, and other assets belonging to Mr. Weinberg."

The two women listened, taking notes. "The estate devolved to his two living heirs: you two, Mrs. Katz and Mrs. Parker. Before any distribution can be made, the Louisiana court must have a final accounting of the assets and any claims against the estate before a judge will render a Judgment of Possession.

"We seem to have all the assets of the estate accounted for—investment accounts, retirement accounts, and a lot of land in Florida. The only debt against the estate is the house in New Orleans. Mr. Weinberg was a co-singer on the loan, and there is a balance due on the mortgage. We'll have to make some decisions on that."

Emma spoke up. "Ms. Fairfax, I think we can move on to discussing the house now."

Ms. Fairfax picked up a paper. "You had federal flood insurance, and the claim has been paid. Unfortunately, the maximum payout of $250,000 did not cover the balance left on the mortgage, and you owe a bit over $50,000."

"On a flooded shell," grumbled Irene.

"Uhh, yes. Your private insurance company, Standard Insurance, has rejected your claim, saying the policy is null and void because the house was flooded, which the policy does not cover."

"That's crazy!" Irene stormed. "George and Emma had hurricane coverage, and they were damaged by a hurricane!"

"You're correct, Mrs. Parker. According to the hurricane rider in the policy, Standard is supposed to cover damages caused by wind and other forces from a hurricane. It does not cover flooding from rainfall. The company claims the flooding was from storm surge. We dispute that. It is our argument that the roof damage on the house is clearly from high winds. Also, the levees and storm walls, built by the US Army Corps of Engineers, were damaged by those same forces, allowing in the flood waters. This is not an Act of God; rather, the damages were caused by foreseeable forces, which could have been and should have been accounted for.

"That's why we have joined in class-action suits against Standard Insurance. We are also joining a class-action suit against the Corps of Engineers and the Federal Government."

Emma looked up. "Where does that leave us with regards to Papa's estate?"

"I have to be frank with you, Mrs. Katz. While we have a reasonable argument against Standard Insurance, this could drag out for years and years, and even then, there is no guarantee of success. The suit against the government is a long shot. Usually, the government and its agencies are immune from lawsuits unless gross misconduct can be proved or if the Congress specifically allows itself to be sued.

"Misconduct is a huge mountain to climb. We would have to show the government knowingly and willfully built the levees in such a manner as to be a danger to the people of New Orleans and covered up that fact for years. Truthfully, I don't know if we can do it. However, by being a part of the class-action, we may be in line for damages if the government decides to settle rather than fight."

"That's unlikely, isn't it?"

"It is unlikely, Mrs. Katz."

Irene took a breath. "So, to sum things up, Papa's estate can't be settled until all claims against the estate are cleared. The major claim is the ruined house in New Orleans, and there's still a $50,000 claim on it from the mortgage company, even though the house is a total loss."

"Yes, that sums it up."

Emma thought back to the few items George had been able to recover from the house when he returned a few months ago. Not much: a vase, some figurines her mother used to collect, and most of the silverware. Anything made of paper—pictures, books, or paintings—was now garbage. All the furniture, rugs, clothes; practically everything else was gone. Emma had fled with her jewelry and important papers. Why Papa didn't allow Emma to keep his papers with hers was a mystery that would never be solved.

Money could never bring back any of it, especially the photographs, but it was still a stab in the heart that the insurance company would pay nothing for these irreplaceable losses.

"How much is Papa's estate worth? Just a ballpark figure," Irene asked Ms. Fairfax.

"Approximately $700,000 before expenses such as legal fees and estate taxes."

"All right, let's just settle the house and get this over with."

Emma turned to her sister. "Reenie, you know George and I don't expect this."

"Mrs. Parker, that is generous. You will be a part-owner in the house, and the lot it sits on, after this settles."

"I'm aware of that, and I'm fine with it." She reached over and grasped Emma's hand.

"Very well. I'll notify my colleague in Louisiana of your decision. I hope we can finally settle matters by the end of the month."

Thursday, March 23:
NOPD Headquarters

THE NOPD PUBLIC INTEGRITY DIVISION OFFICER STOOD AS RICHard Fitzwilliam entered the interview room. "Thank you for coming down, Captain. Please have a seat."

Fitzwilliam took his seat, throwing a hostile look at the PID. "All right, I've got things to do. Let's get this over with."

The officer sat and pulled out a file. "We're looking into the fatal shooting of one Gregory 'G-Daddy' Wickham on September—"

Fitzwilliam interrupted him. "What the hell for? That was a clean shooting!"

His interrogator looked at him over the file. "Was it?"

"You know it was! What is this, some kangaroo court?"

"Captain Fitzwilliam, we are attempting to conclude our investigation into this case, as we do anytime deadly force is used by an officer."

Fitzwilliam spoke without notes. "We were called to the site of a reported shooting at a USCG helicopter engaged in search and rescue. After setting up a command post and deploying personnel on hand, I observed the suspect on a second floor balcony, brandishing a weapon. In my opinion, we did not have time to wait for tactical backup. I made the decision to end the standoff as quickly as possible with the least risk to my people. The sniper was under my orders. I gave the green light to shoot."

The interrogator glanced at the file. "That's all right here: the after-action report, the shooter's affidavit, and the interviews with the other officers present. All consistent."

Fitzwilliam stared at the PID. "The shooter was cleared."

"In the preliminary investigation," the officer clarified. "We need to clear up a few things."

"Ask your questions. I've got nothing to hide."

"Good." He looked at the file. "You've known the victim for some time—years, in fact."

"Yeah. I busted him for distribution over eight years ago."

"You were known to have been on the lookout for him while you were in the Second District."

"Of course. I was working Narcotics."

"Wickham seemed to garner your special attention, though. There's the case about the Bertram/Smith killings in 1999."

"You know about that. It was all tied into taking down the traitor, Officer Jones."

"You also investigated the victim—"

"Perpetrator."

"—Wickham," the investigator conceded, "in conjunction with an alleged sexual assault at Tulane in 1999 without success."

"That's tied into the Bertram/Smith killings."

"You didn't find anything."

"I didn't find *enough*. There's a difference."

"Yes. Then there was the incident at Sacred Heart Academy. Your cousins were involved?"

Fitzwilliam eyed the man. "If you know about that, then you've read my reports. Known drug dealer hanging around an all-girls high school. I don't care if the target was my cousin or not. That deserves some attention."

"Right. Now, on to 2004 and the raid on a house in Gretna."

"Hang on a second," cried Fitzwilliam. "Are you going to review every case I've worked on?"

"Only if it concerns Wickham."

"What's the point?"

The investigator said nothing for a moment, playing with his pen. "How's your wife?"

"What?" Fitzwilliam stormed to his feet. "What the hell does that have to do with anything?"

"She's still in Atlanta with your daughter, isn't she? We've heard reports your marriage is having its troubles. I'm sorry about that—"

"Fuck you!"

"—but we are concerned as to your state of mind on the date of this incident."

Fitzwilliam placed his hands on the table and leaned down to stare the man in the eye. "Get to the point of all this."

The investigator returned the stare impassively. "I think you've been obsessed about this Wickham character. He's been a thorn in your side. He corrupted one of your people while you were working in the Second District, and he's had several run-ins with members of your extended family. You've been on the lookout for him for years, at the Second District and the Third, but you've failed every time you've tried to pin something on him. I think you finally got the opportunity to take him down forever and took it. You acted as judge, jury, and executioner."

Richard Fitzwilliam gazed at his tormentor with no emotion on his face for a minute. "Do you have any other questions for me?" he asked in an unnaturally quiet voice.

"I'll eventually prove this."

"You can try. Meanwhile, I have work to do. My job is to put bad guys in jail and keep the city's streets safe, not badger the men and women trying to police this hell hole." He leaned closer. "And before you ask, I sleep at night just fine. Do you?" Without waiting for a response, Fitzwilliam turned on his heel and left the interrogation room.

A moment later, the door opened again, admitting a tall man in a dark suit. "Well, what do you think?" the PID asked.

FBI Special Agent David Baugham rubbed one hand over his face. "What do I think? I think the bureau agreed to help you finish up this investigation, not to engage in the NOPD's version of waterboarding."

"You worked with Fitzwilliam and planned the raid in Gretna. You watched the interview through the one-way mirror. All we want are your impressions."

Baugham frowned. "If you're asking me if Fitzwilliam really wanted to get Wickham off the streets, I'd say yes. Was Wickham Public Enemy Number One? No. Is Fitzwilliam sorry he's dead? No. But name me a cop who doesn't have one case or one perp who doesn't stand out in his or her mind. It's natural.

"The grenades found in Wickham's Ninth Ward house link him to the 2004 Naquin murder in Houma and to the burned-out boat found floating in the Gulf. Thanks to Capitan Fitzwilliam, we can close those cases. We thank the NOPD for their assistance. Is there anything else you want of me?"

The PID rubbed his forehead. "Look, I think Fitzwilliam's been a good cop, all-in-all. But we can't have somebody go all cowboy and start taking the law into their own hands. He's been under tremendous pressure, and his marriage breaking up isn't helping matters. I've got to know if Fitzwilliam is a bigger threat to the department than he's worth. That's *my* job."

"And you're welcome to it. I know you've got several other cases against NOPD personnel, and the FBI is cooperating. But as for Captain Fitzwilliam, as of now, we are done. You get something more—let us know. Good day."

Chapter 31

Tuesday, April 5
K plus seven months: Washington, DC

Months after independent investigators had demonstrated the levee failures were not due to natural forces beyond intended design strength, the general in command of the US Army Corps of Engineers testified before the Senate Subcommittee on Energy and Water.

"We have now concluded we had problems with the design of the structure." He also claimed the Corps did not know of this mechanism of failure prior to August 29, 2005.

Except for the New Orleans *Times-Picayune*, the story got virtually no play in the national media. They were still busy talking about the mayor's Chocolate City speech—if they were talking about New Orleans at all.

Wednesday, April 13: Downtown

EDNO HELD A SMALL SUMMIT OF LOCAL BUSINESS LEADERS AT the Hilton Riverside. The purpose of the meeting was to report progress to date on rebuilding and to collect ideas on moving forward. Many of the major players in town attended, including DGS.

Elizabeth's job was hobnobbing with the press gathered outside the conference room. She spent most of her time with the local media, making sure they understood the importance of the event. The few representatives from the national media were just interested in photo opportunities. The number of out-of-towners had dropped dramatically since the beginning of the year; a few were known to periodically fly in to grab footage, interview a talking head or two, and quickly flee back home.

This was Elizabeth's last big event for EDNO. In June, she was leaving the economic development firm to run DGS's new Public and Community Relations Department. She was also joining the board of the Darcy Charitable Trust. William, who would become Chairman and CEO of DGS in December, would retain his seat on the EDNO board. DGS did not have rules against nepotism. Besides, Elizabeth was one of the best in town at her job.

Elizabeth was doing deep background with a friend from a local TV station when the conference doors opened. The TV cameramen were the most aggressive, shooting the participants as they left as though they were in a perp walk. One of the out-of-towners shoved his microphone into the face of a tall, young executive.

"Bryan Thorpe of Action NOW News! Can you tell us what the plans are for relieving the crippling unemployment in the city?"

Katrina had made Bryan Thorpe's career just as he had hoped. His bosses had given him a raise and approved a monthly report from New Orleans. His agent was talking to several cable outfits. It was just good timing that this shindig happened during Thorpe's latest trip back.

William Darcy looked at the reporter as though he were a cockroach that needed to be squished. "The press conference will be handled by Mr. Eden of EDNO. They're setting it up in the ballroom. Now, if you'll excuse me…" With that, he stalked off with a little wave at Elizabeth.

Thorpe's producer edged up to his talent. "Oh, no loss with that tight ass. I remember him from…" Justin Middleton's voice trailed off. "Lizzy? Is that you?"

Elizabeth frowned.

"Justin Middleton from the Loyola *VOICE*—remember?"

Her eyes grew wide. Middleton was the slimeball editor of her college newspaper who changed her story about the attack on

Marianne to slander William and the Darcy family. *Because of him, I nearly ruined my life—and William's too.*

"Justin." She greeted him with an insincere smile. "It's been quite some time. How long have you been in town?"

Justin grinned as he shook hands. "Just a day or so, this trip. We were here during the storm. Damn, you're looking great!" He glanced at her name badge, still bearing her maiden name. "You're with this business group?"

"VP of Communications with EDNO. And you?"

"TV producer with Action NOW News out of—"

"A-hem," interrupted Thorpe.

"Ah, yeah. This is Bryan Thorpe, our investigative reporter, and Sam Watson, cameraman."

Thorpe poured on the charm. "Pleased to meet you, Elizabeth. We've got some footage to shoot around here, but maybe we can all grab a drink later?" The smile he gave her made Elizabeth think it had been used with success in his career.

Elizabeth somehow stopped from laughing full into his face. "Sorry, but I have a previous engagement." *Like, for the rest of my life!* "But, here's my card if you need any more background information. You too, Justin."

Thorpe glanced at it. "Elizabeth Darcy."

Elizabeth had a few business cards printed with her married name. She saw no need to have a new badge made up, knowing she was leaving in two months.

Justin made a strange sound and switched his attention between his old college colleague and her business card.

"Darcy?" he finally managed. "*Darcy?* You mean—?" His mouth was flapping like a fish.

"That's right. *Mrs. William. Darcy.*" Smiling, she enunciated each word as though it was the most precious on earth.

"But...how did *that* happen?" Justin cried.

Elizabeth's eyes glowed with secret knowledge. "Let's just say I saw the light, Justin. Maybe one day you will, too. Now, if you would just follow me, the press conference is this way."

Saturday, May 20
K plus eight months: New Orleans

It is a facet of human nature that a sense of sympathy cannot be maintained for an indefinite period of time. Eventually, the hearts of some turned away from the Crescent City. Whether from jealousy, ignorance, selfishness, emotional exhaustion, or schadenfreude, people starting saying out loud what had been whispered before: New Orleans had it coming.

The eyes of the nation fell upon the spring mayoral election, and it seemed to justify this thinking. To say it was a circus was to insult show business. The mayor stood for re-election. Usually in the Bayou State, incumbents had a free ride. Not this time. Twenty-one men and woman registered to run against him, including former close supporters, some of whom broke with him over Chocolate City.

The diaspora had thrown the political make-up into turmoil. Only half the pre-storm residents had returned. Based on state law, a massive absentee voting operation was established to mail and process ballots. All a voter needed to do was request a ballot.

The mayor had won in 2002 by appealing to working-class people and the white business community, which he carried overwhelmingly. Some of the progressives doubted the mayor's "black credentials"; he received only twenty percent of the black vote. The taunts of Oreo ("black on the outside, white on the inside") were still fresh from four years prior.

Thanks to the Chocolate City Speech, he had alienated his biracial base. The mayor then played the race card. He brought in ACORN and the PUSH-Rainbow Coalition to demand satellite voting precincts be set up outside Louisiana. It didn't matter that doing so was strictly against Louisiana law. The people had to be heard!

The courts stubbornly followed the law. Special voting precincts were set up in border cities like Lake Charles and Shreveport. Civil rights groups organized bus trips for refugees to the polls.

Late on April 22, it was apparent the mayor had survived the first round, receiving thirty-eight percent of the vote in the open primary. The white lieutenant governor, brother of the senator and a fellow Democrat, got twenty-nine percent. A run-off between the two largest vote getters was set for May 20.

The pundits fell all over themselves predicting the mayor's doom. The lieutenant governor, a member of a famous and well-respected family, was firmly in the progressive wing of the Democratic Party, and he would likely get more than his share of the black vote. All the public opinion polls seemed to back up the belief the election was over.

Except it wasn't. After the run-off polls closed, the pundits were stunned to learn it wasn't even close. The mayor got eighty percent of the black vote, and enough of the business community, uneasy with the liberal lieutenant governor, decided to stick with the devil they knew. The mayor was re-elected by four thousand votes.

Outside the city, the country was apoplectic. *How stupid were those inbreeds? They re-elected the Chocolate City man? What's wrong with them?* they wondered.

All the New Orleans haters finally found their voice. It didn't matter that the flooding was the fault of the Corps of Engineers. It didn't matter that much of the billions Congress had earmarked for hurricane relief was tied up in red tape, red tape manufactured by Congress. It didn't matter that FEMA was a joke. It didn't matter that people were cheated by their insurance companies.

All that mattered was: *New Orleans had it coming!*

Chapter 32

Saturday, June 11
K plus nine months: Chicago, Illinois

The large crowd that jammed into in the funky, intimate Chicago nightclub was eerily silent as the haunting voice of Billie Joe Armstrong filled the darkness. The place was lit only by images flashing across a projection screen. This was a fundraiser for the Tipitina's Foundation, an organization founded to help evacuated musicians return to New Orleans. The music was part of a video presentation by *Times-Picayune* writer Chris Rose. Photos taken by the newspaper during and after Katina rolled on and on, forever changing the meaning of Green Day's "Wake Me Up When September Ends."

Marianne Breaux fought to keep her composure. She was looking into a scrapbook of all the pain in her heart. She had seen it all before—all the photographs, all the sights—not just Downtown and the Ninth Ward but all over the city. St. Bernard, Plaquemines, the North Shore, Gulfport, and Biloxi. Evacuation centers in Texas and other places. But in this setting, in a darkened club surrounded by strangers nine months and a thousand miles away from the disaster, the effect was more poignant than she could have believed. Again, a traitorous tear slipped down her cheek.

She felt a touch on her arm and heard a soft voice. "Honey, are you okay?"

Chris Breaux, bless him. Her husband always knew what she

needed and when she needed it. She could not lose control of her emotions. Not tonight.

"I'm fine, baby."

He squeezed her hand in reassurance. To distract herself, Marianne tore her attention away from the screen and gauged the audience's reaction. It was with savage satisfaction that she saw incredulous looks of horror and disbelief on the assembled. Chris Rose and his team had done a marvelous job. The crowd thought they had known what happened and had seen the devastation on TV. Realization that they truly had no idea the extent of the calamity was written all over their faces.

Yes, yes, look at it! Marianne thought. *This is what we went through.*

A light came up on Rose, sitting on the small stage next to a guitarist. Like a poetry reading from a bygone era, he read passages from his book, *1 Dead in Attic*, interspersed by accompaniment. Marianne had received the book as a gift from Elizabeth Darcy some months before, but she was spellbound hearing Rose recount his observations, both hilarious and heartbreaking, in his own voice.

The scenes on the screen moved from devastation and despair to reunion and rebuilding. The music changed as well to the unofficial anthem of the Crescent City, "When the Saints Go Marching In." Marianne could not stop herself from lightly clapping, keeping time, with a grin spread over her face.

The lights came up fully, and the manager stepped forward, encouraging everyone who wanted a copy of *1 Dead in Attic* signed by the author to buy them at a table set up against one wall. It was a fundraiser, and the entertainment would continue in a few minutes, but in the meantime, they were collecting donations.

That was Marianne's cue. A few minutes later, she was on stage to light applause. She began by thanking Chris Rose and his guitarist for their inspiring performance. She then got into the theme of her contribution to the evening.

"As you might be aware, I am a Katrina victim, too. My husband and I have relocated to the Chicagoland area, and I have just resumed my jazz singing locally." There were a few loud cheers and whistles from her fans in attendance. "Thank you! Glad y'all could make it!

"But tonight, we want to do something different, and the band has agreed to give it a go. My hubby, you see, is from Lafayette, and we thought we needed something a little more up-tempo to encourage you to give generously to the Tipitina's Foundation. So, here we go!"

Marianne's re-constructed combo included only her original keyboardist; everyone else was new. They were supplemented by two guest performers that night. One, a decent fiddler, struck up the familiar melody of the Mary Chapin Carpenter hit, "Down at the Twist and Shout." Marianne had her hair loose and flowing, and her flirty, red-and-white halter dress danced above her knees as she rocked with the Cajun-country beat. Her eyes were closed, and her face beamed with joy as she sang. She held the microphone in one hand, raising the other above her head as she spun around and around on her heels. It was infectious, and the dance floor was filled.

After the song was done and the applause died down, Marianne introduced her musicians, saving the guest accordionist for last. "The idea for tonight's music selection is rooted way back when I discovered, while packing to move here, a very interesting object among my husband's possessions. I asked him, 'Baby, what's this?'

"He looked at me like he had never seen it before. 'Don't you know what that is?' he shot back. Rolling my eyes, I told him, 'Yes, baby, I know what it is. Can you play this thing?' Then he said something really stupid. He said, 'Of course, I can!'

"Boy, was *that* the wrong thing to say! I drafted him right then and there! Ladies and gentlemen, on accordion, my husband, Dr. Christopher Breaux!"

Cheers followed.

"Our next song is very special to me for two reasons. First, it's almost the story of my relationship with my dear husband. And second, since it's a duet, I get to sing it with him! Usually, it's performed as 'Louisiana Woman, Mississippi Man,' but we've flipped it around, 'cause that's what we are."

Looking each other in the eye, the Mississippi Woman and the

Louisiana Man sang the old country-western song. They sang from the heart, unashamedly, as though the two of them were alone in the world.

Of course, the audience loved it.

Thursday, July 21
K plus ten months: Washington, DC

ANNA ELLIOT FELT LIKE HELL AS SHE TOOK ANOTHER SIP OF CHARdonnay. The hotel ballroom was comfortably filled with the usual crowd for Washington: politicians, military officers, staffers, socialites, and the ever-present lobbyists. The food was tasty, and the booze was plentiful.

She was thankful the senator had allowed her to use her tickets, she really was. She needed the break. Her co-worker, Tony Riviere, was off somewhere working the crowd. She should be doing the same, but she couldn't work up the enthusiasm. While the announced subject of the evening was to salute the federal responders to Hurricane Katrina, she knew most of the attendees were there for a far different purpose.

Only two months residing in the nation's capital and Anna had figured out the ropes. Washington was a town trying to throw off its Southern roots and become one the Great Cities of the World. It thought itself sophisticated, but to disillusioned Anna, the place was just tawdry and corrupt. Everyone in this room was on the make. They were looking for votes, looking for money, or looking for sex—sometimes all three at once.

Anna was tired of the bullshit. She had left New Orleans for a new start, working for Louisiana's senior senator, but found there was little difference between her new home and the old. She had no complaints about her boss. It was the town. She had left one sort of exploitation for another.

She probably shouldn't have worn her tight, deep-plunging gold gown, but damn it, after six months in the hell of Katrina, Anna wanted to feel pretty again! She knew the color was fabulous against her brown skin. Unfortunately, it attracted the wrong kind of attention. She came close to slapping one congressman's aide, and a senator old enough to be her grandfather practically fell into her cleavage.

She was looking about for a waiter with hors d'oeuvres when she heard someone call her name.

"Anna? Anna Elliot—is that you?"

Who could that be? She was new in town; no one knew her. She turned and saw a tall Coast Guard officer in full dress blues working his way through the crowd towards her. She did a double take.

"Freddy Wentworth? Oh my gawd—*Freddy!* Come here, big boy!"

The next moment, she squealed as she was crushed in his embrace. She was so excited she slipped back into her high school accent. "My lawd, it's good to see you! How've you been? I haven't seen you since Warren Easton!"

"I've been doing good, Anna." Wentworth grinned. "And you—man, you're looking fine! What are you doing here?"

A now-bubbly Anna explained she was working for the senator. "And you? I knew you were to go to the Coast Guard Academy." She giggled. "I guess you made it through."

Freddy Wentworth had been Anna's secret crush throughout high school, but the popular senior tight end for the Warren Easton Eagles had no time for the skinny freshman junior varsity cheerleader. And now, he was more handsome than ever! And no ring on his left hand!

She eyed the three gold stripes on the cuffs of his navy blue uniform jacket. "You're a commander?"

"Yeah, just got promoted and transferred to the Pentagon. I was flying helos, but I'm behind a desk now."

"You flew helicopters? Were you—" His face lost all expression and she *knew*. "You were there." It was not a question.

"Yeah." He blinked. "I thought you worked for the city."

"I did." She unconsciously put a hand over the scar at her hairline, a gift from the blown-out window at the Hyatt. She was mortified when Wentworth first turned his eyes to her hand, and then gently moved it. "Freddy, don't—"

"It's all right," his low voice rumbled. "We've all got scars, Anna."

The two survivors locked eyes, and a world of understanding flowed between them. Memories and feelings, both real and imagined. Rational and irrational. The terror and the pain. The relief and the guilt. They were the only ones in the room. It lasted but a moment, but it felt like a lifetime.

Wentworth broke the spell. "Uhh, can I get you a drink or something?"

Anna smiled and held up her half-filled glass. Wentworth chuckled. "Yeah. I'm usually more observant than that. You here with anyone?"

She shook her head. "The senator gave me her tickets. I'm solo. And you?"

His mouth twisted. "I'm one of the 'honored first responders,' giving all the rich and powerful the chance to see a hero. Hell, we were just doing our jobs." He turned to look at the throng. "Now it's time for them to do theirs."

"The senator and the rest of the delegation are trying, Freddy."

"Sure, but that's because they're like *us*." He turned again to the crowd. "The others—they don't get it, do they?"

Both surveyed the crush of the important and self-important. "No, they don't," she had to admit. "They can't. No one can understand who wasn't there."

They stared at each other for a time. Wentworth's fingers danced along her upper arm.

"Look, you want to get out of here? Get something to eat?"

Anna set down her glass on a nearby table. "I'm starved. There's a diner up the street."

His eyebrows rose. "You want to go to a diner in *that* dress?"

She looked up at him. "Something wrong with my dress?"

Wentworth grinned, his brown eyes alight. "Not a damn thing."

Anna felt a shiver down her back, and her dress felt *very* tight. *Damn! Maybe Carrie's right about guys in uniform!* "Let's go," she managed. "We can catch up on everything."

Wentworth offered his arm, and Anna took it. "Sure, and I can tell you what a blind idiot I was in high school." He winked.

Anna Elliot felt the best she had in years.

Tuesday, August 29
K plus one year: New Orleans

ALL OVER THE COUNTRY, IN WAYS LARGE AND SMALL, THE NATION paused to remember the calamity that occurred twelve months before. With all the speeches, sermons, and bell ringing, the most poignant were the small acts of remembrance for those who were lost by those who were left behind.

So it was that Emma Katz found herself again in a cemetery. A year ago, she was in Lake Charles, the sun was hot and unrelenting, and she was alone. Today, it was overcast with a threat of showers, and her husband stood at her side in New Orleans' Metairie Cemetery.

The cantor sang from the Psalms:

My soul, bless the LORD and do not forget any of His benefits.
Who forgives all your iniquity, who heals all your illnesses.
Who redeems your life from the pit, who crowns you with kindness and mercy.
Who sates your mouth with goodness, that your youth renews itself like the eagle.

The Katzes and the Parkers had gathered at the cemetery in this, the last act of their yearlong mourning period. For eleven months, they had avoided parties, concerts, and other forms of entertainment. There was no son to recite Kaddish every day in the synagogue, so Emma and Irene prayed quietly each morning.

The LORD is merciful and gracious, slow to anger and with much kindness.
He will not quarrel to eternity, and He will not bear a grudge forever.
He has not dealt with us according to our sins, nor has He repaid

us according to our iniquities.
For, as the height of the heavens over the earth, so great is His kindness toward those who fear Him.

It took time to obtain permission from the rabbi to disinter Abe Weinberg's casket and move it from Lake Charles, and the expense was not inconsequential. But everything was now as it should be. Abe lay where he always intended to—in the family plot next to his wife, Ruth. At the head of his grave was a large object shrouded by a white tarp.

As a father has mercy on sons, the LORD had mercy on those who fear Him.
For He knows our creation; He remembers that we are dust.
As for man—his days are like grass; like a flower of the field, so does he sprout.
For a wind passes over him and he is no longer here; and his place no longer recognizes him.

It has been a horribly hard year yet a strangely empowering one. George and Emma had gone through some of the worse life could throw at them. Some things had gotten better—George's job and Emma's charity work. The condo in the heart of Baltimore was comfortable. They made new friends and interests. Other things had not improved; the insurance company had proven intractable, and the outlook for a successful lawsuit was dim at best.

But, in spite of death and dislocation and discord, George and Emma had found their rock in each other. Neither was perfect, yet together *they* were perfect. Their love, respect, and mutual admiration had not dimmed but had grown brighter and stronger. Their relationship with Irene and Tyler was closer than ever. There was absolutely no doubt for either Emma or George that theirs was a marriage for a lifetime. Especially now.

But the LORD's kindness is from everlasting to everlasting, and

His charity to sons of sons.
To those who keep His covenant and to those who remember His commandments to perform them.
The LORD established His throne in the heavens, and His kingdom rules over all.[4]

George and Tyler reached down and removed the tarp. The words carved upon the dark gray marble were a mixture of Hebrew and English.

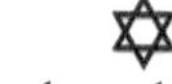

Abraham ben Isaac
24 Av 5765
Abraham I. Weinberg
29 August 2005

Another prayer ended the ceremony. As the Katzes and Parkers walked back to the car, George mused aloud, "I wonder how often we'll return."

Emma's first impulse was to declare an annual pilgrimage, but the words died in her throat. After this terrible year, only truth would do.

"Let's be honest, George. We won't be back here many more times. But we will bring the children here after they come and they are old enough to understand. Papa would agree."

George wrapped his arm around her as the first drops of rain began to fall. "Yes, he would." He kissed her temple as he continued. "But our family is *here*—in us—and wherever we are, so will be our home. You are my home and my life."

What could Emma Weinberg Katz say to that? Nothing, except kiss the man who was her world.

4 From the 103rd Psalm: The Tanakh English Translation, The Judaica Press

Epilogue

We are trav'ling in the footsteps of those who've gone before
And we'll all be reunited on a new and sunlit shore.
Oh, when the saints go marching in
Oh, when the saints go marching in
Lord, how I want to be in that number
When the saints go marching in.
And when the sun refuse to shine
And when the sun refuse to shine
Lord, how I want to be in that number
When the sun refuse to shine.
And when the moon turns red with blood
And when the moon turns red with blood
Lord, how I want to be in that number
When the moon turns red with blood.
Oh, when the trumpet sounds its call
Oh, when the trumpet sounds its call
Lord, how I want to be in that number
When the trumpet sounds its call.
Some say this world of trouble is the only one we need
But I'm waiting for that morning when the new world is revealed.

— "When the Saints Go Marching In"
traditional spiritual

Monday, September 25, 2006: Superdome

Over a year had passed since a monster named Katrina tried to kill the Crescent City. For fifty-six weeks, the people staggered about, collected bodies, cleared debris, and buried the dead. For almost thirteen months, a handful of talking heads on television argued whether the nation should rebuild New

Orleans while countless volunteers voted with convoys of building supplies. For nearly four hundred nights, the survivors worried about the future, lost jobs, lost friends, and lost neighborhoods.

The job of revival was not done—no, not by a long shot. Three hundred ninety-two days of toil and tears had passed, and countless more lay before the people of the Gulf Coast.

But not this day. Today, they were going to party. This was a day to drop their hammers and raise their voices. Today was the day the New Orleans Saints returned home to the Superdome.

This was one insane Monday night. This was football—*Saints football.* Nothing was more important to this battered and nearly beaten city. The town was coming back, and the Saints were the first sign of it.

The NFL and FEMA had poured $185 million into the repair of the stadium. For the first time since the team came into being in 1967, the entire regular-season home schedule was sold out. The team had won the first two games of the season, but that was not the reason for the joyous frenzy. The Saints represented normalcy, a return to pre-K days when most of the housing stock wasn't destroyed, damaged, or deserted.

Excitement in Who Dat Nation would have been at a fever pitch for any opponent. What sent the exhilaration over the edge was the fact that it was the Atlanta Falcons, the damned Dirty Birds, the city's most hated rivals, who had come to play the beloved Black and Gold on Monday Night Football. The nation's eyes were fixed on this game.

It would be ridiculous to try to park at the Superdome, so a stretch limo dropped off the Darcys and their guests several blocks away. As the four couples made their way up the ramp to the plaza, a huge banner on the side of the Dome greeted them, proclaiming, "Our Home—Our Team—Be a Saint." Music filled the air; the Goo Goo Dolls had been hired by the league for pre-game entrainment.

"Where the hell are the Neville Brothers?" Chris Breaux grouched.

Marianne patted her husband's arm. "Poor Aaron can't sing in New Orleans because of the mold. It's okay, sugar, don't be angry.

We're here to enjoy ourselves." She turned to their hosts. "Thanks again for inviting us, guys."

"Don't mention it, Mari," said William Darcy. "We couldn't have this celebration without you."

"You got that right," cried Chuck Bingley, one arm around Jane's shoulders. Suddenly, he began waving at a redheaded woman in the crowd. "Hey, Carrie! Over here!"

Carrie Buford, in a Reggie Bush jersey and skinny jeans, joined the group as quickly as her four-inch heels would allow. She gave hugs to everybody and kisses to the out-of-towners.

"Where's John?" asked George Katz.

Carrie gestured into the distance. "Somewhere over there with the other First Responders. They're going to be honored tonight."

"That's great, Carrie," said Elizabeth. "Are you going to be able to sit with him?"

She assured her she would and then smiled at Elizabeth. "Wow. I can't tell who's further along—you or Emma."

Elizabeth giggled as she caressed her pregnant belly. "It's as bad as you and Jane last year! We're what, Em, a couple of days apart?"

Emma Katz ran a hand over her own six-month baby bump. "December 15 for me."

"And you, Lizzy?" Carrie asked.

"The tenth." She smiled as William's arms enveloped her from behind.

Marianne shook her head. "Jeeze, I don't even wanna know what was in the water back in March."

"Your day's coming, redneck." Emma laughed.

"Redneck?" cried Carrie. "She's in Chicago now. She's a damned Yankee."

"No way!" Marianne assured her. "You can take the girl out of the South, but you can't take the redneck out of the girl!"

"Still, you just wait," Emma insisted.

Chris whispered in Marianne's ear, "It's not for lack of trying."

"Are y'all staying at Dansereau?" Carrie asked.

"Yeah," said George. "We fly back to Baltimore tomorrow."

"Mari and I are staying through the weekend," Chris added.

Elizabeth watched the interaction with a lump in her throat. It was William's idea to have the gang all together again. While the box was reserved for DGS executives and business guests, he had extra seats on the 20-yard line, and that was where their friends would be. They would meet up after the game to return to Dansereau Plantation.

As wonderful and as normal as it was to have her friends in her house, Elizabeth knew it was a temporary joy. The Breauxes would go back to Chicago until Chris got a job back in New Orleans. LSU's Charity Hospital was virtually destroyed. It would be a while before a position opened up again for him in the Big Easy.

It was different for the Katzes. They were not returning even though Tulane Hospital had reopened in February. There were too many bad memories here. Emma and George had established themselves in their new home in Baltimore. They had joined the thousands of others who had been blown away forever by Katrina's evil winds.

Yes, New Orleans would come back, Elizabeth told herself for the hundredth time, but it would never be the same. Just as America now lived in a post-9/11 world, New Orleans would eternally be pre-K and post-K.

"You okay, babe?" William asked, noticing Elizabeth's pensive expression.

"I'm fine," she answered, touching his hand. "It's just…" She jerked her head at their friends, deep in conversation.

"Yeah, I know. I feel the same."

"Live for today, Will," she said into his eyes.

"That's us—that's out battle cry." He grinned. "You can't keep us Cajuns down."

"Damn straight."

"Hey!" Chuck cried. "They're opening the doors."

Carrie turned towards the door. "Oops, that's my cue to scoot. I'd better get back to the others, or Major Buford will put out a search party for me."

"*Major?* He got promoted?" asked Emma.

"Yes. The Guard's trying to get him to reenlist."

"Is he?"

"Haven't decided yet. Gotta run. I'll call you—bye!" Carrie waved as she fought her way through the crowd.

Elizabeth looked around. "Will, didn't you say Richard was going to be here?"

"Yeah, but he's with the First Responders."

Chris leaned over. "How's he doing, anyway?"

"Okay." He paused. "You heard about him and Olivia?"

"Yeah. Is the divorce final yet?"

"Not yet; they're still trying to work things out. But she won't leave Atlanta, and he won't leave New Orleans. It doesn't look good."

"Crap. That's tough."

"Yeah. He's got to make a choice." William's glance at Elizabeth was a clear indication to her where *his* choice would lie.

Elizabeth took his hand. "All right everybody, you've got your tickets? Good. We'll meet up outside this gate after the game. Have a great time."

The Bingleys, Breauxes, and Katzes moved towards their gate while the Darcys headed for the entrance to the skyboxes. They were almost there when they saw Leon Anderson and his wife, both wearing Saints jerseys, standing by the door, being interviewed by a TV reporter.

"Bryan Thorpe, Action NOW News. Can you share with our viewers your feelings about tonight's event? Why was this facility repaired while so many of your people still have no housing?"

"Where the hell are you from?" Leon was clearly ticked off.

"Umm, Hartford, Connecticut."

"Figures. Don't you understand our economy is based on three things—petroleum, shipping, and tourism?" he lectured as he counted off the industries on his fingers. "Many of 'my people'"—he made quotation marks in the air—"are in the tourism industry. How the hell are they going to have jobs if the tourists don't come? Repairing the Superdome shows the rest of the country New Orleans is open for business." Leon looked directly into the camera. "C'mon down, America! Party on Bourbon Street! And while you're here spending your money, you just might see how much else has to be done."

He then returned his attention to Thorpe. "Besides, do you have *any idea* what this team and this building mean to this city? To this whole state—to the whole region? Look around you. There are people here from Mississippi, Alabama, everywhere!

"You think we've forgotten for a minute that eighteen hundred of our friends and neighbors died? This is as much for *them* as it is for us!

"I can't explain it better than that. *It's what we are!* You either understand it or you don't! And if you don't, *then get that microphone the hell out of my face, you idiot!*"

With that, Leon looped one arm around his wife, brushed past Thorpe, and joined the Darcys. "Goddamn asshole," he mumbled. The foursome went inside.

"Uh, Justin?" said Thorpe into his mike. "Cut that from the tape, will you?"

The DGS party made it to the private suite. Unlike the rest of the stadium, the skyboxes had not been completely repaired. The floors were bare concrete, the walls needed new wallpaper, and the missing TVs had not yet been replaced. But the seats were new, and it was all that mattered.

Below on the sideline, the Darcys' guests had a great view of the pregame entertainment. U2 and Green Day blew the doors off the house with a driving cover of the obscure Scottish punk band The Skids' equally obscure song, "The Saints are Coming" before sequencing into U2's "Beautiful Day." A few minutes later, Marianne squealed.

"*Irma!* Look, baby, it's Irma—with *Allen!*"

Sure enough, two legends of New Orleans music were at mid-field to sing the National Anthem: Irma Thomas on vocals and Allen Toussaint on keyboards. Marianne was not the only member of the crowd who had tears in their eyes as they sang.

"One day, babe," Chris promised in her ear, "one day we'll be able to come home." Marianne smiled and nodded.

As one, the seventy thousand faithful rose to their feet as their beloved Saints, in their home uniforms of white jerseys and gold pants, took the field. The visitors weren't impressed. The Atlanta Falcons had heard the roars of Who Dat Nation before and still kicked their NFC South arch-rival's ass. They figured tonight would be no different.

Atlanta, wearing red jerseys with black helmets, won the coin toss. They chose to receive the kick-off, intending to quiet the locals by scoring quickly. The black-and-gold dressed crowd continued to cheer as the teams lined up to begin the game, a noise not heard in Louisiana in over a year.

Things did not work out the way the Dirty Birds planned. Deep in their own territory, they couldn't move the ball. On the fourth play from scrimmage, ninety seconds into the game, Atlanta had to punt. The ball was snapped, punter Michael Koenen took a step, and from nowhere, Saints linebacker Steve Gleason sliced in to block the kick. The ball flew backwards into the end zone, where Saints cornerback Curtis Deloatch pounced on it for a touchdown.

A thunderous roar went up, rocking the newly repaired building. It was though a whole city—those at the game, those without, and those who had departed this world forever—had found their voice:

"WHO DAT! WHO DAT! WHO DAT SAY DEY GONNA BEAT DEM SAINTS!"

For one bright, shining moment, we were all New Orleanians.

The Falcons never stood a chance.

THE END

AND A NEW BEGINNING

Appreciation

When taking on a project of this scope, an author cannot do it alone. I am fortunate to have a number of wonderful ladies who serve as my **Beta Babes**, reading and correcting my gross errors. If the story you have just read speaks at all to you, it is because of these ladies' dedication to this thankless task.

Debbie Styne and **Ellen Pickels,** along with my wife, are the primary editors of this work.

Sarah Hunt, Bonnie Carasso, Amy Robinson, Nicole Newchurch, and **Mary Anne Mushatt** helped make the original manuscript sing.

Ladies, thank you so much.

Thanks go to my fellow members of "The Six-Pack"—**Linnea Eileen, June, Susan, Shelby,** and **Meg**—who whined for me to write a modern. If it weren't for you ladies, *CRESCENT CITY* wouldn't have happened.

A special thank you to my daughter-in-law, **Roni Barzel Hewitt**.

And to my #1 Beta Babe, **my lovely wife, Barbara**, who encouraged me to write this story and supported me while I relived the agony, I love you, my dear.

Bibliography, Sources, and Suggested Readings

Austen, Jane. *Emma.*
—. *Pride and Prejudice.*
—. *Sense and Sensibility.*

Brinkley, Douglas. *The Great Deluge.* New York: HarperCollins, 2006.

Caldwell, Jack. *The Plains of Chalmette: a Story of Crescent City.* Venice: White Soup Press, 2015.
—. *Bourbon Street Nights: Volume One of Crescent City.* Venice: White Soup Press, 2015.
—. *Elysian Dreams: Volume Two of Crescent City.* Venice: White Soup Press, 2015.

Carey, Bill. *Leave No One Behind: Hurricane Katrina and the Rescue of Tulane Hospital.* Nashville: Clearbrook Press, 2006.

Centers for Disease Control and Prevention. "Hurricane Katrina Deaths, Louisiana, 2005." (August 2008)

CNN. "Red Cross: State rebuffed relief efforts." http://www.cnn.com/2005/US/09/08/katrina.redcross/index.html

Dufour, Charles M. *Ten Flags in the Wind: The Story of Louisiana.* New York: Harper & Row, 1967 (out of print).

The National Hurricane Center website archives.

The New Orleans Times-Picayune archives.

Piazza, Tom. *Why New Orleans Matters.* London: Reed Consumer Books, Ltd, 1993.

Popular Mechanics. "Debunking the Myths of Hurricane Katrina: Special Report." (March 2006)

Remini, Robert V. *The Battle of New Orleans: Andrew Jackson and America's First Military Victory.* New York: Viking, 1999.

Rose, Chris. *1 Dead in Attic.* New Orleans: Chris Rose Books, 2005.

Statistics

Hurricane KATRINA:

- Area affected: **90,000 square miles** (233,000 km^2), approximately the area of Great Britain.
- Property damage: **$108 billion** (in 2005 dollars).
- Storm width: **450 miles** (720 km)
- Highest winds: **175 mph** (280 km/h)
- Lowest internal pressure achieved: **902 mb** (26.64 inches)
- Sustained winds at final landfall: **125 mph** (200 km/h)
- Hurricane force winds from eye: **120 miles** (193 km)
- Storm surge height: **28 feet** (9 meters)
- Number of evacuees pre-storm: **1 million plus**
- Number of people rescued: **70,000**
- Electric power loss: **3 million**

2005 Estimated Hurricane Deaths

	KATRINA	RITA	WILMA	TOTAL 2005 SEASON
Louisiana	1,577	1		1,578
Mississippi	239	4		243
Alabama	3			4
Texas		113		113
Florida	14	2	61	93
Other US	5			17
Total US	1,838	120	61	2,048
Outside US			25	1,869
TOTAL	1,838	120	87	3.917

Katrina Victims Identified by DMORT[5] at St. Gabriel and Carville Morgues (as of August 28, 2008)

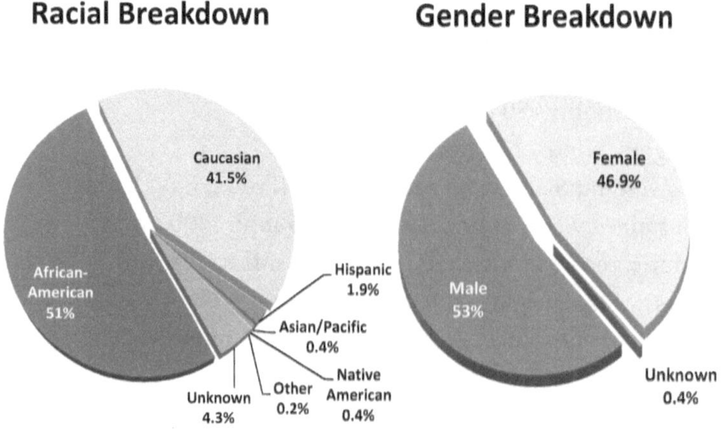

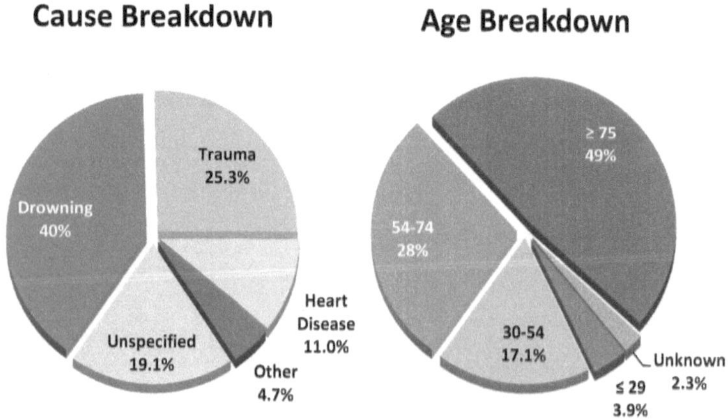

5 DMORT: Disaster Mortuary Operational Response Team

Definitions

It should be noted that New Orleans and Southern Louisiana are not part of what is commonly called the American South. They have a different culture and do not have the southern drawl common to Northern Louisiana and the rest of the Southern United States.

AST: Aviation Survival Technician in the USCG, better known as a "rescue swimmer."

BAYOU: A slow moving stream or river. The term, used primarily in the Southern US, is thought to be derived from the Choctaw word "bayuk."

CAJUNS: The Acadians, the original French settlers in the maritime provinces of Canada. After the British expelled the Acadians from their homes (*Le Grand Dérangement, 1755-1764*), most ended up in Louisiana. The name *Acadian* became corrupted over time to *Cajun*, which is used to describe the country folk of Southern Louisiana, their culture, language, and style of cooking.

CDT: Central Daylight Time.

CHER or CHERE: Sweet, sweetheart, a Cajun term of endearment to a loved one.

CREOLE: The term "Creole" has long generated confusion and controversy. The word invites debate because it possesses several meanings, some of which concern the innately sensitive subjects of race and ethnicity. In its broadest sense, Creole means "native" or, in the context of Louisiana history, "native to Louisiana." In a narrower sense, however, it has historically referred to black, white, and mixed-raced persons who are native to Louisiana. In short, the word means different things to different people, and more than one ethnic group arguably has a claim to the term. The term has expanded and now embraces a type of cuisine and a style of architecture.

DMORT: Disaster Mortuary Operational Response Team

EDA: Economic Development Administration, United States Department of Commerce.

EPA: United States Environmental Protection Agency.

DRESSED: Adding mayonnaise, lettuce, tomatoes, and pickles to a sandwich.

FAUBOURG: A French term for a neighborhood.

FEMA: Federal Emergency Management Agency.

GALLERIES: An outdoor balcony, supported by posts or columns anchored to the ground. Technically, the "balconies" in the French Quarter are really galleries.

HUD: United States Department of Housing and Urban Development.

LANG: Louisiana Army National Guard.

LDH: Landing Helicopter Dock, a type of multipurpose amphibious assault ship capable of operating helicopters and LCATs (Landing Craft Air Cushion).

MONA: A protocol used to treat acute coronary syndrome, such as myocardial infarction (heart attack): morphine, oxygen, nitroglycerin, and aspirin.

NCO: Non-commissioned officer in the military, such as corporal, sergeant, and petty officer.

NEW ORLEANS: How the name of the major city of Louisiana is pronounced has caused great consternation among the locals. New Orleans may be pronounced "nu OR-le-ons," "nu OR-lens" or "NAW-lens." It is never pronounced "nu OR-leens." Yet, the parish where the city is located is pronounced like its French namesake, "OR-leens." Confusing, isn't it?

PARISH: A county, a political subdivision of the state.

PO3C: USCG rank, Petty Officer, Third Class.

PO'BOY or POOR BOY: A sandwich made with French bread, stuffed with almost anything.

PODNA: "Partner." A form of address for men, usually for ones with whom one is not acquainted.

PTSD: Post-traumatic Stress Disorder.

SBA: Small Business Administration.

SHOTGUN: Usually part of a "double"—a single row house in which all rooms on one side are connected by a long single hallway. Supposedly, one can open the front door and shoot a gun straight through the back door without hitting a single wall.

UPTOWN SIDE, DOWNTOWN SIDE, LAKESIDE, RIVERSIDE: The four cardinal points of the New Orleanian compass. "North, south, east, west" do not work in New Orleans.

USDA: United States Department of Agriculture.

VIEUX CARRÉ: French for Old Square. It refers to the original settlement of La Nouvelle-Orléans (New Orleans). The district is now known as the French Quarter.

WHERE Y'AT!: The traditional working class New Orleanian greeting, and the source for the term "Yat", often used (primarily by non-New Orleanians, it is said) to describe New Orleanians with the telltale accent. The proper response is, "Awrite."

Y'ALL: The plural form of the second person verb, "you all." It's NOT pronounced as they would in the south, though—no twang, no drawl. Just "y'all."

YEAH, YOU RITE: An emphatic statement of agreement and affirmation, sometimes used as a general exclamation of happiness. The accent is on the first word, and it's spoken as one word.

About the Author

Jack Caldwell is an author, amateur historian, professional economic developer, playwright, and like many Cajuns, a darn good cook. Born and raised in the Bayou County of Louisiana, Jack and his wife, Barbara, are Hurricane Katrina victims who now make the Suncoast of Florida their home.

Jack is the author of four Jane Austen-themed books. PEMBERLEY RANCH is a retelling of *Pride & Prejudice* set in Reconstruction Texas. THE THREE COLONELS: JANE AUSTEN'S FIGHTING MEN is a sequel to *Pride & Prejudice* and *Sense & Sensibility*. MR. DARCY CAME TO DINNER and THE COMPANION OF HIS FUTURE LIFE are *Pride & Prejudice*-flavored farces.

In 2015, he released the first four of a series of historical novels about New Orleans, titled THE CRESCENT CITY SERIES. THE PLAINS OF CHALMETTE begins the series, commemorating the Bicentennial of the Battle of New Orleans. He marked the tenth anniversary of Hurricane Katrina with three modern novels: BOURBON STREET NIGHTS, ELYSIAN DREAMS, and RUIN AND RENEWAL.

When not writing or traveling with Barbara, Jack attempts to play golf. A devout convert to Roman Catholicism, Jack is married with three grown sons. Jack's blog postings — **The Cajun Cheesehead Chronicles** — appear regularly at **Austen Variations**.

Web site: **Rambling of a Cajun in Exile**:
https://cajuncheesehead.com
Austen Variations: http://austenvariations.com/

Facebook: https://www.facebook.com/pages/Jack-Caldwell-author/132047236805555

Twitter: @JCaldwell25

The Crescent City Series:

All available from White Soup Press

THE PLAINS OF CHALMETTE: a Story of Crescent City

BOURBON STREET NIGHTS: Volume One of Crescent City

ELYSIAN DREAMS: Volume Two of Crescent City

RUIN AND RENEWAL: Volume Three of Crescent City

Other Novels by Jack Caldwell:

Available from Sourcebooks Landmark:

PEMBERLEY RANCH

THE THREE COLONELS: Jane Austen's Fighting Men

Available from White Soup Press:

MR. DARCY CAME TO DINNER: a Jane Austen farce

THE COMPANION OF HIS FUTURE LIFE

www.ingramcontent.com/pod-product-compliance
Lightning Source LLC
Chambersburg PA
CBHW030641260626
47157CB00007B/2435

* 9 7 8 0 9 8 9 1 0 8 0 5 8 *